I0692443

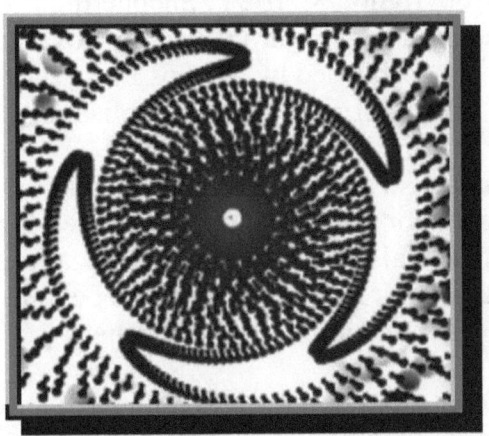

The Scribing of Ishitar

Fall From Grace

By
Carrie F. Shepherd

THE SCRIBING OF ISHITAR: FALL FROM GRACE
By
Carrie F. Shepherd
Copyright © Carrie F. Shepherd 2014
Cover Illustration Copyright © 2014 by Novel Idea Design
Published by Mythos Press
(An Imprint of GMTA Publishing)

Contact:
GMTA Publishing
7405 Beaver Run Dr.
Fayetteville, NC 28314

Printed in the U.S.A.

ISBN-13: 978-0692023419
ISBN-10: 0692023410
LCCN: 2012907481

Dedication

For Riyan Jayde Shepherd
With all of my love.

Acknowledgements

The greatest lesson that I learned during the publishing process of the first installment of The Scribing of Ishitar, Fall From Grace, is that, while an author might have a great idea, no one person can see the bigger picture. Such was true with Ashes to Ashes.

I would like to thank Brooke Funk and Gabby Raines, among others who have asked to remain anonymous, for providing me with their feedback and building the story to make it stronger.

Revelation 12:7-9

Now war arose in heaven, Michael and his angels fighting against the dragon. And the dragon and his angels fought back, but he was defeated, and there was no longer any place for them in heaven.

$\mathcal{M}$ARIUS

"Mr. Talbot?"

Marius stared at his phone, frowning. He was running late this morning and he didn't have time for his executive assistant's ineptitude. Pressing the intercom button he barked, "Yes?"

"Mr. Hamilton is here to speak with you."

Marius froze. It was the fifteenth of the month so Charles Hamilton's visit today wasn't a surprise. What caught him off guard was the time. Mr. Hamilton typically came in at three o'clock so he could sit in the lounge drinking tea and eating the cucumber finger sandwiches Marius ordered for him while he rifled through his safety deposit box.

He licked his lips and swallowed the lump that rose to his throat. "Please tell him I'll be right out."

"Yes, sir."

Marius rose, stepped toward the mirror hanging on the wall beside his desk and ran his fingers through his hair. It was ridiculous to be nervous around Mr. Hamilton. He was an easy going fellow who was always appreciative of Marius' personal attention. But he was the bank's wealthiest client. Which is why Marius always went out of his way to ensure he was well taken care of during his monthly visits.

Forcing himself to smile, Marius stepped out of the office and into the lobby.

Charles Hamilton was a tall, slender man with stylishly cut black hair which was starting to grey. His face was handsome; his features were well sculpted. His lips were full and always ready with a smile. As for his sightless eyes, which were always covered by dark glasses, they were a dark shade of green.

Today he wore light grey trousers and a white button down shirt that was open at the neck. His sleeves were rolled to the elbows, which Marius found slightly amusing because it was out of character for Mr. Hamilton to appear so casual.

Beside him stood his nephew, Mason. He was a young man in his late twenties with long brown hair that he wore tied behind him with a leather string. Aside from this, his physical appearance resembled his uncle's. Right down to the dark green eyes.

Marius wasn't as familiar with Mason as he was with Charles. Though Mason accompanied Mr. Hamilton on nearly all of his visits, he generally spent his time mingling with the pretty tellers, who were obviously enamored by his charms. If he had been anyone else, Marius would have admonished the tellers for fraternizing while on duty. Given he was Mr. Hamilton's nephew, however, he let their behavior slide.

"Good morning, Mr. Hamilton." He stepped forward holding out his hand. Mr. Hamilton immediately reached forward to grasp it. "Forgive me. I wasn't expecting you until this afternoon."

"Will you show me to my deposit box, Mr. Talbot?" He was as courteous as ever, though his tone was far more serious than usual.

"Of course." Marius reached for Mason's hand. Mason hesitated before reaching forward to shake it.

Marius turned away from the pair to lead them to the secured room where the safety deposit boxes were housed. As they followed, he noticed Mr. Hamilton was neither using his cane to guide himself nor holding his nephew's arm. He supposed Mr. Hamilton was used to the path from Marius' office to the secure room so he ignored this curiosity.

When they reached Mr. Hamilton's box, Marius typed in his pass code and stepped out of the way so Mr. Hamilton could use his key to unlock the door. Once unlocked, Marius stepped toward it and pulled the box out, turning to hand it to Mason.

"That won't be necessary." Mr. Hamilton advised him as he pulled a strange wooden box out of the leather satchel he was carrying and set it gingerly into the safety deposit box. It was rectangular and weighty. To Marius it appeared to be the size of a college text book.

Secured to the top of the box was an envelope with tiny bumps—Braille. As for the satchel, it was extremely well crafted, though tattered and ancient.

"A new puzzle box." Mr. Hamilton explained. "I do so love puzzles."

"I see." Marius replied with a nod, although he was confused. A puzzle box this may be, but it certainly wasn't new.

"You may lock it away."

"Of course." Marius slid the box back into its drawer and stepped out of the way so Mr. Hamilton could lock it. He then swung the outer door closed, typed in his code and turned to his esteemed customer. "Will there be anything else this morning?"

"No, Mr. Talbot." Mr. Hamilton gave him a tight smile and turned toward the door. "Thank you for your service."

Confused by Mr. Hamilton's brusque behavior—and, even more so, Mason's silence—Marius watched with furrowed brows as the pair walked away.

REFLECTION

The Guf. The Great Hall of Souls. The Bird Cage. The Mortal Well. Otzer.

Whichever of these you wish to call it, the Guf is located on the Seventh level of the Heavens and is the domain in which Gabriel has ever been charged to work his magic.

Until today that is. Today the Guf belongs to me.

I wasn't surprised when the King of Lords issued me this order. Why would I be? In Gabriel's stead, who else would it fall to? In these days, as we recover from a great war, I am the only being with the capacity of time to see to my own duties as well as this additional task.

But forgive me. I am being rude.

My name is Azrael.

I am better known to you as the archangel of death.

If you are reading this accounting then it means my puzzle has been solved.

Good. I am pleased.

Understand that I came by my knowledge of the facts within this story because I am charged with watching over others, mortal and immortal, to determine innocence or guilt when the time for passing judgment arrives. I am the only being in all of creation with the power of ubiquity. For my tasks, the requirement that I be in all places and in all times so I might witness every event that ever comes to pass is vital.

Now, you must understand that, when I was first given the 'gift' of my magic, I was only burdened with sight and sound. While this was disconcerting to me, it was something I could manage. Listening to many conversations all at once might drive a person mad; though in my case it did not. It was the knowledge of how a person will act before they do so, a punishment set down upon me when I broke the rules and spoke of the events I bear witness to, that I realized I will eventually go insane.

On that day, the rules binding my magic became clear to me. I may speak and, thereby, interfere should I desire to do so. But at a price. As such, I have reverted to making only the barest reference to the facts I witness.

My Lord and Master, whose name is Noliminan, included.

This brings about punishments of an entirely different nature, but we will be discussing this later.

For now, I must explain to you, the sole witness to my life, the consequences which have come about on the three occasions when I found an issue important enough to defy the rules. Only then can you comprehend how I have grappled over the telling of this tale and the bearing of yet another burden.

As I said, the first time I loosened my tongue, I was granted the foresight to understand how a person will behave before they have acted in that manner. The second time I was granted the ability to read others' thoughts. The third was by far the worst. I was to share in the emotions of the worlds.

The fourth time I suffered no consequences. At the time, I didn't understand why not. Now, it is my understanding which drives my motivations. This is another tidbit, as you mortals say, which will have to wait until later in my story. Otherwise, it may be confusing to you. Suffice it to say that, even with the foresight to know that I will be severely punished for this fifth offense, I know I have no choice.

My son is in danger.

Or, rather, a man who I think of as my son.

Though he may not be of my flesh and blood, I love him as if he were. The only manner of protection I can afford him is to bring certain facts to light.

Facts that others will not want disclosed.

Before I begin the tale, itself, I will detail the events which spurned this opportunity.

It begins and ends with the manner in which I have come by the management of the Guf.

PART ONE:
THE AFTERMATH

-1-

Gabriel sat low before the King of Lords' chair, his brown and white wings stretched wide behind him and his gaze lowered. He waited with his breath caught deep in his chest for his punishment.

For my undeserved punishment.

The bitterness of the thought swelled in his throat, forcing him to swallow.

He had not joined in Lord Regent Lucias' rebellion. What he had done was voice his opinion to King Noliminan that he understood the ideals of the revolutionists.

Understood them; not supported them.

In Gabriel's mind, one did not equate to the other.

Yet here he sat, ready to be persecuted for his empathy.

Where in the name of the Thirty Hells is the justice in this?

He felt King Noliminan's accusatory, light brown eyes as they trailed over his face. He bore this humiliation as he sat before the Council of the Gods, who were staring at his back. Because it was the gaze of his eleven brothers and sisters which weighed most heavily upon him. These eyes embodied a mixture of sympathy and self-preserving fear.

If Gabriel could be put on trial, were any of the members of the Quorum safe?

"I am grieved." The King of Lords advised the Council, his tone far heavier than his words. "First Lucias stands opposite of me—and with him a legion of Gods, angels and demons who would take up arms—but Gabriel?" He shook his head in frustration. "A member of my Quorum? Come before me today to beg for forgiveness for agreeing with Lucias' words and ideals?"

"Your Grace," Gabriel whispered, "I beg only for your understanding."

He looked up, eyes stinging with tears, to the face of his maker. It was clear to him that King Noliminan had already made up his mind. Gabriel would be punished. His only hope was that the worst fate he would face would be exile.

Scared as he was, he decided to speak for those who remained in King Noliminan's service. Perhaps he could save his brothers and sisters from his own plight.

This was a doubtful supposition and he knew it.

"I beseech you to understand how it is for those of us who serve rather than rule."

The King of Lords sighed heavily and fell against his throne. He raised one of his large, bronze hands to his nose and began to rub the bridge of it. "I tire of your complaints. I have not, even once, mistreated you."

This was not exactly a lie. King Noliminan had done far worse than mistreat him. And it had happened many more times than once.

But this was a secret which Gabriel would keep for his Master. Despite everything, he did love him. He wouldn't humiliate his God by arguing with him before the Council members.

He raised his hand to indicate his brothers and sisters. "The Quorum are not the only servants who sit at the feet of the Gods. There are angels and demons—"

"Must we go through this again?" Lord Marutuk inquired. "We have already listened to this tripe from the servants. The King of Lords has deemed Lord Regent Lucias guilty of treason. It's inconsequential."

"Indeed it is." King Noliminan agreed with a sigh. "Gabriel, we have heard your views. What we are left with is what to do with you. Unlike your brethren, you have committed no true sin by agreeing with Lucias' views. Yet I cannot permit for animosity to exist against the mortals within a member of my Quorum."

"Your Grace, I have no animosity against the mortals!" Gabriel replied, angry and frustrated. He would pay for his words and he knew this. Yet, he was unable to hold his tongue. "Nor does Lord Lucias! Have you not bore witness to the testimony given you by those who have come to my defense? This is not about the Gods be damned speaking apes!"

The King of Lords' nostrils flared with cold fury. He growled, burning at Gabriel's insolence. "If your animosity is not directed toward the mortals then who is it directed toward? Lucias' very point—"

"Lucias' very point," a sultry voice purred from the sidelines, "was that you—nay, *all* of we Gods—love our mortal races more than we love our servant children."

Gabriel looked upward to see his mother, the Goddess Raziel, who had taken over the management of the Hells bound entities in Lucias' stead and was now known as the Lady Regent. She was sitting upon his father's throne and looking, as if extremely bored, at the shine of her fingernails. Her face, which was delicate and fair, showed no emotion whatsoever. Her lanky body was set in such a manner to suggest she would rather be elsewhere.

"After the travesty of ousting Luke from his throne—without giving him the benefit of a single word to this Council in his own defense—I am forced to agree with Gabriel."

The expression on King Noliminan's face was stoic, though the frustration and anger directed toward Raziel burned in his eyes. Raziel, who seemed not to care about having upset him, simply continued to examine the shine of her well buffed nails.

She believed that, along with Lucias' crown, she had earned the right to speak her mind to him. Lucias, after all, had been afforded this courtesy.

"You cannot be saying you agree with Lucias' stand, Raziel!"

Raziel turned her bored, molten eyes upward and met King Noliminan's gaze.

"I do not agree with his method of deliverance," she contended. "However, your Grace, after listening to the testimony presented on Gabriel's behalf, I cannot disagree with his message."

"Have we been sitting through the same trial?" Lady Moira, the Goddess of fate, sighed.

"No law has been broken by Gabriel." Raziel said, fanning her hand toward her son, ignoring Lady Moira all together. "What have we come to, your Grace? Putting the child's loyalty into question simply because he has the intelligence to think on his own?"

"We cannot have them thinking without our guidance." King Noliminan replied, rather coldly, to this.

She will pay for her insolence, Gabriel thought. *She will pay dearly.*

"Oh, no, of course not." Raziel rolled her flaming eyes. "Next thing, they might be demanding our approval that they have dreams and—Loki's beard, pray it never be so—fall in love with who they choose rather than who we demand."

"Actually," Lord Loki interjected with a slight chuckle to his tone, "they call this, here, a goatee."

King Noliminan shot Lord Loki—always joking and laughing at the most inappropriate of times—a stony glance before returning his gaze to Raziel.

"You know very well what I mean." He admonished. "Our servants were made to follow our orders. Not to act without our command or complain about their treatment. If we cannot depend on our angels and demons to follow our orders, without question, then where are we?"

"Further advanced by their aide." Raziel suggested, her raven brow lifting above her calculating, shimmering eye. "You do not see me holding Zamyael to—"

"And look at the mess of *her*." King Noliminan growled, turning his eyes to the demon in question.

Zamyael, who was beautiful in Gabriel's estimation, had been born a Goddess. She had been pulled from Lucias' soul rather than sired and birthed. But she was a demon, now, because she had defied King Noliminan and, to punish her, he had demoted her. Hers was a cautionary tale of what could happen to a body should they dare refuse the King of Lords' commands.

"Can we not get this over with?" Lord Evanbourough, the God who lorded over the exiled demons, grumbled. "We are not being fair to Gabriel by dragging this thing out to quibble."

Gabriel, who had been grateful for anything which might distract King Noliminan from him and his punishment, sighed as his Master turned to meet his gaze.

"Very well." He glared down at the archangel. "Gabriel, I have no choice but to turn you out."

"No!" Gabriel cried, flying forward and grasping desperately at the hem of King Noliminan's thigh length toga. "No, your Grace, please! Do not send me away! Do not—!"

"There's nothing else for it." King Noliminan pronounced. "Since your misunderstanding of my decree of free will amongst the mortals is so profound, the only lesson I might grant you is that you must live amongst them until you can find love and compassion for them."

Thus decreed, he flicked his hand.

Gabriel cried out again, flying forward as he did so. But it was no use. By the time the King of Lords' hand returned to his lap, the world began to spin around Gabriel before growing dim and, inevitably, dark.

When he awoke, he was bitterly alone but for the mortals that resided upon the world to which he had been exiled.

-2-

Raziel did not wait for Noliminan to release the Council before standing and storming out.

The entire proposition had been madness; unfair and unjust.

Noliminan hadn't listened to a Gods be damned word she'd said! He made up his mind regarding what he meant to do before entering Council!

She understood, now, how little influence she wielded over him when antiquity demanded.

Zamyael followed upon her heel. She spoke not a single word in one direction or the other as Raziel stormed to her living quarters. Once within the foyer of her suite of rooms, Raziel turned to the door and slammed it, her anger burning in her heart and in her mind.

"It's centaur dung, Zamyael." She growled. "Every single bit of it."

"Yes, my Lady." Zamyael agreed in a docile tone.

This only served to enrage Raziel all the more.

Once upon a time, Zamyael had been free and open with her. She would speak any opinion which must be shared. Since Lucias had lost his damned war, however, Zamyael hadn't uttered a single word to Raziel but for 'yes, my Lady' or 'no, my Lady'. Her response, of course, was based upon whichever was appropriate to the conversation at hand and agreed with Raziel's current opinion.

"Mayhap Luke deserves what he got." Raziel muttered, more to herself than Zamyael. "I cannot say what is right where that worthy is concerned. But Gabriel? My dear, sweet Gabriel? Who never harmed a soul?"

"Yes, my Lady." Zamyael answered. Her dark eyes narrowed upon Raziel before she turned away to walk toward the opposite end of the room. Once there, she pulled a vat filled with red wine downward so a glass could be poured.

Raziel watched this, frowning at Zamyael's back. Her love for Zam, which had once been strong, was now nearly non-existent. Now, Zamyael was nothing more important than her servant and slave.

Zamyael turned around, caught Raziel's irritated regard, and immediately looked toward the floor. The fire burning within her black eyes infuriated Raziel to no end.

Where does your infernal sense of superiority come from?

"Just . . ." Raziel shook her head and waved her hand at the demon. "Leave me if you aren't willing to console me."

"As you please, my Lady." Zamyael replied coldly, granting Raziel a curtsey after the glass of wine was thrust into her hand.

Raziel tried to stay her anger with Zamyael's all too feminine ways as the demon turned and walked gracefully away. She may have wanted to be a woman when they were forced to revert to the essence they were born in. But Raziel hadn't. She preferred to use her sex to manipulate others.

Prior to the rebellion, the Gods and Goddesses were able to take on forms in whatever essence they desired. And, they were able to change their servants from male to female at their whim as well. Zamyael, herself, had been forced to live as a male. But

19

something had taken place near to the end of the revolution which stripped them of this ability and forced them to revert to their natural forms. That Raziel no longer had the choice to be a male, when to be so furthered her aims, infuriated her beyond all telling.

Not that it mattered, she supposed. In the end, even as a woman, she now wore Lucias' crown. Really, the only reason she had been touting herself as male in the first place was because she had coveted the power this bauble would bring its wearer.

Once—the first time Lucias and Noliminan were arguing to the point where she believed Lucias meant to stand against Nol— she had asked Noliminan why he had given the power to Lucias rather than to her. Yes, he had been created before she had. But she was Noliminan's wife at the time. If either of them deserved to sit at Noliminan's side it was her. Not Lucias.

Knowing him as she did, she should have anticipated his response. He told her that women were weak and unfit for such power. He would never be content to rule with a Goddess at his side. Her job was to lay in his bed without complaint, spread her legs when he had a whim and deliver his offspring.

Infuriated, and craving Lucias' power more than Noliminan's approval, Raziel immediately amended her essence to male whenever she knew she would be in his presence. This ensured that, when the day came and Lucias finally lost his tether, his crown fell to her.

As for her current state, she came to peace with it when she realized she could use her femininity to her advantage. She could, given the circumstances of the war, reconcile with Noliminan in their marriage contract. She would gladly keep her legs spread to him and give him his damned babies if it meant that she was to become the most powerful woman in all Sixty Realms.

He hadn't, yet, asked for her hand again. But she was confident that, eventually, he would.

Sighing, she shook her head and walked through the room to the fire pit. She lowered herself onto her preferred chair and stared into the flames, her mind spinning.

She knew there was only one way to retain power. Just as there was only one way to reconcile their marriage. She had to keep Noliminan angry with Lucias.

The real reason for the travesty that had taken place between Noliminan and Gabriel was because the angel wore Lucias' face. Noliminan's anger with Lucias was triggered by the sight of Gabriel.

With Lucias locked away and Gabriel in exile, how was she going to keep Noliminan's rage with Lucias enflamed?

Unable to bear the weight of her frustration, she let out a deep sigh and buried her face into her slender hands. She sat in silence for several long minutes before lowering her hands to her lap.

She needed to do something to convince Noliminan that Gabriel should be returned to the Guf.

There has to be a way to restore the boy to his rightful place without Noliminan coming to understand my true motivation for suggesting he does so.

With this thought, Raziel raised her gaze and fell back upon her chair. As she did, her eyes landed upon her copies of the many Tomes she had written over the years. These Tomes were filled with the history of every important event ever to have taken place since her creation.

Her eyes dancing over their bindings, she had a glimmer of an idea regarding how she might assist Gabriel. And, in so doing, protect herself and the progress she had made toward achieving her goals.

In the darkness, and in the silence of the evening, her laughter echoed in a cloak of comfort around her.

- 3 -

When Raphael opened the door to find his mother and Zamyael standing on the other side, he shuddered. There was an inward chill that washed over him as he looked upon the expression on Raziel's face. Given the mood of her parting from Council, he was not, entirely, surprised to see her.

"Raphael, is he in?" Her tone was as icy as her gaze.

"Yes, my Lady." Stepping back, Raphael pulled the door with him. "But he's in a mood."

"When is he not?"

He had no response to this. Ever since Raphael had returned from being a prisoner of war in Lucias' camp, King Noliminan had, indeed, been in foul temperament. Raphael, whose own shadow terrified him these days, was less than able to manage him.

The night before, he had walked in on King Noliminan, his hands clenched tight around Gabriel's neck, screaming Lucias' name at Gabe and blaming him for Lucias' betrayal.

"I shall advise him you are here." He gave the Lady a small bow and turned away from her. His irritation that she would follow him through the apartment, rather than waiting in the sitting room, overwhelmed him. He gave her a cold scowl and slipped through the library door.

His Lord and Master sat on the opposite side of his desk with his head lowered into his hands and his fingers buried in his long brown hair. His masculine features were dark with heavy shadows. His tone, when he spoke, was gruff. "What is it, Raphael?"

"Lady Regent Raziel is here to speak with you."

King Noliminan snorted at her lately come by title, lowered his hands to his desk and raised his head. His eyes were full of storming fury. "I am in no mood to placate her."

"I understand, your Grace." Raphael swallowed. "But she's in one of her moods."

King Noliminan rolled his eyes and turned his head from side to side. He was beginning to get tired of Raziel and her lately come by attitude toward him. He didn't like that she took the liberties with him which Lucias had done before being imprisoned.

"Let her in." He commanded. "But stay here. I want her gone swiftly and she won't linger if she understands at the start of it that she will not gain my private audience."

Raphael was grateful for this. He loathed the days when Raziel spent the night with King Noliminan in the room adjacent to his own.

An occurrence which was increasing in frequency, much to his dismay.

He bowed to the King of Lords and returned to the door to let Raziel in. Zamyael, he noted, had stayed by the front door and lowered herself into her waiting stance. He hated seeing her so. He missed his beloved Zamyael of old.

He offered her a haunted smile which she weakly returned and followed his mother through the door.

"You sent my son away from me today."

King Noliminan crossed his arms over his chest and glared at her. "He disobeyed."

"How?" She sneered. "By refusing to play your little dress up games?"

His eyes narrowed and his lips pursed. Raphael shivered. "Ware that tongue woman. Lest I rip it from your throat."

Wisely, she let the matter of Gabriel drop.

"It's time to write the Tome detailing Lucias' petty little war."

"So write it."

She sighed dramatically. "You know I am unable. Everyone who had any involvement has been locked away with Loki's damned."

"Then ask Loki to unlock the door so you might visit them."

A strange expression crossed her pretty features. Raphael knew she loathed the Thirteenth level of the Hells. Especially given the fact that she had spent the majority of the rebellion locked up in one of its cages. Raphael had never been told who had sent her there. Certainly Lucias never admitted to having done so.

"Wouldn't it be easier to simply order Azrael to tell the tale?"

King Noliminan watched her with faint interest. After a shift of the shadows he reminded her, "You know that he cannot speak with you. He's hanging in the gallows of the Great Hall even now for denying *me* a conversation."

"Nol," she stepped toward his desk and lowered herself into one of the chairs on the other side. "Please be reasonable. I do not wish to write this Tome based on word of mouth alone. Azrael is the only one who knows what took place!"

"No."

"But, your Grace—"

"I told you no, Raziel." His fist flew downward, slamming onto the desk. The sound of it made Raphael flinch. "I will not permit it, let alone order it to be so."

Raziel didn't seem to be affected. "I wouldn't utilize him to my personal ill gain."

His eyes flashed before narrowing. He knew better.

"Do you want a biased accounting—?"

"You have my answer." His tone held a warning quality that made Raphael shudder. "Now leave.

"Fine!" She stood and spun away from him, stomping to the door. She looked to Raphael to be a child throwing a temper tantrum. "I'll figure out another way to find out what took place!"

"You do that." He sat back and crossed his arms over his chest again. "And don't come back to me until you hold a copy of the damned thing in your hands."

Infuriated with him, she stormed out of the door, slamming it behind her.

Raphael had never been more grateful to see her go.

- 4 -

"This has to be your decision, Azrael." Lucias tells me through the door. "I will support you. You can be assured of that. But it will be you who pays the ultimate price."

"He's focusing too much attention on the youngling." I share. "He's starting to ask questions."

"I cannot tell you what to do."

"But you can tell me what you *want* me to do."

"You already have your answer to that question."

I do. I knew what Lucias would ask of me before I entered the Thirteenth level of the Hells so we might hold palaver.

"You are the one who will pay for your decision." Lucias reminds me. "Either by your action or inaction. You must decide if the risk or punishment is worse."

Swallowing, I nod at the closed door. Lucias is right. This is my decision. The only one who can weigh the consequences is me.

"Thank you for your candor." I raise my hand to set it upon the door that separates us. I want to see Lucias' face. But that face, along with Noliminan's, is one of the few that I cannot look upon without first gaining permission to do so. "I know what I must do."

Silence stretched between us before Lucias let out a low, tired sob. It wounds me to hear this. Rarely, if ever, has Lucias shown any type of weakness to others. That the sob was made in gratitude, as much as it was in sorrow, did not decrease the nature of its significance in my mind.

"I must go." This I say regretfully. "There are many tasks which must be seen to before I speak with her."

"I wish you love and luck in all things."

"And I you, Pipa." My voice is little more than a whisper. "I shall speak with you again when I can."

No response. I didn't expect there to be one.

We both know there is a very real possibility that, if I do not succeed at my task, we will never have the opportunity to speak with one another again.

-5-

Evanbourough sat soaking in his tub, his eyes closed and his mind spinning. Though he had been fundamentally wrong in his understanding of many facts, he regretted none of his actions.

A knock on his bathing room door pulled him out of his reverie with a frown.

Who, exactly, would be calling on me at this hour?

And, better yet, who would dare to come into his rooms without his allowance of it to knock on his bathing room door?

"Who is it?"

A familiar, yet unexpected, voice sighed. "Azrael."

Irritated, Evanbourough glared at the bathroom door. "What do you want from me?"

"I demand a word."

"Fine." Evanbourough scowled.

What choice did he have but to agree? One didn't deny a member of the King of Lords' Quorum an audience if it had been requested. Especially when their request was verbally classified as a demand.

"Wait in the sitting room. I shall join you there momentarily."

"As you will."

Evan sighed, standing as he did. The air around him was cool compared to the water in which he had been bathing and he shivered slightly as he stepped out of the bath. He reached for his black silk robe and wrapped it around his body, cinching it tight at the waist before stepping out of the room and into the hall.

As much as he disdained my presence, he understood well that it did not do to keep one of the Quorum waiting. More than likely, he reasons, I have been sent by Noliminan, himself.

He stepped into the foyer and frowned as his eyes found my back. My gaze was held upward to the oil paintings of the only three lovers Evan had ever taken to his bed.

"How may I help you, Azrael?" He asked frostily.

He had never been comfortable with anyone who delved into his emotions or his past. The paintings on his wall were a window to both. As such, my contemplation of them was unsettling to him.

I continued to look at the paintings for a moment before languidly turning to face Evan with what he considers to be a strange expression upon my drawn, brown skinned face. "Forgive me for interrupting your bath."

"Let us get on with it so I might return."

My lips twitched slightly and my crimson eyes narrowed. Evanbourough was uncomfortable with my obvious amusement over his discontentment. "Just so."

"What does the King of Lords want of me?"

"You have the wrong of things." I replied with a cold tone as I lowered my gaze. "It is actually I who seek your favor, my Lord. And, more than likely, against Noliminan's desire."

This made Evanbourough start. "Really? How so?"

"Is your confidence mine to count upon?" I asked, my gaze still lowered.

"Ta." Evan answered, softening his tone as he did so. "Yes. Of course, Azrael. Forgive my rudeness, child. You do, indeed, have my confidence."

I nodded. As I did so, my eyes narrowed, causing Evanbourough to shiver. "I held palaver with my father this morning."

"You don't say." Evanbourough swallowed his surprise. To visit anyone on the Thirteenth level was forbidden. But given the sheer magnitude of the crimes Lucias had committed, I could be found guilty of treason, myself, for my disobedience. "Is he well?"

"No." I said bluntly, almost rudely. "But that is not the point which I am here to discuss with you."

"No." Evanbourough agreed, a twinge of fear for his own skin for having upset a member of the Quorum flushing through him. "Of course not."

"He has done something terrible." I said softly.

Evan considered me with disbelief. Could there be anything more terrible than revolting against the King of Lords and his Council?

He was unable to suppress his cold smile. "And what, pray tell, would that be?"

"He is the one who hid the dathanorna." I answered.

This was a cold slap in the face.

"Loki's beard." Evanbourough muttered.

"You *will* help, Lord Evanbourough." I demanded, my crimson eyes—which, he thought, look more like two pools of blood to those who look upon me than seeing orbs—danced with instruction over Evanbourough's face.

"Why *me*?" Evan's question was choked.

"Because you are already aware of its existence." I snapped. "Yet you have told no one. And nor would you for fear that you would be betraying Tristan."

Evan crossed his arms over his chest and glared at me. He didn't like being commanded by a servant. Especially against the King of Lords' desires. Aside from that, he suspected he was being blackmailed.

Which, he realized soon enough, he was.

"I mean to visit Raziel and speak with her about the revolution for the sake of prosperity. In the retelling, I may be required to divulge the story of the mistake made between the demon and the angel and the child that was begot. You must move the dathanorna from its current hiding place." I commanded. "And if you do not, my retelling of your own part in this will be more brutally honest than, perhaps, you would care for."

"Very well." He shivered. He knew that I would make good on this threat. As such, he had no choice. "How much time do I have?"

"That depends upon Raziel." I continued to watch him with a penetrating gaze. "It depends on if she is willing to listen to what I know or if she is just trying to appease herself for the purposes of the Tome." My brow furrowed slightly. "Her current thoughts run to her own purposes. What her final motivation will be when we actually speak is unclear."

"Raziel wouldn't ask you to lift your tongue if she wasn't interested in what you have to say." Evanbourough, who was disconcerted regarding the reminder that I could read his thoughts, assured me.

He marked that an odd shimmer stained my blood red eyes. He swiftly looked away, unable to bear such disdain from one so powerful.

"Go to it, Azrael." He said, his voice gentle as he tried, unsuccessfully, to block his thoughts from me. "With no fear regarding me. As you command me at Lucias' will, I shall see to the replacement of the dathanorna's living quarters straight away."

-6-

I am grateful, when I knock upon my mother's door, to see Zamyael has been waiting for me. Because I told her almost immediately after speaking with Lucias what my intentions were, she has been expecting me. Her following my request that it should be she who answers the door pleases me.

"Here." I raise the lock of hair that I have acquired to be used later to show her. "Hide this. I'll explain when I am able."

"*If* you are able. Azrael," her eyes implore me, "do not put yourself into harm's way! You know not how your magic will punish you this time."

"I know not." I agree. "But I care not." Pressing the lock of hair into her palm I squeeze her hand. She knows I am lying to her because I am trembling. "When the time comes, promise me you will do as I say."

"I promise." She nods. "Must you tell her—?"

"To save Lucias?" I interrupt her. "I must tell her everything."

Zamyael sighs. She knows that my father's safety is not my primary concern. "Of course you must."

I grant her a smile which I hope tells her that I understand her fear. She makes no response, though her thoughts do seem to settle. She leads me to the sitting room, where Raziel waits for us. I notice, as she does, that she tucks the lock of hair that I have given her into the waist of her skirt.

Dear Zamyael. If the love between an angel and a demon were not forbidden, I would confess my adoration to you.

Lowering myself to the seat across from Raziel, I look over the table filled with meats, breads and cheeses that Zamyael has prepared before meeting Raziel's chilling gaze. I shift uncomfortably and I force a smile.

Even though it is my choice to be here against Noliminan's wishes, I am more fearful of the harm I might do to others by speaking secret words than I am of what will befall me. This is my nature. Perhaps, as I recognize this trait, I understand why Noliminan granted me this magic. Even if his intention was that it was meant to be a punishment.

"I know you wish me to speak with candor." I decided before walking through the door that misdirecting my mother as to my intentions was my only hope of achieving my own gains. In fact, she believes that I am here because Noliminan ordered me to be, rather than on my own accord, because I instructed Zamyael to mislead her in that regard. "I am unsure as to what help I might be, my Lady."

"You shall be a tremendous help." Raziel assures me, her nose curling at the title. She had insisted to Noliminan that she become Queen of Ladies and he had refused her. As a result, she was touting herself as Queen Regent rather than Lady Regent.

Enough ill will has formed within me for her at this point that I care little and less about how she prefers to be addressed.

"If we can only make Noliminan see. Mayhap, then, he will allow Gabriel to return to the Guf."

"You trust in his ability to forgive far better than do I." The words were said before I considered them.

Raziel's flaming eyes narrow and her brow furrows. I know my mother is angry with me. She might defy Noliminan when it suits her, but she doesn't stand for such behavior toward him from others.

Especially we lowly servants.

"I only mean to say he is stubborn." Reading the turn of her thoughts, I backtrack. "Once he has made a decision regarding punishments, he very rarely backs down. Look to Queen Raguel if you need evidence of it."

"Ta." Raziel nods, her forehead smoothing. Queen Raguel is one of those topics of discussion which always brings about fear in Raziel. Needing her to forget my insolence, I use this knowledge to my advantage. "Poor Raguel."

I ignore her false empathy. "I am in a quandary. I do not know where to begin."

"At the start of it." Raziel shrugs her shoulders. "The first of it which started the upheaval."

"It is impossible, my Lady." And here I throw in a jab. "You see, you did not breathe life into me until all of this was well on its way. And I did not anger Noliminan enough that he should trouble me with my tasks until much later than this."

Raziel actually frowns in response. It makes my heart glad to see it because it means she understands that my magic has never been my choice. It also means she understands this punishment has been born from trying to aide one of my brothers from Noliminan's oft times cruel punishment and that her interference where Gabriel is concerned might cost her dearly.

Now, you might find this selfish of me, but—though I love Gabriel and do not begrudge him any small advantage her games might earn him—I loathe her for trying to interfere. She never raised the first hand where I was concerned. Nor Zadkiel. Nor Camael. Nor Metatron.

So why, this time, has she become so damned motherly?

I understand you might be thinking that this is a silly question to be brokered within my mind given I can read her thoughts.

"As long ago as that, then?"

"Upon your very birthing." I put a soft spin to my tone, though my intent truly was to wound her with my words as she has, numerous times, wounded me with hers.

"Father loves you dearly. Never doubt it."

"I do not."

"Lucias faithfully serves Noliminan."

"I—" She swallows and shakes her head. "I know."

"So where shall I begin?"

I'd rather she set the rules of the game out to me with words. If she tells me where to start, then I can decide by her question how much she really needs to know as I spin my yarn and how much of it I can omit.

"What of when he first started taking action against his anger and jealousy?" Raziel suggests.

"It is a fair place to begin, I suppose." And it is. Though I would have started much earlier had I not been directed otherwise. The knowledge that I have played my mother to my own gains makes me smile. "The meeting where Lucias finally lost his patience with Noliminan, I should mean."

"Yes." Raziel's eyes dance, shimmering fully orange in the light of the fire.

She thinks she has gained the secrets holding the most scandal from me. She doesn't understand that far more delicious facts live in the past of that moment which she may not, now, entice me to share. "It's as good a place as any."

I force myself to smile at her. When Raziel smiles in response, I nod. "May I have a promise first, my Lady?"

"What would this be, child?" Her irritation that I would ask anything from her buzzes fitfully through her mind

"I beg you . . . if some of this does not need to reach the King of Lords' ears . . . ?"

I lower my gaze to the fire and watch the flames for a moment. I, too, know how to play games when the playing of games is required.

"Azrael?"

"As the story unfolds," I add a pleading note to my tone, "I would—Lucias is in enough trouble as it is. I would that you not speak of some of it to Noliminan if it can be avoided."

"I cannot make such a promise as not to share this tale with the King of Lords." She snaps. "He will demand to see my scrolls."

Her tone is filled with so much anger that I force myself to flinch. Having witnessed a great many events, and having read each and every one of Raziel's Tomes, I know their inaccuracies for what they are.

So, too, I suspect, do Noliminan and Lucias.

I nod and decide to take Lucias' sound advice. If Raziel can spin the truth for her own gain, so can I. "Of course, my Lady. Forgive me for my insolence."

"It is accepted." Raziel looks up to watch Zamyael, who slips past me and steps toward her to lower herself obediently into her waiting stance.

I hear the turn of her thoughts as she watches her. I loathe her for them.

"Tell me your tale." She returns her gaze to me when she is no longer interested in admonishing Zamyael for something which has never been within the demon's control. "And leave not a single sordid detail aside.

PART TWO:
THE ARGUMENT

-1-

I shall begin with the moment that I was pulled violently into a conversation in which I understood at once I had no business overhearing.

This knowledge, even now, is painful and disconcerting.

As I formed within the King of Lords' dining room, I shook my head in an attempt to gain my composure. Looking around myself, I saw only Noliminan and Lucias.

At the time, these two Gods were the only two, out of all of souls, that I was not able to direct my attention toward or to read their thoughts. Never had I been privy to any conversations taking place between them without a third party in the room.

That I was standing in a room where they were the only two present was terrifying to me. Whatever they had to say to one another was not meant for my ears.

"Free will?" Lucias glared at Noliminan across the table. Having never been privy to Lucias' true thoughts, I wanted to scream as my mind reverberated with words which were not my own.

More the fool am I for actually believing, for once, we might simply bide one another's company. I've only been invited to sup with you so you might tout your ridiculous notion of free will.

"And without consequence, you say?"

Terrified of the thoughts running through my head, I shivered. I wondered what was happening to me. How would I, one who is banned from the minds of these two betters, know the turn of Lucias' thoughts?

"Not exactly." Noliminan's tone was docile as he assessed Lucias' mood. He reached for Lucias' hand, covering it with his own. "They must ask for forgiveness and absolution should they abuse this privilege. Nor would we simply hand redemption over to them."

"And if they *do* ask for forgiveness and absolution?" I watched in silent fear and fascination whilst Lucias' eyes narrowed.

"Then they have the opportunity to make better choices on their second journey." Noliminan shrugged.

"Just how many journeys are they to be afforded?"

"As many as it takes."

Though I still do not know how, I became aware that Lucias was biting back his immediate remark to settle for a more politic response.

"Do you plan to allow them the knowledge that their little 'say sorry' is your only requirement should they wish to avoid me?" Noliminan appeared taken aback by the question. "Or will you let them stumble into the epiphany by themselves?"

"Of course I shall allow them the knowledge."

"My halls will be empty within a matter of days!" His temper was flaring as he pulled his hand away from Noliminan's.

"You will still be the Ruler of your Thirty Hells. And the angels and demons will still be yours to—"

"You do not mean to give the children the same absolution as you plan to give your speaking apes?"

Lucias voicing my own thoughts made me smile.

Noliminan shrugged. "A servant of the Gods must be held to a higher standard than a mortal."

"I agree. But you—"

"Why must you argue every matter I discuss with you?" Noliminan asked with a note of irritation to his tone.

"Because you never think things all the way through." Lucias pulled his napkin from his neck, where it had been tucked into his shirt, and threw it to his plate.

I knew something to be true in that moment: Lucias was violently ill. And not because of the conversation at hand. Something was physically not right with him.

"The very fact that the angels and demons do serve the Gods should lend them higher measure for choice. Yet, should they displease you, you would throw them to me and my cages without thought or reason."

"Where I am certain you will coddle them." Noliminan placated. "Really, Luke. You are being silly about all of this."

Noliminan sighed, reaching again for Lucias' hand. Lucias, who I suspect was conflicted by his feelings for Noliminan, let him take it.

"Adam is to be *your* child—*your* son! He is ever as much, by your seed, your creation, as mine."

"All I am saying," Lucias sighed, not wanting to dwell upon the fact that he had, at Noliminan's request, impregnated an ape, "is you are going to have an uprising on your hands if you do not take into consideration the already existing current between the mortals, the children and the Gods. Even more disturbing yet, between the angels and the demons and the Gods of each Realm."

"You have already and thoroughly spoken of this untrue current."

"I do not speak untruths!" Lucias seethed, pulling his hand away. His anger was raging again. "The Gods be damned, every one of us, but there will come a day of reckoning. When such a day comes, it shall be on *your* head for ignoring the signs of it."

Noliminan's lips pursed as his eyes danced over Lucias' face. I wondered if, mayhap, for the first time in all of the years they had this conversation, Noliminan was seeing reason.

I realized all too soon how foolish a prospect my supposition was.

He smiled. "I think Adam should be made in your image."

Lucias lowered his gaze, his thoughts ringing out strong and clear in my mind once again.

Noliminan and his speaking apes! There are more important matters to consider than the damned apes!

His answer was made through his teeth. "I do not wish for Adam to look like me."

"Ah, but I do." Noliminan said his voice somewhat a purr. Lucias, biting back his anger, lowered his gaze to the napkin he had discarded upon his plate. "I have always said you are my finest creation."

"I have never heard you say half as much." Lucias replied, unable to hide the smug satisfaction the compliment inspired.

"No, but you are." Noliminan grasped Lucias' hand again, squeezed it tightly and then released it. "Oh!"

Lucias glared at him. By his expression, I kenned he was wondering what asinine idea had occurred to Noliminan now.

I certainly was.

"I have been remiss! That new demon of yours—"

"Loki." Lucias said, his smile softening. I understand why. I am fond of Apprentice Lord Loki, myself. "But he's not a demon. Is he?"

"How did you come by that knowledge?" Noliminan asked with narrowed eyes.

"Aside from the fact that he bears no wings?" Lucias asked in irritable tones. "I sent him to the brothels so he might lose his virginity and he returned upset by his discovery that the female demons also bear male genitalia."

Noliminan nodded dismissively. It was another tired conversation between the two of them and Noliminan was wise to let the hermaphrodite state of we angels and demons sit where it was for the moment lest it raise Lucias' temper again. "Just, please—tell me this one is working out for you."

"His service to me is adequate." Lucias agreed. Though his response seemed guarded to me. "But Sappharon—"

"I do not wish to discuss that atrocity." Noliminan slammed his fist down on the table. "You had no right making her without my permission."

"You are extremely unreasonable where Sappharon is concerned." Lucias said nonchalantly, in no mood to argue with Noliminan about his bratty demon. "She has a good heart."

"A good heart?" Noliminan snorted. "She's as devilish as any I have ever met!"

"She has to be." Lucias snapped. "I made her so she could see to the tasks she would need to without compunction or compassion." Lucias sighed. "For the work we must do, it is sometimes what is required."

Noliminan snorted again.

"By any road," Lucias seethed through his teeth. "Loki is eager to learn and he is willing to take the less desirable tasks without complaint." Noliminan nodded. "Also, he seems to get along well enough in his daily duties with Martiam and Azrael, so the collection and disposition of souls upon death and judgment is better served."

"I am pleased by it." Noliminan conceded. "Azrael's job will be all the more difficult with an added third possibility to contend with."

"Have you spoken with Gabriel?" Lucias asked, trying to sound glib. My job wouldn't change a wit. It was Gabriel who would find himself overwhelmed. "Have you told him of the immeasurably increased workload you expect out of him once you grant the speaking apes their 'free will'?"

"I have not." Noliminan answered, the corners of his lips turned down. He knew Lucias' endearment of the humans had ever been to call them that. "He shall be honored by the task."

"So you say." Lucias dismissed, not at all convinced. Gabriel, aside from me, was already the busiest of the twelve servants who bow to Noliminan's throne. Gabriel, alone, was responsible for creating and tracking the souls going toward the various times and worlds.

Now he is to also track those asking for absolution from their sins as well?

"I only worry over much about Gabe because he is my son."

"Of course you do." Noliminan placated him, seemingly happy to address what he assumed to be the true problem at last. "I promise I shall advise him of his new tasks with the greatest of all delicacies."

"Then he shan't deny you." Lucias used docile tones. "They never do. Even when they know damn well and good they ought to."

Noliminan shrugged. The matter of Gabriel's denial was moot.

The entire point of this heated discourse was that Gabriel *couldn't* deny him.

Gabriel and we others would do the bidding of the Gods without question. Should the task prove to be too much, or if we had qualms regarding the consequence, we would be dealt with appropriately.

"I must leave you." Lucias said, needing to put as much space between them as possible lest he say something he would later regret.

"So soon?"

The Gods pray! Lucias' thoughts reverberated through my mind, causing me to close my eyes tight and shake my head against the pain of my discontentment. *He has actually been wounded!*

"I'm afraid so." Lucias said. He gave Noliminan a cruel smile. "Raziel cornered me in the gardens this morning and asked if I am free to spend the night."

That did the trick.

Noliminan's expression was one of a man who has just been slapped.

His eyes blazed as they narrowed. "Oh, I see. Raziel is more important to you than I."

"No." Lucias' smile was cruel and cold. "The shadows with Raziel simply shift more pleasurably."

The strangeness of Noliminan's expression was overwhelming. His anger with Raziel over her choice to present herself as male to him, rather than as female, has always been profound.

He looked away.

"That's disgusting." He muttered. "I fail to see the attraction between the pair of you now that she refuses to supplicate sexually as a female."

Lucias opted not to correct Noliminan by sharing with him that the only time Raziel refused to take on her female essence was in Noliminan's presence. Otherwise, she was ever the woman she had always been meant to be. I understand that Lucias believed Raziel's reasons for playing games with Noliminan were her own. He was not about to get into the middle of the quarrel given their long, tumultuous past.

"Your loss on both counts."

Noliminan's gaze flew to Lucias. An odd light burned within his eyes that I had never seen within them before. "Tell her I said hello."

41

"Tell her so yourself." Lucias snorted. "I'll see you tomorrow to discuss matters of the Court."

Noliminan returned his strange gaze to Lucias, but I barely had time to recognize this before Lucias was gone.

With him, I was forced out of the room.

-2-

Lasterian chased after Lord Tristan who, contrary to his peaceful nature, was storming through the castle of the Hells' Realms in seek of Lord Aegir. Though he knew not why his new Master was enraged, there was no question that this was the case. He was spouting out profanities in such a string that the demons guarding the doors of their Masters' houses followed Lord Tristan with wide eyed gazes and turned down wings.

Wings, Lasterian thought as he stumbled past one of the demons, nearly falling at the creature's knees, which were charcoal black. Not pristine white like his own.

He thought to the peculiarity of the differences between angel and demon for but a brief moment before hearing Lord Tristan spout out another string of curse words that pulled him out of his reverie so he was, once more, running at a mad dash after him.

Finally—the Gods be praised—they reached Lord Aegir's door.

Not bothering with the formalities of knocking, Lord Tristan threw the door open and stormed within. Lasterian, unknowing of what was to pass but ready for anything, hovered outside the door and peered within with wide eyes.

Though rumors abound that those who bowed to Lord Regent Lucias were lesser Gods, these rooms were as congenial as any Lasterian had ever visited within the Heavens!

The commotion of the door flying open forced the demon on the other side—a beautiful female with silver hair which glistened in the light of the fire—to fly away from her post at Lord Aegir's feet (he was an odd looking being with hair the color of moss, almost iridescently blue scaled flesh and eyes that matched his strange hair) and huddle, frightened, against the far wall.

Lasterian tried to pass her a smile to calm her, but she had no eyes for him. They were glued, tight and frightened, upon Lord Tristan.

"What is the meaning of your meddling in the mediation between the fairies and the sea dragons?" Lord Tristan seethed. "I have worked for three thousand years to get them to meet and you destroy all of my efforts with a single, misplaced word."

"I see no reason to allow your mischief fairies Atlantis." Lord Aegir answered, shrugging his shoulders. His tone, unlike Lord Tristan's, held no anger. "Why should they be granted an underwater kingdom?"

"This mediation has nothing to do with Atlantis." Lord Tristan growled. "Or with my mischief fairies. Your sea dragons and my water fairies have been destroying each other for nigh on eight thousand years! If they would simply sit down and talk—"

"You and your talk-talk." Lord Aegir sighed, turning his mossy eyes in Lord Tristan's direction. One of his hands was raised and his webbed fingers flapped together around the words 'talk-talk'. "It doesn't ever solve anything."

"It does when nosy sea dwellers aren't putting their gills in it." Lord Tristan seethed. "Why do you not take your issue with the underwater peoples to Triton? It is he who is pushing the issue. Not me."

Lord Aegir snorted. "That overblown sea horse?"

"And the King of Lords wonders why nothing ever gets done!" Lord Tristan cried, hands in the air, palms and gaze to the ceiling.

"Really, Tristan." Lord Aegir yawned through his response. "You do take your work far too seriously. Take a day off, why don't you." His strange eyes flicked to Lasterian. "Take advantage of your new plaything."

Lasterian's brow furrowed at this. He was unsure as to why Lord Aegir was looking at him in such a fashion or why he had been called a plaything. Lord Tristan didn't help matters by shaking his head and glowering at the cowering demon in the corner of the room before turning his gaze back to Lord Aegir. "You are troubled in more manners than I can even begin to describe."

"*You* are a prude." Lord Aegir retorted. "You and Evanbourough; the pair of you. Always it is you fighting for children's rights." He stuck out his tongue, which was forked and as green as his hair and eyes. "Blah to equality, I say. They should count themselves lucky."

"Lucky." Lord Tristan growled his gaze returning to the beautiful demon. He held a hand to her. "*This* is lucky? Cowering in the corner because she's frightened to death of you." The tenor of his laugh was cold. "How I wish I were as lucky as her."

Lasterian's gaze returned to the demon. Her skin had gone ashen and her eyes had grown wide as she flew her gaze to the floor. If he wasn't mistaken, she was even trembling. He could not understand what was wrong with her. What had she to be so frightened of?

"My treatment of Saristia is neither here nor there." Lord Aegir answered Lord Tristan. "And nor is it your concern."

"The day of repayment will come, my friend." Lord Tristan forewarned. "I should hate to stand in your shoes when it does."

"Ha!" Lord Aegir snorted. "What day of reckoning? The King of Lords cannot say anything about it. Look at how he treats his own!""Zadkiel defied a direct order." Tristan seethed.

Lasterian had seen Zadkiel only once. Though Lasterian rarely classified any male as beautiful, this angel was. His features were masculine and handsome, but his hair, skin, wings and eyes were solid gold in color.

Despite Zadkiel's beauty, Lasterian found the archangel difficult to gaze upon because the left side of his body was a crippled mass of bone and muscle.

Curious as to his uncle's plight, Lasterian had braved to raise the question regarding why one of the Quorum should be so horrifically disfigured. Lord Tristan had advised Lasterian that Zadkiel, who was the only being with the magic to extinguish the force of life once it had been created, had used his powers to dispose of a Goddess against the King of Lords' command. His punishment, Lasterian had been told, was to be flung from the Heavens by Michael and Metatron toward the farthest away of all of the inhabited worlds.

"Zadkiel's situation is much different than this innocent—"

"Oh." Lord Aegir purred. "She's far from innocent. Want to have a go at her so you might judge her skills for yourself?" He leered at Lasterian. "I *share* my toys."

Lord Tristan glared at him, lips pursed tight. Finally, he shook his head and spoke in a dark tone through clenched teeth. "Will you speak to the sea dragons and ask them to attend tomorrow's council or will you not?"

"Not." Lord Aegir returned with a smile.

"Then I have no choice but to take the matter out of your hands." He spun on his heel and bolted toward the door, shooing Lasterian out of the way with a gesture of his hands as he did so.

The sound of Lord Aegir's laughter followed them as the door slammed shut behind them.

Lord Tristan let out another frustrated cry before storming in a new direction all together, throwing out another string of curses behind him. Lasterian, who had never before been in the castle of the Hells Realm, tried desperately to keep up lest he become lost.

He would never be able to find his way out should Lord Tristan leave him behind. And after hearing what Lord Aegir had said . . .

He shuddered.

Lord Tristan turned down a long hall which seemed to have fewer doorways distributed farther apart. When he reached the door making up the end wall of the hall he knocked loudly. Standing there, waiting, he turned his pale blue eyes to Lasterian and forced a tired, less than confident smile.

"The Sovereign Lady lives here." Lord Tristan explained. Lasterian's eyes widened as he swallowed back the immediate lump of fear that had risen in his throat. The Lady's reputation of being indomitable proceeded her. "I trust you shall be on your best behavior. Make me proud and such."

"Lady Raziel, my Lord?" His father, the archangel Camael, had told him Lord Regent Lucias was the ruling God of the Hells. Given this, Lasterian didn't understand why Lord Tristan would seek aide from Lady Raziel rather than Lord Lucias. "Not Lord Regent Lucias?"

Lord Tristan averted his eyes slightly. "Lord Lucias is a powerful God, Lasterian. He has better things to trouble himself with then petty politics."

"Yes, my Lord." Lasterian agreed. "But if he is Lord Aegir's King—?"

"Just as I bring my issues to the Queen of Ladies rather than the King of Lords, it is equally appropriate that I speak with Lady Raziel rather than directly to Lord Regent Lucias." He gave Lasterian a patient smile. "We let the two rulers discuss matters between the Heavens and the Hells when their interference is required and bring our issues to their women. It isn't the place of lesser Gods to speak with them directly."

"Yes, my Lord." Lasterian nodded in understanding.

The door opened to a beautiful, feminine looking male demon. His eyes were black, as was his hair, which was braided in small rivers. He wore nothing to cover the upper half of his lithe body, though his shimmering black skirt (which scooped in a curve from his hips to below his navel and, then, fell in a silky curtain to the tops of his delicately made feet) aptly covered him.

Lasterian shivered as the demon spoke.

"Tristan. What an unexpected surprise."

"Is Lady Raziel in, Zamyael?" He asked, warmth now added to his tone. "And is she granting audience?"

"She is in." Zamyael said, cocking his head slightly to the side. "Though she is otherwise engaged at the moment." An odd expression darkened the demon's features. "I'm certain you are welcome to come in and wait, however. I shall simply tell her you are here and speed things along."

"I shouldn't want to interrupt something important." Lord Tristan offered.

"She's only tarrying with Lucias over a game of kings' castles." Zamyael shrugged his shoulders. "Not making plans to change the course of our worlds."

"I see." Lord Tristan chuckled slightly. "Well, then, yes. If it is all the same I should very much like to wait."

Zamyael nodded. He stepped back and indicated a chair to the left of the fire. "Please do sit."

Lord Tristan put his foot out with a clap before him and bowed to the demon. The strange offer of fealty puzzled Lasterian. Zamyael seemed pleased by this, however. He grasped his skirt and gave a slight curtsey, much as a woman would do. He wore a faint smile.

After Zamyael turned and left them, Lord Tristan summoned Lasterian that he might lower himself to his hunkers at Lord Tristan's side. Lasterian did so without ceremony, looking up at his God and watching him as his blue eyes danced with amusement and his lips twitched to avoid a smile. A moment later and he turned his eyes down to Lasterian and then, just as swiftly, away.

Having missed something, however, he returned his gaze to meet Lasterian's own.

"Are you are alright?" He asked.

"Yes, my Lord." Lasterian's voice was shaking to his own ears.

"Do not be frightened, child." Lord Tristan reached his strong, slender fingers to pat Lasterian's long brown hair. As he did so, he held Lasterian's gaze with warm regard. "Lady Raziel is kind."

"Of course, my Lord."

"Do you find Zamyael pretty?" Lord Tristan asked.

"Ta, my Lord?" Lasterian answered, not knowing how he was supposed to respond to such a question about a male demon. He lowered his gaze and added. "But not as pretty as the demoness. I should very much like to spend time alone with her."

"Saristia?" Lord Tristan yanked his hand away as though scorched.

"Yes, my Lord."

Lord Tristan's eyes narrowed. "Never let me hear you speak thusly about a demon again, child." His tone was icy. "Male or female. Do you understand? Angels and demons must not pass time in solitude together. It is against the laws of the Gods."

Lasterian's brow furrowed. "Why?"

"It simply is." Lord Tristan seethed. "Just . . ." He looked away. "We'll not talk of this again. Be a good lad and mind my words."

"Yes, my Lord." Lasterian lowered his gaze, unable to stomach the strange coldness within Lord Tristan's eyes.

What have I done to disappoint my Master so? To anger him?

"Do not be upset, child." He said, the bite out of his tone. He appeared to be slightly irritated with Lasterian, however. "I meant not to harm your feelings." His lips twitched. "I forget you are still so young. You do not understand our laws and our ways." He reached forward again and entwined his fingers in Lasterian's hair. "I should hate to have you make such a fatal mistake as falling in love with a demon when naught that is good could come of it. One, or even both, of you might find yourselves a permanent resident in Lord Regent Lucias' basement."

"Yes, my Lord." Lasterian said, gaze still lowered.

From the direction of the hall, Zamyael cleared his throat. "Excuse me, Tristan. Raziel and Lucias will see you in the library." His smile was tight as he looked upon Lasterian. "Only you. Lucias is not in a current mood for angels and their penchant for wagging their tongues."

"Of course." Lord Tristan said, standing. He didn't realize Lasterian was affronted by the accusation that he was a gossip. Or, if he did, he didn't care. "You will stay here. And behave."

"Yes, my Lord." Lasterian promised.

As good as his word, Lasterian stayed in his waiting stance while Zamyael led Lord Tristan down the hall. After a few moments, his ears tuned toward the soft sound of bare feet upon marble. He raised his eyes to meet the demon's ebony gaze. Lasterian forced a smile that felt ugly and untrue upon his lips.

"Is he kind to you?" Zamyael asked as he stepped forward and lowered himself—rather gracefully—into one of the chairs belonging to his Goddess. Lasterian's mouth dropped open and his eyes grew wide at the brazenness of the act. He should never dare sit upon any one of Lord Tristan's chairs without first gaining Lord Tristan's accord that he might do so. "Tristan, I mean."

"Oh." Lasterian nodded vigorously. "Ta. Extraordinarily kind."

"I'm pleased to hear it." Zamyael said as he reached for a fat red grape upon the fruit plate at the table and plopped it into his mouth. "Such is rare."

"Rare?" Lasterian licked his lips as he watched Zamyael reach for another grape.

Zamyael, seeing Lasterian was watching him, threw it toward Lasterian. The angel deftly caught it in his mouth and closed his eyes to the pleasure of the taste of it as it popped upon his tongue and then slid down his throat.

"Does he give you time away from him?" Zamyael asked, his eyes narrowing. "For you, I should mean?"

"Oh, yes." Lasterian opened his eyes and nodded. "Every Seventh Moon I get to myself. He lets me do whatever I want without ever a question."

"If that's so, I can arrange for you to meet with her." Zamyael nodded. "For a price."

Lasterian was confused. He swallowed back the flurry of butterflies that took flight within his stomach. "Meet with whom?"

Zamyael chuckled. "Did I not hear you telling Tristan that you wish to tarry in the land of the demons?"

"Forgive me." Lasterian said, as confused as ever he had been in his young life.

"Saristia." Zamyael offered, somewhat irritated by Lasterian's slow wit. "You did say you wish to spend time alone with her?"

Lasterian forced his attention to the hall, half expecting Lord Tristan to jump out and announce this as a trap. Assured that the

God was not lurking, he licked his lips and returned his gaze to Zamyael. "Yes. But Lord Tristan told me such is forbidden."

"Znit." Zamyael snorted. "He wouldn't care about such a silly thing. He was merely marking his words in the event Raziel or Lucias where to overhear him."

"But he said spending time with her would be against the law."

"Whose law?"

"The King of Lords' law." Lasterian's head was beginning to ache.

Zamyael rolled his eyes and swatted his hand in Lasterian's direction. "Why on which moon would Noliminan make a law such as that?" Lasterian started at the sound of the King of Lords' name. Though all knew the name, very few dared to voice it's syllables. "There's nothing different between you and she but the color of your wings."

"Lord Tristan was quite insistent—"

"Do you find her pretty or do you not?"

"Pretty." Lasterian nodded. "Yes. She's very pretty."

"She, like you, is not fully a she." Zamyael said with an amused smile.

"Her essence is that of a female." Lasterian felt his lips curl downward. "She has breasts and everything."

"Ta." Zamyael chuckled. "And, unlike you, she can breed your seed. But she cannot seed your breed."

"By any road," Lasterian was becoming irritated with him. He didn't know what games were afoot, but he didn't need the demon to tell him how his own body worked. "She is beautiful to me."

"Then you would meet her?"

"Yes, if I—" He stopped, frowning. "What price?"

Zamyael smiled. It was a smile that was as terrifying as it was beautiful. Lasterian found himself confused by his sudden desire for this strange man given he had no taste for such tremblings. "You are a clever one."

"What price?" This time, his voice sounded slightly desperate.

What is wrong with me?

For having made only one glance at the demoness, how was it that he now plotted against an order which had, but a moment ago, been given him by his newly Mastering God?

Never mind his strange, disconcerting attraction to Zamyael. Lust for another male was completely out of his character. Even if that male appeared more feminine than masculine.

Zamyael shrugged and wore an air about him which suggested his price for arranging a meeting would be both small and pointless. Lasterian, young but not foolish, sensed otherwise.

"It really is something rather small." He said. "I only need a tiny favor."

"What 'tiny' favor?" Lasterian was confused as to why Zamyael would trust him to keep his lips shut about this given he had made it a point to insult Lasterian's kind regarding their penchant for gossip.

Zamyael's eyes narrowed. "You find a way to arrange time for me to be alone with Camael."

"With—" Lasterian snorted. "With *Camael*?"

"He is your father, is he not?" Zamyael asked, his eyes widening. "You are his exact image. I thought—"

"Well—Yes!" Lasterian snorted. "But he serves the King of Lords as a member of the Quorum! How am I to arrange something such as that?"

"The *how* is not my concern." Zamyael shrugged. "I only need ten shifts of Countenance's shadow with him alone. Give me ten shifts of the shadows to speak with him without the eyes of his Master, or mine, and I shall grant you however many more you need with the demoness."

"About what?" Lasterian asked eyes wide.

"*That* is not your concern." Zamyael said, lowering his gaze. "And it's best you do not know." He looked up swiftly. "We haven't much time before your Master returns. Do we have barter?"

"I—" Lasterian shot his gaze to the hallway. He shook his head and then returned his gaze to Zamyael. "I shall speak to my father and let him know you request a word. But he is a stubborn man. Who is above my station. I cannot make any commands upon him."

"Do what you must." Zamyael said, lips pursed. "But you do not get the pretty unless I obtain the opportunity to speak with Camael without the benefit of Raziel or Noliminan's ears. Do you ken?"

"I ken." Lasterian answered, frowning.

Zamyael nodded, shooting his eyes to the hallway and raised his finger to his lips to silence Lasterian. Lord Tristan, done with his business with Lady Raziel, was returning.

"Raziel is so pleased to have Camael's son chosen and exonerated as an angel servant." Lasterian started, surprised by the strange demon's sudden words. "Ah! Tristan. I was telling your dear Lasterian how pleased my Lady is to know her grandson has been promoted from the hall of the mortal souls to the service of a God."

"Lady Raziel told me the same thing." Lord Tristan beamed at Lasterian. Despite Zamyael's words that there was nothing wrong with meeting the demoness, Lasterian likened himself to a treacherous traitor. "I knew the moment I laid eyes upon him . . . Well. He is Camael's son, after all. And Camael is, indeed, a fine and loyal archangel."

"You flatter, my Lord." Lasterian said, lowering his gaze, trying desperately to prevent himself from panicking.

Lord Tristan chuckled and reached forward to pull one of Zamyael's braids. "Thank you for interrupting them. And thank you for keeping Las occupied."

"No matter." Zamyael said, giving him a slight—and very womanly—curtsey.

"We should go now." Lord Tristan said, turning his gaze to Lasterian. "Are you ready, child?"

"Ta, my Lord." Lasterian said as he found his feet. He smiled weakly at Zamyael. He wasn't sure if he liked the demon or if he did not. He did know that he would be wise to watch his back in Zamyael's company. "Thank you for your company."

"Oh. You are welcome just *anytime*." Zamyael answered and gave Lasterian a slight curtsey as well.

"Thank you, my Lord." Lasterian said, not raising his gaze.

"Come on home, Las." Lord Tristan said, throwing his arm around Lasterian and pulling him forward. "You shall cook me a good, hot meal and the two of us will palaver about how we proceed with the water fairies."

"I should like that." Lasterian whispered.

"Goodnight, Zamyael." Lord Tristan said, bowing his head to Zamyael. "Thank you, again, for your aide."

"Anytime, Tristan." The womanly faced demon winked at Lasterian. "Just anytime at all."

-3-

"Loki!"

Loki stopped at the sound of his Master's voice and turned toward Lord Regent Lucias, who was running down the hallway to catch up with him. He was laughing, for a change, which told Loki he was in a good mood. Loki found himself smiling in return, grateful for this small wonder.

"You walk far too fast! I've been trying to catch your attentions all the way from Raziel's!"

"I didn't realize, my Lord." Loki said, smiling at his new Master. "Please do forgive me."

"Znit." Lord Lucias laughed, still trying to catch his breath. "How could you know that I was seeking you?" He clapped Loki on the back. "I must put you on task."

"Me?"

What a stupid question. You are *his apprentice.*

"Ta." Lord Lucias scoffed, his eyes dancing with his amusement. "Are you not my slave?" Loki chuckled, not offended, and nodded. "The mischief fairy, Zev, has sired a son who, he hopes, will be his crowned prince."

"Hopes?" Loki asked with a raised brow. "But he shan't?"

"Moira's business." Lord Lucias reminded Loki. "I only require you to attend the birthing and then tell me what you think of him."

"Forgive me, my Lord. Is he truly Zev's son?"

"No." Lord Lucias answered, lowering his gaze. "The seed that made him is my own."

How oddly vulnerable he looks.

"I merely wish for you to advise me if he is princely."

"Of course." Loki grinned at him.

It didn't need to be said that neither Zev nor the mother was to learn the child was not Zev's. Zev had been trying for far too long to sire a suitable heir. It would break his spirit to learn he had, yet again, failed.

Though, it must be said, Loki rightly found it odd that Lord Lucias had chosen to sire a son with that particular race, given Lord Tristan was Heavens bound. He reasoned, however, that his Master had his own agenda.

"I shall see to his features."

"Good lad." Lord Lucias clapped him on the back again, causing Loki to grin. "And then return to me right away with the news."

Eager to please Lord Regent Lucias, Loki granted him a hearty nod. "I shall return as swift as I can."

Lord Lucias chuckled, his eyes dancing with a strange light, and clapped Loki on the back yet a third time. It was a strange gesture which pleased Loki because it was only ever afforded to him. Lord Lucias' affection toward Sappharon was quite different. He treated her in a much softer manner.

"Is something troubling you?" Lord Lucias asked him, his smile faltering.

Loki pulled himself out of his reverie and shook his head.

"No, my Lord." He hesitantly, clapped Lord Lucias' back in return. He was rewarded with a very strange and baffled grin for his effort. He instantly regretted his attempt at intimacy. "I was reflecting on my luck."

"Luck?"

"That I may be of service to you."

This earned him another strange smile. "My servants do not generally refer to their assignment to me as *luck*."

"Well." Loki shrugged. "We can't all be fools."

"Too right you are. But I think it is I who am the lucky one in this situation, my friend. I am a hard master. You've taken my moods and tasks in stride."

"I guess I've yet to see the moods." This answer was honestly meant. "You've been nothing but kind to me."

"Give it time." His expression was one of regret. "You are sure to see my darker side eventually."

"We all have them, my Lord."

"Too right." He agreed. "Let us just hope that you love me yet on the other side of them."

Loki's brow furrowed at this. He couldn't imagine that the God could do anything which would cause him to lose his regard for him. Though, he'd heard stories from others in respect to Lord Regent Lucias' temperament and actions.

Stories that both concerned and terrified him.

His hesitation to respond earned him another strange smile. "I must take my leave, Loki."

"Of course, my Lord." Loki nodded, regretting that he hadn't promised his Master that he would love him no matter what he said or did. "I shall see you soon with news."

Lord Lucias nodded, clapped him on the back again and walked away. Loki watched him, his mood dampened by the very real possibility that he had somehow disappointed his Master, until Lord Regent Lucias turned a corner and was out of his range of sight.

-4-

Gabriel sat at his kitchen table with his shoulders slumped and his eyes rolled up so that he was staring blankly at the ceiling.

He was frustrated and he was angry.

And he had a right to be neither one.

It was just that, as of late, everything seemed to be done on a whim. There was no planning. No care of how decisions affected others. It was all about what King Noliminan or Lucias wanted, right here and now, and damn the consequences.

He knew that there was no possible way for him to perform the tasks that were being asked of him. There were only so many shifts of the shadows in the day. Yet, now, he was not only to create new souls, he was to recycle old ones as well?

It was madness.

At least, now, Gabriel could set his own pace. Or, perhaps, take an evening off should he wish.

Who cared if, for a period of sixty shifts of Lord Countenance's shadow upon the newest world, no mortals were being born?

But if he, now, had the added requirement of meeting every soul ever recycled and replacing and then removing their memories of past lives every single time they took a trip around one of the various inhabited worlds, what did that leave him?

He had posed his concerns to King Noliminan. But in the end, as he ever did, he had simply agreed to the task that was demanded of him. He had no choice. The consequences of saying no to one's Master were damning.

Especially when one's Master was the King of Lords.

Gabriel, tired and frustrated as he may be, was not willing to test King Noliminan's patience.

A knock played at his door, irritating him. He had had all of the unexpected guests that he could stand and was truly in no mood for more. But the knock was persistent and when he heard an all too familiar voice call his name he knew that turning *this* guest away was not an option.

He sighed, forced himself to stand and walked toward the door. "Father."

"Gabriel." Lucias' expression was unreadable. "I have come to the understanding that you spoke with Noliminan this morning."

"He spoke *at* me." Gabriel agreed, correcting him regarding the fact that the conversation had been entirely one sided.

A strange expression clouded Lucias' features as he turned toward his son. "And how do you feel about what he had to ask of you?"

Gabriel's brow furrowed as his gaze trailed over his father's face. He wondered if Lucias wanted a true answer to his question or more supplication toward the task. He didn't know which side of the argument his father had taken. As such, his response needed to be tempered to avoid an explosion. He had been on the opposite side of Lucias' argument in the past and he hadn't fared well for his honesty.

"It will create a lot of extra work for me."

"Can you succeed?" Lucias' expression was stony and impossible to interpret

"I do not believe I have another option." Gabriel settled on this as the most honest, non-contradictory answer that he might provide.

"I did not ask you what you were ordered to do, Gabe." Lucias sighed. "I asked you what you believe you can do."

"What answer are you looking for?"

"I'm not ordering your answer out of you." His father replied, his temper flaring. "I want you to truthfully answer my question."

"Then, no, Father." He replied, steeling himself for a blow. "I do not believe that I can succeed with the task at the rate the King of Lords expects me to. Yet, I also believe that I had better figure out a way to do so lest I find myself punished for my failure."

"Did you share this information with Noliminan?"

"He wasn't asking for my opinion on the subject."

"Precisely my point." Lucias growled, his fist flying into his open palm. Gabriel watched with relieved silence. "He infuriates me to no end."

"He believes that his idea is a good one."

"Of course he does." Lucias carped. "Because it was *his* idea!" His expression evened out again. "And, on its merits, I suppose that it *is* a good idea."

Gabriel, who didn't think that it was a good idea at all, bit his tongue. Lucias was looking for his opinion no more than King Noliminan had been.

"Though I pity you, your work load is not my greatest concern." Gabriel was not surprised by this. "I don't even care that he's decided that free will should rule the day." He began pacing, his tone rising. Gabriel knew it was best to let him get it all out without interruption. He had been on the wrong side of this type of behavior, too. "Yet, if it must rule the day, every soul concerned should be afforded the same benefit. Not only the speaking apes!"

Gabriel, realizing that his father had gone silent and was staring at him, understood that this is where he was meant to interject. "He's affording the same luxury to all of the races."

"Not to *your* race." Lucias corrected him coldly. "Not to your brothers or your lesser peers." He shook his head. "Not even to me and mine."

"He has never stopped you from doing what you do." Gabriel clamped down on his tongue after he had said the words.

Speaking to Lucias in such a manner was a mistake.

"If you don't think that he punishes me for my actions then you are sadly mistaken." His eyes were dark and angry. Gabriel took a step back from him, not trusting that Lucias wouldn't take his anger out on him. "Zadkiel and Azrael are my doing and we are all excruciatingly aware of that."

"Zadkiel should have told you no." Gabriel muttered under his breath. "And Azrael shouldn't have attempted to speak reason with King Noliminan about something that was not his to concern himself over."

"A-ha-ha!" Lucias' stony expression grew crazed as he shook his finger back and forth in the air. Gabriel took another step back, now certain that this conversation was not going to end well for him. "Precisely! He couldn't tell me no because I gave him a *direct order*! Which was precisely Azrael's point!"

"Yes, Father." Gabriel held up his hands, trying to calm Lucias. "I agree with you; I stand on your side." His father's brow furrowed at this. "What can I do but obey? He's told me his requirements of me and I must meet them." He shrugged. "My plight is as simple as that."

"It *is* as simple as that," Lucias replied, calmer now. "But it isn't fair."

"How on which moon does fairness enter into this?"

His father frowned at him. They had passed the point of Lucias' anger and Gabriel knew, now, that he would come out of this conversation unscathed.

"What do you need from me to allow you some freedom?"

"I do not yet know." Gabriel sighed, exasperated again. "I have not yet made a plan. Where am I going to keep all of these souls? How am I going to give them all the attention that they are going to require between the dying and the rebirth? I . . ."

The expression on his father's face stopped him from going on as he predicted, "We are, none of us, going to come out of this for the better."

"No." Gabriel agreed, reaching for his father's hand. "We are not."

"How can he not see that he is beginning the end?" Lucias squeezed Gabriel's hand and then, rather violently, let it go. "That he is pushing my tolerance?"

Gabriel did not like the position Lucias was putting him in. Any answer he gave would place him in the middle of an argument which was meant to be waged by the two ruling Gods. "Because he believes you will, eventually, come around to his way of thinking." He steeled himself and said, "In the end, you always do."

"Not this time." Lucias advised him. "And the Gods will damn *me* for it. You wait and see if they won't."

"They cannot if you do not over react." Gabriel cautioned him. "You are clearly passionate about this, and I thank you for your love and concern on behalf of all of my brothers and sisters. Yet, for once, I beg you to cry off."

"I will bide for now." He muttered in response to this. "But I can hold no promise to you that my blood will not eventually boil."

Gabriel nodded, knowing that if he were in his father's position, with all of his father's powers, he, too, would allow himself to feel the same righteous indignation.

But he wasn't, so he couldn't, and he didn't.

He couldn't afford to. The price was simply too high.

It is better sometimes to just make do.

"I think that I may have to replace Loki." The sudden change in subject startled Gabriel.

"What—why?" He asked, surprised by this turn of events. "I thought you were pleased with him."

"Too pleased." Lucias muttered scratching his cheek. "I'm afraid he was not made for complete servitude."

"Meaning what?" Lucias' smile was sly. Gabriel, understanding almost at once, laughed at him. "When has *that* ever stopped you before?"

"Fair point."

"You aren't going to find anyone who is perfectly suited to you." Gabriel sighed. "Give him time. He'll come around." He shrugged. "Eventually we all do."

"Sometimes I wonder how you can."

"The binding magic forces us to." Gabriel replied tonelessly.

Lucias frowned at that. "It isn't right that you should be forced into adulation. And the Gods I rule take advantage of the magic."

"As do the Gods of the Heavens." Gabriel reminded his father. "Many wear false smiles in King Noliminan's halls."

"I know." He groused. The rest was said through gritted teeth. "Which is why the infernal sense of superiority of the angels over the demons infuriates me so."

"This springs from living quarters and proximity." Gabriel tried to explain. "A false sense of understanding exists that living close to you is not as good as living close to King Noliminan." Lucias frowned. "Everyone thinks that because you are separated it was because you lost his favor."

"I made the *choice* to leave!" He looked dumbfounded. "And we had to separate the Gods to temper them!"

"This isn't what everyone understands." Gabriel explained. "On either side. It happened long and away before most of us were even born."

"I bet that Noliminan isn't quick to correct anyone who raises the issue." Lucias snorted. Gabriel smiled at the truth of his statement. "Whatever." He smiled in return. "Let them all live with their delusions."

"There's my Pipa."

Lucias smiled at this endearment. Gabriel was pleased.

"Will you stay a bit? And talk me through my ideas?"

"Yes." Lucias smiled again. "I'd like that very much."

-5-

Loki stepped into the bridging Courtyard wearing a cocky grin. He had finished his task in the Oakland Grove and could report, upon seeing Lucias, that the baby was, indeed, comely.

Now what he wanted was the company of a beautiful woman whilst he ate his midday meal.

He allowed his eyes to dance over every table until they landed upon such a woman. The stunning creature had long copper hair which curled over her shoulders and danced across the generous swell of her bosom in beautiful waves. Her features were curved to perfection; her mouth was generous and swelling.

Loki's own split into a grin as he imagined kissing those lips.

Her eyes, which were dark but whose color was impossible to ken from the distance in which Loki stood from her, were turned to the curve of her long fingered hand.

She appeared, by her stoic expression, to be bored.

His smile grew. Boredom was a state of mind that Loki believed his wit would immediately cure.

He made his way toward her table, noticing that she raised her gaze to look upon him as he approached. Smiling to himself that she noticed him, he stepped past her, appearing as if he hadn't even seen her, and then came to a comedic halt.

"By the love of all of the Gods!" He cried, spinning dramatically back in her direction and lightly stepping toward her so he could lay his hand upon her table in a false swoon. "But I have long been told that when I bridge the Courtyard to the Heavens the faces I might see would be those of only the most beautiful of Goddesses!"

She blinked at him, almost as though surprised.

"My Lady," he fell to one knee, "will you not grace me with the courtesy of your name!"

Loki realized almost at once that the Gods and angels sitting at the surrounding tables were turning their attentions toward him. He marked immediately that the chatter around them had completely ceased.

He ignored all of this, holding his gaze to the Lady's own.

Her eyes were green, he saw now that he was close to her. Two glittering emeralds which danced with clear surprise under a copper brow.

Finally, with a voice like a melody, she said, "My Lord, forgive me. But I haven't an inclination for your dramatics."

"Sweet Lady," he flew the hand upon the table to his chest, "I have no dream in my heart but for that a drama must be played. For I fear if you do not favor me with the sweet syllables of your name I might go mad in my quest to otherwise claim them."

"Then mad you must go," she replied with a tight smile as she pushed away her lunch and stood. "As I must bid you good day."

"Mad I will go." Loki replied with what he hoped was a charming smile. "And good my day shall be. For this night, when I lay down my head, 'twill be your face my mind's eye sees."

Her porcelain cheeks flushed slightly pink at his prose as she reached for the sides of her crushed velvet, emerald green dress, granted him a slight curtsy and turned to leave him staring impishly after her wake.

-6-

Camael was not one to meet in private with anyone. Let alone demons. But his curiosity had been piqued by Zamyael's request to speak with him.

As a result, he now stood in Raziel's sitting room with his hands on his hips, staring in disbelief at Zamyael for her cunning and almost treacherous plan.

Though she no longer wore her female form, she bore no semblance of masculinity and, thus, he could not think of her as otherwise.

"Was this your idea? Or Lady Raziel's?"

"Raziel wouldn't dirty her hands with something like this." Zamyael shrugged her slender shoulders. Camael understood what she was trying to do with that shrug, but her all too feminine wiles no longer held any fascination for him. "She has bigger fish to fry, as they say on some world or the other."

"Then yours?" Camael demanded.

"I did not say that." Zamyael's black eyes turned swiftly away.

"If you were not ordered to roll this along, why are you?" Camael was frustrated with Zamyael. She knew better than to interfere with the plans of her betters!

"Because my idea is a good one. With free will comes consequence when a bad choice is made." As she spoke, her gaze flicked swiftly down to Camael's nether regions and back up. Camael, humiliated, looked swiftly away. "As you well know. And they should learn this early on."

"The point is there are to be no consequences." Camael seethed.

Damn Zamyael's black heart!

"For anything."

"Which is a mistake," Zamyael growled through gritted teeth. She shook her head, sending her braids to dance. Though a smile immediately danced to his lips—she was a damn pretty thing to look at—this was another trick which would no longer work on Camael. "The nature of the soul is to find the line that cannot be crossed. If there is no line then there can only be chaos."

"But to give them a false test—"

Zamyael's eyes turned to the door.

"Your mother will be home soon. There is no time for this dispute." She smiled softly. "Noliminan has far less than gently put you in your place. As a result they now both believe every word you say to them lest you find yourself in worse straits. This makes you the only one who can start an argument between the two without the suspicion of manipulation." Camael felt his lips thin. "Stroke their great egos! Convince them into argument and have them barter on the outcome. When Noliminan learns of the folly he created he may change his tune."

"He will never—"

"Not all the way." Zamyael raised her hands to stop Camael from finishing. "But he might bend when he learns you do not give children knives and expect them not to cut themselves."

"It seems cruel to me." Camael muttered.

As Zamyael had so callously reminded him, he had, very recently, been put violently in his place. He wasn't sure what else King Noliminan could do to him. Yet, he was unwilling to risk whatever love he had finally snatched back from his Master to find that out.

"Maybe. But you must admit that it makes sense."

Camael rolled his eyes.

It did make sense. Regardless of his personal shortcomings, he liked the idea that King Noliminan might temper a small amount of fairness into his Divine Plan. Certainly, if there were not some rules, Zamyael's prediction of chaos was right.

"You shall do it?"

"Yes." Camael grouched at her. "In any event, I'll try." He frowned softly. "But with those two?" He shook his head. "The outcome you want and the outcome you will get may just not be the same."

"I know them both well." Zamyael's voice was flat as she said this. This caused Camael—who held his own—to shiver against the animosities she rightly held against her betters. "They will respond exactly as I have predicted. Mark me."

"If this goes bad, you may count upon the fact that I shall."

-7-

Watching Raphael and Michael strategize over a game of kings' castles, a smile danced across Raguel's lips. Though they were both in service to her husband, she had long been fond of each of them in her own way.

Raphael's face mirrored Noliminan's. Thus her attraction to him had long stemmed for her love of his Master. Whereas,

Michael was her champion, always jumping to her defense when an insult was flung her way.

She believed in her heart that Michael coveted her.

He had never given her a blatant sign of this fact. Rather, it was the turn of his eyes to the swell of her hip or the hungry smile he would sometimes wear when he looked at her lips.

She was, though she would never tell him, grateful for his tender regard.

Until this afternoon, no one aside from Noliminan had ever openly flirted with her. As Noliminan's wife, no one would have dared.

Michael caught her gaze and offered her a smile. She smiled in response and lowered her eyes. Her cheeks flushed with heat as his own darted swiftly away.

Ruminating on Michael's regard, Raguel's mind cast to the brazen youngling who had approached her in the Courtyard.

Clearly, his playful drama in asking her name had been honestly meant. Otherwise, she knew, he would have never approached her. Never would have *dared* to approach her.

Certainly not in such a public setting as the bridging Courtyard.

Pondering upon the brazen youngling, she didn't take notice of Noliminan as he stepped into the room. When she raised her gaze to the pair at the kings' castles board, she found him standing behind Raphael, pressed against him with his hands grasped together in front of the archangel's chest. He was leaning over Raphael, looking at the board, wearing a smile which was somewhat tight. Raguel wondered, as her eyes danced over his smile, what thoughts were causing him such obvious displeasure.

"Raphael, pay attention to Michael's dragons."

Michael looked upward as a troubled smile played on his thick, masculine lips. His dark eyes were burning with discontentment. He had ever been uncomfortable with Noliminan when he was physically intimate with one of his archangels in such a manner as he was being intimate with Raphael now.

"No cheating, your Grace. He must learn the game of kings' castles for himself."

Noliminan chuckled at this. "I think we both know his skill is no match for yours."

"Then perhaps you would care to take his place once we have finished." Michael, who rarely, if ever, spent time with Noliminan when not mired in Noliminan's tasks, offered.

"Another time, min 'lasupita." Noliminan replied, turning away from them both and walking toward Raguel. Raguel felt a stab of sympathy for Michael as he watched Noliminan's back. Though he was obviously pained by the rejection, not a line of his disappointment appeared on Michael's stoically handsome face. "My Queen."

"Your Grace." She replied, forcing herself to meet his gaze as she nodded in supplication to him.

"I understand that you were molested in the courtyard today." His tone was tight. She finally understood his earlier smile.

"Never think it, your Grace." She replied, noting that Michael had snapped his gaze in her direction. His black eyes danced over her with grave concern. "A youngling approached me." She shrugged. "I think he simply didn't know I am yours."

"He'd best not have." Noliminan snorted. "Who was it?"

"I know him not, your Grace." She sighed. "The bearded one."

"Loki." He flared, his eyes narrowing. "He belongs to Luke."

Raguel's lips pursed.

Of course he belongs to Lucias.

Lucias had the distasteful habit of surrounding himself with extraordinarily handsome men.

Who could deny that the charming Loki was both virile and comely?

"Why does he wear a beard?" Raphael braved. "I've never met a God or angel with a beard before."

"His mortal life was spent among the centaurs." Michael muttered as one of the sea dragons Noliminan had warned Raphael about took out a water fairy. "The goatee is a sign of virility amongst those people."

"He was a centaur?" Raguel asked, surprised.

"No." Noliminan shook his head. "A nymph. He was spirited from the Isle of Borasphith on the world known as Hetuktah by his mother. She rightly feared the mermen would smash his head upon a rock for the mistake of being born male. The centaurs took him in as one of their own."

"Queer." Raguel replied.

Centaurs did not typically accept any creature who could walk upon two legs into their herd. Loki was lucky they had chosen to do so rather than trample him.

"Loki's a queer creature." Noliminan snapped. "Best you keep your distance from him."

"As you say, your Grace." Raguel agreed.

She knew better than to pass her time with any one of the male Gods. Let alone one who had been borne of nymph blood. The nymphs, when they set their mind upon you, had the magic to trick you into their beds.

Even against your better judgment.

"He made a mistake in his approach of me. It really amounted to nothing more than this."

"It had better not have been." Noliminan growled.

She nodded and returned her attention to the archangels. Michael wore a strangely sad expression. She gave him a secret smile which he seemed to accept in his heart before returning his attention to the game.

Only three moves later, Raphael's villages were all utterly decimated.

-8-

Raziel wasn't sure what she had stepped into. Though, clearly, the two cats holding palaver in her sitting room had most certainly eaten her canaries.

She looked from Zamyael to Camael and their false smiles. She decided not to question them. It wouldn't do any good. If she asked, they wouldn't tell her the truth anyway.

Not wearing those damned expressions, they wouldn't.

"Having a pleasant chat, are we?" She asked. Camael had the better sense to blush as he averted his navy blue eyes to the floor.

"Very pleasant." Zamyael responded without the slightest pause. That worthy didn't have the sense to care about Raziel's suspicions.

"I should take my leave." Camael muttered and stepped briskly past Raziel, his gaze still averted. "Mother."

"Good evening." Raziel said, shrugging off the coat of conspiracy which hung heavily in the room. Whatever they were up to would play itself out soon enough. No need to worry about the matter until it did.

Though she did add to Zamyael after Camael took his leave, "Whatever you are up to, do not set the fire free in my rooms."

"You were adequately dismissed from the conversation, my Lady." Zamyael countered. "I was clear on the point that you have nothing to do with my plans."

"Alright." Raziel believed him. But this made her even more curious. "Loki will be here shortly." Zamyael sighed, but nodded. "Call me out when he gets here. I need to speak with him." She cocked her left eyebrow. Zamyael wouldn't like the rest of what she had to say. "Ours will be a private conversation. So I should like it if you would find something other to do."

"What can you possibly have to talk to Lucias' demon about in private?" Zamyael spat.

"That is not your concern." Raziel chuckled under her breath, not correcting Zamyael that Loki was a God, and not a demon, as this would only broker argument. The child was so damned jealous of everything and everyone when it came to Raziel's attentions. "And our meeting is not what you think or I would have asked you to send him to my bedchamber." Raziel narrowed her eyes. "As I think you well know."

"I do." Zamyael's expression softened as he gave a curt nod. "I shall make myself scarce."

Raziel nodded and left him to his own devices. She'd had a long day and she wasn't in the mood to placate the child with reassurances.

No more than was she in the mood to placate Lucias. But where that worthy was concerned, she found it hard to say no. They may no longer be the great lovers they once had been, but they still cared for one another and were careful to look out for one another.

Besides. He was the only piece of Noliminan left to Raziel.

She supposed she was selfish to use Lucias in Noliminan's stead, but she cared about this not a wit.

She was determined to win this fight and then she wouldn't need to use Lucias anymore. Noliminan would eventually tire of his own childish behavior and crawl to Raziel on his hands and knees, begging her forgiveness.

The thought of this made her smile. She didn't intend to be an easy win. Noliminan was meant to work hard for her favor; to pay her back for the humiliation Raziel, herself, had faced at their extremely public divorce.

Lost in her own thoughts, and enjoying just being alone for the first time all day, Raziel found great irritation with Zamyael when he poked his head in to announce Loki's arrival.

Yet, Raziel had agreed to the conversation and so she followed Zamyael back to the sitting room amiably enough.

Until, of course, she saw the expression on Loki's face. The sheer terror there stopped her dead in her tracks.

"Zamyael." She sighed. "Please leave us."

Zamyael made his distastefully feminine curtsey and departed to the depths of his rooms. Alone with Loki, Raziel indicated a chair. "Please. Sit."

"My Lady, thank you. But I think I prefer to stand." A tremble of palpable fear darkened his tone.

"I am not going to bite you, for the love of the Heavens." Raziel sighed again.

"Perhaps not, my Lady." He agreed. "But whatever you have in mind for me I would rather not sully with false pleasantries."

Raziel snorted at this.

"What on which moon are you talking about?" She asked, taking the seat.

Why had Lucias insisted on spooking the boy before sending him to me?

"I only wanted to talk to you to see how you are faring. And if you are being treated well."

"But I displeased him today and I thought—" The handsome young God shook his head. "I apologize, my Lady."

He smiled and Raziel, finally, understood Lucias' nearly obsessive draw to him.

In fact, she suddenly wanted him. Knowing that he was borne of the nymphs, she asked herself if this was true hearted desire or magic at work.

But no.

Under that smile, this was nothing more base than desire.

"I thought he meant to sever our ties."

Raziel chuckled at this.

"He has said nothing about displeasure to me." She indicated the chair. "Will you not sit down? You make me uncomfortable." And then under her breath, yet loud enough so Loki could hear her, "You should never elevate above your betters."

Loki nodded his apology and found his seat.

Though, Raziel would soon learn, making his betters feel comfortable was never to be Loki's primary concern.

"Why, exactly, do you believe you have displeased him?" She asked. Loki looked suddenly away. "Did he tell you that you did?"

"He did not say so." Loki shook his head. "No."

"Then what are you prattling on about?" Raziel asked. She was becoming impatient.

"I was too familiar with him."

"Funny." Raziel answered, raising a brow. "I heard he had the opposite complaint." Loki looked suddenly quizzical. "What did you do which was so *familiar*?"

"I—you know?" He raised his hand and slapped the air. "Clapped him on the back."

To this Raziel snorted laughter and immediately threw her hand over her mouth to cover her smile.

"It's not funny!" Loki cried, but he was grinning so Raziel didn't take his admonishment seriously. "He started acting put out after that."

"Well you aren't exactly his chum!" Raziel could no longer hold in her laughter. "You touched him without his giving you permission to do so first. Your action merely surprised him. Nothing more."

"He does it to me all the time." Loki looked bewildered but amused. "I imagined this was his way of showing me affection so I just, I don't know, hit him back."

This made Raziel laugh even more. Such masculine affection was not at all Luke's style.

"It is, Loki." She let her laughter settle. "Leastwise, where you are concerned." Her eyes travelled the young God's face and her smile came easy. "He is not used to tempering himself."

Bless the child, but he looks even more confused than ever.

"What I mean to say is that he isn't used to his servants refusing his command of certain kinds of duties."

Understanding dawned on Loki's face like Apollo's morning star. He blushed profusely and shook his head. "He hasn't asked anything in that regard from me."

"Nor would you be overly receptive if he had." Raziel answered him with a shrug.

Lucias had told her Loki held no fascination for the masculine sex. And Lucias—violently offended the only time Raziel had asked him to change so that she might take him as a man does a woman—refused to utilize his female essence.

"Which is why he," Raziel had to repress her smile again as she raised her hand in the same gesture as Loki had earlier and slapped the air, "claps you."

She waved her hand at Loki.

"Rejection has never been in it for him. He's tempering himself with you." She shrugged. She didn't understand why. If Loki were hers she would have put him in her bed kicking and screaming if it were required. "Given his temperance where you are concerned, he simply does not know how to behave around you. He is worried he may have offended your virtue or sensibilities."

"Not at all." Loki said with a sure clear voice. "I adore him. I mean . . ."

"Don't worry about something which is not your problem." Raziel reassured him. "He'll figure out a way to live with this issue in his own manner and in his own time."

"Thank you, my Lady." Loki nodded to her. "I will try my best to help him along his way."

"Good." Raziel stood, pleased to see Loki had the common sense to stand as well. "If or no you want him to know of our conversation is your business."

"I believe I shall tell him."

"I believe honesty with your Master is always your best course of action." Raziel counseled. "You can find your own way out?"

"Yes." He nodded, bowing as he did so. "And thank you. Again, I mean."

"You please him." Raziel assured him. "And that pleases me. So I beg you seek my counsel where that devil of a man is concerned at any time."

Loki lowered his gaze and gave her a small, courteous nod. He had been granted an important favor and he had the sense to understand this. Raziel nodded in response and watched him with great interest as he turned and then made his way out of her rooms.

Lucias couldn't have been paired with a more appropriate servant had he chosen the youngling for himself.

Hopefully, this time, Lucias could temper himself long enough to hold on to him.

-9-

King Noliminan smiled as he passed one of his fauns over the kings' board and knocked away Camael's own. It wasn't the game which seemed to please him, but the rare chance to spend time alone with a member of his Quorum.

Camael told King Noliminan that he and Lucias had fought and he needed King Noliminan's counsel to patch it. Oddly enough, King Noliminan offered no true advice. He told Camael that he, himself, was left with the sting of Lucias' tongue before their last parting.

Contemplating his next move, Camael cleared his throat and raised his gaze. King Noliminan gave Camael what the archangel hoped was a pleased smiled.

"Michael is hosting a dinner party next Sixth Moon." He said, holding King Noliminan's gaze. "It's the Quorum's annual feast."

"Have the moons waxed and waned thusly?' King Noliminan mused, sitting back and lacing his fingers behind his neck. Camael nodded. "How does Lord Countenance while away his damned hours?"

"That's his business." Camael shrugged as he, finally, made his move. "Will you and the Queen of Ladies be coming?"

King Noliminan's smile grew. "Of course we shall come!"

"I wasn't sure this year." Camael answered softly. "There has been much mistrust amongst the Small Council this past season."

King Noliminan looked away. It was almost as though he had, for the moment, forgotten his quarrels.

"I knew you would be the one honorable enough to put your bides aside for the sake of your children."

"I think all four of us can put aside our pettiness for an evening."

"I know *you* can." Camael smiled adoringly at him. "You've always been so forgiving when, at times, we do not deserve it."

"We all make mistakes."

"Most of us do." Camael reached across the kings' board and grasped King Noliminan's hand. "But you are wise and, so, rarely do."

King Noliminan's eyes flicked to Camael's hand and narrowed. He didn't pull his hand away, but he did suddenly freeze. As he flicked his gaze upward to meet Camael's own, Camael shivered. He hadn't touched King Noliminan since he had been punished for siring Lasterian. That he had taken the liberty to do so now clearly upset his Master. He quickly pulled his hand away lest he earn greater ire.

King Noliminan responded to his statement, "Not always. But I can bide a night."

"I thank you for it, your Grace." Camael swallowed and lowered his gaze.

His soul was singing with discord. This was the first time he had been alone with King Noliminan in over two thousand years. And now he had, once again, lost the King of Lords' favor over the stupid mistake of taking his hand.

"I love you, your Grace."

"And I you, child." King Noliminan replied tersely. "But I think I'm done playing games for tonight." He flicked his gaze to the kings' board. "Perhaps tomorrow you and Raphael can pick up where we left off?"

"Yes." Camael swallowed. King Noliminan had just told Camael, in his cruel, backhanded way, that he was being cast aside.

"Good." He stood and gave Camael a long, searching gaze. "Goodnight."

"Goodnight, your Grace."

-10-

Evanbourough had been skeptical as to Camael's request that Evanbourough should have him, Lady Raziel and Lord Regent Lucias to dinner. But he was practical in his desire to garner political gain and so agreed to the meeting.

"That was fine, Evanbourough." The Sovereign Lady sighed as she laid her napkin over her cleaned plate.

"Yes." Lord Lucias agreed, smiling. "And what a good idea. I'm glad that you thought of us."

Evanbourough flicked his gaze to Camael, who was looking slyly at him but saying nothing.

"Well. Yes." He answered them. "It has been too long since I've seen either of you and I ran into Camael whilst he was visiting his son and thought, perhaps, a foursome should be more enjoyable for us all."

"I appreciated the invitation as well." Camael smiled softly at him. He turned swiftly to the other two. "In fact, I've been meaning to speak with the pair of you about something rather important."

"Oh?" Lord Lucias asked as his brow rose. Lady Raziel wore a sudden, knowing expression as her eyes darted to Evanbourough. There was nothing for this but to just shrug in response and silently admit the dinner invitation for the sham it was.

"Yes." Camael nodded. "You are planning to attend Michael's annual family dinner this year?"

"Of course." Lady Raziel returned, still watching Evanbourough intently. As for his part, Evanbourough finally understood why he was there. "Why wouldn't we ?"

"The situation is delicate." Evan nodded at Camael. Lord Regent Lucias turned his gaze in Evanbourough's direction at this. "Raphael told me that he supposed you would refuse given the current air of politic." Lord Lucias smiled softly at the Sovereign Lady. "And your current . . . eh . . . domestic quarrels with a certain carvetek mouk who need not be named."

Lady Raziel chuckled at this and looked to her well made hand. "I see."

"Forgive my ruse." Evanbourough's lips twitched in amusement. "Raphael did ask me to intervene."

"You can tell the carvetek mouk we'll be there." Lord Lucias grumbled. "Though he may not find either a one of us in fond company." He smiled then, and met Evanbourough's gaze. "Of course I speak not of Raphael."

"Of course." Evan nodded his agreement.

"I, for one, think his current manner of planning is just mad." Camael said, far too innocently. Evanbourough and Lady Raziel exchanged another knowing glance across the table. "I'm all for free will for the mortals, but there must be consequences should they break the rules."

"Just so!" Lord Regent Lucias piped up, leaning toward his son. "To just let them get away with whatever they want."

He shook his head violently. His passions were obviously enraged.

"But you know," Camael, far too innocently, responded, "you can't speak with King Noliminan. If it's not his idea, or entwined in some sort of barter for his pride, there is simply no winning."

"Is that so?" Evanbourough asked, trying to hide his amusement. He felt a kick under the table and smiled as he watched Lady Raziel raise her hand to cover her lips. "And what kind of barter do you think could be waged to make him change his mind?"

"On, no." Camael laughed heartily. "You'll never get him to change his mind." He shrugged his shoulders. "But it would be fun to put by a test of his theories if only to prove to him that he's wrong."

Lady Raziel turned her gaze to Camael at this. Her smile was soft but no longer amused. She was now, if Evanbourough interpreted his perception correctly, extremely interested.

"I don't know, say . . . Put a couple of Tristan's fairies together and give them some sort of temptation they can't act upon. You know the minute you tell them not to do whatever—"

"The sooner they will." Lady Raziel finished his sentence for him. "And then he'll have to change the rules of his own game." She laid her hand upon Lord Lucias' and squeezed it. "Of course, that is, if someone were brave enough to stand against him to *propose* such barter."

"I see." Lord Lucias chuckled under his breath. "So this is the sudden interest in dinner?" He smiled grandly at Evanbourough. "You know me well enough, don't you?"

Evanbourough shrugged. He'd had no part in this. Yet, he found it delicious all the same.

"I do live to serve you."

"It's a trap." Lord Lucias responded to this. "And not fair to the participants. You can't tell someone not to think of his sister's bum because, by the very nature of telling them not to do so, they will go mad trying not to and end up doing so anyway." Evanbourough shrugged. "Which isn't fair."

"Maybe not." Lady Raziel answered. "Nor is the game he's playing at. The sooner he realizes his folly the better. There is too much at stake this time to worry about playing fair."

"You're the only one to make the proposition who will get away with it." Camael reasoned. "If only to prove you wrong and himself right." He sighed. "He cares not one wit what we think. But he'll play the argument out with you if only to put you in your place."

"I'll consider."

"The children's party—"

"Raziel," Lord Regent Lucias' admonishment was extremely stern. Evanbourough had never heard him use such a tone with the Sovereign Lady before. It wasn't pleasant to hear now. "I said I shall consider this."

She lowered her gaze. She looked every bit the child who had been put in her place. It was strange to see her so submissive. "Of course, my Lord. Forgive me."

"It is forgiven." This response was in a completely different tone than had been his admonishment. Evanbourough was pleased to see Lady Raziel understood Lord Lucias' concession.

Wanting to change the subject, Lord Lucias brought the conversation in the direction Evanbourough had hoped, eventually, someone would. "Is that the Lady Thea, Evan?"

"Hmm?"

"The woman." Lord Lucias nodded toward the wall where Evan's paintings hung. "Is that Theasis?"

"Oh." Evan shrugged. "Her. Yes. That is Thea."

"You don't say." Lady Raziel, who hadn't been interested enough to look, raised her gaze to the painting.

"So are you and she . . ." Camael asked. "Are you as stringent with her as you are with Lord Tristan?"

"No." Evan shrugged. "We bide the time now and again, that's all. She's good for a certain itch that Tristan can't scratch."

Lord Lucias chuckled lightly. "Indeed."

"Yet she graces your wall, Evanbourough." Lady Raziel replied softly to this. "You must have feelings for her to have placed her in such honor."

"This is true." Evan nodded. "But she does not belong to me and I wouldn't want to stand in her way to find whatever she is looking for by making it seem she does."

"Good news for the rest of us." Camael muttered.

Evanbourough found his eyes darting in Camael's direction. He had heard rumors about Camael which, if true, would render Theasis' ability to bed whom she wanted moot. He wondered, as the archangel's navy blue eyes danced over the curves of Thea's prettily made face, whether his desire for her was borne of fascination or lust.

"Quite so." Evan tried to tame the jealous flare of his nostrils. Lord Regent Lucias and Camael might have missed his reaction. Lady Raziel, however, did not. Her expression was one of curious understanding.

"You should have invited her." Lord Lucias offered. "Maybe next time—"

"Tristan is tolerant of her." Evanbourough snapped, not meaning to. Lord Lucias actually started at the unexpected attack. "That does not mean I can parade her around my home and under his nose." He softened his tone. "Besides. Odd numbers at the table make for bad luck."

"Of course." Lord Lucias' smile was apologetic. "And we have bad luck in spades these days." His eyes softened. "Why tempt Moira?"

Evanbourough acknowledged his silent apology with a small smile of his own.

"Well." Lord Lucias sighed, standing. "As much as I hate to do so, I must be off to home." He smiled apologetically about the table. "I've not graced my own halls since Third Moon and I think my natives are getting restless."

Evanbourough chuckled at this. "Tell the little brat I say hello."

"She'll be glad for the tidings." Lord Lucias' smile was broad and bright as he held out his elbow to the Sovereign Lady. "Met paken? May I walk you home?"

"I shall very much enjoy that." She rose and took the proffered arm. "Thank you again for dinner, Evan."

"I should be going too." Camael said as he stood and grabbed the coat he had taken off and thrown over the back of the chair where he had been sitting.

Evanbourough followed them, seeing them all out with pleasantries and swiftly shut the door behind him. As he did so, he heard a door down the hallway open. He looked upward, smiling warmly as his gaze fell upon Tristan, now standing in the hallway with his arms crossed over his chest.

"Well?" Tristan smiled softly at him. "Did they fall for your silly little lie about bedding Thea?"

"Whilst tripping over their own tongues." Evanbourough replied softly. "Thank you for aiding me in the telling.

"It isn't me who is going to have the difficulty in living with the lie."

"I don't see another way."

"That's because, for now, there isn't one." Tristan pushed open the door he had just stepped through and held his free hand toward Evanbourough. "Come to bed. We'll worry about tomorrow when tomorrow comes."

Evanbourough, exhausted by the day, obeyed.

-11-

Seeing the Queen of Ladies sitting alone at a table, Loki stepped swiftly in her direction and offered her a bow.

Knowing, now, who she was, he understood what a complete and utter fool he had made of himself the last time he had seen her.

He also understood that he owed her an apology.

"Excuse me." He said, his tone gentle. "Your Grace?"

She turned her beautiful green eyes in his direction and gave him a smile with her sensual lips. The same melodic tones he remembered from their last meeting danced between them as she said, "Loki."

"I fear I must cry your pardon." He tried to keep his eyes from dancing down to her bosom and found it was nearly impossible to do so. "I didn't realize you are the King of Lords' wife."

"Thank you." Her smile, which had been guarded, became real. "But it's not necessary. I understand you are new to our Court."

"I am." He said, his tone hesitant. "But that isn't an excuse for putting you in harm's way."

She laughed at him. "What on which moon makes you believe you put me in harm's way?"

"I just assumed he wouldn't be pleased."

Loki, who had been worried about her since he had discovered her true identity, felt the relief wash over him as she laughed at him again and waved her hand in his direction.

He had heard stories about punishments the King of Lords had dealt to those who he believed trespassed his property. And, though Loki, himself, didn't believe women were to be treated as chattel, there was no telling how the King of Lords viewed the politics of his marriage.

"I'm glad to know otherwise."

"Honestly, Loki," she said, her beautiful smile widening, "it was in a public setting and you weren't behaving lewd."

"May I join you?" He asked. Then with a playful wink, "I promise to behave."

"I would be pleased." She replied as she indicated the chair directly across from her. Not, he noticed, beside her. "Your time among the centaurs is a curious thing to me. Would you share with me your tales?"

Oh, I'd share my tail with you alright.

He chuckled at his lascivious thoughts and forced himself to give her a more innocent grin.

"Your Grace," he said with another wink, "sharing the stories of my mortality with you would be my great pleasure."

-12-

Lasterian was smiling as he watched Saristia swiftly don her robes so she could leave him to return to her Master. This was the third time Zamyael had been able to arrange a meeting for them while Raziel was out of her rooms, but only the first time they had actually given into their desire for one another.

Zamyael opened the door to find them still there and snorted. "The pair of you had best make haste." He warned. "You are pushing your luck as it is."

"You said we had ten more shifts of Countenance's shadow." Lasterian smiled lazily at him.

"Twenty shifts ago!" His tone was impatient. "I'm risking my hide for you." Zamyael continued, frowning. "If Lady Raziel comes home early—"

"All right, all right."

"I've been gone far too long as it is." Saristia told them. "Zamyael, when do you think we can meet again?"

"I think at this point it is best left up to you." Zamyael replied, somewhat nonchalantly. "You need to find somewhere other than Lady Raziel's suite now you have stepped beyond the rules I have lain."

"But there is nowhere else she can go that Lord Aegir will not find her." Lasterian replied to this, suddenly feeling desperate. "He is a cruel God, Zamyael."

"Do you think I do not know that?" Zamyael was picking up Lasterian's clothes and flinging them at him. "You promised me you would refrain from coupling. And today you broke your promise. Then you promised me you would be out in time so I will not get caught. And now you are breaking *that* promise." He shook his head, exasperated. "I cannot risk my own tail for your amusement anymore."

"We're going now." Lasterian assured him, pulling himself out of bed and swiftly beginning to dress. "Please. Just one more time."

Zamyael sighed, his dark gaze flicking from one to the other of them. "Fine." He finally spat. "But only one more time. And then you must be left to your own devices."

"When?" She asked him desperately.

"I know not." Zamyael frowned. "I shall send you both word when I can." Seeing Saristia was finally fully dressed, he pushed her out the door. "Now go!"

Regretfully, and with a reluctant wave, she disappeared into the hall. Lasterian's gaze lingered behind her as he let out a long, satisfied sigh.

"And you too!" Zamyael huffed.

Lasterian hadn't finished dressing, but he was decent.

Before he could stop himself, he flew forward, wrapping his arms around Zamyael's neck and taking his lips in his own.

Zamyael froze, taken by surprise by Lasterian's appreciative kiss, and then, slowly, raised his hands so one was on the small of Lasterian's back and the other wrapped around the back of his neck.

When he reciprocated the kiss, Lasterian, surprised by the softness of his lips and skin—he felt more like a woman than even Sarista did—found himself pressed against him, his recently sated passion exploding through his body again, leaving him hungry.

He felt Zamyael pulling away, but it was a reluctant move. When Zamyael spoke, it was in an angry whisper. "Get out of here."

Lasterian pulled away, confused by both the sudden rejection and his strange desire for the lady beneath the cloak of masculinity. "I'm sorry—I—"

"Now!" Zamyael cried as he lifted his arm toward the door with a long, slender finger pointing at it.

Feeling as though he had been slapped, Lasterian backed slowly to the door and, once on the other side, bolted.

-13-

Loki, who had come home late after having a surprisingly enjoyable dinner with the Queen of Ladies, stormed to the door, irritated.

He knew Sappharon was here and her bed chamber was much closer to the main door than Loki's. He would never understand the brat's sense of superiority or failure to serve Lord Regent Lucias in the manner in which she had been created to do.

Yet, someone had to serve their Master. So Loki had roused himself from his bed, thrown on some bed close and, irritably, opened the door. "He's not here."

And then he started.

The woman behind the door was breathtaking.

She had long black hair and pale white skin. The tight red dress she wore plunged low enough to tease his eyes with her full bosom, yet managed to be modest enough to tempt his curiosity. Her skirt fell to her feet with a slit up the left side which exposed the better portion of her perfectly sculpted leg. Her face was delicately made with a small, slender nose and lips so thick as to tempt him to want to take them in his own then and there so he might feel the softness of them.

Though his thoughts had, minutes ago, been on the Queen of Ladies and her reserved manners, they were now directed completely upon the beautiful creature standing outside of Lord Lucias' door.

"I apologize." He managed. "For my rudeness." Stumbling over his words, Loki bowed, holding her ebony gaze as he did so. "Lord Regent Lucias is out at the moment."

"Might I wait for him?" Her voice was seductively low and pleasing to his ear.

"I don't know how long he'll be." Loki answered. "Sometimes he doesn't come home for days at a time."

"My business with him is important." She smiled winsomely at him. He was helpless but to smile in return. "But if you'd rather turn a lady out then I shall return at a time which is more convenient."

"Yes—No—of course not." Loki stepped back, pulling the door open for her and thinking *I'd love to turn you out.* "Please come in. You can wait for Lord Lucias in his library if you like."

"Thank you." Her black eyes danced over his face. His hands flew up to straighten his hair and adjust his collar. He wished he had chosen not to answer the door in his sleep attire.

"May I offer you a drink? Mayhap, a bite to eat?" He granted her a broad smile.

"Wine if you have it." She stepped past him.

As she moved the scent of her intoxicated him. Jasmine in bloom, mixed with hydrangeas and, if he wasn't mistaken, a wisp of vanilla. He knew many things as Lord Lucias' servant, but women's perfumes remained an alluring mystery.

The buxom maid looked over her shoulder and gave him an astute smile. There were probably goads of men hammering down her door. "Wine made with the white grape, if you please."

"Sure." He muttered with the presence of mind to look abashedly away as he stepped past her and led the way to the library. He indicated Lord Lucias' most comfortable chair as much for her sake as for the affordability this would give him to study that one bare leg.

Her eyes darted around the room. Obviously this was her first time visiting Lord Lucias at his living quarters. This small knowledge made his heart sing gleefully. He smiled his newfound cheerfulness and walked to the bar to pour her a drink.

"Only the wine?"

"Ta." He met her gaze over his shoulder and licked his bottom lip.

"Can I get you a book or—?"

"No, thank you." She smiled coquettishly at him as she lowered herself into the proffered chair. As he had hoped, she pulled her left leg forward to cross over her right knee. Her calf was as pale and slender as a swan's neck. Staring upon this, he saw the shoes she wore were as red as her dress with heels so slender and high it was a wonder they were able to balance the weight of her. "I wouldn't want to disturb his things."

Loki had completely lost his senses for clever words and so, instead, nodded. "I will read to you if you'd like." She wore an amused expression at this. "Do you like poetry?"

"Of course." Her amusement only served to make her more beautiful, baffling his senses.

"I have a book in my room." He offered.

"No, thank you."

"Oh, no." He laughed, understanding her misconception. "Of course not. I only meant I can retrieve my book and then read from it if you would like."

"Perhaps another time." She answered, still wearing her sweet smile.

Loki held out his arms and shrugged. "Would you prefer I stand on my head and sing 'hi-diddle-diddle'?"

At this she laughed an honest, hearty laugh.

"No." She shook her head, her dark eyes dancing. "If you must entertain me than simply sit with me."

"You don't know what you're missing."

"My loss." She held her hand to the chair across from her. "Please."

"Thank you, my Lady." He swept her a gracious bow and then found his seat. "Would it be rude of me to ask your name?"

"No." She answered, still wearing her bemused expression.

"Well, thank you." He replied. "My curiosity is satisfied."

She lowered her gaze, shaking her head, and chuckled. "It's Theasis."

"Theasis." Loki furrowed his brow. "What a feminine name."

Theasis nodded, smiling. "I'm a feminine girl."

He scanned her from head to toe, unable to contradict her statement. Though he had known she'd said this in jest. "My name's Patricia. So who am I to critique?"

She threw her head back and laughed. "It is not!"

He laughed in return. "You're right. I lied. It's Helen."

She raised her delicate hand to her mouth, still shaking her head. "What is your name really?"

He stood, clapped his heels together, snapped his arm to his waist and bowed. "Loki, my Lady. At your service."

"Lord Loki." She nodded to him, still smiling.

"Nah." He assured her. "Nothing as fine as that." He bowed again. "Just Loki."

"Unfortunately, my name truly is Theasis." She answered him, her smile broad and beautiful.

"It's a lovely name." Loki assured her with another brilliant smile. He hoped she found him as charming as he meant to be. He felt like a complete and utter ass. "For an extremely lovely woman."

"You flatter." She returned with her head cocked, but still wearing her beautiful smile. "Ware to the woman who falls for you."

"Oh, no!" He responded. "No, no, no." He put his hands behind his back, conjured a single rose and then stepped forward, handing it to her. "Such a lady would be held in my highest regard."

She looked at the rose, her expression softening. He pushed it toward her and she, hesitantly, accepted the flower. She brought it to her nose, sniffed it delicately and smiled up at him softy. "A lucky girl indeed."

"I should be the lucky one," he assured her, "to be held in any type of regard from such a woman."

Her cheeks became two pink roses. "Thank you."

"It's not required." He assured her, bowing one last time before backing up and lowering himself in the chair opposite from her. "You remind me of someone I know."

She chuckled. "You've probably seen me at Council."

"I've not yet been." He smiled at her. "I've not been in my Lord's service for long."

"Oh?" She asked, her delicate brow rising over her shapely eye.

"I served him at the last, but he took Sappharon rather than me." Loki explained. Then with a shake of his head and a smile. "I have a problem holding my tongue."

"I hadn't noticed." She grinned, amused.

"It's true, you know." He nodded at her. "I'm not always this shy."

She chuckled at him. "Well, whoever you saw, it couldn't have been me." Her gaze fell to her feet as she uncrossed her legs, crossed her ankles and started smoothing her skirt. "I'm a Heavens bound Goddess." She explained. "So if you haven't seen me at Council, chances are you haven't seen me at all."

"I see." He swallowed back a minute bit of despair at those words. Being in service to Lord Regent Lucias, he had no business flirting with a Heavens bound Goddess. Not that this would stop him. Though, he did understand the potential consequences. "I must be thinking of someone other."

"Probably Lord Evanbourough." Theasis offered. "In my male form, we are similar in appearance."

Loki's eyes danced over her face again as he thought that, should she wear any form other than her female form, such would be a pity.

"Yes." He smiled at her. "Of course." He ran his hand through the air, mimicking running his fingers along the curve of her face. "You could most definitely be Lord Evanbourough's much more beautiful sister."

She nodded. "We both descend from the line of Raziel." She lowered her gaze. "But if you should hear anything about us . . ."

"Oh." Loki nodded, suddenly understanding he had less right to court this beauty than simply her divination. He was well aware of Lord Evanbourough's possessiveness. As for her blood relationship to Evanbourough, he found no offense that they courted. They were all ultimately either from the line of Lord Lucias' or the King of Lords' given that pair had started it all. The blood line was so diluted at this point that it was impossible to tell who came from which line.

"Of course. I apologize for my indiscretion."

"You misunderstand, my Lord." That she gave him the underserved title pleased him. He was an Apprentice, not a Lord. "While we bide our time together, he does not own my hand."

"The rest of us shall count ourselves blessed." He smiled at her, pleased by her downturned gaze and the new rise of the roses upon her cheeks. He looked swiftly to her hand and found her glass empty. "Would you like another glass?"

She followed his gaze and seemed surprised to find she had drank all of the wine. "I should go."

"Of course." Loki bit back his disappointment.

"But yes." She held the empty glass toward him. "I should like another glass." He smiled at her. "If, that is, you intend to stay."

"Wild centaurs couldn't drag me away." He assured her, pleased by her small nod and sultry smile. "Do you mind if I join with scotch?"

"You take after your Lord."

"Yes." He laughed as he stood and grabbed her glass. He walked to the bar and talked to her over his shoulder. "Before I met Lord Lucias I was happy with water. Now . . ." He waved his hand over the bar. "I understand why he drinks as much as he does. I sometimes wonder if it's enough."

"It's a hard world." She responded softly.

Loki started. He hadn't meant to become melancholy. Nor had he been seeking her sympathy. He turned swiftly, both drinks in hand, and gave her a charming smile. "Good for me that I like the smell of brimstone."

Her soft expression wasn't amused. She turned in the words she truly wanted to say and parried instead with, "Lucky for me that I enjoy the smell of hypocrisy."

To this Loki threw his head back and burst into uproarious laughter. The truth in the words was all too pointed. When he heard her approach he turned and handed off her glass of wine. "I hadn't expected that."

"There's a lot I didn't expected when I knocked on Lord Lucias' door." She said enticingly close, her beautiful smile wide and her dark eyes studiously taking in his features. "You are quite handsome, Loki."

"You should see my mother." Loki was unused to flattery and, so, answered in the only manner he knew how: with bad jokes.

"Does she also wear a beard?" She asked, bemused.

"It's a goatee." He corrected her.

"Whatever it is," she lowered her gaze and the pink roses returned to her cheeks, "it's comely." She cleared her throat. "Virile." She raised her gaze. "None of the other Gods wear one."

"What the other Gods fail to understand about true masculine vanity can fill volumes of the Sovereign Lady's Tomes." He smiled at her with amusement. "Don't get me wrong." He ran his finger along her delicate arm. "I was raised by centaurs so many of my mannerisms tend to bend their way where masculine custom is concerned."

"Centaurs? I should like to hear stories about them."

"I should like to share them." Puzzling over the fact that nearly every female he had ever met was fascinated by his time with the centaurs, he went over the stories which had most amused Lady Raguel in his mind. He put down the glass of scotch and tentatively reached for her dimpled left cheek.

Surprisingly, she didn't pull away.

He lowered his own gaze and—unused to his flirting actually resulting in an immediate response—blushed furiously.

"I would enjoy that." She moved her hand from his arm to his chest to feel his heart palpitations

"Then, perhaps, I might call on you?" He raised his gaze and met hers. "For a walk or a picnic."

"I should like that."

"Yes." He smiled, turning his face to press his lips onto her soft fingers. "I should be honored to escort you."

-14-

Sappharon hadn't been in her bed. This was why she hadn't answered the door when the Lady had come calling.

Of course Loki had no way of knowing that.

Then again, neither did Lucias.

For the past two hundred years, Sappharon had been a member of a certain coalition she knew Lucias would—one day—be proud of her for joining. For joining and for gathering what information was required in preparation for when the moment of rebellion came.

It was far closer than Lucias, or any other of the Gods, expected it to be. Sappharon's involvement with it was solely in the service of making sure her dear Lord Regent was knowledgeable when the time for taking sides came.

Sappharon was well aware that Lucias viewed her more as a responsibility than a confidant. Though this knowledge wounded her, it also martyred her pride. She knew that one day he would see her as his most faithful servant, not a burden to bear.

After the meeting Sappharon and an angel she had long ago come to count on as a friend took a walk along one of the long beach shores of the world known as Tontkika. This world had been chosen because it was one of the oldest and, because its people had destroyed one another, one of the least inhabited.

She didn't know the angel's name. Familiarity was forbidden for the protection of the brewing rebellion. But she trusted him and, by the angel's own words, understood that he was near to ready to meet Lucias to voice his concerns for himself.

"Do you think he will receive me?" The angel asked, brushing a lock of his long blonde hair behind his ear and turning to meet Sappharon's gaze. "That he will listen to me?"

"I think his frame of mind is bending our way." Sappharon said. "He reveres Noliminan, but enough has happened between the pair of them lately that I think if I ask for a private audience for you it will be granted."

"Will he punish me?" He whispered. The moment she had said Noliminan's name aloud he had paled. "Or return me to my Master?"

"No." Even if the events of late hadn't taken place and a surprise meeting had been sprung on Lucias at Sappharon's request, Lucias never would have betrayed the angel simply for seeking his succor. It wasn't who Lucias was. It was too bad no one other than Sappharon understood the greatness of her Lord. "He is very discreet."

"I need to speak with him soon."

"I know." Sappharon sighed, her eyes surveying the scar on the fair angel's face. It hadn't been there at their last meeting. It was a testament to the increasing violence of the angel's God.

Sappharon wished she knew who his God was so she could smite him herself. The physical abuse, above all other things, infuriated her the most.

"Would you like me to speak with him tonight?" Sappharon asked. "Where can you meet him? And when?"

"I don't know when I'll be able to get away again." The angel wore a broken and tired expression. "May I come to him? When I can?"

"I don't know." Sappharon frowned. "If you get caught wandering through any one of the Hells without an escort then any number of misfortunes may befall you." Her soul raged for this man. "I cannot grant you any certainty that you would even make it to Lucias' door."

"Just let me in." He whispered. "If I do make it to the door . . . Please promise me you will let me in."

"You have my word." Sappharon reached for her friend and pulled him forward, touching his forehead with her own. "If you knock on my Lord's door then I swear you will have his audience." Her eyes narrowed as she thought to the new one; the favored one. "If the bearded freak answers the door, tell him only that you are there to see me."

"I will."

"I'll do my best to see it isn't an issue." Sappharon promised. "But this pig . . . he's . . ." She didn't finish. From her friend's expression she thought it best she didn't. "Just come when you can."

"Thank you, Dame Sappharon." The angel whispered, his eyes glistening with his gratitude. "No matter what befalls me, I shall never forget your kindness toward me." Sappharon smiled at him and nodded. She knew it was better to leave with nothing else to say. There was too much at stake.

-15-

Zadkiel frowned at Gabriel. "I will not be your lamb."

"Did I ask you to be?"

The archangel shook his head, his golden eyes downcast.

No. Not directly.

He had merely asked Zadkiel if he would be the one to question King Noliminan regarding his Divine Plan. He believed that Zadkiel had already faced their Master's wrath and so couldn't be further punished for this. Zadkiel wondered if Gabriel truly understood the depths of their Master's ability to make his point.

"If the conversation arises then I will respond with my heart as I ever have done."

"Which is all I ask."

Gabriel reached for Zadkiel's arm to bring him comfort, but his touch had the opposite effect. It merely managed to rise his indignation that his brother would request that he raise an issue with King Noliminan which was, truly, not his own.

"Damn you." Zadkiel groused standing and swatting Gabriel's hand away. "The conversation is *never* going to arise! King Noliminan isn't going to speak with me! He never does!"

"Approach *him* for palaver, then." Gabriel suggested. "He cannot still be angry with you after all of this time. Not truly. Mayhap it is time to request that he releases you from your punishment."

Zadkiel glared at his brother. He had asked King Noliminan to forgive him a thousand times and a thousand times King Noliminan had told him no.

"Can't he?" Zadkiel raised his golden finger and poked it toward Gabriel. "What do you—one of his favored angels— know about his ability to forgive?"

"You should have told Lucias no."

"Then *he* would have punished me!" Zadkiel groused through gritted teeth. He turned and faced his brother. "You have never in life been put between King Noliminan and Lucias. As such, you cannot understand how I labored over which of them was right and which of them was wrong."

The rage he had long ago pushed into the depths of his soul threatened to surface.

"I had to choose between them knowing I would pay by one hand or the other regardless of my actions." He found and held Gabriel's gaze. "I made the right choice for the betterment of us all. And, dear Gods, but I have paid for doing so."

Gabriel floundered. He, wisely, held his tongue and Zadkiel relented. It was the first time Zadkiel had ever explained the predicament his King and his father had placed him in and Gabriel was kind enough not to needle him for doing so now.

"My advice to you, brother, is to refrain from meddling with King Noliminan's desires." Zadkiel counseled. "I beg of you." He swiftly looked away. "When it comes to the pair of them and their quarrels, you must stay as far away as you can."

"I do not intend to interfere." Gabriel assured him. "I only wanted your counsel on how I might approach King Noliminan and beg that he see reason. Will you grant me your aide?"

Zadkiel loathed self-pity, yet there was another question in need of response. "Where were you when I needed your aide?"

"Azrael was the only one who could have saved you." Gabriel replied, not unkindly.

"Azrael was the only one who tried." Zadkiel frowned severely. "His punishment for doing so was a magic so great it is driving him to the brink of insanity."

Gabriel paled. Like the rest of them, he knew that my magic is the most burdensome to bear. They have all watched me transform from the carefree creature I had once been to a detached shell.

"Knowing this, what would you have asked of me?"

"I know not Gabe. Mayhap the defense of my position as you are asking for this from me?"

"I ask you only because when King Noliminan and Lucias are approached by you they will look upon you with regret." He sighed. "And mayhap consider the consequences of my fate as they do so."

"Gabriel," Zadkiel responded, softly and without anger, as he tapped at his disabled leg with his cane to make his point. "Where King Noliminan and Lucias are concerned, their choices never beget regret."

-16-

Gabriel, frowning, knocked lightly on Lucias' door. He didn't like the state he had left Zadkiel in and he knew only King Noliminan or Lucias could sedate him. Of the two, he could guess who may be convinced to help.

It was Sappharon who opened the door. She wore an eager expression on her face which immediately turned to irritation.

"Oh." She groused. "It's only you."

"I do not have time for your games today." Gabriel pushed her out of the way and forced himself into his father's apartment. He had never liked Sappharon and he never would. "Is Father here?"

"If he were, would I be answering the door?" She grumbled.

Gabriel refused to dignify the question with a response. It was Sappharon's Gods be damned job to open the door.

"Do you know where he is?" He asked irritably.

"In the basement." Sappharon snapped back, using Lucias' term for the Thirteenth level. He called it this because, even though it was on the Thirteenth floor, the only access to it was through a hidden door in his library. Literally, you see, the Thirteenth level was, indeed, Lucias' basement. "Playing with his pretties."

"Fine." He made to turn away from her.

"I wouldn't intrude if I were you." She warned with a lazy drawl. "You don't have the stomach for it."

While this was probably true, Gabriel believed the matter at hand was more important than whether or not he would be able to bear watching his father at his work. He waved his hand at Sappharon and made his way to the library. There, he found Apprentice Lord Loki sitting on one of the sofas with his right leg propped up on the table, reading one of his father's books.

Gabriel reflected on the fact that he had often seen King Noliminan sitting precisely that way when he was reading. Though the two looked nothing alike, the striking resemblance in their mannerisms in that moment was somewhat amusing.

Knowing the turn of Lord Loki's sense of playfulness, he walked toward the young God and bumped his knee with his own, forcing his leg to fall off of the table.

"Heil." He greeted the youngling with a grin.

"Good morning, Gabriel." Lord Loki gritted his teeth as he looked, irritably, up at Gabriel. "Feeling a bit above our station this morning, are we?"

Gabriel started. His mouth fell open and his eyes danced over Lord Loki's handsome features. "Not at all, my Lord. I—"

Lord Loki's face split into a sudden and unexpected grin. "I'm only playing with you, Gabe."

Gabriel granted him a nervous laugh. "Oh."

"Quiet in the Guf this afternoon?"

"Is my father down there?" Gabriel shook his head, amused for having been taken in by Lord Loki's pretend propriety. He raised his hand and pointed repugnantly toward the bookcase which concealed the stairs leading down to the Thirteenth level of the Hells.

"Ta." Lord Loki nodded. "I wouldn't recommend interrupting him, though. He's in a mood."

"I really do not have a choice." Gabriel replied, regretfully.

"Would you like for me to come with you?" Lord Loki asked with a dark brow raised over a purple eye. "Or, if you prefer, I can go fetch him for you?"

"Would you fetch him for me?" Gabriel smiled at him, grateful for his understanding.

"Of course." Lord Loki pushed his book aside and stood. He walked toward Gabriel and clapped him on the back. The strange, masculine gesture made the archangel smile. "I wouldn't go down there if I didn't have to either."

"I thank you for your understanding, my Lord."

"Of course." Lord Loki winked at him and then walked away. He pulled the book case open and then disappeared as he pulled the false door closed behind him. He hadn't been fast enough to hold back the crying agony of the damned, the sound of which made Gabriel shiver.

Curious, Gabriel stepped toward the book Lord Loki had been reading. When he realized it was one of Raziel's Tomes, he felt himself pale. No one was allowed to read those Tomes aside King Noliminan and Lucias. In fact, so far as Gabriel knew, no one else could.

Was he wrong on that count?

Could Lord Loki read the ancient language which was spoken only amongst the Small Council and Zamyael? But how could that be? His father wasn't so brazen as to teach Lord Loki the ancient texts, was he?

Gabriel wouldn't believe that.

The only people, other than Small Council and Zamyael, who were able to read the Tomes, so far as Gabriel knew, were his brothers, Uriel and Mihr. And they were only able to read the text because Raziel had spirited off with them during her pregnancies and raised them on a plane which was hidden from everyone else's view. Gabriel learned, later, that Raziel often hid there when she didn't wish to be found by King Noliminan or Lucias.

Lord Loki must have only been curious regarding history and was trying to work the writings out on his own. There were too many secrets the Small Council preferred to keep to themselves for Gabriel to believe otherwise.

The book case opened, tearing Gabriel from his thoughts. When he saw his father, tired and disheveled, he suddenly regretted calling him from his tasks. "My Lord, I beseech that you forgive me."

"What troubles bring you here, Gabe?" Lucias asked, his expression concerned. "You've never bid me out of my work before."

"I apologize for doing so now." Gabriel bowed to him. As he did so, Lord Loki stepped out from behind the bookcase and skirted around Lucias.

"What is so important?"

"I've come in regard to Zadkiel." Gabriel softened his tone as he saw his father's expression darken at the mere mention of his brother's name. As for Lord Loki, his lips pursed tight as he shook his head. "I just left him and he was not himself."

"In what manner?"

"He was extremely upset." Gabriel swallowed. "He was raging."

Lucias lowered his face so Gabriel was unable to read his expression. Gabriel knew his father well enough to understand that, where softer emotions were concerned, he was extremely guarded. "That isn't very much like him, is it?"

"No." Gabriel sighed, relieved that his father understood why he had felt compelled to seek his aide. "It isn't. And it worries me."

Lucias raised his gaze then, giving Gabriel the very briefest of nods accompanied by the tightest of all smiles. "And you believe I should go and speak with him."

"I thought you might be able to help."

"Mayhap." Lucias grumbled his agreement as he started walking out of the library. Gabriel followed. Lord Loki waited, only following after Lucias raised his hand and flicked it toward himself indicating he should join them. "However, given I am the cause of his affliction, sometimes when he sees me it merely makes matters worse."

"Yes, Pipa." Gabriel nodded. "I understand this. Won't you try?"

"I shall see to it straight away." He flicked his eyes to Lord Loki. "I loath to ask this of you, Loki, but will you speak with me as I bathe?" He looked down to his disheveled clothes and ran his hand through his unkempt hair. "I cannot greet Zadkiel like this."

Lord Loki's eyes flicked swiftly to Gabriel and then away. He wore a very strange expression on his handsome, masculine face. It was hesitation, Gabriel sensed, toward serving his Lord and Master. Gabriel didn't understand a lick of it. He, himself, coveted such a request to accompany King Noliminan in his bath. He had been born to serve King Noliminan completely. It was blasphemy, in Gabriel's mind, that Lord Loki should shirk such a basic responsibility. "Of course."

"I only wish to palaver. The bath I shall see to myself."

Gabriel shook his head, bewildered.

"Of course, my Lord."

"You will see yourself out, Gabe?" Lucias asked. Gabriel nodded. "I'll stop by your Guf after I've calmed Zadkiel down."

"I would appreciate your update as to his mood, my Lord."

Lucias nodded and turned away, walking down the hall. Lord Loki, his hands deep in his pockets, met Gabriel's gaze. His lips were pursed and his eyes set in a strange expression that flabbergasted Gabriel's mind.

Nor did he have time to contemplate it as Lord Loki raised his brows, turned away and followed after his Master.

-17-

"I beseech your forgiveness for having asked you to palaver with me whilst I bathe." Lord Regent Lucias muttered as he began removing his clothes. "I do understand your sensibilities but there was an uprising last night and everyone in the basement is bristled."

Loki chuckled at Lord Lucias' reference to the Thirteenth level of the Hells as "the basement" as he stepped forward to help him pull his shirt over his shoulders. They were broad. His figure—buried beneath his clothes—was deceiving. Loki had always imagined his body to be lithe. But it wasn't. Not at all. Rather, Lord Lucias was much more muscular than Loki would have ever suspected.

Lord Lucias looked over his shoulder to meet Loki's gaze. "I told you, you are not required to assist me with my bath."

"It's no trouble." Loki replied, his finger brushing along the length of Lord Lucias' arm as he pulled the shirt off of his back and stepped away. "What are they fighting about?"

"Only Azrael knows." Lord Lucias muttered as he began unfastening his belt. He raised his gaze and gave Loki an exasperated smile over his shoulder. "It happens every once in a while. One of them goes mad from the imprisonment and acts out and then next thing you know they're all screaming at one and another."

"I can't imagine how hard it must be to be one of them."

Lord Lucias shrugged his well made shoulders and lowered his gaze to his task. He didn't care how it felt to be one of them. They'd put themselves in that position by their own actions as far as he was concerned.

Loki needed to take a page from Lord Lucias' lesson book.

He still felt guilty merely *watching* Lord Lucias punish the damned souls. The day would come when he would have to take over the task and he wasn't sure if he would be able to do so with the conviction with which he had watched his Lord and Master go about his work.

While Lord Lucias' attention was distracted, Loki found his eyes traveling the length of his back as he pulled off his trousers and stepped out of them.

His body was absolute perfection.

When he turned around to step into the water, Loki got the full view of him. His mouth fell open and, as he always did when he was nervous or upset, he reverted to his wit. "Good God man! Is that a cock or a tree?"

Lord Lucias froze and looked upward with a startled expression. He had a slight blush on his cheeks, which Loki found endearing. After the shocked expression passed, Lord Lucias found a disinterested smile. "There's one in particular who you have to watch out for today."

Loki was grateful he had ignored his discomfort and turned the conversation back to work. "Just for today, or is he always agitated?"

"Just for today." Lord Lucias muttered before dunking beneath the water. When he rose he said, "I think *she's* about to break."

Loki acknowledged his assumption with a smile. As he did so, Lord Lucias rubbed his left eye with the back of his hand. He looked tired, suddenly. And childlike.

"But that's a good thing for her because once they break it isn't generally long after that I'm allowed to set them free."

"Then you do set them free?"

"Only after they are truly sorry for what they did." Lord Lucias smiled softly and met Loki's gaze again. "I can always tell when I am being lied to."

"I'm . . ." Loki bit back the smile that rose to his lip as he lowered his gaze. "I'm glad to hear it. I thought once damned, always damned."

"It happens." Lord Lucias admitted. "Not often. You will learn true evil rarely ever exists in mortals. Generally it's just a string of bad decisions they made during their lifetime which bring them into our care."

True evil rarely exists in mortals. Which was not to say that it is uncommon in immortals.

Loki ignored the clear distinction.

"Do you think this is why the King of Lords is changing the structure?"

"Yes." Lucias grumbled. He returned his gaze to hold Loki's. "This is why I don't squabble over the whole issue of free will." He offered another distant smile. "It is much fairer than the current system. It's just that it should apply to everyone."

"Do you think you can change his mind?" Loki's tone was very curious.

"I do not." He admitted.

"I'm sorry to hear that."

"There are other issues that I think he may meet me half way on if I push them hard enough." He shrugged. As he did so, his eyes narrowed. "If, that is, the carvetek mouk knows what's good for him."

"How far are you willing to push them?"

His eyes narrowed even further and his lips twitched. He assessed Loki long and hard before giving him an answer. When he did so, his words were dripping with venom.

"All the way, tukte 'aasifa."

-18-

Zadkiel's expression as he opened the door to his cottage was one of guarded irritation. He sensed no retribution for his displeasure, however, and he swiftly forced a thin, tired smile. "Good morning."

"Gabriel is worried about you." Lucias pushed the door open to let himself in.

I often find it amusing that my father never bothers to consider that his actions might be rude. He is, after all, the Lord Regent of the Sixty Realms. All doors are expected to be open to him.

"I am certain Gabriel has greater concerns at the nonce than me." Zadkiel replied to this as he limped out of Lucias' path, his gold staff tucked under his arm to support his weight. "Ours was no more than a brotherly quarrel."

"You know, I doubt that, Zadkiel." Lucias wasn't in the mood for gentle supplication. "And if so, what was your argument regarding."

"It matters not."

"It mattered enough to Gabriel to raise it to my attention." Zadkiel's gait was slow as he made his way into his kitchen. Once there, Lucias slipped past him, pulled out a chair and lowered himself at Zadkiel's table. "He is worried about you."

Zadkiel leaned awkwardly against his counter as he reached upward with his left hand to grasp at a glass. It was obvious to me that my father was just ready to find his feet and fetch it when Zadkiel's fingers snatched it and brought it quickly down.

I was grateful for this.

Showing favoritism to Zadkiel by performing his menial tasks would belittle and embarrass my brother.

"He's merely being overly kind. There is nothing new under the sun to trouble you about, Father."

"Then this is an old quarrel?"

Zadkiel stood with his back to our father, toying with the glass he had just pulled out of his cupboard. Lucias watched him, waiting. After a long pause, Zadkiel lifted the bottle of scotch,

101

poured our father a drink and turned to face him. He took two painful steps toward Lucias, who took the glass away from him wearing a patient smile.

Finally, Zadkiel advised him in docile tones, "I've determined I shan't go to Michael's party."

This seemed to surprise my father. "No?"

"No." He replied, dragging himself toward the table.

It's a painful thing to watch having known him in prime health.

"If this is regarding your quarrel with Gabriel then I must insist that the pettiness be set aside." Lucias sighed as he watched my brother, searching for any clue regarding the depths of his misgivings by his expression. "We are, all of us, making sacrifice this year for the sake of peace."

Zadkiel's golden eyes slowly rose until Lucias was finally granted the courtesy of his gaze. "I assure you, I shan't be missed."

"*I* shall miss you." Lucias corrected him. "As will your mother."

"She won't." He shook his head. His gaze had lowered again into supplication. I felt Lucias' entire body lament with the grief that he felt for his son. "And nor will King Noliminan."

"What nonsense is this?" Lucias asked him. "Of course they shall miss you."

"No." He replied. "They shan't. None of them pay me any mind any more unless such is required in my servitude."

Lucias' brow furrowed. He knew what Zadkiel was telling him was true—he had bore witness to Noliminan's smug, self-satisfied grin whenever he looked upon the child.

"Haven't I paid my dues, Pipa?"

"Yes." No hesitation. "You have. But then, if my opinion held any import in the matter you never would have been punished to begin with."

"Punished for *your* sins." And there it was. The heart of the matter. Said by Zadkiel in docile tones and followed with an expression of pure horror that the words had actually escaped his golden lips.

"It was the right thing to do." Lucias answered him softly, choosing not to admonish him for his honesty.

I had hoped his soft tones would calm my brother's fear, but this was impossible. Every moment of Zadkiel's life since the day he had been thrown from the Heavens has been lived in fear.

"Anael was insane. She would have destroyed him. She had to be extinguished and you are the only one with the power to release the life force for good."

"King Noliminan shall never see it that way." Zadkiel shivered as he raised his gaze again to meet Lucias'. "He loved her."

"Noliminan never loved her." Lucias corrected him, lowering his own gaze to hide his anger. "He merely wanted a female version of me."

"He never should have made her." Zadkiel braved. Lucias, startled by his sudden burst of unbridled anger, looked upon his son with honest, open regard. "Who punishes him?"

He hit his staff against the floor. The sound if it echoed around the small cottage within which Zadkiel lived. Rather ominously, in my opinion.

"He can make and destroy lives without retribution." Lucias reached forward, trying to calm his son with his touch. His attempt must have worked. Zadkiel's tone became softer, even if his words did not. "And he's made more fatally unforgivable mistakes than all of the rest of us combined."

"Noliminan is very powerful, Zadkiel." Lucias gave a very unnecessary warning. "The most powerful of us all." He lowered his gaze again. "The decision as to whether or not to stand up to him is never an easy one to make. You should be proud of yourself for having done so when what is right required your action."

"He is not more powerful than you." It wasn't meant to stroke Lucias' ego and he clearly knew that. "He is all of you and you are all of him. His only power comes from some cosmic mistake of being here first."

103

"His power comes from the fear and the greed of the Council which supports him." My father corrected Zadkiel. "And that's my fault. The system of democracy was my idea."

"The system would work if the Gods who sat upon the Council weren't corrupt." Zadkiel replied. "But there is no care among them for what is the greater good. Only what barters they can make for their votes."

"Some of them care." Lucias corrected him.

"Not enough of them to support you." Zadkiel prodded him, knowing, as I did, where Lucias' mind was already going. Knowing what our father ultimately meant to do if he could not meet Noliminan half way through discussion alone. "The majority will hold to the current ways because it serves their needs."

"It will be a close thing." Lucias admitted.

"Direct confrontation will not be the way." Zadkiel lowered his gaze. "A vote at Council will never pass." He reached forward and grabbed Lucias' hand. He squeezed it tight. "Do not raise the issue at Council until you have the majority, Pipa. The consequences of losing this vote will be too great for you to bear." He raised his gaze to hold Lucias' own. "Those of us who would support your cause hold no vote."

"Another injustice."

"Which is a fight you shall never win."

Lucias smiled at him. He had come to calm Zadkiel's anger and, in the end, it had been Zadkiel talking sense. "Come to Michael's party."

Zadkiel sighed. "I'd rather not."

"Do not let them win, my son." Lucias entreated. "Every time they look at you they are forced to deal with their own atrocious behaviors. Eventually they will realize their folly."

"You have more faith in them than I do."

"And you have more compassion than *I* do." Lucias ran his hand lovingly over his son's wounded leg. "For once, let us allow compassion to rule the day."

-19-

Tristan stepped out of Evanbourough's suite with a smile, grateful they had both been able to free their afternoon schedules so they might spend some time together. He had no intention of tarrying in the halls of the Hells for overly long. Rather, he planned to will himself to his apartment to retire for the evening after grabbing a bite at the Hells bound Courtyard where the Gods and demons of this level found their leisure.

Moira's laws being what they are, however, stopped Tristan dead in his tracks.

Far down the hall, looking lost and confused, an angel was wandering. The child was obviously terrified of the catcalls made by the demons set outside in the hallway. He kept turning this way and that, darting toward freedom before bolting in another direction after another demon taunted him.

Tristan thought about yelling in the lad's direction but decided to do so would only scare the angel more. Instead, he started walking swiftly toward him.

The boy tried to run. He knew the moment he saw a God coming toward him he was in trouble. But Tristan was faster than him and was easily able to catch up. When he reached the angel, the child started flailing his arms, trying to hit Tristan.

This was a foolish game the angel would not win.

Tristan danced around him until he stood at his back and grabbed him from behind, cinching his arms to his chest to bind him. The child kicked—trying to get away—but Tristan would have none of it.

The demons who had been taunting the boy immediately fell still. They knew Tristan to be a Heavens' bound God and they weren't about to push their luck that the scared, lost angel didn't belong to him.

"Calm down, child." He growled into the angel's ear. "What are you doing here?"

"Let me go!"

"Where are you going?" Tristan asked him through gritted teeth as the boy's heel struck his knee.

"I need to palaver with Lord Regent Lucias!"

"Then you're a damn fool." Tristan shook him. Any words which were to be passed to the Lord Regent were required to first be passed by the angel's God to either the Queen of Ladies or the Sovereign Lady. Not to Lord Lucias directly. He had more important things to concern himself with than the complaints of the Heavens bound children. "What about?"

"That's my business!"

"Not when you're wandering these halls without your guardian, it isn't." He reached one arm down and was, finally, able to pin the angel's legs. "Do you know how dangerous it is here for you here?"

"I must palaver with Lord Regent Lucias!" The boy repeated, still trying to struggle but failing under Tristan's strength.

"And I didn't say I wouldn't deliver you to him to do so, now did I?" Tristan shook the angel and held him against his struggle. "But you're nowhere near Lord Lucias' quarters and I'm not about to set you free to get yourself raped or worse."

The angel gave one last kick before falling limp in Tristan's arms.

"That's better." Tristan tried to sound kinder than he felt in that moment. "Now. If I put you on your feet, I want your promise that you aren't going to run."

"You'll take me to Lord Regent Lucias?" The angel's frightened voice was a whisper.

"I'm a God of my word." Tristan promised him. He couldn't imagine what this angel might possibly want with Lord Lucias. And he was more curious to find that out than anything else. "I'll walk you right through his door."

"I won't run."

Tristan wasn't sure about that, but he put the lad to his feet anyway. Though he could carry him, it would be easier on them both—after this fracas was done—if the angel were to walk.

They would be remembered as it was.

Once the child was released, Tristan held out his hand. "It will be better if they think you're with me a purpose. And given you aren't my servant, it would be better if they think you have been loaned to me by your Master as my pretty."

"Yes, my Lord." The angel, very tentatively, wrapped his fingers around Tristan's hand. "But I'm not your pretty." Then, in a very small voice, "Am I?"

Tristan felt the corners of his lips dance.

"My pretty lies in his own bed sleeping in yon apartment." Tristan pointed to Evanbourough's rooms. "And, lucky for you, he fell asleep when he did."

"Yes, my Lord." Looking at the angel, Tristan realized he wasn't a boy at all. He looked young, but he was definitely a fully grown adult.

The angel didn't say a single word to Tristan as they made their travels. But this didn't concern him. He was more concerned with what the angel had to say to Lord Regent Lucias than anything he might want to say to Tristan.

When they reached Lord Lucias' door, Tristan stood before it and turned the angel toward him for one final demand. "I intend on sitting in on your meeting."

"No!" The angel's blue eyes were filled with the fire of his panic. "You can't! My business is between myself and Lord Lucias!"

"Either you agree to me being included in this meeting or I take you back to the Heavens right now to return you to your Master." Tristan narrowed his eyes as he spoke. His threat was disingenuous but his charge didn't know that. "I'm the last one to be seen with you. And when you don't return to your Master, he or she is coming after me." The angel's blue eyes grew wide. "I believe—given my personal risk—I deserve to know what I'm putting my hide on the line to protect you from." He bent down so he was on level with the angel's gaze. "Don't you?"

His voice was a whisper. "You shall betray me."

"I told you before," Tristan raised his hand and laid it on the angel's cheek. "I'm a God who keeps my word."

The angel's terror at being returned to his Master overwhelmed his mistrust. He gave an almost non-existent nod and lowered his gaze.

Satisfied, Tristan raised his hand to the door and knocked. He was less than surprised when Sappharon opened the door.

The brat wore an expectant expression which first turned to relief but then quickly changed to fear.

"Lord Tristan. How may I help you?"

"None of your games, Dame." Tristan said in a voice low enough so only they three would hear. "I've seen you darting in dark halls where you don't belong. Now I believe I understand why. So are you going to let us in before more people than already have see your new friend darkening your Master's door?"

Sappharon lowered her head and stepped backward, opening the door for them. "Please do not betray me, my Lord."

"If I had intended to betray you, then I already would have." Tristan assured her. "I'm not blind to what has been going on. Nor are Evanbourough and Theasis. We side with you and your kindred, Sappharon."

"Thank you." Sappharon whispered as she looked upward and met Tristan's gaze. "You have always been kind to me."

"I am sure that the day will come when you will give me reasons why I should not be." Tristan grinned at her. "But that day is not today."

Sappharon lowered her fiery red gaze, so alike to Lady Raziel's, and turned to the angel at Tristan's side. "Come with me."

"I promised him he could meet Lord Regent Lucias with me." The angel's face was ashen. "Please do not be angry. It was the only way I was able to gain his escort."

Tristan didn't correct the lie. Rather, he decided, for the angel's sake, that he would add to it. "He came to Evanbourough seeking guidance of direction. I answered the door instead."

"Very well." Sappharon reluctantly agreed. "Just—both of you. Be aware that Lucias is feeling ill and is in a very dark mood. So temper your words."

"I think his mood is about to get darker," Tristan prophesized.

"Just so." Sappharon nodded. "Since you're already in this—"

"I shan't betray you, brat." Tristan reached forward and gently grasped her bicep. Relief etched on every line of her odd looking face.

She would be devastatingly beautiful, Tristan thought, *if she took more care in her grooming. And I would take her if I were not with Evan.*

As it was, he *was* with Evan.

And she was a red hot mess.

"I owe you."

"Careful." Tristan smiled at her. "I may come to collect."

Sappharon smiled winsomely and turned away. They followed her down a hallway Tristan had never been through before and waited at the last door on the very end. Sappharon slipped in without knocking. When she slipped out, it was with a thoroughly chastised expression.

"I've gained you an audience." She turned to the angel at Tristan's side. "Make the first words your best. Or he won't listen to the rest."

"I'll speak on his behalf." Tristan pronounced. "If you will let me talk to him."

The angel looked up at Tristan, his blue eyes huge and filled with gratitude. When he spoke, his voice was a shaking whisper. "Thank you."

Preparing for anything, Tristan slipped into the bedroom, catching his breath to find Lord Lucias in his finely made bed with red silk sheets pulled to his waist to protect his modesty. He swallowed his fear, and brought the angel around so he stood in front of the Father of the Hells. He knew, given the craze in Lord Lucias' eyes, that Sappharon had been right. If his first words weren't the right ones, neither he nor the child would survive this meeting.

"This angel is damned by the hand of his Master if we don't protect him." He watched as Lord Lucias' expression softened slightly. His gaze slowly fell from Tristan's face to the terrified face of the angel before him. "Will you grant him succor?"

109

"There is an apartment on the Thirteenth level which is reserved for Gods." Lord Lucias' voice was weary. "Right now it is empty. There is no safer place for him in either the Heavens or the Hells." He forced his gaze upward to meet Tristan's. "Stay there with the child tonight to keep him from being frightened by those outside the door. I shall decide what to do with him tomorrow."

Without a word, Tristan pushed the terrified angel behind him, bowed and left Lord Lucias' bedchamber.

A safe place for the night was, clearly, the best they would be able to hope for.

-20-

Loki smiled as he met Lord Tristan's gaze. Tristan smiled in return and stepped back to let him into the apartment.

"I have an apology to make on behalf of my Master." Tristan's expression faltered. "He wants me to speak with you and the angel." He lowered his gaze. "He is not well this morning."

"He didn't look well last night." Tristan didn't ask the underlying question and Loki was grateful. Honestly, he didn't know what was wrong with Lord Lucias. Only that he had been violently ill for several waning moons. "I trust you will convey the child's words true?"

"Honest." Loki raised his gaze and held Tristan's, "I have a fair idea this is Lord Regent Lucias' first test of me." Which frightened him. "So yes." He assured Lord Tristan. "I will judge fairly and repeat what I believe to be true."

"I think the child will receive you better anyway." Tristan told him. "I do not know what in the name of the Sixty Realms he has been through, but I've never met a more devastated soul in all of my existence." Tristan's expression was taut. "He hasn't said a word to me regarding his cause for audience."

"Did he really knock on Evan's door as Sappharon is trying to ploy?" Loki didn't believe for a minute that he had. If the child wouldn't speak with Tristan—a Heavens bound God with a reputation of love and fairness—he never would have sought out Lord Evanbourough.

It was reputed that Evan felt nothing but disdain when it came to children—angels and demons alike. Loki didn't believe these rumors for a moment given Evanbourough was charged with the protection of the exiled ones. Yet, he had heard that more than one demon assigned to Evan's service had begged for their release from Lady Raziel due to Evanbourough's temper.

"No." Tristan was honest to the question put directly to him. "I found him wandering through the Hells on his own. Demons down the hall from Evanbourough were taunting him and I happened to be stepping out as it was happening." He shook his head. "He was so frightened when I tried to grab him. Imagine if someone else would have found him." Then through his teeth. "Imagine if Zuko would have found him."

"He never would have made it." Loki agreed.

Zuko was the God who had been charged with tempting mortals with a propensity to abuse their children so Lord Lucias could damn them for it. Loki didn't personally know the cruel God, but from what he'd heard the last thing in the world that Zuko would do is protect an immortal child. Rather, Loki suspected, he would take the child to whatever God he knew had the sickest passion for it.

He felt himself shiver. "He's damn lucky, Tristan."

"I know."

"So why is Sappharon lying?"

"Who knows why Sappharon does anything?" Tristan's gaze was averted. Loki knew he was hiding something to protect Lord Lucias' brat. He thought, as he watched Tristan's lips twitch into an unwanted smile, Tristan admired her.

Admiration? For Sappharon?

Surely he was mistaken about that.

"Don't play me." Loki snapped. "I cannot help you if you do."

Tristan, frowning, met his gaze. "Can I trust you?"

"If not then I have no business serving a God as mighty as Lord Regent Lucias."

Tristan considered this for a moment. Loki understood that anyone who didn't know who Lord Lucias truly was wouldn't take such a vow as it was meant to be made. But Tristan nodded in agreement. "I believe the angel told Sappharon whatever was going on with him. She took pity on him and, perhaps, went so far as to promise him Lord Lucias' aide."

"I don't want to know how they met." Though he was hard pressed to believe that Sappharon would act on any one's behalf but her own, Loki meant this sentiment honestly. He and Sappharon loathed one another. Loki didn't need to add knowing something he couldn't keep from Lord Lucias to the list of supposed betrayals he had made against the brat. "Tell the angel not to bring it up when he's speaking with me."

"I will." Tristan's voice was soft and his gaze was lowered.

"Did he ever tell you his name?"

"No." Tristan shook his head. "I think he's still afraid I'm going to betray him to his Master. I doubt we will find out either his name or that of his God."

"How can we protect him if we don't know who we are protecting him *from*?" Loki asked, exasperated with the angel.

"If you were tortured every day would you want anyone to tell the person who had been torturing you that you had told on them?" His tone was sharp. Loki looked at him, startled. "I do not blame him for not trusting us. I've heard from the Gods' own lips what they do to their charges. Azrael alone knows what they *aren't* bragging about."

The door to one of the bedchambers of the apartment very hesitantly opened then and the angel stepped slowly out. He looked from one to the other of them, his distaste for Loki clear upon every line of his face.

"Oh." Tristan stood and pointed to Loki. "This is Lord Regent Lucias' other servant, Loki."

The mistrust on the angel's face was almost like a slap to Loki's own. "I am here to talk to you on behalf of Lord Lucias. He is not feeling well enough to receive you."

112

"I cannot talk to you." The angel whispered. His face was ashen and his eyes were bright with their fear. "Sappharon warned me about you!"

"I am what you have." Loki replied to this, not at all surprised by this reaction given Sappharon's obvious intent to protect this terrified child. "I have to report back to my Lord Regent with my own opinion. If you do not talk to me, then there is no offer of succor."

The angel's already ashen face paled further. He turned his gaze to Tristan. "Do you trust him?"

"With my soul." Tristan assured him, smiling softly at him. Loki held back a snort. He and Tristan knew each other only by word of mouth.

"Just tell me what he does to you." Loki softened his tone. "First, who he is?"

"I cannot tell you who he is." The angel whispered.

"You have to." Tristan stepped forward and set a hand on the angel's shoulder. "We will not tell anyone but the Lord Regent. We have to be able to keep an eye out so your persecutor does not come after you while in our care."

The child was still frightened, despite their reassurances. Yet, he was intelligent enough to know he had been backed into a corner and was left with no other choice. Returning to whence he had come was not an option.

"My God is Lord Regan." He whispered. Then swallowed. His voice grew steadily louder. "He cuts me up and sells my parts in the various worlds for barter and trade."

Loki felt the blood drain from his face. "What do you mean that he cuts you up and sells your parts?"

"He took my liver last time." The angel replied, his voice now cold. "I thought it was the end of me. I lay in agony for three cycles of the sun while it grew back." He lowered his gaze to his feet. "I could have gone on bearing his abuses. But his new barter with the black market is for my heart."

"Piss on the Gods!" Tristan whispered. "If Regan cuts out your heart . . ."

"I may as well visit Lord Zadkiel then." The angel, his gaze still at his feet, completed the thought. "Given it is the heart which holds our life force, I will be forced to lie host to whatever mortal it is put within or become a passenger taking a backseat through life. This is why I had to run."

"Excuse me." Loki whispered.

He stepped swiftly to the bedchamber where the child had been. Once inside, he softly shut the door behind him. His mind swelling with the words the angel had said, he fell against the door and allowed himself to slide to the ground. He pounded both fists to the floor with every bit of force that he could muster and a satisfying bolt of pain ran up both arms as the marble floor buckled inward and around his fists.

Lord Lucias had warned him of the evil in the worlds that they ruled. He had even warned him that those around him were not to be trusted.

But this? It was vile; black-hearted . . .

Forcing someone to choose to either possess his host or live as a witness to his own life in the mortal's undermind . . . it was the most evil of all propositions that Loki could imagine. Either way, one life or the other was forfeit to the worst of all imaginable manners of thievery.

In that moment, he loathed his position to serve at Lord Regent Lucias' side.

-21-

Zamyael sat at the desk staring blankly at the book which lay open on top of it. Lasterian's kiss had raised turbulent emotions long buried as deep within her soul as she could send them. Reconciling those feelings was proving to be a fruitless task as she listened, through a slightly ajar door, to a conversation between Lucias and Raziel which she had no business hearing. They were discussing days long ago passed and she was thrown into a deep, unpleasant reverie.

Zamyael, like Raziel, had been born a Goddess. Not a demon. Certainly, not male.

Raziel's purpose had been to serve and love Noliminan as his wife. And Zamyael, upon her birth, was gifted to serve and love Lucias as his.

She never minded the gifting; Lucias was extremely patient. He waited until she came willingly to him rather than claiming what was his to take from her from the start.

Noliminan was never inclined to be so caring or understanding. He mistook Lucias' patience as indifference toward her and, in so doing, cornered her and stole her maidenhood. She never admitted to Lucias the rape, but believed he suspected such to be the case as her behavior became withdrawn after the incident.

Lucias never made any attempt to verify his suspicions as far as she knew. Still, there was no mistake to be made about it. The first falling out which ever occurred between Lucias and Noliminan was her doing.

Shortly after she went to Lucias' bed, Lucias took her from the palace the Small Council shared. The two of them hid in a small cottage upon the first world Noliminan had created.

Despite the beauty of the forest surrounding them, Lucias paid attention to only her. His patience knew no bounds, for he allowed her to come to him only when she wanted him.

Which, because of his gentleness toward her on the rare occasions when they coupled, became more and more frequent over time.

Eventually, Raziel came searching for them. Though Raziel's love for Noliminan was palpable, it didn't stop her from imploring them to come home.

Zamyael didn't want go with her. However, she knew Lucias missed his home and so beseeched him that they return.

To his credit, Lucias refused.

Zamyael was stubborn in her own right, however, and would not keep him from his home. His kindness and patience with her was sufficient to see her through the worst of times. Or so she had believed. In her heart, she recognized the beginnings of the disdain he was coming to feel for her for keeping him. She pleaded with him that they return and he, eventually, agreed.

They were not long home before she became the subject of Noliminan's twisted desires. Whether Lucias knew this and simply turned a blind eye, or if Noliminan's advances were discreet enough that Lucias never suspected them, the subject of Zamyael's abstinence toward Lucias did not raise angst amongst the pair for quite some time.

At which time, she found a new champion in Raziel.

Cornered by Noliminan as she showered beneath the waterfall gracing the long balcony, Zamyael was forced against the wall by the neck when Raziel stepped out of the castle. Raziel caught sight of the scene of the two of them coupling and screamed in rage as she never had before.

Zamyael feared that Raziel would believe the worst of her as Noliminan tossed her to the floor. To her astonishment, Raziel turned on Noliminan, raving at him for taking something which belonged to Lucias, insisting he had overstepped his bounds.

Enraged at being chastised regarding his power and his possessions, Noliminan kicked Zamyael into the castle, adding insult to injury, and advanced upon Raziel. The doors through which Zamyael had been flung slammed shut and, though she pounded desperately on them, trying to get through so she might aide Raziel, locked.

Noliminan did not lie regarding his power. She was unable to do more than stand on the wrong side of the doors and scream as he and Raziel vanished into nothingness. Noliminan had taken Raziel away to do with her as he would in a place where neither Zamyael nor Lucias would be able to interfere.

When they returned, it was with the first angel, Raguel, as a babe in arms.

It was upon their return that the second battle between Noliminan and Lucias occurred. This battle, unlike the first, culminated in such destructiveness that both Raziel and Zamyael believed one or the other of them would be utterly destroyed.

But neither of them had been.

The women didn't know who had ultimately won, though both suspected that Noliminan had been the victor after Lucias' subsequent supplications.

The men didn't discuss the matter with them and the pair didn't push the issue. An uneasy peace settled between the four of them.

But peace like that is not lasting.

Shortly after Lucias and Noliminan returned from their warring, Raziel—for reasons unknown to Lucias and Zamyael—began to appear not as a Goddess, but as a God. Though, only when Noliminan was in the room.

Zamyael couldn't be certain of what spurred this rebellion. What she did know was that this happening continued with greater and greater frequency until it became acceptable and expected.

Eventually, Noliminan grew tired of Raziel's mutiny and began to seek Zamyael again in Raziel's stead. Zamyael avoided his attentions by refusing to be alone whether in or out of his presence. She knew he was becoming incensed with her as well.

When Noliminan's patience with her had dissolved, Zamyael paid dearly for her unwillingness to bend to his sexual demands.

Yet, none of them were prepared for the lengths to which he would go to prove his superiority over them.

Over dinner one night, he casually raised the subject of Lucias' pleasure with Raziel and Raguel in his service. He, Noliminan, complained for having been left to his own devices. Lucias, in his attempt to shelter Raziel from what he perceived to be Noliminan's ill treatment, did not argue the point. Noliminan decided this was a concession; that Lucias was releasing Zamyael from his care for Raziel. He flicked his evil hand nonchalantly toward Zamyael so that she was immediately seized with pain.

Two black wings forced their way through her shoulder blades. The force of their growth and their sudden heavy weight pulled her chair backward so she lay sprawling on the floor. Raziel cried out in surprise and ran to her. Raguel sat staring, mouth agape, fearful of them all and so not knowing how to react to Zamyael's sudden writhing.

"What have you done?" Lucias cried, his dark brown eyes flying to where Noliminan sat at their table.

"I made you." Noliminan said calmly. "Each and every one of you. Never forget that, what I have made, I can just as easily destroy."

If or not this brokered argument from Lucias, Zamyael would never know. The pain was excruciating and Zamyael, afraid and confused, lost all consciousness.

What followed was chaos.

While she was still unconscious, Lucias skirted Zamyael away and hid her. When she woke, the body she had once inhabited was no longer hers.

She pieced together from what Raziel was willing to share with her that Lucias had been afraid for Zamyael and, unable to reverse the magic which had turned her from a Goddess into the first demon, Lucias changed her physical essence so Noliminan would no longer covet her.

When Lucias returned with a male Zamyael, Noliminan was infuriated. So much so that he demanded Raziel to return to her natural form.

Raziel refused.

When she did so, Noliminan turned his frustrations onto Raguel. The magic that he had taken from Zamyael was granted to the angel, but only on the condition that he, ever thereafter, live as a she.

Raguel, present during Zamyael's demise, had been too terrified of Noliminan to refuse. Over time that terror turned into supplication. Now, Zamyael thought as she listened to Raziel and Lucias through her door, her initial supplication was genuine regard.

Sighing, Zamyael reached for the book upon her table and closed it.

There was no room for such melancholy after all these years. There was no changing her plight and to dwell upon her past would only destroy what sanity she had managed to retain.

Besides, she thought as she stood at her doorway, opening it just enough so she could see Raziel sitting perched on Lucias' lap with her strong arms wrapped around Lucias' neck and Lucias wearing a tender smile as he looked down upon her, she still had the two Gods who had always loved her best and protected her from what ill will they could.

Zamyael would learn in the all too near future just how foolish she was to believe in such tripe.

-22-

"His God cuts him up into pieces and sells his parts to the earthbound." Lord Loki snapped, every word like acid on his tongue. "He means to cut out his heart and sell it to a mortal!"

Lucias, his mood sated for the nonce, didn't look up when Lord Loki entered his library. He had seen the damnation on the face of the angel when Tristan presented him the night before and, so, he hadn't needed to hear the child's words. As a result, he decided that, no matter how painful, Lord Loki needed a lesson in what would come to be if he were to truly embrace becoming his apprentice.

"And?"

Lord Loki said nothing. But his indignation at Lucias' lack of compassion resonated throughout the room.

Lucias refused to look upon his face. I suspect he understood Lord Loki's discontentment. Lord Loki, he rightly assumed, believed he was owed some type of warning regarding what he would be forced to bear witness to.

Lucias held his tongue. He would not always be there to warn Lord Loki about the evils that existed; the evils which he would be forced to judge.

"I cannot do this." Lord Loki finally said, his tone cold and unforgiving. His anger toward Lucias was palpable. "I *will* not do this!"

"You can and you will." Lucias said no more than this.

"No." Lord Loki's voice took on a desperate quality which was not at all like him. Hearing this, Lucias finally raised his gaze from his paperwork. "I had no idea . . ."

He asked, pointedly, "You cannot laugh at all of it. Can you?"

"No." Lord Loki's face was pale as he shook his head. His purple eyes were dark with pain. "I do not know if I can ever laugh again."

"You can." Lucias said cautiously. "Which is what will make you better at this task than I am."

He held his hand out to indicate a high backed chair on the other side of his desk. He appeared pleased that Lord Loki walked forward to lower himself within it. I know my father well enough to understand that Lord Loki makes him extremely nervous when he hovers over him. He prefers them to be on a level playing field.

"Hold on to your sense of humor, Loki." He counseled. "No matter what you see or hear and no matter whom you offend when it is inappropriate that you do so." He lowered his quill and tented his hands. "In the end, it will serve your sanity."

Lord Loki, so fresh and young, mistook Lucias' melancholy for apathy.

"What would you have me do, Loki?"

"Protect that child!" He cried, his anger blazing like hot coals in his eyes. Lucias, who clearly understood where such anger came from, seemed not to take offense. "Damn that God!"

"I will protect the child." He promised. "In exchange, I will not punish his God." Lord Loki's immediate indignation was palpable. "Yet." Lucias qualified. "This God is but one cog in a giant wheel. I want him—make no mistake—but I want those who enable him as well."

He stood, walked around the desk to take the chair next to Lord Loki's, leaned forward and grasped the arm of Lord Loki's chair. Had Lord Loki been anyone else, he would have reached for his hand to comfort him.

"I assure you that his God will be damned to antiquity in my own time." He sighed heavily. "What I must ask you now is if he would be better served to remain free for the nonce. As a tool."

"Yes, my Lord." Lord Loki acquiesced, though it pained him to do so. He avoided his Master's gaze at all costs. "I understand."

"What would you have me do?" Lucias asked him. He would have Lord Loki direct this schooling.

"Bide." The word was cutting on Loki's tongue. "Until the time is right. And then damn them all, as you say, to antiquity."

Lucias nodded, raised his hand lest he be tempted to comfort the youngling, and laid it on his own knee.

"Whatever I do, met paken," he sighed, "and whenever I do it, you are to have no part in it."

Lord Loki turned toward him, his fury awash upon his handsome face. "Why? I want my hand on all of it!"

"No. I need you far more here—understanding my decisions and reasoning—should something happen and you need to take my place."

"I am not ready to take your place!"

"Perhaps not yet." Lucias sighed. "But the day may come. We are, all of us, replaceable. Your purpose is to be my apprentice. You shall take my place if or when I choose to step down."

Lord Loki's expression became hard with those words. "The King of Lords will never replace you."

This earned him a small and patient smile. "I have no intention of going anywhere, Loki. Yet, you must be prepared for that eventuality all the same."

Rolling his eyes closed, Lord Loki silently placated him with a nod.

-23-

Michael stood over the table where the Small Council sat in palaver, ready to intercede should it become necessary that he must. He had witnessed far too much discontentment between the four of his betters as of late to truly believe any one of them would bide their tongues for the full course of the evening. As a result, he decided before opening his door to the festivities that he would separate the Small Council if their tempers ran over.

If I am able.

Thus far no arguments had been brokered amongst them. Rather, it was teasing banter between King Noliminan and Lucias whilst Raziel and Queen Raguel both held their tongues and simply glared at one another in antiquated animosity.

Thank all of the Gods that are or ever were for that!

He was grateful for their silence.

As for King Noliminan and Lucias, he understood the teasing between his father and his Master for what it was. The same debate had been ringing in docile tones for more years than he cared to remember.

Though he would never in life admit it, his thoughts ran that if free will were to be granted, the angels and demons had more right to it than the mortals. He, like every one of his brothers, longed to be able to speak his mind.

But his job was to protect King Noliminan, not debate with him. He understood why his Master needed for him to follow every order he issued without question. Because of this, and because strict obedience was buried deep within his nature, he could forever hold his tongue.

"I disagree with you, Nol." Lucias managed to keep his tone pleasant and his expression content.

Michael, who knew both his father and his Master better than either of them, probably, cared for, watched as Lucias attempted the lie of it.

"I say that if you put a temptation right in front of the pair, and tell them to it is forbidden, then they will not be able to resist the prize."

"And I say that, if given plenty to make them happy, then they will avoid it a purpose so as not to displease their God." King Noliminan responded.

His argument sounded reasonable enough. But Michael had learned much as the General of King Noliminan's army and had seen people act less than reasonable. Thus, he silently disagreed.

"Why would they risk my anger for the sake of an extra bauble?"

"It is the nature of desire." Raziel spoke for the first time all evening.

Michael watched as King Noliminan's eyes darted toward her.

"If you tell me, for example, I may not rut with Raguel, then I should rape her simply to spite you." Raziel flicked her flaming eyes to the Queen of Ladies and sneered. "No matter how distasteful I find her."

Queen Raguel sighed at this but—wisely—held her tongue. Michael, who was standing directly behind her, laid his hand upon his Queen's shoulder and squeezed it.

He was in love with her. This, he understood, damned him.

It wasn't his place, as an angel—even as an archangel—to covet a Goddess. Certainly not his Master's wife.

He was pleased when she covered his hand with her own and held it there. Despite his better judgment, he felt a shiver of lust for her at her touch.

"Haven't we all learned that lesson well?" King Noliminan replied chuckling. "But then I think it is a different matter when you are not a God. They require our approval."

Michael, pulling his thoughts away from his desire, was furious that his Master didn't defend his Queen from Raziel's quip.

As ever, he held his tongue.

He was not the Queen of Ladies' champion, after all. Though he was bound to protect Queen Raguel in a subversive manner, he belonged, wholly, to King Noliminan.

As did she.

"They neither require nor *want* our approval." Lucias, who noticed Queen Raguel's discomfort and passed her what guarded understanding he could without actually appearing to be kind, muttered. His expression was suddenly stormy. To Michael it was troublesome and foreboding.

"I know I am right on this count, min 'lasupita." King Noliminan responded haughtily as he waved Lucias off with a flick of his hand. "They would not tempt my anger by touching whatever it is I told them they could not have."

"Would you care to raise a friendly wager?" Lucias asked in overly eager tones, leaning back, rather than forward, as if the wager was a new idea to him.

Uh-oh, Michael thought. *Here it is. This is what has been driving him all night.*

King Noliminan's eyes sparkled. Rather foolishly, in Michael's opinion.

"I relish the thought of putting you in your place."

"It *is* where I belong." Lucias' smile broadened.

Michael rolled his eyes and, again, shook his head. His father amused him. He wished more than anything that he could openly laugh at his quips.

"My terms: They must be of the same race. One male and one female. And they must be told that, if they touch whatever it is we decide to tempt them with, there will be damning consequences for all of mortality."

King Noliminan nodded his agreement. "They must be placed in an exotic setting with all of the food and comfort they could ever care to have. They should have no need of anything. Especially not whatever it is we tempt them with."

"And what is the wager?" Raziel asked, sounding bored.

Almost.

Michael knew his mother's cunning for what it was.

"I say that if they give in to their temptations then you let me lay down the rules in regard to the consequence when it comes to your new plans of free will." King Noliminan's eyes narrowed slightly. Lucias, seeing he was on the losing side of raising barter, raised his palms to King Noliminan and lowered his chin. "Just in regard to the mortals until the Council agrees that myself and our children might be afforded the same regard."

"If I win, you drop this madness of asking for me to give free will to the Gods, demons and angels and accept things the way they have rightfully always been."

"It seems fair to me." Raziel drawled. "On both sides."

"What should we put in the garden to tempt them?" King Noliminan asked with a thoughtful expression.

"If you truly want to test them, then the best way to do so is to put the forbidden fruit in the garden." Lucias suggested.

Michael felt his eyes turn to his father. Every God, angel and demon had been ordered upon the lifting of their mortal veil to resist their desire to eat the fruit of which Lucias was speaking. To do so would result in a visit to Zadkiel.

King Noliminan snorted. "Why?"

"Since you believe your mortals have the restraint of the Gods, why not put them to the same test as you have put the rest of us?" He shrugged. "Give them your ridiculously stupid fruit tree and forbid them, as you have forbidden us, to eat from it."

King Noliminan smiled at this. Michael shivered under that smile.

"As you will it, Luke."

"What race do you think?" Lucias asked, his eyes rolling away.

"Why not Lucias' beloved Adam." Raziel purred, reaching toward King Noliminan and running her fingers lovingly over his hand. "I am certain Raguel can seduce him into handing over one of his rib bones so she might create a female of his race."

"As if a woman can be born out of a bone." The Queen of Ladies groused, obviously wanting no part of it.

Michael, whose hand was still set upon his beloved Queen's shoulder, squeezed her again. The thumb of her hand which still covered his own danced upon his wrist, causing him to shiver.

"I shall make a woman for Adam if it is what you require. But from the seed of another ape in my womb. Not from a piece of Adam's stupid failing body."

"I like it." King Noliminan clapped his hands together, ignoring the byplay between the women altogether. "We can make Adam immortal until Raguel's female is birthed and they have bore children to propagate their race. I will make the barter so in the morning."

"And may the best of us win." Lucias' smile was contemptuous. His expression, and his tone, was as cold as ice. "And may the loser hold to his barter when it comes time to close the bargain."

-24-

"It's done." Camael, who had been hovering in a hidden spot behind Raziel until that moment, whispered into Zamyael's ear. "They've just sealed the barter."

Zamyael flicked her gaze swiftly to where the Small Council sat in their palaver. She smiled as her eyes danced wickedly over each one of their faces. "Noliminan hasn't the barest of clues as to what he's just gotten himself into."

"He does seem overly pleased with himself." Camael agreed.

"Damn fool." Zadkiel's amusement danced between them as he leaned forward on his staff. Zamyael started, unaware that he had been standing beside them and listening to their conversation. "He didn't even put in any rules other than 'don't touch it'. What is he thinking? You know well and good that Sappharon is going to have Adam's ear."

"Well, yes." Zamyael purred. "But, then, apes that can talk have no desire to displease their maker."

She chuckled to herself. She was pleased with her plan to wedge greater distance between her 'betters' on so many levels.

"He gave them a voice, by all of the Gods that are or ever were! So they must be just *ever* so grateful of this fact that they shall exhibit such immortal restraint over their senses so that even Sappharon's forked and silver tongue couldn't entice them to break the rules."

-25-

For only the second time in all of my life, I felt the jarring slam against my soul of being propelled to stand directly behind Noliminan. There was no one else in the hallway from which my perspective could have been pulled.

Only Noliminan.

He was standing directly outside of Lucias' door, waiting to be granted entry. He knocked two times before, irritably, letting himself in.

It was very quiet, but there were signs all over the main room that Lucias had been biding his time here after Michael's party. Two empty glasses sat on the hearth of the fire and coals still burned red in the pit.

Noliminan glared at them. He understood at once that the second glass belonged to Lord Loki. He was very clearly displeased with the level of pleasure Lucias found whilst biding his time with the youngling.

After glaring at the glasses, his gaze rose until it fell upon the coat Lucias had been wearing to the party that night. It had been flung over the back of his favorite chair, most likely discarded the moment Lucias returned home.

He smiled and then walked toward it to raise it upward, breathing in Lucias' scent.

I started as I watched Noliminan react to Lucias' essence. He very clearly found Lucias' scent pleasing.

He returned the coat to its previous position over the chair, ran his finger over the fabric of it almost tenderly, and wandered, slowly, down the hall toward Lucias' bedchamber. He took stock of each painting and every bric-a-brac on every shelf, smiling to see many of the baubles he had given Lucias throughout their years displayed rather than hidden away or lost in some closet.

When he reached Lucias' bedchamber, he raised his hand to knock. He hesitated, however, and, instead, reached for the door handle.

Peering within the door, I was able to see Lucias laying on his bed, his limbs splayed and his face peaceful in his sleep.

Noliminan allowed himself the luxury of watching him for a few shifts of Countenance's shadow before, with seeming reluctance, stepping toward his bed and lowering himself upon it.

He reached his hand out and very gently ran his finger along Lucias' dark and troubled brow. When he spoke, it was in quiet tones lest he raise Lucias' ire. "Luci."

Lucias' eyes rolled under his lids, but other than that he didn't respond. Noliminan chuckled at the childishness of it and tried again, this time a little louder. "Luci."

"Go away." Lucias muttered and curled away from Noliminan, pulling his silk sheet with him. He was now curled in a ball on his left side with the sheet clutched in his strong hand.

I don't believe I have ever seen my father looking so vulnerable. Seeing him so now touched me in the most fundamental of all ways.

Noliminan smiled once again and then reached for his shoulder. "Lucias. Tukte lolo. It's me. Wake up."

Lucias, still half asleep, grasped Noliminan's hand and rolled onto his back, pulling Noliminan with him so he was covering him. His face, only inches below Noliminan's own, wore a soft, hungry expression. His eyes, as yet, hadn't opened. "I've waited a millennium for you to return to me."

These words surprised me to the point that the parts of me which were performing tasks requiring them to be corporeal let out a startled gasp. This caused each of them to be forced to explain to whomever they were speaking with at the time some excuse that mislead them as to why I would react in such a manner.

He hadn't said he had waited a millennium for Noliminan to come to him. Rather, he had waited for Noliminan to *return* to him.

I understood almost immediately that this wasn't the first time Noliminan had visited Lucias' bed.

Noliminan wore an embarrassed smile. "Tonight I have come only to talk."

"Mmm." Lucias tittered as he rolled his eyes open. When they came into focus they danced over Noliminan's face. They were soft with his obvious love for the King of Lords. "Have we not done enough talking for one day?"

Noliminan smiled. "I have something new to talk about."

Lucias reached upward, lacing his hand behind Noliminan's neck. Very slowly, he pulled himself upward and took Noliminan's lips in his own. Noliminan closed his eyes and fell into the kiss for the very briefest of moments before pulling gently away.

Lucias allowed him to do so.

I marked very clearly the pain of an old wound burning bright in my father's eyes. It was only there for a moment before Lucias threw his guard up, but I could tell by his reaction that Noliminan had seen it as well.

And that he regretted having caused it.

"Your loss." Lucias muttered as he spun upward, putting his back to him. These were words I had heard him speak to Noliminan before. "What do you want?"

"Why do you not get dressed?" Noliminan suggested. "I'll wait in your sitting room for you."

"No, tukte 'aasifa." Lucias answered in a soft, patient tone. "I haven't been feeling well lately and I intend to go back to sleep when you are done with whatever it is you must say to me."

"Tukte lolo, please?" Noliminan sighed. "If only your small clothes." And then he grinned. "Kostluk prilnth tat Luci?"

"Nanxta miente kostluk." He shook his head. His tone was still gentle. And he, too, was smiling. "And I don't wear small clothes. So unless you have a need for me to leave my bed for something other than talking, then no."

Though I have no idea what the words they exchanged meant, I hold a belief in my heart that Noliminan knew Lucias had no intention to attack.

I also suspect that Noliminan knew what I did, which was that he had no hope of forcing Lucias to do anything he did not want to do without another argument.

Noliminan was very clearly tired of arguing with Lucias.

"Very well." Noliminan reached forward and grasped a lock of Lucias' shoulder length, dark brown hair. He let the silk of it dance within his fingers for a moment before letting it go. "One of the angels has gone missing from my court."

Lucias, finally, looked over his shoulder and met Noliminan's gaze. "I'm sorry to hear about that but how might I help?"

"He was last seen at your door with Tristan." Noliminan explained. "I must know if you talked with him and, maybe, know where he was going."

"No." He shook his head. "I didn't talk with him."

I did not miss that Lucias had answered only one half of his question.

"But you do know where he was going?" Lucias looked quickly away. "Please, Lucias. Whatever this is about, I shall never be angry with you for providing any one of our children your succor should they have asked for it."

"If we are talking about the same child, then yes. He did request from Loki that I grant him my succor." Lucias' tone was tight. "And when he did so, I obliged."

"What did he want?" Noliminan was clearly trying not to be accusatory.

"Sanctuary." Lucias muttered. He was looking down now, to his hands.

"From whom?"

Lucias let out a long, tired sigh through his teeth. His breath made that odd whistling sound he never intends to make but which I have heard many, many times before.

Noliminan seemed to finally understand. I knew this by the manner in which he asked the next question. "Tukte lolo, what did Regan do to him?"

"Black market trade." Lucias' voice was still taut.

"Please." Noliminan sighed. "I need you to be open with me right now and to be specific."

"His organs are traded on the black market. His liver. His kidneys. Only Azrael knows what not. From what I understand Regan removes them, sells them, lets them grow back and then removes and sells them again."

Noliminan frowned.

"He isn't the only one doing it." Lucias muttered. "It is a very lucrative practice."

"This has been going on for some time." Oddly enough, it was put as a statement. Not a question. I remember my brow furrowing with the tone of the words.

Lucias looked over his shoulder with angry, narrowed eyes. His tone, now, was pure venom. "This is one of those 'untrue' currents you asked me not to sully your senses with."

I was puzzled by Noliminan's strangely curious tone as he asked the next question.

"What are you going to do about it?"

Lucias, obviously not expecting any quarter from Noliminan, turned on the bed so one knee was pointing in Noliminan's direction. He had a very cautious expression on his face. "For now? I intend to let it bide."

Noliminan appeared to ponder over this statement for a moment before asking, "Why?"

"Because as I said: Regan is not the only one practicing such arts." Lucias' tone was unreadable. But his expression was cold. "I do not want to stop just Regan. I want to stop the practice all together."

"Then we shall put it to vote at Council." Noliminan advised him, clearly not intending his suggestion to be a request. "But we have to take care of Regan now."

"No." Lucias shook his head. "We don't." He held his hand out and grasped Noliminan's bicep. "I've already spoken with Lady Martiam about Regan. If he asks for another angel, the Lady is going to stall him."

"She can't stall him forever." Noliminan responded calmly.

"She doesn't have to." Lucias pulled his other leg on the bed and turned the set of his shoulders so that he was facing Noliminan full on. "Once I know who he is trading with I intend to cut him up into a million little pieces and scatter them on each of the various worlds so he cannot reform himself together. I intend to do so to make an example out of him."

"Then let us make an example out of him." Noliminan sighed irritably. "Why wait?"

"Because the others must be punished too." He carped. "Not just frightened."

"Why would you—?" He shook his head. "Never mind. The punishing of the damned is your responsibility. Not mine." He lowered his gaze. "I still believe we must put the matter to vote."

"Nol, if we do so now then we will not win." Lucias responded. His expression was serious in its sorrow. "The trade is far too lucrative for those who make practice of it. The majority rule would go to the house."

Noliminan shook his head. "Then we'll just order them—"

"You cannot." Lucias reached forward and grasped a lock of Noliminan's hair. His eyes danced lovingly over it for a moment before raising his gaze with a tired, knowing smile. "If it is not the majority vote then they will just do it anyway." He let Noliminan's hair fall to his chest. His tone was reasonable and pleading. "They *all* deserve to be damned, met tukte 'aasifa. Not just Regan. And I cannot damn them if I do not know who they are."

"You wish that I should trust your judgment with this one." Noliminan muttered.

"I do." Lucias held his gaze. His dark eyes were dancing over Noliminan's own, waiting for his response. "Because I understand what I am dealing with whereas you do not."

Noliminan sighed. "In the meantime, how do you intend to prevent Regan from stealing a servant from the workhouses or brothels?"

Smiling, Lucias grasped Noliminan's hand. "You must avoid the details."

Noliminan shivered. "I will leave it to you then."

"I thank you for allowing my discretion." He lowered his gaze as he said this.

"But if you need my intervention—"

"I promise you, if it goes that far, I will ask for your aide." He allowed, raising his gaze again.

"I hate to ask what those purchasing the organs do with them." Noliminan whispered.

"Loki is looking into the matter." Lucias replied, too fondly.

Dark jealousy streaked across Noliminan's handsome features at the mention of Lord Loki's name. At the time, I believed it was because he was aware that Lord Loki and Queen Raguel had developed a strong—though completely platonic—friendship.

"What we do know is that some of them perform surgery, replacing their own mortal organs with those of an angel or demon. It is rumored to prolong mortality." He suddenly wore a very ugly, angry smile. "Which has not yet been proven as it is a relatively new trade."

Noliminan sighed heavily. "Are you still happy with my appointment of him to you? Loki, I should mean?"

"I am." Lucias appeared surprised by the question. "I believe we respect one and another."

Noliminan frowned. He must have had the same question in his mind as I did: What does respect have to do with a master and servant relationship?

"He doesn't please you in his general service to you?"

Lucias blushed and looked swiftly away. "He doesn't sate his lust with other males."

"The only one you've ever stopped yourself in that regard to before is me." Noliminan snorted. "God or not. Why not just force him to give you what is rightfully yours?"

"It wouldn't be right to do so in this situation." Lucias gave him an angry glare. "You should know me well enough by now to understand that, where my servants are concerned, I refuse to resort to rape. It is impossible to command respect out of someone you've humiliated."

Noliminan's silently contemplated this. His actions have always shown he disagreed with that sentiment. He thought nothing at all of humiliating we members of the Quorum. In fact he seemed to thrive off of his ability to do so.

Finally, he said, "Why do you not force Loki to shave his beard? It's unnatural."

"It pleases me." Lucias' voice was warm. As was the smile he wore at the mention of Lord Loki's beard. "It is of his people. I shouldn't ever offend him in the asking."

Noliminan, clearly not amused with Lucias' repeated attempts to protect his charges, gave Lucias a tight smile. "Tell him to shave it off. Gods do not wear beards."

"I won't." Lucias returned, stubbornly. "It is of his people. It isn't a bother to me."

"It's a bother to *me*." Noliminan asserted. "He prances about the court with a harem of bitches falling around him like foolish adolescent girls. It has caused more than one complaint to be raised to Raguel's attentions by the other Gods of the Council. So if it goes against your sensibilities, then I shall order him to do it myself."

"Careful." Lucias' tone was tight. His eyes were blazing. "Loki is a sensitive being who might not appreciate the request."

"It isn't going to *be* a request."

"By request I meant order." Lucias warned him with a smile that Noliminan obviously didn't much care for.

"If I tell him to then he has no choice."

"Pick your battles with that one, Nol." Lucias warned again. Though, this time, he turned his gaze away, relinquishing his will. "You may need him in days yet to come. Is it really worth ostracizing Loki over his conquests or his beard?"

"If an example must be made, then yes. It is."

"If you *dare* . . ." Lucias seethed in a whisper. Noliminan, seemingly surprised by this sudden attack, pulled slightly away. "He is *my* property to do with as *I* bide. Not yours."

"Tell him to lose the beard." Noliminan warned, his anger and a fair bit of hostility was clearly evident at this juncture. "By next Council."

"Get out of my bed. *You* aren't welcome *here*."

I have never, in all of my days, seen Noliminan angrier.

He reached forward, grasping Lucias' erection in his hand and using every bit of his sensual magic he could muster. Lucias immediately rolled his eyes backward, unable to hide his surprise, and let out a long, hungry groan.

Oh Gods, I thought, *I finally understand why I have no business watching them when they are alone together.*

I was horrified.

I wanted nothing more than to turn my attention elsewhere.

As with everything else I was seeing at that moment in time, however, I had no control over what my magic forced me to witness.

"Never in life." Noliminan, clearly humiliated by Lucias' orders toward him, bent forward and pressed his lips against his ear. "Never in life shall you ban me from your bed." He grasped

Lucias tighter, pulling on him to make his point. "Do you understand me, Lucias?"

"Yes." Lucias groaned. "Please . . . I understand."

"Good." He let Lucias go, ignoring his plea and leaving him hungry. "See to the issue of Loki's Gods be damned beard by next Council." He growled as he stood. "*That* is an order."

As violently as I had been pulled into the conversation, I was brutally pushed away.

Trying to collect my thoughts, I shivered.

I suddenly had the distinct impression that, for one reason or another, this was one conversation that Noliminan had wanted me to bear witness too.

I have no doubt that I will be pondering his motivation for many years to come.

-26-

Loki was reading, not sleeping. He threw the book he had no business holding in his possession aside swiftly and covered it with his blanket lest Lord Regent Lucias see he had stolen a Tome. As he did so, his gaze flew to the open door as Lord Lucias stormed within, towering above him.

"That mouk!'" The Lord Regent seethed through his teeth. "That crude, ugly, carvetek mouk!'"

Loki stared at him for a moment, not knowing how to respond. When his mind reasoned that only one person ever made Lord Lucias this angry, he braved an answer. "The King of Lords?"

"I am to order you to shave off your beard!" He stormed. "By next Council!"

Loki, frowning, raised his hands to his chin and stroked his goatee. He didn't want Lord Lucias to face retribution, but his goatee meant all of the worlds to him. He had earned it only after passing the trials of manhood amongst the centaurs, who had raised him as if they had foaled him into their herd. "My Lord . . . Must I shave it?"

"Not a whisker of it." Lord Lucias assured him. His eyes darted away from Loki. His anger was palpable. "He gave me a direct order." His brown eyes were blazing as they returned to meet Loki's gaze. "Me!" He threw his fist to his chest in what Loki assumed was righteous indignation. "The ruler of all Thirty of these Hells!"

"But, my Lord." Loki frowned. "What good can come of you arguing with him over my goatee? Yes. It is important to me, but—"

"You believe I would make you deny your own rites of passage?" Lord Lucias snapped at him. "Do you think so little of me as that?"

Actually, Loki was surprised that Lord Lucias had not supplicated to such a simple demand. There were more important issues than his facial hair to contend with. As much as Loki loved his goatee, he would have supplicated had he been in Lord Lucias' position.

"You are walking in with me proudly to the next Council sporting that beard."

"Goatee.'" Loki swallowed the fear he suddenly had the sense to feel.

"And to all of the Hells with him for the way he ordered me."

Loki didn't know the way he had been ordered. But the pain in his voice was palpable. He had been humiliated. All because of Loki's pride. "I will shave it if you ask—"

"I would *not* ask!" Lord Lucias seethed. "Never placate that carvetek mouk against the truths of your soul. Don't you ever let him make you someone you are not." He shook his head. "And who cares anyway? It's a beard! Not the ends of all of the worlds."

To this Loki had a response.

"He doesn't care about my goatee." He muttered, "He's merely trying to prove he's in charge of you."

Lord Lucias looked away suddenly. His cheeks were flushed with his obvious embarrassment.

"You bet he cares about your beard." He answered. "He knows you are coveted for it."

Loki looked away. How was he supposed to respond to that?

"Forgive me, Loki." Lord Lucias grumbled. "I meant not to embarrass you."

Loki cleared his throat. "Truly, my Lord. If it creates such problems—I *will* shave it."

"No." Lord Lucias responded in a tight voice. "You shall not."

Loki swallowed. "I wish I were not the contention between the pair of you."

"Oh no." Lord Lucias snorted. "As you say, this is not about your goatee."

Loki lowered his head. He knew this wasn't the time to be amused by Lord Lucias' sudden acknowledgment of the fact that a goatee was not a beard. But the acknowledgment made him smile all the same.

"I do not care what he says to the contrary."

"I'm tired."

Loki, who was not at all tired, wanted out of this conversation. He would not fare well in any war between the King of Lords and Lord Lucias. The last thing in all of the worlds and moons he wanted was to become one of the King of Lords' targets.

"Of course you are." Lord Lucias sighed, granting him an understanding smile. "Forgive me."

Loki shook his head and met his Master's gaze with a small smile. Lord Lucias smiled at him in return and took his leave.

-27-

Heavy pounding on the door followed immediately by Zamyael's surprised cry startled Raziel from the thoughts she had been having in regard to plans she had made for the following day. It was far too late for visitors and the insistent raps on the door were irritating. Zamyael stood to answer but Raziel stayed him. "I'll take care of this."

She walked through the sitting room to the door, barely unhinging it before it came flying toward her as Noliminan stormed in with all the rage of soul he could possibly muster. "How do you live with that carvetek mouk?"

Frowning, Raziel turned to follow him with her gaze. She couldn't remember the last time Noliminan had graced her home with his presence. "I'm afraid he is the Queen of Ladies' problem."

"I meant Lucias." Noliminan spat before adding, "And I'm in no mood for your cattiness."

Raziel turned to Zamyael, frowning. "Will you leave us?"

"Yes, my Lady." Zamyael rose, gave them one of his disgusting curtsies, and made his way back to his room.

"What has he done to so affront you this time?" Raziel asked when Zamyael—and the constant irritation that his womanly ways wrought—was gone.

She was truly curious but she used the most bored of tones she could find knowing, of course, it would infuriate Noliminan to no end that she had no interest in his temper tantrum.

"He ordered me from his bed!" Noliminan raged.

Raziel, surprised and hurt at the very thought of Noliminan in Lucias' bed, did not respond. The words she had would only serve to make matters worse.

"Me!" He slammed his chest with his fist. "And over something so trivial! So stupid!"

"And what would that be?" The rage building within Raziel poisoned each word. Yet, somehow, she managed to hold her affronted tone.

It was in moments such as these, when she understood Noliminan held Lucias in higher regard than he did her, that she loathed them both.

"All that I asked of him was to make Loki shave that damned beard of his." The indignation spread like wildfire over his masculine features. Raziel marked this with cold, narrowed eyes. "I even told him that I would make the order myself so as not to offend the child at Lucias' hand."

"You should know by now to never demand anything of Lucias whilst sharing his pillow." Raziel seethed with narrowed eyes.

Noliminan started at this, his eyes glowing with embarrassment and discontentment. It seemed to be in that moment that he realized that Raziel was still wearing her woman's form. The dark fury in his eyes was suddenly mixed with unguarded hunger.

"You know damn well that his head did not cross my pillow tonight." He spat, forcing himself to ignore both his hunger and his surprise. "I was there on business and that's where I happened to have found him."

Raziel felt her rage flood away. Having never witnessed even the most remote overtures of romance between the pair of them she had no choice but to believe him. As such, she deflected Noliminan's attention from her ill begot statement. "Why is it so important to you that Loki shaves his goatee?"

"It was just a simple request." Noliminan seethed. "I did not know that Lucias should be as affronted as to think that I had asked Loki if he wouldn't mind cutting off his most offending parts!"

"No request you make of Lucias is simple these days." Raziel warned him, ignoring the underlying threat to Loki's masculinity. The last time Noliminan had been enraged enough to make such a threat he had made good on it. "Even if your intent is. Take care in how you treat him right now. Lucias is apt to bite."

"He had best follow my orders." Noliminan had not heard a word of Raziel's warning. She sighed and rolled her eyes. She didn't want to be caught in the middle of this fight. "That youngling had better have a clean face come Council."

"Do not raise barter upon it." Raziel warned him. "And do not take your anger out on young Loki when the time comes. Leave Loki out of it."

"You can damn well bet that I shall take it out on Loki." Noliminan stormed. "Who is he to defy me?"

"He is not your plaything. You would do well to remember that." Raziel cautioned. "You made a promise to both Lucias and I that you would never again interfere with us where our servants came to concern. You had better stick to that promise or you'll have more than just Lucias to contend with."

"You're *threatening* me?"

Raziel stepped forward with eyes narrow and cold rage in her heart.

Loki was young. He was innocent. He didn't need to be trapped between the egos of the two most powerful Gods in creation.

"By threatening Loki you threaten Zamyael and me. I know you do not want both of us on your other side. So you'd best leave Loki alone."

"Lucias shall not get away with this constant defiance of me for much longer." Noliminan muttered. Raziel knew she had won her point. "Who does he think he is?"

"Your Shitva." Raziel replied gently.

Shitva was the ancient word for soul mate. Raziel's meaning was not intended to be romantic in nature, as the term was commonly mistranslated to mean. Lucias had literally been born of a good portion of Noliminan's soul. She and Zamyael had pondered on more than one occasion just how much of himself Noliminan had given up in creating Lucias.

Noliminan stopped his ranting in his tracks. He snapped his head in Raziel's direction and appraised her with cool, narrowed eyes. "He cannot be so bold as to think he is my equal."

"Do not put me in this position, Noliminan." Raziel glared at him in response and raised her hands, palms toward him. "Your fight with Lucias is not mine." She swiftly looked away and lowered her hands. "You have made it all too clear that you have no care of me so do not beg me your counsel against him. He has proven to me time and again that he needs me."

"It is *you* who turned *me* away." Noliminan said coldly.

"Never in life." Raziel snapped at him, taking on her male essence. Now was the time to make her point. "You are always welcome in my bed."

"You lie!" Noliminan stormed, his eyes darkening as her appearance changed. "The last time—"

"I said *my* bed." Raziel returned with her eyes narrowed. "She is no longer part of me where you are concerned and nor shall she ever be again."

"You're acting foolish." Noliminan rolled his eyes and flung himself onto one of Raziel's chairs. Now, it would seem, was not one of the times that he would argue with her that he could force her to remain female if it was his desire. He had certainly done so before when her refusal to give him what he wanted willingly had angered him. "I know that you give over to Lucias in your natural form."

"Am I being foolish where you are concerned? By making you force me to be female when you order me to your bed as such?" Raziel asked, still standing. "Then why do we not turn over our tables?" Noliminan looked up at her with disgust. "Go on. Let me see her. And take her if that's what I should like."

"Never in life." Noliminan grunted, waving his hand at Raziel.

"But, Noliminan," Raziel purred at him. "You are acting so *foolish*."

Raziel could have sworn that she saw a small smile dance on the corners of Noliminan's lips. His expression, she marked, had softened. "I miss you, you cat."

"I miss you too." Raziel answered honestly.

"Are you free tomorrow evening? In this form?" Raziel met his gaze, gave a false frown and shrugged. Noliminan smiled brilliantly at her in response. "I am only asking you to the evening meal."

"I suppose I can clear up sixty shifts or so." Raziel responded, trying to keep the eagerness in her heart at bay. "But only if you will promise not to discuss politics." Noliminan nodded. "And only if you can refrain from rising up your wife's name."

Noliminan smiled softly. "Hasn't that last ever been your rule?"

"Where will you find yourself, met paken," Raziel braved the question, "should you fall in love with me and I refuse to return to my female form."

"I already am." Noliminan's voice was heavy with regret. "You know I am. You were once bound to me with a marriage contract. And you gave me my first true born child. Which, at the end of it, is why I am patient with your ill-founded games."

"This answer will do for now." Raziel allowed. She refrained from mentioning that this true born child had been forced to become his current wife. Or that he was correct in his statement that she was able to defy him by being male rather than female in his presence only because he allowed it.

Noliminan, clearly thinking these thoughts as well, smiled in response. "Thank you for allowing me my outrage."

"You are welcome to my counsel any time." Raziel returned. "I just hope, where Lucias' sensibilities are concerned, you will take it."

"As you said, he is the father of your children." Noliminan muttered jealously. Raziel refused to reflect on the fact that he had no right to be jealous. He had left Raziel's bed eagerly enough to seek out Zamyael. "You must know him better than any of us."

"I do." Raziel agreed. "This is why I bid that you take care when his jaws are snapping." She felt suddenly conflicted by her desire to usurp Lucias and her affection for him. "When the day does come that he takes his stand against you, I fear you both shall find the true depths of your regard for one another in your heart."

Noliminan frowned at this.

"By then, met paken, it will be too late for both of you to reflect upon anything but your regret."

-28-

Zamyael followed Loki out of his bedchamber and toward Lucias' sitting room, where Raziel and Lucias were waiting for him. Once there, Zamyael stayed in the shadows of the hallway, smiling as Loki walked to the sofa and lowered himself beside Lucias without a thought or a care. Zamyael was pleased that Loki wasn't intimidated by Lucias, like the last one had been. She imagined this one might last; that it might be worth her time to get to know him.

"Loki." Raziel smiled cattily at Loki.

142

This was a game to her. She didn't care a wit for Loki's goatee. She was merely trying to find a way to manipulate the situation while still appearing to remain loyal to Lucias.

Loki smiled coolly in return. It was almost as if he conned her deception. This only served to raise his esteem in Zamyael's mind all the higher.

Raziel nodded and turned so she was facing both of them.

"I wanted to speak with you both because last night Noliminan paid me a visit."

Zamyael snorted. She wasn't quiet about it in any way and both Lucias and Loki raised their gaze to look at her. She quickly turned her back on them both. Her feelings regarding the fact that Noliminan and Raziel were courting again were none of their business.

"I know you, Luke." Raziel's tone was falsely soft now. Zamyael looked over her shoulder, watching in silence. She was waiting to see what game was afoot. "I know you intend to defy him."

"He had no right to order me anything where Loki is concerned and you know *that*." Lucias snapped.

"I reminded him of this as well." Raziel reached forward and grasped Lucias' hand. It seemed to calm him well enough. She raised it to her lips and kissed the back of it. "He's prideful, Lucias. Can you not give him an out? Must you defy him openly and in front of all of the Gods?"

"He came to my bed and demanded that I force my servant to change his appearance." Lucias growled.

"I understand." Raziel conceded. "He was wrong for doing so."

Raziel stroked Lucias' cheek with her free hand. Zamyael rolled her eyes, understanding Raziel's motives. She had lived with the Sovereign Lady long enough to know that should the opportunity ever present itself that Raziel could replace Lucias, she would not only take it but she would also facilitate it. This might or might not be her intent during this conversation, but Zamyael understood Raziel's desire to usurp Lucias lived vibrantly in the back of the Lady's mind.

"Please. With everything else you've been able to bide, do not let the turn of your patience be over something as foolish as Loki's goatee." She gave Loki a tired, and falsely understanding, smile. "I concede that such is not foolish to you, child, but in the larger turn of things, it *is* rather trivial."

"I agree with you, my Sovereign Lady." Loki's voice was even. It was, from his tone, difficult for Zamayel to interpret his true meaning.

"It is not trivial." Lucias sighed. "After Noliminan issued the order, I demanded that he leave me. In response he stoked my passion."

This, Zamayel was interested in. By the odd expression on Raziel's face so was she. Loki just looked surprised.

"He purposely left me hungry with words to suggest that I am nothing more than his plaything. It was a lesson, Raziel. Its intent was all too clear."

"He fancies himself better than you." Raziel sighed. "He will use what wiles he has within him to hold onto his self-deception. It has never been a secret that you covet him."

"It was very pointedly meant to put me in my place!"

"Yes." Raziel agreed. "It was. And it was cruel."

She smiled softly. Zamayel shivered because the smile was deceptive. She loved Lucias and she wanted to warn him. But she served Raziel. She could never betray her.

"Please. You are better than this. Give him an out."

"If it is such a big deal, I'll shave the damn thing off." Loki's voice was laced with anger.

"No you will not." Lucias insisted. "If we give him an out, it isn't going to be concession."

"There has to be a way that you can both win." Raziel's voice was a manipulative purr. Lucias, however, buckled under it as he ever did.

Zamayel snorted again, this time looking away and so not knowing if anyone had heard her.

"We'll think on it." Lucias promised. "Loki and I. We'll talk about it and if we can come up with an out, then we shall give it to him."

-29-

Raphael was surprised when he opened the door to find Lucias and Apprentice Lord Loki standing on the other side. "Raphael, is he in?"

"Ta, my Lord." Raphael stepped back to let them in, beaming at them both. "And he's in a fair enough mood today." He leaned forward to give them a conspirator's whisper. "I believe he is readying himself for a date, but with whom I know not."

This made Lucias smile. "The old boy always has been happiest when he's in pursuit of a bit of tail."

"Just so." Raphael agreed with a hearty laugh. "Come."

"Do you want me to stay out here?" Lord Loki asked, very quietly.

"No." Lucias answered him, rather brusquely. "Given this is about you, you have the right to know what is said."

"Thank you, my Lord." To Raphael his tone was a mixture of both fear and relief.

"He really isn't as bad as all that." Lucias assured Lord Loki in a very gentle tone. "Is he Raphie?"

"Not at all, Lord Loki." Raphael smiled at Lord Loki, hoping it was a reassuring smile, "Except where *this* one is concerned."

Lucias chuckled. "There's a bit of truth."

"Come." Raphael repeated and began leading them toward King Noliminan's bedchamber.

When Lucias realized where they were going he let out a soft, deep chuckle under his breath. "His time to turn me out, is it?"

Raphael smiled. King Noliminan had shared part of the story with him the night before when he had returned from speaking with Lucias. Even though he had not sought Lucias out for pleasure, he had been extremely affronted that he had dared ask him to leave his bed. "Forgive me, Pipa. I know not what you speak of."

Lucias snorted his disbelief. "Of course not, Raph."

Raphael smiled softly at him over his shoulder. He wished the war between his father and his beloved Master would abate because he loved and respected them both in equal measure. "The only thing he shared with me is his great affection for you and his sadness that you must always—just lately—quarrel."

"I regard him in equal measure, I assure you." Lucias nodded at Raphael. His expression did grow softer, however, and Raphael was glad to see it.

He was tired of listening to them argue. Lately, it seemed, if a rooster crowed at dusk rather than at dawn one or the other was accused as being the cause of it.

"Hold while I announce you?"

"Of course." Lucias said as he leaned casually against the wall with one boot and his back to it and his arms crossed over his chest. "Take your time."

Raphael smiled at him, gave Lord Loki another smile, for good measure, and then stepped quietly into his Master's bedchamber. King Noliminan, who sat at his vanity studying his jaw line, looked up in surprise.

"You have guests, your Grace." Raphael bowed to him, smiling under his soft regard. "Lord Regent Lucias and Apprentice Lord Loki."

King Noliminan chuckled as he sat the brush aside. "Come to apologize, have they?"

Raphael, who hadn't been told why they were here, had an idea that an apology was nowhere in it. "They do wish to palaver."

"How do they seem, Raphael?" He asked with a curious smile. Curious, Raphael noted, and serious. "Honest, now."

"Of good cheer." Raphael replied. "Apprentice Lord Loki seems frightened. Not that he said so. His demeanor is simply quiet today."

"Just when I could do with a good joke." King Noliminan smiled softly. Finally he nodded. "Show them in." Raphael turned to go. "Raph?" Raphael stopped, turning to meet his gaze. "Join us. Your presence tempers me."

Raphael, elated by this admission from his Master, turned and went about his task. He slid out, his smile growing as he was met with Lord Loki's curious regard. "Come."

Lucias kicked himself away from the wall and began walking toward him. It was a happy, graceful movement and it made Raphael smile as he turned away and opened the door for them.

Nothing about his father or his King had been happy for as long as he could remember.

"Nol, a tukte 'aasifa." Lucias offered King Noliminan a half-hearted inclination of the head as his eyes danced over his face to see if there were to be some sort of trickery or sudden fit of anger.

"Lolo a tukte, Lucias." King Noliminan bowed his head in response then turned his regard to Lord Loki, who wore a strange expression upon his brow. Raphael, who didn't understand some of the words the pair spoke to one another when they reverted to the old language merely marked Lucias' lips thinning in his attempt to repress a smile. "Loki."

"Your Grace." Lord Loki mimicked Lucias' half-hearted attempt at fealty. Raphael forced himself to repress his smile that Lord Loki would brave his veiled contempt.

"What pleasantries bring you to my bedchamber, tukte lolo?"

"If only such pleasantries were mine to claim, tukte 'aasifa." Lucias bowed to him again, now wearing a sloppy, playful grin. "As I remember, you were less than receptive to my requests when you last visited mine own."

King Noliminan chuckled. "Snet, snet, tukte lolo."

"You look well today." Lucias' voice drawled. Raphael watched him, waiting for whatever trap had been set to spring closed. He sniffed the air slightly. "A new scent? Very nice." King Noliminan's eyes widened and then fell to their normal form. "Raziel will be pleased."

King Noliminan's eyes darted first to Lord Loki, who appeared disinterested, and then to Raphael, who was happily stunned. "A rare occurrence where that one is concerned."

Lucias chuckled at him. King Noliminan had not been baited and it obviously pleased Raphael's father.

"Loki and I have a proposition for you." He looked over his shoulder to Lord Loki and winked. Lord Loki gave him a small, hesitant smile in return and then Lucias returned his attention to King Noliminan. "We propose that you allow us to address the Council on the matter of Loki's beard."

"What are you up to, Luci?"

"Listen." Lucias held up his hand. "Please. I beg."

King Noliminan's eyes narrowed slightly. "Very well."

"We propose that the ever so important matter be wrapped into my barter with you in regard to Adam and his temptation."

"You cannot re-open the barter now!" King Noliminan began laughing. "You've already fairly lost!"

"Then you shan't care if we add Loki's offensive and atrocious beard as one of my concessions." Lucias smiled wickedly in return. He pointed to Lord Loki. "Loki has agreed that if I lose this barter he will shave the beard without any ado. And, as you know, given there are no greater Gods than you and I, the only way to reopen the magic is by a vote."

King Noliminan's playful gaze turned from Lucias to Lord Loki. That worthy just stood there wearing his tight, silent smile. He clearly didn't trust the vote of the Council any better than Raphael did. "To shave it off and keep it off."

"And keep it off." Lucias answered for Lord Loki. "If, of course, I lose."

The trap Raphael had been waiting for had been sprung. Raphael felt himself smiling at his father's clever guile. He had managed to defy a direct order yet keep Lord Loki's beard—and King Noliminan's great ego—intact while doing so.

"Hah!" King Noliminan cried. "If the Council agrees to re-open our barter to add this concession, then I agree."

"My goatee thanks you, your Grace." Lord Loki said in a very playful tone as he bowed.

His expression isn't very playful.

King Noliminan's attention remained fixed on Lucias. "No added concessions aside the matter of Loki's beard, Lucias. I want none of your general trickery!"

"Never think it, Nol." Lucias replied in a voice that was laced with both false indignation and good humor.

King Noliminan nodded at him, his expression contemplative for a moment. When he spoke, his tone was soft. "It's a fair solution, Lucias. I'm glad you raised it."

"Well." Lucias replied with the strangest of smiles. "We can't let a little thing like Loki's goatee come between us. Can we?"

-30-

Lasterian sat in the room Lord Evanbourough had made for him to sleep in on the occasions when he and Lord Tristan stayed the night in Lord Evanbourough's apartment. He hadn't seen the demoness, Sarista, since he had angered Zamyael with his ill begot kiss and he missed her.

He wondered if he could sneak away and ask Zamyael when he could arrange for them to see one and another again, but he had been warned by both Lords Tristan and Evanbourough that he was never to go wandering in the halls of the Hells without one or the other of them escorting him.

Desperate, he had asked Lord Tristan if he ever wandered the halls of the Hells if he might join him. He had fashioned this question with the curiosity he thought Lord Tristan might understand. Lord Tristan was, after all, a God of the Heavens who spent the majority of his time with a God of the Hells. Given that, was it so peculiar that Lasterian, an angel who served this same God, would be curious about both Realms his Lord chose to abide within?

Lord Evanbourough had been less than receptive to Lasterian's curiosity to explore the Realms of the Hells, but Lord Tristan argued that Lasterian must understand both Realms given that Tristan was Evanbourough's lover and, therefore, spent his time in both worlds.

Lasterian didn't care. His goal, at the moment, was to find the demon Zamyael to determine how he would find Saristia. Thus, he had been hinting to Lord Tristan that he should like to visit with Zamyael, his only friend amongst the demons, so that he might freely learn.

He heard a knock on the door. He meant to answer but Lord Evanbourough stepped through, frowning at him. He reflected upon the fact that had he barged into Lord Evanbourough's room he would have been punished, but rather than raise any issues he had no right to raise, he smiled. "Lord Evanbourough?"

"I am leaving for the Sovereign Lady's now." Lord Evanbourough's black eyes danced over him. He knew the God didn't care much for him. He understood it. The bond between a God and his or her angel was unbreakable. Lord Evanbourough had no demon of his own and had not hidden the fact that Lord Tristan's bond with Lasterian displeased him.

Now, however, was not the time for Lasterian to care. He had the opportunity to see Zamyael. He knew if he could just speak with Zamyael for a moment then he could be convinced in helping him find Saristia.

Smiling, he bowed to Lord Evanbourough.

"I am in your service, my Lord."

Evanbourough gave him a strange, cold look in response.

"Yes." He said. "Let's hope you remember that."

-31-

When Zamyael awoke to find a very female version of Raziel with Noliminan, unabashedly copulating in the sitting room, her anger finally overcame her.

She had been able to hold her fury at bay when she learned that Raziel had forgiven Noliminan enough to begin courting him again. That he had spent the night in Zamyael's home—that Raziel had allowed him to do so understanding Zamyael's rancor toward him—was an unforgivable betrayal.

Never mind that the pair hadn't even the courtesy to lock themselves away behind Raziel's bedchamber door.

Had Raziel forgiven what Noliminan did to Zamyael? Was not her disgusting demon—and *male*—body enough of a reminder to Raziel of how cruel Noliminan could be?

Unlike her peers and betters, Zamyael had become unforgiving to the point where any love or respect she might have once felt for Noliminan had forever been destroyed.

She understood the power Noliminan could wield better than any other creature under the sun. Even stupid Zadkiel, who was always whining about the fact that he now had a gimp leg, had not been destroyed on such a fundamental level as she had been.

Yes, she feared him.

Though, never again in life would she revere or adulate him.

That Raziel was flaunting her lately come by reconciliation with Noliminan was an insult of the greatest proportions. And Zamyael had every intention of making her pay.

Of making them both pay.

She raised her gaze and glared at the source of her contention, sitting behind her desk wearing a stupid, sloppy grin as she worked on the Tome she had been asked to write for the sake of prosperity. Zamyael wondered, angrily, if Raziel were journaling the night's acrobatics.

Perhaps Raziel would visit this particular Tome and gush over the wonder of her devotion, feeling oh so Gods be damned pleased over the fact that she had stolen Noliminan's heart from Raguel.

And giving Noliminan just one more reason to give her Lucias' throne should he abdicate.

When the knock on the door came, Raziel raised her gaze to finally look at Zamyael. Her expression faltered slightly as her eyes met Zam's. She merely continued to glare at Raziel with her nostrils flaring and every piece of her heart being ripped into a thousand tiny pieces by the dumbfounded concern Raziel *finally* had the good sense to manage.

She knew who her Mistress was and she knew her ultimate goals.

Even if Raziel had, yet, to realize them, herself.

"Zamyael . . ." Raziel's voice was as gentle as the breeze. This only served to anger her more. "Answer the door."

Zamyael sneered at Raziel as she rose to her feet. Her journey to the door was not so much a walk as an angry storm which began to blow around them both.

She stepped out of the library, pulling the door furiously behind her. The crash of it against the door frame echoed around their living quarters much as thunder rang when Zeus was throwing his electric arrows toward the various worlds during one of his childish temper tantrums.

When she reached the door she pulled it open and glowered at Lord Evanbourough and the pathetic little angel who had braved to kiss her without her permission. The strangeness of the angel standing at the side of a Hells bound God was not lost on her, however. Even in her rage. "What?"

"I have an appointment with the Sovereign Lady." Evanbourough advised her with a raised brow.

"She's in the library."

Evanbourough gave her a curious frown. She immediately regretted the flare of her temper toward him. He had always been kind to her.

He turned toward Lasterian and gave him an impatient smile. "Do mind Zamyael."

"Yes, my Lord."

When Evanbourough returned his attention to Zamyael, he did so with quiet concern. "My Lady."

"My Lord." She replied, softening her tone and granting him a curtsey. She no longer deserved the courtesy of his granting her title.

He nodded at her and left them, stopping at the library to grant her another concerned smile before slipping through the door for his appointment with Raziel.

When they were alone, Zamyael turned her attention to Lasterian. He was watching her with unguarded fear. She found herself frowning at that. "What, exactly, are you doing here?"

"Lord Evanbourough told me I might come." He replied, lowering his gaze.

"I told you I never wanted to see your stupid little face again." She snapped at him. "You should have told him no. You aren't *his* pretty after all."

"I wanted to apologize to you." He lifted his gaze and she saw that the apology was truly written in his eyes. Still frowning, she sighed and turned away from him. "For my inappropriate kiss."

"It isn't accepted." She muttered. Though it most definitely was. She now coveted that kiss in the light of Raziel's rejection of her. And she wanted more. "You shouldn't have come."

"Please, Zamyael." He stepped forward and set his hand upon her bicep. "I didn't mean to offend you. I was merely grateful for your help." Then hesitantly. "Have you seen Saristia?"

She rounded on him then.

Men and their pleasures! Did none of them think of anything but dipping their pathetic little wicks?

"How dare you ask me about your ridiculous little plaything on the heels of an apology?!"

"Zamyael, I'm—"

"Have you no idea who I am?" She seethed. "Why is *she* more important to you than *me*? After such a kiss as you gave me?"

"Zamyael . . ." He swallowed. He was obviously terrified of her, but she didn't care. "Because you're male."

Her fury at those words manifested itself in a guttural roar. She grabbed Lasterian by his infuriatingly white wing and flung him down the hallway toward her bedchamber.

When she was finished forcing him to pleasure her, forcing him to pay for the cruel acts that every man she had ever cared for had inflicted upon her, she felt not even the slightest tinge of regret.

Not then, anyway.

-32-

(I stop my telling for a moment, my eyes darting first to Raziel and then to Zamyael. Raziel wears a contemplative expression; Zamyael's expression is a study in pain.

(After a moment, Raziel raises her gaze to meet my own. "And?"

("I required a moment to catch my breath." I lie as my gaze darts to Zamyael. Raziel follows my gaze, reaches for the back of Zamyael's head and irritably begins to toy with her braids.

("I am not angry with you over something that happened so long ago." She snaps at her. "You are faithful to me now."

(*Faithful to me now?*

(I ponder these words as I raise a glass to my lips to hide my disappointed frown. In my mind, if either of them were to forgive the other it should be Zamyael forgiving Raziel for the manner in which she has always mistreated her.

(As ever, I keep my opinion to myself.

(My task is to watch and listen and delve so, when the time comes for judgment, the appropriate actions are taken. My witness to Zamyael's thoughts gives me an understanding as to her behavior. As such, I find no contempt regarding her actions against Lasterian.

(I also believe that Zamyael has already paid tenfold for any sins she might or might not have committed through the events that she has been subjected to during the natural course of her life.

(Should the day for judgment against Zamyael come, I will have no part in it.

(As for Zamyael, she wisely holds her tongue.

(I know it is a hard thing for her to do, however, and not just by the buzzing nest of thoughts scrambling through her mind. Her jaw has visibly clenched and her eyes have dropped. Looking upon her, one would think she had suddenly found renewed interest in the curve of Raziel's bare foot.

(Raziel, herself, takes Zamyael's downcast gaze as nothing more than supplication.

("I am grateful, my Lady Regent. I know I have betrayed you."

("Mayhap this bit of it can stay out of my Tome." Lady Raziel mutters.

154

("It would be wise if Noliminan was less than aware of the turn of Zamyael's thoughts." I agree, though hesitantly. Raziel brokers no input when it comes to what does or does not get written down for the sake of prosperity. Her mind is abuzz with her irritation that I should insert my opinion.

(Yet, Raziel is far from blind to Noliminan and his sometimes cruel ways. She knows if he were to ken how deeply Zamyael's discontentment toward him runs that naught but ill could come of it for the beautiful demon.

("Yes." She finally nods her agreement. Then, very hesitantly she raises her gaze to meet my own. "Please." She says in gentler tones. "Proceed.")

-33-

Evanbourough stepped through the door which separated the library and Lady Raziel's sitting room and stopped short. The room had an unnaturally cold vibe to it that enveloped him like a tattered old coat.

His eyes found Zamyael first. She sat in the Sovereign Lady's favorite chair wearing an expression of cold satisfaction. Her eyes were turned to the doorway; her raw smile was thin and contemplating.

Evanbourough followed Zamyael's gaze and shivered as his eyes fell upon Lasterian. The angel's haunted, navy blue eyes— so alike to those of his father—were as round as saucers. His mouth was slack; his skin was sallow. Behind him, one of his beautiful white wings hung disturbingly crooked. Several of his feathers had fallen to the floor beneath him, pooling around his knees, creating the illusion that he was sitting on a pillow rather than the hard marble of the floor.

Evanbourough swallowed and returned his attention to Zamyael. The expression on her face terrified him, so he tempered his words with caution. "My Lady? May I ask what games are afoot?"

Her cold calculation swung in his direction. He saw nothing but madness in the black coals which made up her eyes. "Games, my Lord?"

"Did Lasterian misbehave?" Evanbourough felt no love for the angel. But he did know the child was nothing if not obedient. He suspected whatever enraged Zamyael had nothing at all to do with Lasterian's behavior.

"No." She replied, her smile still raw. Another shiver passed over him. "He was the picture of a perfect guest. A real *pleasure* to entertain."

"I see." Evanbourough replied, frowning.

What he thought was, *I must get that child as far away from that crazed woman as is devilishly possible.*

"Well, then." He forced a smile in Lasterian's direction. Stepping toward him, he held out his hand. "Come, Lasterian. Let us get you home."

Lasterian turned his disconcerting gaze upward and met Evan's. "Home?"

Evan smiled at him and grasped his hand. Once standing, Lasterian wobbled. Evanbourough sprang forward, wrapping his arm around the child's waist and pulling him close to give him purchase.

What in the name of these Thirty Hells did Zamyael do to you?

He looked over his shoulder and gave Zamyael a smile. It was waxy upon his lips. "Have a pleasant morning, my Lady."

Her eyes flashed; Evanbourough's stomach curled. When she spoke it was in frigid tones which chilled him to his bones. "Oh, yes, my Lord. I intend on doing just that."

Evanbourough thrust the angel into the hall. Once there, he pushed him toward the wall. He shook his head, meeting the cold fear in Lasterian's eyes.

"Boy . . ." He whispered. "What has happened to you?"

"You said you would take me home . . ."

His tone was so deadly cold that Evanbourough shivered. He nodded, took the boy's hand and spirited them to Tristan's living quarters.

Tristan wasn't there, giving Evanbourough his only opportunity to find out what, exactly, happened to the child.

"Lasterian." Evanbourough cleared his throat. "I brought you home. As I promised you I would."

"Yes." The child looked around himself with a haunted expression. "Home."

"What occurred?" Evan tried to speak in a soft, caring tone. He was ill equipped and he knew that. He hated the angel for Tristan's love for him. Yet, he understood that his hate was ill placed and so he tried, desperately, to comfort the lad. "Your wing is broken."

"Broken?" Lasterian asked, so distant and unaware that it was painful.

Evanbourough shook his head, reached for Lasterian's wing and did the unspeakable by healing it. No one but for a servant's Master was allowed to touch the wing of an angel or demon. Yet, Evanbourough thought some allowances must be made given what had befallen the angel against his will.

If, that was, Lasterian would talk to him and barter his protection.

"What did Zamyael do to you?"

"He . . ." Lasterian shivered. His eyes were wide as he met Evanbourough's own. "He raped me!"

"Raped you?" Evanbourough sighed his relief. No harm could come of a male angel being raped by a male demon other than humiliation. "I'll poultice you. You'll be healed before Tristan finds out." He raised his gaze and met Lasterian's haunted eyes. "Tristan cannot find out. He won't forgive you for your trespass."

"Trespass?" Lasterian cried. "Why would Lord Tristan be angry with *me*?"

"He just would be." Evanbourough shook his head. He based this off of his own feelings rather than any reaction that Tristan might or might not respond with. But, he knew how much Tristan loved the angel and he thought it best that nothing come between them. "It is better that Zamyael took you." He forced a smile. "Rather than you taking him."

Lasterian paled.

"Lasterian?" He shivered under Lasterian's strange expression. "Why do you look as you do?"

"He . . ." He shook his head and lowered his gaze. "Zamyael forced me to take his woman parts."

"What?" If these words were ever spoken aloud to anyone who would spill them to the Sovereign Lady, it would be the end of the child.

One did not take such liberties with Lady Raziel's servant.

"He forced me to enter him." Lasterian's blush was blazing. "And not from behind." His blush grew. "I didn't want him, my Lord!" He cried and turned his attention toward Evanbourough. "He forced me! My body betrayed me when he did due to his soft nature!"

Evanbourough shook his head. "If you took Zamyael's female parts with an erection then you weren't raped."

"My Lord!"

"You weren't raped!" Evanbourough growled. "And you have ruined me for protecting you from your punishment!"

"My Lord, I didn't . . ."

"I tire of helping you, you little idiot." He growled. "Shut up before your accusations ruin us all."

-34-

Tristan frowned as Evanbourough paced back and forth at the foot of his bed. "I never liked him and I don't want you to bring him to my home with you anymore."

"Why?" Tristan asked with a sigh. "What did he do to displease you this time?"

"He has done nothing." Evan stopped his pacing and turned to meet Tristan's gaze. He held it true enough but there was some darkness within the black of Evanbourough's eyes that Tristan neither understood nor trusted. "He's handsomely made, Tristan. And if he bides his time in these halls, only ill can come of it."

"What happened?" Tristan tried again.

"I told you. Nothing has happened." Evanbourough snapped and turned away. "He is not welcome in my presence anymore. If that is not enough for you then, mayhap, you should keep your distance as well."

Angry with him, Tristan sighed. "Fine. I'll leave him home when I visit you from now on."

"Which is all I have asked of you." Evanbourough responded, though he kept his back to Tristan rather than acknowledging him.

Tristan, frustrated, rolled his eyes and looked away. He wouldn't get an honest answer out of Evanbourough as to what had passed between the God and the angel.

So, quite frankly, why in the name of all that was right should he bother to try?

-35-

"Evan!" Theasis smiled as she stepped toward him. "How are you? Where is Tristan?"

"We aren't joined at the hip, Thea." Evanbourough looked up from where he was sitting, his black eyes darker than normal. His expression reflected the depths of his mood.

"Do you mind if I join you?" Theasis asked. It was a good position, not too far to the front nor too far to the back. They would be able to hear and see everything.

Evanbourough, always the gentleman, stood and scooted over so Theasis could take the nearer seat. Thea smiled her thanks in Evan's direction, lowering herself into the chair which Evanbourough had recently occupied. Evanbourough waited for her to find her comfort before slowly lowering himself as well.

"Do you believe we shall see fireflares today?" Theasis wondered aloud.

"I know not, Thea." Evanbourough returned distractedly. "There has been a lot of politicking since the last Council. I think we had best be prepared for anything."

"Probably wise counsel." Theasis nodded. She let her eyes wander over Evanbourough's troubled profile for a moment before reaching for his hand and squeezing it tight. Evanbourough looked upward, his dark expression now sad. "Are you alright, min 'lasupita?"

"No, met paken." Evanbourough forced a smile in her direction. "But it isn't anything I wish to sully your heart with."

"You can tell me anything." Theasis responded to this, honestly meant. "Maybe I can help."

"Not this time." Evan raised Theasis' hand and kissed the back of it. "Thank you all the same."

"If you change your mind, I am here for you." Theasis reminded him.

Evanbourough smiled at her and nodded.

The door to the Great Hall of the Gods opened and the King of Lords and Queen of Ladies stepped through. Their twelve servants, which made up the Quorum, followed after them, each one as different from the other as he could possibly be. Theasis smiled as her eyes trailed over them, hovering longest over Zadkiel as a familiar pain and anger rushed through her. "I wish the King of Lords would release that child his bind."

"The time for forgiveness will come." Evanbourough sighed. "Eventually."

The Sovereign Lady entered next, followed by Zamyael.

Evanbourough snorted and looked swiftly away.

Theasis furrowed her brow at this but decided it best not to ask. Whatever ill passed between Evanbourough and Zamyael would have to be let past. Zamyael was Lady Raziel's right hand. It would not bode well for Evanbourough to hold his grudges.

"Lord Regent Lucias is late." Theasis tried to turn Evanbourough's attentions to something different.

Evanbourough chuckled at this. "He's usually the first one here."

"Maybe he's making a point." Theasis offered.

"What point?" Evanbourough snorted again. But he was smiling and Theasis took his jest in good stride. "That he's too proud to mark the shift of the shadows?"

"With that one?" Theasis laughed gently. "You never know."

She squeezed Evanbourough's hand, happy that Evan hadn't let hers go. Evan raised her hand and kissed the back of it again before, hesitantly, setting their clasped hands on his own knee. Theasis relished in the intimacy, hoping the affection was truly meant and not part of their ruse that they were lovers to barter votes for those children headed toward exile.

They sat like that, each one in their own thoughts, watching the others of the court, until, some fifteen shifts later, Lord Lucias entered the Hall with Loki and Sappharon close on his heels. His step held no urgency. He looked at The Queen of Ladies and King of Lords almost as if bored.

It was only to Lady Raziel that he offered his bow.

Once Lord Lucias was seated, the King of Lords raised his hand and Gabriel stood. The archangel stepped forward and blew upon his trumpet, calling the Gods to their Council. When everyone had finally fallen silent, he returned to his waiting stance and the King of Lords rose.

Theasis started slightly as, watching the Goddesses who constantly followed Loki around and who were surrounding him now, the realization finally came to her. "Loki still wears his goatee."

Evanbourough turned to her with a brow raised. "And?"

"He told me the Lord Regent has been ordered to force him to shave it." Theasis explained.

She didn't add that Loki had sought her out from fear for comfort. What passed between she and Loki had nothing to do with their ruse. She honestly liked the youngling. She had claimed his virginity and this knowledge pleased her.

Even if, now, he passed himself with willing fervor amongst the geese of Goddesses, angels and demons making up his gaggle.

"He said Lord Lucias refused, but that he knew he would give in."

"He doesn't know Lord Lucias very well, then." Evanbourough shrugged.

The King of Lords was glaring at the pair of them and they both knew it was time they fell still.

The pleasantries were taken care of first: This God has this new servant; that God has done this or that. Lord Lucias sired a new child in Aiken Darklief of the Oakland's mischief fairies.

Finished with news of varying import, the King of Lords delved into the Divine Plan and glances were exchanged all around.

There were rumors abound of the Plan and the discontentment it harbored amongst the Small Council. But the evidence was clear given both Lady Raziel and Lord Lucias began looking, clearly bored, away from the King of Lords' back and on anything else they could possibly land their gazes upon.

Meanwhile, the Queen of Ladies, as she ever did, held her dazzling green gaze on the King of Lords' back with sheer adoration clear on every line of her beautifully made face.

When he was finished explaining the ins and outs of his plans, he smiled grandly around the room and waited. When no one said anything one way or another, Lord Regent Lucias sat forward in his chair, stood, and then, mockingly, clapped.

Theasis' eyes widened and her hand clasped Evanbourough's all the tighter. Such a display against the King of Lords, even if it came from Lord Lucias, rarely boded well for the person making the outburst.

"Luke?" The King of Lords' face grew taut. "You have something to say?"

"I do, your Grace." Lord Lucias stepped forward. "As surprising as this must be to you."

"The podium is all yours." The King of Lords smirked at him and rolled his eyes as he backed away. When he found his throne, his gaze seemed to hit the Gods of the Council whom he knew would vote his way.

The message was clear. He was placating Lord Regent Lucias, allowing him to speak his mind but silently bidding the Council the manner in which he expected them to vote.

It wasn't the first time Theasis had watched this behavior and, given she served him and would pay for any disobedience against him, she understood precisely how she was meant to vote.

Lord Lucias didn't bother to bow to him. Rather, he stepped to the podium and looked swiftly around the room.

He was, obviously, judging his audience.

"I have no problem with the Divine Plan." Lord Lucias said, his voice gentle.

The entire room buzzed with surprise.

"I believe free will is a beautiful thing." He smiled up at them all. "Though, I do have one small concession I should like the Gods to consider before a vote is passed." He looked around again, his smile growing. "I propose that all creatures are allowed the same courtesy of free will as are the mortals. And by this I mean you and I."

Followed by the heavy words that Theasis knew would one day damn him.

"And, by this, I mean the angels and the demons."

"My Lord, forgive me, but you cannot be serious!" A God Theasis was not close to cried as he found his feet. Theasis believed his name was Aminos, but she couldn't be sure. "If we can't order our servants to do our bidding, what is their point?"

"When their bidding includes turning their tail for your profit rather than their own, I should think much." Lord Lucias glowered at the God, his brown eyes narrowed and his face contorted with rage. His head instantly turned to another; this one Theasis knew as Ragen. "Or being chopped into parts for barter or gold."

The King of Lords stood, clearing his throat.

"The Gods should never abuse their children." He agreed. "But I must side with caution and agree that we cannot allow our servants free will." He smiled brilliantly at the court. Regardless of whatever else Theasis had ever felt for the King of Lords, she coveted such a smile. "I need my Quorum to follow my orders without question. I know the same is true of you."

"Some of us have children who follow us without question and without the requirement of an order, your Grace." Theasis turned toward the familiar voice and frowned as she realized it was Tristan who spoke.

And without Lasterian sitting in his waiting stance at his feet. How curious.

"Because loyalty is born of kindness. Never cruelty."

"Yours is still a pup, Tristan." This from Lady Martaen. "Wait you until he finds his tongue and then speak to us of blind loyalty."

"While I agree with Lord Tristan," the King of Lords inclined his head to that worthy, ignoring the Lady all together, "the truth is that sometimes a punishment must be made. If we take the authority from the God most qualified to determine such our servants will rule in chaos."

The Sovereign Lady stood and walked forward.

"I, personally, rely on Zamyael." She pointed to her demon, bowed in the waiting stance at Lady Raziel's chair. "He knows more about what is going on in this Court by word of mouth than I ever could."

She looked around the court. Theasis sat forward, intrigued by every word. She understood by some of the things shared with her by Loki and Michael, whom she had befriended long, long ago, that Lady Raziel was not a Goddess who should be trusted. Whatever side she took in this particular debate would be mired with her manipulation to meet her own personal means.

"Zamyael is able to dance among your children and learn the truths that would never, otherwise reach my ears. He understands more about any given consideration than any of the four of us," she indicated the four chairs of the Small Council, "could even imagine." She shook her head. "I for one, agree with Lucias. We must rely on our servants. Not bind them."

"Which goes to the point of our servants not being able to bide our secrets as they are." The Queen of Ladies said, not rising. "I do not want Raphael spewing my personal stories." She looked around the room, seemingly meeting each gaze in its turn. "I want him to keep my secrets." She indicated the King of Lords. "Where would His Grace be if Raphael let loose his tongue on the secrets you share with him in his presence?"

"True that." Another God announced. "Our servants are present at all of our most important councils." Theasis looked over her shoulder and recognized Lord Coeyren held the floor. "Many of these conversations are private. I shouldn't want that they would be shared."

"Just my point." The King of Lords nodded, rising from his throne. He looked over his shoulder and gave his Queen a winsome smile.

"While I agree with this part of it," Lord Lucias sighed, almost reluctantly, "the abuse against the children has got to stop."

"Sappharon is breathing lies to you again." Ragen seethed.

"Can we not ban abuse?" The Sovereign Lady grumbled, ignoring Ragen. "Both Lucias and I agree on many of your points for the nonce. But can we not be kind to those who we are charged to protect?"

"Forgive me, my Lady. But we are not charged to protect them." The Queen of Ladies addressed Lady Raziel with obvious distaste. "They are charged to protect us!"

"But must we beat them into supplication to make them do so?!" Lord Lucias snapped at her. "Must we chop them up into little bits and sell them for a bauble?"

"No one does that." The Queen of Ladies waved her hand at him.

"The issue in question is can the Divine Plan be passed to the mortals." This was said in soft tones by the King of Lords. "Shall we vote on this and make the other a separate discussion after each one of us has had time to conduct our own research and provide our own opinions?"

"One cannot be decided without the other." Lord Lucias grumbled and turned away so he could walk to his throne and fall into it.

"I agree." Lady Raziel bowed before settling herself into her own seat.

"But given this is my Court," the King of Lords said, "and my cause, I raise only the issue of free will where the mortals are concerned and agree to reserve the greater issues in regard to Gods and servants to the next debate."

Lord Lucias turned to the Sovereign Lady. The two whispered for a moment before Lord Lucias returned his attention to the

Council. "We disagree. But will concede if the issue remains open." Then through his teeth. "For now."

"It is agreed." The King of Lords seconded. "Raguel?"

"I can agree to these terms."

"Very well." The King of Lords looked around the Council. "In favor of the Divine Plan?"

Theasis eagerly raised her hand.

She saw that Evanbourough raised his as well, though hesitantly. Theasis wondered on this but wouldn't question it as she knew better than anyone that Evanbourough always voted with his conscience.

"And without such?"

It was a close thing. Theasis couldn't say, in that moment, which way the vote swayed.

She watched as the King of Lords turned to Gabriel. "The vote?"

"The majority votes that the Divine Plan passes." Gabriel's voice was tight. He immediately lowered his head, as though bowing.

To Theasis, however, it appeared more as though he were hiding his disappointment in his betters.

Theasis, being charged with the well-being of all angels, was well tuned to Gabriel's displeasure.

"Very well." The King of Lords smiled grandly. "The motion is passed."

The majority clapped.

Though she had voted in its favor to placate the King of Lords, Theasis would not celebrate until all creatures were afforded their will and so held her hands down. She was pleased that Evanbourough continued to hold her hand and did not raise his own to clap either.

"To the next issue, Lucias and I have made barter." The King of Lords smiled winsomely and turned his attention to Lord Lucias. He bowed, charmingly enough, though, again, without necessity, and extended his hand. "My Lord?"

Lord Lucias stood and nodded. "As you all know I've sired a son with an ape to create a thinking mortal race which we shall call human."

There was a strange energy which passed through the court at this. Some of it was amusement. Some of it was disgust. Quite a lot of it was a dark sense of superiority.

Theasis found it strange all the way round.

"It is these humans who have inspired our Divine Plan." Lord Lucias smiled. "But there were disagreements and Noliminan and I formed a bit of barter."

"We've heard of such." Evanbourough braved, a smile to his voice. It was a reminder as to what Theasis loved about him best. "And we beg you must share."

"Thank you," Lord Lucias said to Evanbourough.

Theasis felt the hand holding her own grasp hers all the more tightly.

"I shall leave the original details of the barter to our benevolent King."

"In short." The King of Lords smiled grandly. This Thea also found captivatingly beautiful. "The original barter is that I can supply a world of full sustenance and joy to Lucias' Adam and Raguel's Eve and neither, should then, wish for more." His satisfaction with the idea of his own plan was clear. "Lucias believes that, given they have everything they could desire, if we plant something simple to tempt them, they will fall for the trap and take it." He looked around, assessing the Court. "I believe that if they are sated enough they would not risk our wrath for their desires."

"The barter is made and not up to vote." Lady Raziel explained. "Luke and I shall not voice our disagreement." She gave Lord Lucias a small—somewhat cold—smile. "The peculiar situation here is that the original barter is made up of certain terms and your betters wish your permission to re-open an already sealed barter to add a new concession."

"Just so." Lord Lucias chuckled and stood. "And, as you know, given a closed barter can only be opened by better Gods than the higher ranking or a vote of our Council, we turn to you."

The Council muttered its agreement to this sentiment, though which God was the better had long been up for debate.

"If I lose, I must never again raise the fact that I believe we immortals deserve our freedom." He smiled and looked around the room. "This Noliminan has agreed to."

"And if I lose, I must allow Lucias to guide me with some proposed changes as to the treatment of the mortals if they fail their tests." He raised his hand. "Only the mortals." This was a clarification made when the buzz of disagreement enveloped the room. "Your vote on your servants will remain yours."

After the King of Lords finished his statement, Lord Lucias stepped forward to stand directly before the podium, facing them all. His expression suddenly became extremely serious. Theasis wondered what gravity must exist to warrant such heavy contemplation and waited with bated breath for whatever argument stood between them to fall.

"My problem, you see, is that my servant, Apprentice Lord Loki, has the audacity to believe that he has the right to wear a beard on his face."

He turned and pointed to Loki. That worthy, who was surrounded by his ever growing gaggle, held his head high as though he had a right to his defiance.

Theasis—and everyone else in the room—stared at Lord Lucias in disbelieving silence.

"And Noliminan has ordered me to force him to shave it off."

The King of Lords nodded, his eyes darting around the Court with what could only be described as quiet amusement.

"Given, as I have explained, that custom is a closed barter with only a higher ranking God available to open it," Lord Lucias spoke in serious tones, "we simply wish your approval to reopen the consequence by your vote."

"Excuse me?" It was Lord Countenance, the God of time, who stood at this. His strange, not quite there eyes were shimmering with the confusion that every one of the members of Council was experiencing but were fearful to voice. "Do you truly wish for us to vote over the fate of a beard?"

"We do." The King of Lords nodded.

"But this is madness!" The child God, Armand, who would forever be too young to grow a beard of his own, cried.

"Mayhap." Lord Lucias agreed. "But it's *Loki's* beard." He countered with a smile, rushing forward and grasping Loki's hairy chin in his hand.

Loki's mouth was forced open in a manner so comical that Theasis was unable to hold back her laugh. This earned her several irritated—if not confused—glares.

The fawning women who surrounded him giggled, relieving her of the Council's attention.

"And that's not just *any* beard."

"We are to vote on the fate of Loki's beard?" This was Lady Moira, the Goddess of fate, who obviously found the situation as amusing as Theasis did because she was also laughing. "But no one cares!"

"Noliminan cares." Lord Lucias corrected her, slamming his hand comically onto the podium, to which he now returned. "And we agreed I shouldn't have to force Loki to shave it unless I lose this barter."

"Loki's beard?" Another God Theasis did not recognize—because he was extremely shy and so seldom spoke at Council—asked, his expression mirroring his confusion. "With all else which is important? I am to vote if Apprentice Lord Loki should wear a beard?"

"I'm extremely fond of it." Loki retorted, his tone implying that this was the most serious matter ever to have been raised to vote. "Though, truly, it isn't a beard."

His eyes danced. Theosis understood why. Loki never thought of his goatee as a beard. And his quips to correct others regarding its nature were something Loki took deep to heart, regardless of the joviality in which his disputes were raised.

"It's a goatee!"

His gaggle tittered. One of them, Thea noted, began dancing her fingers through his hair. As she did so, his grin split his handsome face. He was obviously pleased with his gaggle's adulation.

Thea, chuckling to herself, shook her head. She didn't begrudge Loki, who was charming to a fault, the flocks of women who, clearly, adored him.

"My Lords, I truly do not believe anyone but Loki cares." It was Tristan this time. "Let him wear the damn thing if he likes it! Whatever its name!"

"Ah." Lord Lucias returned. "But I agreed to re-open the barter to add the concession if the Council so agreed. So might we?"

"I think we can all agree that if that's the only concession we should open the barter." The Queen of Ladies snapped.

Theasis thought this queer.

Loki had shared with her that he and the Queen of Ladies had developed a strange, platonic friendship which was thick with its confidences. She would have thought, as Loki's friend, that the Queen of Ladies would have understood the importance of his goatee to him.

She would reflect later that the Queen did.

Her flippant attitude toward it was her way of protecting him from having to shave it lest the King of Lords believe she coveted him for it.

As, obviously, Loki's gaggle of geese, did.

"Call the damned vote." The Queen entreated.

Theasis was not surprised that the majority reigned.

She held an honest belief that those who didn't vote in approval were simply stymied by the simple fact that there was a vote at all. It was the most foolish thing they had ever, since beginning their Council, voted on.

"Good." Lord Lucias chuckled as he turned away to find his scat. "Then may Loki's dammed and hated beard prevail."

-36-

"What, precisely, just took place?" Countenance asked Moira as the two of them exited the Great Hall of the Gods together. "What in the name of the Sixty Realms was that about?"

"Only Azrael knows." Moira returned with a chuckle. "Loki's beard? Has the Small Council lost their minds?"

"By Loki's beard they have." Countenance muttered. And he smiled at his own joke, thinking to himself that the jest was as ridiculous as the vote, itself. "I hope his luck prevails."

Moira, whose magic possessed that tricky devil, luck, smiled grandly. "By Loki's beard it shall."

-37-

Zamyael lay upon her bed with her hand rested upon her stomach. Her mind was reeling with truths that she wanted to deny.

Her nipples had become red, swollen and were painful to the touch. And she had vomited every afternoon after consuming her lunch.

After long consideration, she knew what was wrong with her.

She was pregnant.

(Raziel spins violently toward Zamyael, her eyes wide and her mind buzzing with discontentment. I ignore the turn of her thoughts because—given she has done far worse than Zamyael—her condemnation against the demoness is annoying to me at best.)

She had forced the angel to copulate with her and the result was that his seed had impregnated her.

She shivered.

This was as bad as it could get.

Her womb was home to what might be—if she understood her current situation to be what it was—an abomination.

Dear Gods! Her sins were as great as any ever committed. *What am I to do now?*

-38-

Tristan stood in Lord Lucias' sitting room, waiting for the appointment he had arranged to speak with the Lord Regent about his suspicions regarding Dame Sappharon.

He didn't want to tell on the brat.

But, lately, Evanbourough and Theasis had seen signs of more and more secret meetings. If Sappharon was involved, as Tristan knew by the altercation with the angel whose parts were being stolen she was, Lord Lucias needed to find that out before the King of Lords did.

The King of Lords already loathed Sappharon and he made no bones about this to anyone who would speak her name.

Not, Tristan understood, because he ever bothered to get close to the brat. Rather, because the demon was the only thing Lord Lucias had ever created on his own and without the King of Lords' permission or direction.

Dame Sappharon hadn't been made by birthing, as was natural. Rather, she was made from a piece of the Lord Lucias' soul.

In short, Sappharon was the one piece of factual evidence which suggested that Lord Lucias was as powerful as the King of Lords.

The King of Lords simply couldn't abide that.

Loki stepped into the room with an apologetic smile. "Sorry to keep you waiting."

"It matters not." Tristan replied, grinning as his gaze landed upon the beard which had caused so much contention—and good humor—just lately among the Gods.

"He shouldn't be much longer." Loki assured him. "Do you want a drink while you're waiting?"

"Yes, please." Tristan smiled appreciatively at him. "Brandy if you have it."

"I believe we do." Loki turned away from Tristan. Tristan allowed himself to trail his gaze over the youngling's strong, shapely back. He looked swiftly away when Loki turned to face him.

"Here you go."

"Thank you." Tristan stepped forward and accepted the glass.

"Of course." Loki smiled at him. "I truly am sorry that his earlier appointment is running over."

Tristan shook his head. "He's a busy man. And I understand. As long as he doesn't cut me short then I—"

"I never would." The Lord Regent stepped out of his library with Lord Parsiphany at his side. He dismissed Parsiphany saying, "Thank you for your promised assistance."

"It is my pleasure, my Lord." Parsiphany replied with a bow. "Thank you for thinking of me."

"My pleasure." He turned to Tristan then as Loki led Parsiphany away. As for Tristan, he allowed his eyes to follow them. Parsiphany was another God who insisted upon his masculinity and so was, therefore, extremely attractive to Tristan. "I apologize for my delay, Tristan."

"No need for an apology, my Lord." Tristan assured him as he gave Lord Lucias his full attention. "My visit is one of a personal nature."

"Oh?" Lord Lucias, who was walking toward his library, looked over his shoulder and met Tristan's gaze. "I'm intrigued."

He waited to speak any further words until they were within the chambers of Lord Lucias' library with the door soundly closed. He looked around to make sure they were alone and then smiled, pleased with Lord Lucias for his discretion. He had asked for a meeting where neither of their servants were present and he was pleased that Lord Lucias was complying.

"What troubles you?" Lord Lucias asked as he found a seat on the sofa rather than behind his desk. "That you would bring your issue to me rather than through your rightful channels?"

"Something has come to my attention . . ." Tristan cleared his throat. "It's about Sappharon."

Lord Lucias shifted uncomfortably in his seat. He crossed one long leg over the other and laced his fingers around his knee. "I see."

Tristan sighed and lowered his gaze to his feet. He didn't take a seat. He knew his place and so he wouldn't until it was offered. "As you know, Theasis and Evanbourough are charged with watching the comings and goings of the angels and demons and then taking them into their care should they be exiled."

"This I do know." Lord Lucias' gaze narrowed. He raised a hand and indicated a high backed, comfortable leather chair at the end of the sofa.

Tristan nodded, slid around the chair and lowered himself within. He smiled nervously, knowing he was on the wrong side of things given he was governed by the King of Lords and not Lord Regent Lucias. Rightfully, he should be discussing this matter with the Queen of Ladies.

"Given my peculiar relationship with both," Tristan tried to put this as delicately as he could so Lord Lucias knew that what he heard from the Heavens didn't necessarily cross his pillow when he lay with Evanbourough, "I know much of both the Heavens and Hells bound Realms."

"It is rare that a Heavens bound God should spend as much time as you do in the Halls of the Hells." Lord Lucias conceded with a smile. "But let us not sully our conversation with what is custom."

"Custom has never been in it with me." Tristan smiled softly in response. "As far as I am concerned, our nation is still one."

"As far as I am concerned, as well." His expression softened with the sentiment. "And I'm glad to know such a belief still crosses both fences."

"It does." Tristan assured him. "In more cases than you might know."

Lord Lucias nodded, still smiling. "So what has your understanding of truths to do with my brat?"

Now, Tristan found a sigh and a bit of fear. He lowered his gaze to his hand and muttered, "I've always been fond of her." He raised his gaze and met Lord Lucias'. "And I don't mean to tattle or get her into more trouble than she already is in."

"Of course not."

Tristan lowered his gaze again, trying to find the words he had practiced but which were now lost to him. Finally, knowing there was no better way, he said the words as they must be said.

"She's involved with certain meetings between the angels and the demons." Tristan muttered and then raised his gaze to seek Lord Lucias' pained, but not entirely surprised, expression. "And not just by word from Theasis and Evanbourough. I fear someone who oughtn't see her lurking in the shadows might."

"I have suspected the children are comingling." He sighed. "If such was happening, I would never find surprise that Sappharon is at the heart of it." He looked swiftly away. "I don't find myself angry with any of them for it."

"Nor do I." Tristan sighed his relief. "But others will."

"Others have a rude awakening coming their way." Lord Lucias muttered. "How many times?"

"It started out as one meeting every few cycles of the sun or so." Tristan counseled. "Now?" He shook his head. "Two or three by each Seventh Moon."

"So often . . ." He was silent for a moment, but eventually shook his head and forced his gaze to meet Tristan's. "They mean to rebel."

"I believe this to be the case."

"And if they do?" Lord Lucias asked in a kind, patient tone, "Which side shall you be on?"

Tristan swallowed the lump in his throat, knowing the betrayal of his answer. But his potential punishment did not change his conviction regarding right and wrong.

"Yours, my Lord." He replied softly. "And theirs."

Lord Lucias bent forward and held out his hand. Tristan took it with no compunctions. "You are brave, child."

"It isn't my brevity which is required. It is you and the children who will pay the greatest of all sacrifices for the rest of us."

"Anyone who is willing to stand against Noliminan, in any measure, shall pay." He lowered his dark eyes. "Thus, so shall we all."

-39-

Sappharon slipped into Lucias' suite, grateful it was still dark within. She quickly fixed the locks and began making her way to her bedroom, relieved she hadn't been caught.

It was to be a short lived pleasure.

"Where have you been?"

Sappharon's heart immediately fell into her stomach and her blood ran cold. She stopped and turned toward Lucias' favored chair, forcing herself to smile as she saw the dark outline of her God set within it. "Just for a walk, my Lord."

"I hear you've been taking a lot of walks lately." Lucias growled at her. "Are you a fool? Or do you just lack enough guile that you know not how to sneak about without getting caught."

Sappharon felt as though she had been physically slapped. Nothing harmed her more in life than Lucias' disapproval of her. "I'm only restless lately."

"Do not sully me with your lies." He snapped at her. "I know exactly what you have been up to."

"You don't understand—"

"I understand perfectly well." Lucias countered. "What I fail to approve of is your not asking my permission first." There was a level of coldness to his tone which Sappharon did not much care for. "Do you realize you have been *seen*? That you jeopardize your own cause because you fail to trust me enough to ask me how to best go about it?"

"I thought to keep you out of it." Sappharon whispered. "That you might not be forced to take a stand."

"I have no choice. Especially now." Lucias snarled. "I would have preferred to do it my way rather than yours." He shook his head and flicked his fingers to the fire pit. The fire blazed, lighting up the room. Sappharon saw, then, that his mood wasn't tempered with anger. It was tempered with fear. "You've put me in a very precarious position, Sappharon."

"I'm sorry." Sappharon whispered. And she was.

Lucias sighed and turned his profile to her. "I want to attend your next meeting."

"Yes, my Lord." Sappharon stepped swiftly around the furniture, braving to fall to her knees to grasp his hand. "Whatever is your will."

"I know of a place where we can all go and no one will find us." His expression was distant. "A sort of base camp if you will. Where we will be free to come and go." His eyes narrowed. "Mayhap some of us can still mingle among the others after we make our first strike without being detected."

"Where?" Sappharon asked, surprised. They had been searching for just such a place for years.

"On the first of all worlds. On Anticata." Lucias muttered. "A castle we lived in once long, long ago." Sappharon felt her brow furrow. "Noliminan never goes there." Lucias' voice was so far away as he spoke that Sappharon felt she might lose him. "It pains him too much."

"Why?" Sappharon whispered.

Lucias finally turned his head downward to look upon Sappharon. His dark eyes were blazing. "It does not concern you." Sappharon flinched. "It is enough for you to understand that it is a safe place for us to bide."

Sappharon nodded and lowered her head so her cheek rested on Lucias' knee. She thought, when she felt Lucias' hand moving toward her, that she would be pushed away in anger. Rather, Lucias began stroking the back of her head, giving her a sense of peace and safety.

She whispered, "I'm sorry I displeased you."

"I'm not displeased." Lucias muttered. "I was scared for you. Were it someone else who had seen you, it wouldn't have been me who they would have told."

Sappharon nodded and looked upward. "Who saw me?"

"It doesn't matter." Lucias smiled kindly at her. "What matters is that Moira blessed you that it be so." He pushed Sappharon away so he could stand. "On the morrow I want you to contact your friends and let them know they are to have no meetings until they hear from you. Let them know you've found your place and that you are securing it." Sappharon nodded at him. "I don't think Noliminan would ever visit that place again, but I want to put spells around it so we can be sure."

"I will see to it first thing."

"Good." Lucias sighed and began to walk away. "Sleep well."

"Yes, my Lord." Sappharon returned. "And you."

-40-

The castle had been built upon the side of a large mountain, cut from marble and granite in delicate curves. On the south side of the castle was an expanse of woodland and on the north a great ravine between the mountain upon which the castle had been carved and an adjoining mountain on the other side. A great waterfall fell at the very edge of a long balcony which extended the length of the castle on the ravine side. It was at this end of the castle where the greatest apartments were located.

As I was pulled to this place, I shivered. Unlike the conversation that Noliminan and Lucias had last shared, I do not believe Lucias either wanted me there or detected my presence.

And unlike the last two times, Lucias' thoughts were not mere whispers.

They were outraged screams.

It was as though I were watching any other soul in creation rather than one of the two ruling Gods.

It was here, I knew as I watched Lucias, where Lucias' most vivid memories had been borne.

The castle had become overgrown with brambles and roses. Ivy hung in drapes over windows and doors. Spiders had spun their delicate webs in every crack and crevice. And woodland creatures had taken up residence within and without.

But the structure itself, which had been forged by Lucias and Noliminan's own hands, was still sturdy and strong. It would take Lucias but a minute bit of spell work to cut back the overgrowth and clean up the castle to its original, ancient glory.

After that, he had much more difficult spell work to perform.

Lucias had to come up with a border which Noliminan would be unable to bend or cross. He had a fair idea he would be successful. Yet he also understood that Noliminan was, by the barest fraction of his soul, stronger than him.

Lucias' only hope of besting Noliminan where magic was concerned would be to outwit him.

Also, he knew that the spell could not be open to the inhabitants of the castle. He understood the game of kings' castles well enough to know that Noliminan's greatest tool would be spies he could set free in Lucias' camp. No one could be trusted completely.

His allies may not appreciate becoming prisoners within the base camp. But he hoped they would see the sense of it and find contentment in the fact that the castle grounds were grand and expansive.

Once the cleanup work was complete, Lucias found himself wandering through his old living quarters. He felt an oddly ambivalent surprise that Noliminan had kept it exactly as he had left it. He would have thought Noliminan would have emptied it of his things, if only to rid himself of his memory.

Yet, even the book Lucias had been reading, its binding now soft and its paper yellow and frail, sat upon the bed where he had thrown it while arguing with Noliminan over his mistreatment of Zamyael before storming out of the castle for good to begin the creation of the first level of the Hells.

He walked over to the bed and raised the book to his chest. He was grinning, but it wasn't a happy grin. His entire face ached from it but he was helpless to stop it. Every bit of his emotion was welling up within him; every bit of anger he had experienced that dreadful day when King Noliminan had been so affronted by Zamyael's behavior that he had turned her into a demon.

His grin tightened. His entire face aching, he walked to his library to file his book away. He understood that returning to live in these halls was going to be harder on him than he had intended. He was suddenly glad he had come alone on this first visit so no one could see his hideous grin and all of the pain in his soul it represented.

If he had but known that I was watching him, he would have been mortified.

"Past is past." He finally growled at himself. His voice echoed through the bedchamber. Somewhere a bird heard it, cried and took flight. Lucias listened to the sound of its wings beating the air until it was out of earshot and then forced himself out of his silent reverie.

There was too much to do, now, to dwell.

And precious little time to do it in.

He made his way out of his apartment, through the castle and into the cellar. Here, he and Noliminan had set up all manner of tools which would aide them to best master the most difficult of spells.

He looked around, found what he thought he would need to begin, and set to work.

-41-

Loki stepped out of his room, walked down the hall and stopped short when he reached the sitting area. Zamyael, her already too pale face ashen and her eyes wide with fear, stood just inside the door with her arms crossed desperately over her bare chest and her expression set to panic. "Zamyael?"

"Where is Lucias?" Zamyael asked, her tone matching the panic of her expression.

"Out for a few days." Loki said, walking toward her and taking her hand. "Sit down. Let me get you a drink."

"No." She shook her head. "Thank you. Do you know where he went?"

"He said something about a castle in Anticata but—"

"Thank you, Loki." Zamyael forced a smile in his direction. "It is probably best you don't tell anyone else." Her eyes were blazing. "Not Noliminan; not even Raziel."

"He didn't say it was a secret." Loki shrugged his shoulders.

"If this is where he truly went, then it is very definitely a secret." Zamyael curtseyed to him. Watching her, Loki wondered—not for the first time—how devastatingly beautiful she must have been as a woman. "Thank you for your aide, Loki. I'll take my leave now."

"Wait." Loki grasped her hand before she could bolt. "Something is obviously troubling you. Is it something I can help you with?"

"No." Zamyael said, the queerest expression crossing her femininely beautiful face. "I'm afraid there is no one who can help me now."

With that, as though she still bore the magic she had commanded as a Goddess, she was simply gone. Loki stared at the spot where she had been, as much taken aback by Zamyael's ability to transport herself by apparition as by her strange mood.

He wondered if he should seek Lady Raziel and speak to her about the demon's odd behavior. But then, he reasoned, he should not.

Not until he gained Lord Lucias' counsel, by any road.

He decided he would let the matter go. He had other things to attend to just now. Lord Lucias had made it clear that he wanted Adam to begin falling into temptation before his female was born.

The sudden timeline on a thing which hadn't needed to be rushed was disconcerting. Coupled with Lord Lucias' strange need to make himself scarce, Loki found himself suspicious as to his Master's motives.

But his business was not to meddle.

Lord Regent Lucias had made it clear that whatever he was doing was not Loki's concern. All that was Loki's concern was to make excuses for him if anyone should come looking for him and that he was to see to Adam's failure.

So far these had proven to be easy enough tasks.

Soon, though, the King of Lords would be looking for Lord Regent Lucias.

Loki wasn't sure that worthy would take his absence—and Loki's inability to explain it—with as little suspicion as everyone else had.

But Loki would cross this bridge when it came. Now was the time for the sport of attempting to save his precious goatee.

Loki had the idea that he was going to enjoy convincing Adam to take the fruit much more than he probably should.

-42-

"Lucias?" I watched my father start at the sound of an all too familiar voice.

He turned swiftly in Zamyael's direction, raging with anger that she should be there. He didn't want Zam to get into trouble. If she were caught in his game, her past punishments would seem like child's play compared to what might happen to her.

His anger abated, however, when he saw the expression on Zamyael's face. "Whatever is the matter, met paken?"

"I'm in trouble." Zamyael whispered, her black eyes wide. She gnawed on her lower lip for a moment, almost as if wanting to change her mind about sharing whatever mischief she had been up to with him. "I've done the unforgivable." She swallowed. "Raziel will turn me out! I will be damned!"

Lucias, who couldn't think of anything that Zamyael would ever do to make Raziel angry enough to turn her out, shook his head and stepped forward. As for her being damned, that was under his control. Not Raziel's. "Nothing can be as bad as all of that."

"But it is." Zamyael's eyes were wild. Her expression was a study in complete and utter fear. "I've copulated with an angel!"

Lucias felt his brow furrow at this. The fact that Zamyael had copulated with an angel didn't surprise him as much as the fact that Zamyael had strayed from Raziel's bed.

Still, he thought Raziel would understand.

So, he forced a smile, pulled the demon into his arms and gently kissed her forehead. "If you have, then nothing can be done about it now. Yet, I doubt Raziel will be angry with you about it."

"She will when she finds out I am pregnant." Zamyael's voice was a quiet whisper.

Shocked, Lucias felt his comforting hands freeze. "You're certain the child belongs to the angel?"

"Raziel makes me take her as a man would a woman." Zamyael raised her face. Clearly this admission was humiliating to her. She was waiting for him to judge her, or Raziel, for utilizing the organ which belonged to her which she loathed.

He didn't judge her.

He knew Raziel well enough that he understood. And he knew Zamyael was in the precarious position of being forced to supplicate completely to Raziel after the argument which culminated to put her in Raziel's care rather than Lucias' that had placed her in this predicament.

Understanding that he wasn't judging her, she grasped desperately at his shirt as the tears fell freely down her cheeks.

As for his distaste toward Raziel, in that moment, he bit his tongue. He would share his anger with her when the time was right. Now, given he must protect Zamyael, was not the time.

"How can I get pregnant, Luke? I'm male now!"

"No. You're a hermaphrodite. As with all of your kind, you have a womb." He muttered against her braids. "And you know this well." He shook his head. "Damn it, Zamyael. What were you thinking?"

"I wasn't." She buried her face against Lucias' chest again. "Raziel was seeing Noliminan again and I was angry because she would want to be with him after every horrible thing he has done to me. It was a moment of revenge!" She cried, her eyes flashing with the indignation which Lucias supposed she had the right to feel given Raziel had long ago promised to protect her at all costs. "I raped the angel! It was only one time! I didn't think—I didn't know—it was possible for me to become pregnant!"

Lucias sighed and shook his head. He swallowed the bile rising in his throat and, once again, buried his lips within the fine braids of the demon's hair. Zamyael was right on one count: being impregnated by an angel was as bad as it could get where a demon was concerned.

And then this unrelated thought rang through my mind: *I'm coming mother.*

I wanted to cry out. I wanted to grasp at my hair and pull every strand of it from my head. This thought had come from neither Lucias nor Zamyael.

It could only have come from Zamyael's baby.

Lucias, who must have been as concerned by Zamyael's fate as Zamyael, herself, shivered. His eyes widened.

"I shall protect you, Zam." He muttered. He looked around, his brow furrowed and shook his head. "How far along are you?"

"Not very." Zamyael whispered.

"Well it's not too late to root it out if—"

"Never!" Zamyael pulled away. She actually looked affronted. Lucias clearly found it hard not to chuckle at her for her motherly instincts. Yet, he kept his amusement at bay. There was nothing funny about the situation Zamyael had placed herself in.

"Has Raziel noticed?" He asked, softly.

"It's too soon for signs." Zamyael shook her head. "I just . . . I know."

"I understand." Lucias reached for Zamyael's chin and forced her to raise her gaze. "I'll figure something out, Zamyael. I'll make certain that no one aside you and I learns of this."

"How are you going to do that?" Zamyael asked, her eyes desperate but hopeful.

"I know not." Lucias admitted. "While you can carry this child as you are, it would be better if you were to return to your natural form. Male angels and demons rarely carry their babes to full term."

Zamyael's eager expression at returning to her female form was painful to bear witness to.

If I thought Noliminan wouldn't take you the moment he crosses paths with you, I would let you remain as you were born even after the birthing.

"Will it be a dathanorna?" Zamyael asked, her eyes hopeful this would not be. "I mean—" She swallowed. "Given I was born a Goddess, the baby will be a God. Won't it?"

"I cannot say one way or the other, met paken." Lucias replied lovingly. "I honestly don't know."

"I'm sorry for sullying your heart with my misfortune." Zamyael smiled sadly at him. "You have enough of your own troubles."

"Oh, my beloved first and only true hearted wife." Lucias smiled adoringly down at her. "Nothing is more important to me at this moment than you." He looked around himself. "Especially in this place." He found another smile. "When I was at my lowest, it was you who came with me rather than let me wander alone in my pain."

"Because I love you." She said simply.

"And I love you in equal measure." Lucias bent down, caught her lips and kissed her softly and lovingly. "I'll figure something out, Zamyael. I promise you. Raziel will never know."

Zamyael, closing her eyes in relief, laid her head against Lucias' chest once more. "Thank you, my Lord. I shall never forget your kindness."

"It is a debt long overdue repaid."

-43-

(Raziel flinches as she listens to this last part. I know she feels betrayed. Not because Zamyael had possibly birthed the child of another. But because she hadn't trusted Raziel enough to ask her for her help or forgiveness.

(Never mind my father's classification to Zamyael as his only true hearted wife.

(She had, instead, gone to Lucias.

(This is a trespass that I know, by the buzz of her thoughts, she will not forgive. I hope, as I think ahead to the rest of my tale, that I might protect Zam.

(Even now, I know my desire to do so is a foolish proposition.)

-44-

Loki was surprised when he suddenly felt Lord Lucias' presence, which had been absent for far too long, in Eden. He swiftly slithered away from the tree with the odd red leaves and strange and low hanging yellow gourds and, when he was no longer within Adam's sight, changed himself into his own form from that of a serpent to walk swiftly in the direction from which his Lord silently called him.

When Loki saw Lord Lucias, he smiled.

He was sitting on a large stone with one leg pulled against him and his long arms wrapped around it. His profile was to Loki. His gaze was held in the direction of a beautiful flower garden. He wore a soft, tender expression.

Loki thought he looked peaceful.

In these days, when Lord Lucias never seemed to be able to find serenity, Loki was glad for it.

When he reached Lord Lucias he raised his hand to clap him on the back and, instead, set it tenderly on his shoulder. Still looking at the flower garden, Lord Lucias allowed his smile to broaden. He raised one of his own hands and placed it upon Loki's.

"It is beautiful here." Lord Lucias' voice seemingly came from far away. He squeezed Loki's hand and then allowed his own to fall back to his leg to, once again, entwine his long fingers. "Peaceful."

"It is peaceful."

Lord Lucias turned his gaze upward to hold Loki's own. His brown eyes seemed troubled. "How goes your task?"

"Adam is weakening. Once Eve is here, I give it little to no time." He shrugged

"Good." Lord Lucias nodded. "But I need your help with something other than tormenting the poor ape for the time being."

"Anything." Loki smiled at him. "Name it."

Lord Lucias nodded and looked away. "I was hoping you would say that."

He sighed and, reluctantly, lowered his leg and stood.

"I need you to stay with Raziel." Loki watched as he hurriedly turned his gaze away. "For three sun cycles. Maybe longer."

"What?" Loki started at this. His stomach churned. "Why? Have I done something to displease you?"

"Never think it." Lord Lucias returned his gaze to Loki. His eyes studied Loki's face. His expression was kind and his regard was warm. Yet his eyes were still smoldering with some unpleasant thought which Loki could neither read nor understand. "I need to borrow Zamyael and the only way I can ask for her aide is to trade your service to Raziel."

"She came looking for you." Loki heard the anger, distaste and jealously in his own voice. He didn't want to serve Lady Raziel in Lord Lucias' stead. Not even for sixty shifts. Let alone for a span of sun cycles.

He was Lord Lucias' servant. And he had ever been proud to be chosen to be so.

Lord Lucias nodded. "She found me."

"She seemed upset." Loki swallowed back his displeasure. He had no doubt in his mind that Zamyael was responsible for this farce. For the moment, he loathed her for it.

"She was." Lord Lucias nodded. "But it isn't something you need to dwell on."

"I didn't tell Lady Raziel." Loki assured him. "I thought it best to get your counsel before I did."

"Thank you." Lord Lucias raised his hand and set it upon Loki's shoulder. He held it there, his eyes dancing over Loki's face. He must have sensed Loki's displeasure because he was obviously trying to determine how deep it ran. "I'd like to speak with Raziel myself about borrowing Zam. I intend to leave that part out of it."

"She shouldn't keep secrets from her Mistress." Loki snapped.

"That's for me to worry about." Lord Lucias' brow furrowed. "Why are you angry?"

Loki sighed, rolled his eyes and looked away. How could he tell him he felt abandoned by him? Or that the abandonment was painful?

"Loki?" Lord Lucias' eyes were like ants crawling over every inch of his face; scratching and nipping with each step they took.

Finally, Loki was unable to take any more of it. In a hard, growling voice he snapped, "Why can't Sappharon aide Lady Raziel? Why must it be me? I've done everything you've ever asked of me without compunction or complaint. I'd rather bed you—if that's what you require of me—than serve that cunt!"

Lord Lucias recoiled from this. His expression was a study in surprise. Both from the sentiment and his offense with Loki's mortal obscenity. His dark eyes were slightly rounded and his lips were slightly parted. His nostrils flared outward for a moment—but only for a moment. When he spoke, his voice was calm. This only served to infuriate Loki all the more.

"If you would rather I send Sappharon than I shall. But I need to send someone I can rely on. I trust you more than I do her. If you would prefer I put her in my counsel over you—"

"No." Loki shook his head and let out a long, tired sigh. He would rather himself be Lord Lucias' personal spy than Sappharon. "You must think me a spoiled child."

"No."

His mind at ease, Loki whispered. "Is Zamyael going to be alright?"

"That's Moira's business." Lord Lucias muttered. "By her will, yes. But I must make sacrifice to her for it to be so. Even if I do there is no guarantee." He shrugged his shoulders. "Her hand only reaches so far."

Loki shivered at this.

What would the Goddess of the Fates require from the Father of the Hells in repayment for the protection of another Goddess' demon? And knowing such a favor still may not aide Zamyael, what terrible thing was Zamyael hiding from Raziel that it should be so?

"Things with Zamyael are that ill?"

Lord Lucias nodded. Loki turned to face him and, seeing his frown, shivered once again.

"I'm sorry." Loki shook his head. "For calling the mother of your children a cunt." Lord Lucias gave him a tight, understanding smile. "I wish I could help."

"You *can* help." He smiled sadly at Loki. "Stay with Raziel with no further complaint."

Loki nodded and forced himself to smile in return. "Yes, my Lord."

"Thank you." He leaned forward and kissed Loki's cheek.

Strangely, at least to Loki, Loki took no offense to this rare show of affection.

"Finish up here and then report to Raziel's apartment. I'll let her know that you'll be there in but a few days."

Loki was not even given time to respond. With his final word, Lord Lucias simply vanished.

-45-

Moira frowned slightly at the knock on the door.

It was late and she was in no mood for visitors. She had just had to unstring the tapestry of her predictions for the entire human race due to the King of Lords and Lord Regent Lucias' damn barter over their Divine Plan.

She hoped to at least have a basic history restrung before Apollo rode the sky with the morning star.

When she answered the door, she felt her brow furrow. Lord Lucias had never, in the entire course of her life, paid her a visit.

"My Lord." She said, backing away as she pulled the door open to grant him entry. "Please. Come in."

Lord Lucias gave her a tight smile as he stepped through the open doorway. He looked swiftly around, taking his measure of her personal belongings, before turning to Moira with his arms crossed tightly over his chest. "I need to make barter with you."

Moira felt her brow rise. "With me?"

"Yes." He nodded. "Are you willing to make terms?"

"My Lord Regent . . ." Moira felt her brow furrowing. "Whatever you have need from me I shall gladly give you without the need for barter."

"I need you to cease meddling in Zamyael's business from this day forward."

Moira started. Her very purpose was to meddle in other people's business.

"I can't—have you spoken to the King of Lords about this?"

She swallowed. Hard.

The last thing she wanted was to be in Lord Lucias' bad graces.

But this request was something she could not concede to without permission from the King of Lords. To assist Zamyael at Lord Lucias' bidding was one thing. But to stay out of her business altogether? And from that day forward? This was an entirely different proposition.

"I have no intention of speaking with Noliminan about this." Lord Lucias said. His expression grew extremely stern. Moira felt herself shiver. "I am not issuing you a direct order and so I do not *need* to speak with Noliminan about it. I am merely asking to barter with you for a favor."

"My Lord, I—"

"I expect the price for such a request to be high, Moira." His tone softened and he unfolded his arms. "I am willing to meet your required payment."

Moira shook her head and looked to the mess of the tapestry she had been in the process of restringing.

"I . . ." She cleared her throat. "I could use some help with the speaking apes."

Lord Lucias gave her a tight smile in recognition of her use of his term of endearment toward the humans. "What type of help?"

"Eventually they will need a God to live among them." Moira replied, turning to meet Lord Lucias' gaze. "My Lord, this can be a powerful race if given the opportunity."

"They are non-magical entities." Lord Lucias replied, his expression impossible to read. "What power do you perceive they might have?"

Moira shook her head. She wasn't, yet, sure. But she said, "I want you to create a powerful soul." She couldn't meet Lord Lucias' gaze. What she was asking for was blasphemy. "The most powerful soul of all other souls."

"A God?"

"Yes." Moira nodded and raised her gaze again. "But not just *any* God. I want a God to be born in the image of the humans who has the power to destroy worlds if the inhabitants of those worlds act in such a way that destruction is required."

"A God who can bring about an apocalypse?"

"Yes, my Lord." Moira nodded. "A God with that power—"

"Could be born to live among any race at any time without detection." Lord Lucias sighed.

"Just so, my Lord."

"If I were to give you such a God, Moira," Lord Lucias said, his eyes narrowed, "it would be with the understanding that you do not meddle in this God's business. You do understand? A God this powerful cannot be controlled by anyone but me and Noliminan. Not even by you."

"My only request would be to put the God into play when it is required. Beyond that, the God would have to make up his own mind in regard to whether or not he uses his powers based on his own personal experiences."

Lord Lucias considered Moira for a long moment. Finally, however, he nodded. "Stay out of Zamyael's business and I will give you such a God. But *I* will choose when he is to be born among the mortals. Until then, he remains in the Guf with Gabriel and no one else is made aware of his existence."

"I agree with those terms, my Lord."

"Very well, Moira." Lord Lucias held out his hand. Moira looked at it for a long moment before reaching forward and grasping his wrist. As Lord Lucias wrapped his own fingers around Moira's wrist, the magic of their promises to one another joined them together as one and their barter was officially sealed.

-46-

I watched with dire fascination as Noliminan looked up from his desk, frowning as his gaze fell upon Lucias' face. He wore an expression which Noliminan did not much seem to care for. It was tight and his dark eyes were blazing.

"Lucias? He lowered his quill, seeming to prepare himself for anything. "It's late. What do you need from me at this time of night?"

Lucias shook his head. He held both hands out, almost as if in supplication. Noliminan watched as his expression softened slightly and his eyes darted, almost nervously, over Noliminan's face. "Peace?"

"Peace?" Noliminan's brow furrowed as he crossed his arms over his chest. "I didn't realize we are at war."

Lucias shook his head.

"We're not, but . . ." He raised his gaze and gave Noliminan a tired smile. "I've come to advise you of what I believe fundamentally to be an unavoidable truth."

"Oh?"

"I fear that I . . ." Noliminan was frowning as Lucias' cheeks flushed pink. "I'm ill equipped to speak of this outright."

"Luci?" He stood and slipped around his desk. He raised his hand and set it upon Lucias' shoulder. Lucias raised his dark eyes upward and met Noliminan's gaze. "Whatever you must say to me I must hear."

He nodded and looked swiftly away. "Whatever I must say to you?"

"Yes." Noliminan sighed. "I know we have our arguments. But arguments are the extent of what they are."

Lucias nodded. "I fear that I'm . . ."

He shivered and lowered his gaze.

I shivered with him.

"I fear that I'm in the family way."

Lucias? Pregnant?

I stumbled backward upon hearing this news. Not as much from surprise as from understanding.

If I had been paying even the smallest bit of attention to Lucias or the events that allowed me to be standing in this room now, watching the pair of them, I would have seen this coming.

But I hadn't been. I suddenly felt like an unobservant fool.

Noliminan merely blinked. He lowered himself onto his desk, crossing his arms over his chest as he did so. "I suspected as much."

Lucias bit his top lip, swallowed, and raised his gaze. "You and I haven't . . . And you're the only one who I've ever allowed to . . ."

"I believe you." Noliminan sighed. "I've felt Azrael around you." He muttered, as his eyes fell right upon me. That he would know exactly where my presence lingered in the room caused me to shiver again. "I'm assuming your child has just been slow to kindle."

"Slow to kindle?" Lucias shook his head. "Nol—it's been hundreds of thousands of sun cycles!"

Noliminan sighed. "A child such as ours wouldn't come until it was time for him to come."

"That's just . . ." Lucias shook his head. "Madness!"

Noliminan shrugged. "Any baby you and I have created together will be powerful. It's a child who would bide his time until he was needed."

His eyes shifted away. I saw, before they did, an old, nostalgic pain.

I worry on what that look meant to this very day.

"You promised Moira you would put him into play."

"I—" Lucias shook his head. "How do you know?"

"Why else would he choose now to make himself known?" King Noliminan smiled sadly at him and shrugged. "I'm not angry, Lucias."

"But you're not happy either."

"Yes." He leaned forward and sat his hand upon Lucias' cheek. "I am. I'm simply . . ." He shrugged. "Afraid."

"I didn't tell Moira the child is ours. And I made her promise that she would allow the child his own fate." Lucias assured him. "She's not to direct him."

"Good."

"In what manner would you tell the Council?" Lucias asked, his gaze averted. From what I know of my father, he would prefer to keep this child a secret from the likes of Hades and Odin.

"We are *not* to tell the Council." Noliminan shook his head. "No one must know about this. Not until it's time that it be known." His eyes searched Lucias'. "We must put him with the Quorum. Lest someone use him for ill gain." He lowered his gaze. "Zadkiel would be the perfect solution. And Azrael. We already have an excuse for keeping them out of sight."

"My Gods, Nol." Lucias growled at him. "That is unforgivably cruel."

"This is why I haven't allowed you to interfere where they are concerned." Noliminan corrected him. "Their punishment will deem that they aren't called into question. Zadkiel has been exiled, for all intents and purposes, and Azrael has been forced to eliminate his corporeal body but for at his cottage unless he is on task."

"Nol . . . ?"

"I demand your supplication, Lucias. If the Council learns about him then they will use him for ill will."

"Yes, but—"

"For once in your life," Noliminan sighed. "Please. Just follow this request without questioning. I do know what I'm talking about on this particular point. The influence over this child must be limited until we are ready to put him into play lest someone use him for ill gain. When he is old enough, you may take him from Zadkiel and Azrael and select the education you believe will serve him, which he must learn from you."

Dear Gods.

I wouldn't share this thought with Raziel but I was helpless, in that moment, to do anything I understand.

Noliminan, who had insisted Zadkiel and I never be forgiven for our sins, was now manipulating his reasons to punish us so that Lucias would follow his orders with no further question!

"Yes, my Lord."

For a third time, I shivered. Aside from my complete understanding as to Noliminan's true reasons for not forgiving Zadkiel and I, I had never seen Lucias supplicate in such a complete and fundamental way.

I understood, as I watched the pair of them, that the politics of their relationship were a thing I would never, under any circumstances, comprehend.

"No arguments."

"Good." He gave Lucias a soft, loving smile. "Kostluk prilnth tat Luci?"

"Prilnth tat Luci?" Lucias raised his gaze and met Noliminan's own.

"Ta." He whispered, his hand extended toward Lucias. His eyes were blazing. Lucias opened his mouth to speak. Noliminan, smiling sadly at him, shook his head. "Hakteshu grof 'lasupita. En toppe dor ame."

Swallowing, Lucias reached for his hand. As he touched it, his form immediately changed.

Standing before me now was the first man and the first woman in the whole of existence.

And the Gods pray, I thought as I looked upon them, *what a beautiful pair they are to behold.*

He bent at the waist, his lips meeting hers as she wrapped her slender arms around his neck. He carried her to his bedchamber and gently lowered her onto his bed.

As he looked down upon her I fully realized the true depths of their regard for one another.

And as he took her with a tender restraint I had never before seen him master, I understood that they were not simply making love.

Rather, they were fighting desperately to rejoin their fractured souls.

-47-

Raguel lay back on her bed, her heart breaking.

Her bedchamber was connected to Noliminan's. And, though he never brought his menial conquests to their apartment, tonight he had brought a woman whom Raguel knew he adored.

She didn't need to hear the name of his lover to know who it was. There was only one woman that Noliminan would have cared enough about to have brought her into his own bed.

That woman was Lucias.

This wasn't the first time she had been forced to listen to them couple whilst lying lonely in her bed. And, she knew that, even if their couplings were scattered and rare, it wouldn't be the last.

But this time, for some reason she couldn't fathom even within her own mind, hurt worse than all of the rest.

Needing to seek comfort, she slipped out of her bed and found a dress she knew she looked pleasing in. She then made her way to the one man she knew coveted her for who and what she was and who would never turn her away if she were brave enough to approach him.

Standing before Michael's cottage, it took every ounce of her courage to raise her hand. But she did, and she forced herself to knock.

When he opened the door, it was with an irritated scowl. A scowl which immediately turned into a surprise grimace.

Clearly, he hadn't expected her to be standing on the other side of his door at this time of night.

"Your Grace?" His voice was gentle, yet heavy with his surprise.

"May I come in, Michael?" She asked, lowering her gaze.

"Of course you may." He stepped back, pulling the door open with him.

Raguel had never visited him at his cottage. As she stepped in, the scent of him—which was that of rain on the meadow—overwhelmed her. With it was the love she had buried for him and pushed deep into her soul lest they both be punished for giving into their abandon.

She didn't say anything to him. Rather, as he closed the door, she stepped toward him. She flew her arms around his neck and stood on her toes so that she might pull him downward and press her lips against his.

She felt him moan against her lips. She felt the hunger he had for her dance against her stomach.

But rather than taking what she offered him, he shook his head, his lips still locked to hers, and then, almost desperately, pushed her gently away.

"I . . ." His tone was thick with his desire for her. "Please, your Grace . . . I beg it of you that you do not tempt me . . . I must . . . No."

She started. Her eyes grew wide as she looked up at his face. His expression was painfully regretful. But it was also set and determined.

"You are my Master's wife." He whispered this unforgivable explanation. "We would both be damned."

"Then we are both damned." She cried, desperate, the tears jumping into her eyes.

He swallowed and looked away. The pain upon his features was palpable.

"No." He muttered. "I'm not . . ."

He turned his back to her then.

This hurt worse than his pushing her away.

"He's ordered that I remain chaste." His dark eyes returned to hers as he looked over his shoulder. "Even if I were to break that vow, it could never be with his wife."

"Michael . . . ?"

"No, my Lady." He whispered, looking away again. "If you were anyone else but his *wife* . . ."

Shaking her head in desperation, she turned away from him. Knowing Michael well enough that she would not be able to tempt him to break his vow, she left him to find another brand of solace.

-48-

Loki wasn't even certain what he needed to pack. Would he be able to return to the privacy of his own home should he require time to himself?

Shaking his head, he decided he didn't care. If he needed time to himself he would take it. Lady Raziel be damned.

He started grabbing everything he thought he would need and stuffing it into his bag. He was just ready to snap it shut when he heard a knock upon the door. Surprised, he looked at the hourglass he kept in his room and frowned.

Judging by the sands that had passed it was extremely late.

Knowing better than that Sappharon would answer the door, he made his way through the apartment and opened it himself. When he saw who stood on the other side he was helpless to do anything but blink.

"Your Grace?"

Her eyes puffy and red from crying, Raguel wrung her hands.

"I know Lucias isn't here." She said. "May I come in?"

"Of course." He shrugged and stepped out of her way. "Can I get you a drink?"

"No." She shook her head. As she did so, she raised her gaze. It was then that he saw the true depth of her pain. "Loki, may I ask you a question?"

"Of course, met paken." He replied, reaching for her hair and allowing it to run through his fingers. It was just as soft as he had always imagined it to be and, though her face was puffy and her eyes red, he wanted her completely. "You may ask anything of me."

She swallowed, nodded, and lowered her gaze. "Am I . . . ?"

He waited, his concern growing for her with every shift of the shadows.

"Am I pretty?" She whispered.

"Oh, dear Lady." He sighed. "No."

She flinched.

"You are not merely pretty. You are breathtakingly beautiful."

She braved to meet his gaze then. Her eyes were round and hopeful. "You aren't just saying that to be kind to me?"

"Raguel, no." He shook his head and cupped her cheek with his hand. As he did so, he stepped toward her and pressed against her. "Can you not feel for yourself that I desire you?"

She let out a sorrowful laugh. It was followed by a smile. "Yes."

"Where is this self-doubt coming from?" He asked as he stepped away. He didn't want to offend her.

"Noliminan is bedding—" She stopped herself, blinking.

It seemed to Loki that she had surprised herself by sharing such intimate information with him. He didn't understand why. She had recently told him that her husband was bedding Raziel again. And she had felt no remorse for having done so. He wondered who this new affair must be to cause her such angst.

"And then . . ." She laughed again. "It doesn't matter."

"Obviously it does."

"I know you do not love me." She muttered.

"I love you."

"As a friend." She smiled softly.

He couldn't deny that. But it had been her who had set the boundaries of their relationship. Not him. So he nodded.

"But perhaps . . . ? Would you be willing to add another goose to your gaggle?"

Throwing back his head and laughing loud and strong he wrapped his arms around her. When he recovered from the bout of humor which had overcome him he lowered his face into her hair and nodded.

"Your Grace," he grinned, "yours are feathers I have long desired to ruffle."

-49-

Lucias willed himself to Raziel's door and knocked. He seemed pleased that Loki was the one to receive him.

"Lord Regent Lucias." Lord Loki's cocky grin was the medicine he needed. His heart felt lighter. "Lady Raziel's gone to bed for the night. But I can rouse her if—?"

"No." He shook his head. "Are you tired? Or will you sit with me for a moment and palaver?"

"I can sit with you." Lord Loki replied, running his hand through his moppish brown hair. I smiled to myself as I heard Lucias make a mental note to tell the lad to cut it. He thought Lord Loki's hair was getting too long.

"Come in." He looked to the bar. "Scotch?"

"Not tonight, met paken."

Lord Loki gave him a strange smile. "Okay."

"I've finished my barter with Moira." He lowered his gaze as he slid into Raziel's favorite chair.

"Good." Lord Loki replied, surprised. "That was fast."

"By necessity." Lucias looked exhausted. "I'm going to go away for a while, Loki."

Lord Loki frowned, but nodded.

"I'll be at the castle on Anticata if you need me." He forced himself to smile. "I don't want you to tell anyone this, though."

"What if the King of Lords asks me where you are?"

I watched in silent fascination as Lucias' brow furrowed at the question. He thought on his answer for a moment before speaking.

When he did answer, his motivation was all too clear in my mind. He wanted to know how Lord Loki would react to him. He wanted to know if Lord Loki would be jealous if he knew Lucias had gone to King Noliminan as a woman.

"Loki." He lowered his gaze. "You should know that I went to him."

"My Lord?" Lord Loki looked confused.

I found this endearing. Lord Loki seemed to always be confused by Lucias and his traits and desires.

"As a woman." His smile was tight. "I'm pregnant. And he needed to be told this."

Lord Loki flinched backward.

Being privy to his thoughts I understood at once that he was recalling Queen Raguel's admission that she had come to him because King Noliminan was bedding someone new.

He didn't share this, however, and I kenned by my father's expression that he would have given everything and all to know what Lord Loki thought about his admission.

But Lord Loki, wanting to protect Queen Raguel, would not share his true feelings. Even the small bit of knowledge that he had realized it was Lucias, in his woman form, that had so upset Queen Raguel seemed a secret he must share with no one but her.

Why else would she have been so damned upset? Lord Loki thought, *I mean,* who *else could it have been who could have upset Raguel enough to risk Noliminan's wrath by straying from his bed?*

Especially into mine! When he already mistrusts me due to my lascivious nature and my gaggle.

How stupid have I been? How blind?

Ah, my Queen, forgive me for not understanding the true extent of your painful plea for help.

"The King of Lords?"

"Ta." He sighed. "I was born a woman. And quite honestly it's the form I prefer. When I know I will be alone—when you and Sappharon are both gone for the night—it is the form I wear."

Lord Loki's eyes danced over his face.

My Gods, he thought as he looked into Lucias' eyes. *If you are this handsome as a man, how beautiful would he have made you in your true female essence.*

The thought alone brought on a rush of restless curiosity. He looked into Lucias' eyes and he saw, for the first time, the softness, the affection and the desire which had been there all along.

He immediately amended his way of thinking about Lucias. Knowing female was the form Lucias preferred, he would ever, thereafter, think of Lucias only as a Lady.

I understood he did this for two reasons.

The first is that Theasis had once told him that she loathed it when people insisted upon speaking or thinking of her in the male vernacular. And the second was that it allowed him to reconcile his more tender regard toward Lucias in his own mind.

If he thought of Lucias as Lady Lucias, then he would let his adoration and desire take hold.

Given he is my father, and though I agree with Lady Theasis and would generally do the same, in this instance I find I cannot, for reasons which should be clear, think of Lucias as a woman.

"We have been lovers from the beginning. When I didn't catch pregnant we decided we had to come up with other ways to propagate. He demanded, then, that I change my essence." He lowered his gaze, embarrassed by this admission. "I loathed it. But I understood his designs. So I did."

He looked timidly upward. Seeing only understanding in Lord Loki's eyes, he sighed.

"Thus, Raziel and Zamyael." He lowered his gaze again. "I hadn't been with him in quite some time. So the pregnancy has taken me rather by surprise."

Lord Loki cleared his throat. "Pregnant?"

"Yes." Lucias sighed. "This is not a secret you can share, Loki. You must promise me you will speak of it to no one aside Nol, himself."

Lord Loki gave him a stiff nod. "What, exactly, should I tell him if he comes looking for you?"

"If he doesn't ask about the baby?" Lucias gave him a teasing smile. "Tell him if he had cared he would have asked about the child and otherwise he can shove his requests up his ass."

Lord Loki paled.

This was a phrase Lord Loki had used once in front of Lucias, but he'd never before heard Lucias speak thusly. Generally when he was angry he reverted to the old words and Lord Loki didn't understand what he was saying half of the time. Hearing Lucias repeat this particular phrase, therefore, seemed somehow vulgar to him.

Especially given Lucias was now Lady Lucias in his mind. A Lady would never tell someone to shove anything up their ass.

Yet, he could forgive Lucias this trespass as it had clearly been intended to convey his true desire that he would be angry with Noliminan if he showed no interest in the child growing within Lucias' womb.

"Is this what you truly ask of me?"

"It is an order, Loki." Lucias said, not meaning it. He gave Lord Loki a smile which he hoped his apprentice understood meant his statement should be taken the joke that it was. Being privy to Lord Loki's thoughts I knew he didn't take it this way. He thought Lucias was being serious. "All you need tell him is that I ordered you not to disclose my whereabouts."

"As you will me." Lord Loki replied, staring at his hands, which were folded on his lap.

"Are you up for a game of storming stones?"

"Yes." Lord Loki looked upward and smiled. He wanted to play a game far more important than the stones. But he would take from Lucias what Lucias would give him. "I covet spending time with you before you leave me."

"Good." Lucias grinned. "I covet spending time with you as well."

-50-

Michael's soul beat with discord as he slipped through the door of King Noliminan's apartment and made his way through the sitting room to the ornate glass doors leading to the patio. He knew King Noliminan and Raphael were not at home and that this was a rare chance to make right what he had gotten horribly wrong.

When he saw her standing against the marble railing, looking over the edge upon one of the worlds below, he was no longer the master of his own emotions.

He ran toward her, swallowing the rush of desire for her which seemed to overtake him. When he reached her, he pressed himself against her back as he swept her into his arms and forced her to turn to face him.

His lips sought and immediately found hers. Her mouth was, at first, soft and yielding but then, inexplicably to him, became drawn and hard.

"Your Grace . . ." He whispered, looking down into her beautiful, emerald green eyes. "Will you forgive me? Will you come to me now?"

"Michael . . ." Her eyes were dancing over his face. The desire he had always found within them for him was burning. "Oh, min 'lasupita."

He closed his eyes and tried to kiss her again. As he did so, she raised her hands to his chest and gently pushed him away.

"No, Michael." She sighed. Her tone was sad. Almost regretful. "I cannot. You had the right of things."

"I didn't . . ."

"You did."

"I will defy him for you!"

An expression shadowed Queen Raguel's face that echoed a sadness deep within her. "After speaking with you, I found myself seeking the bed of another."

The pain which consumed him was overwhelming.

But it was not borne simply from her rejection. It was also from the thought that, when he had turned her away, she had sought solace in the arms of another.

"I do not understand, your Grace." He whispered. "There is another who commands your heart?"

"No." She sighed. "Merely a friend. But as I left his bed I understood too poignantly that laying with him had been a mistake." Her smile was thin. "But, Michael, laying with you would be an even greater one. Because you I do love. And once yours, I could never return to Noliminan."

"Then I shall hide you!" He cried. "I will protect you! Come with me! We will both leave and—"

"And go where?" She asked, her eyes trailing over his features. "Noliminan is the creator of all things. There is nowhere we can hide from him. He isn't going to let either one of us simply walk away."

"But he doesn't love either one of us!"

"No." She agreed. "He doesn't." Then, pushing him away, "But we *are* his property. And you've seen for yourself how he treats his damaged goods. Metatron would be unable to rest until we were brought before him and punished."

"I would beg Metatron to—"

"Where did begging get Zadkiel?" She tried to make him see reason. "Where did it get Camael? Or Metatron, himself, for that matter?"

Michael flinched.

"Love me enough to leave me alone." She begged of him, her green eyes memorizing his face. "Love me enough that you might live. You know as well as I do that, if he learned that we have even considered consummating our desire for one another, it will not be merely castration that will be your fate."

"I don't care." He shook his head. "Let him tear me limb from limb. One night with you would sate me for the rest of my days."

"No." She sighed. "It wouldn't. And I'd rather know you are still alive and that I cannot have you than that you perished at Zadkiel's hand because of me."

"Your Grace, I beg it of you!" He fell upon one knee and reached for her hand. He searched every line of her beautiful face to commit the moment that he was alone with her, pleading for her, to his memory. "Do not turn me away."

"I'm afraid," she whispered as she looked upward and toward the doors behind him, "that I have no choice." She swallowed. "And that he is here. So best you stand and step away from me before he comes through those doors and sees you groveling at my feet."

Michael felt as if he had been slapped by those words. Yet, when he heard King Noliminan barking commands at Raphael, he understood the sense of them.

He rose to his feet, looking over his shoulder toward the sound of them and then turned to face her before bolting away from her, through the door leading to King Noliminan's bedchamber. There was a little known passage way which was built behind a tapestry in the wall that he could use to escape without being seen.

As he reached the door, he turned to give her one last, regretful smile. Before he left her he said the words that he had longed to share with her for the full of his adult life. "I love you, Raguel."

She gave him a sad, tired smile before returning her attentions to the marble railing and whatever world spun below them which held her captivation.

-51-

Raziel hated being summoned by Noliminan. It was her contention that, if he wanted to speak with her, he could just as easily come to her living quarters as she could to his. But Raphael had warned her of Noliminan's mood and so, despite her discontentment, she now stood in Noliminan's sitting room awaiting his demanded audience.

The least he could do when he does demand my ear is to be available when I show.

Raziel's time had grown of import, as of late, given Lucias and Zamyael had been missing for three waning moons.

She was loathe to admit it, but she wanted Zamyael back.

She had no true hearted complaints about Loki's service. But he just wasn't Zamyael. He didn't know Raziel's moods or what was important to her and what was not.

Because Raziel was the first line of defense when it came to the Hells bound Gods and their requests, she didn't find the need to listen to every single compliant which was raised. Nor did she feel as though she owed anyone an explanation when they disagreed with her orders or views. Loki, used to announcing all audiences to Lucias due to the import when it raised to Lucias' level, had yet to learn that there were times when it was permissible to send someone away.

As if sensing Raziel's discontentment, Loki shifted uneasily at her side. Raziel let out a frustrated sigh at this and gently set her hand upon Loki's arm. It wasn't Loki's fault that Lucias had traded his service for Zamyael's. Raziel needed to mark well her attentions toward the youngling lest she hurt Loki's feelings.

If she succeeded Lucias' crown, as she eventually intended to do, she would need Loki's help in the future.

Finally, after what seemed to Raziel an extremely rude and unreasonable amount of time, Noliminan stepped into the hallway and began walking toward them. His eyes flicked first to Raziel and then landed, furiously, upon Loki. He offered neither of them a smile.

"Thank you for coming to see me."

"Thank you for making me wait." Raziel rebutted. "How might I serve you?"

"I can't seem to find Lucias." Noliminan was still glaring at Loki "He's been missing for months. Do you know where he is?"

"Yes, your Grace." Loki responded. Raziel marked that Loki didn't answer the underlying question, however, and she was forced to hold back a smile as she watched Noliminan waiting impatiently for him to do so.

Finally, "Well?"

"I told you that I do." Loki shrugged. "Should I make you a hat so you might wear it for the occasion?"

To this, Raziel was not able to hold back her bray of spitting laughter. Noliminan, obviously incensed, snapped his gaze to Raziel and then back to Loki. "Where *is* he?"

"I'm not at liberty to say, your Grace." Loki shrugged again.

Noliminan's nostrils flared wide at this. "*Why* can't you say?"

Loki looked this way and that, his eyes darting down the hallway, around the sitting room and then, finally landing on Noliminan. He stepped forward, placed his hand at the side of his mouth to curve his fingers around his lips and whispered. "Because, your Grace. It's a secret."

"Damn it, Loki!" Noliminan growled at him, pushing him away. "I am in no mood for your childishness! I demand to see Lucias! Now!"

Loki shrugged his shoulders again. But he made no response and this seemed to anger Noliminan all the more.

"Well?"

"What do you want me to do about it, your Grace?" Loki asked, his voice calm and his tone reasonable. "I'm *his* servant— not the other way round. I can't order him to appear before you if he doesn't want to do so."

"Go and tell him I demand to see him." Noliminan said through gritted teeth.

"I cannot."

"You cannot?" Noliminan growled, his face flushing red with his rage.

Raziel swiftly took a step away from them both. She had been on the other end of such a rage before and it hadn't boded well for her. She hoped, desperately, that Loki understood what he was up against and would back down swiftly.

Her hope, however, was in vain.

"How dare you tell me no!"

"I'm not the one telling you no, your Grace." Loki's voice was chanting, melodic. "Lord Regent Lucias is." He shrugged again. "I'm merely following his orders, which are to tell you that had you really cared about him then you would have asked me about the baby rather than his whereabouts. Since you chose not to, I have been ordered to tell you to take whatever demand you have of him and stick it straight up your—"

Noliminan exploded in his rage. The violence of the brilliant tawny light and the force of the explosion cut off Loki's last word so Raziel could not hear it—though she watched in utter horror as his lips formed around it.

She watched in greater horror still as Noliminan reformed himself and backhanded Loki so hard that the youngling was literally blown off of his feet toward the apartment's main door— which was torn off of its hinges upon impact—and out into the main hallway.

A loud boom echoed around Raziel and Noliminan, followed by a second and third thud as Loki hit the wall and then the floor.

Raziel, frozen where she stood, stared through the now open doorway to the limp, crumpled body of her temporary servant where he had landed on the cold marble of the floor.

The wall above Loki had folded in half over the place where he had hit it and the floor, itself, bowed in a great circle beneath him. Deep cracks spiraled outward along the full width of the hall and for a good ten feet in either direction.

Loki's arm twitched horrifically backward at the elbow, startling Raziel from her dumbfounded immobility. She ran swiftly forward and fell upon her knees beside him. She pulled the youngling into her arms and snapped her own head backward so she was glaring at Noliminan over her shoulder.

Noliminan, still seething, began walking toward them.

"Noliminan! Come to your senses!"

Noliminan, not expecting defiance from this quarter after such a display of his power, snapped his gaze to Raziel. His light brown eyes narrowed slightly and his nostrils flared outward again. Raziel steeled herself for the inevitable flailing which never came.

Instead, Noliminan turned angrily on his heels, let out a deafening growl and stalked moodily back down the hallway and into the room from which he had first appeared. Once he was gone, Raziel returned her attention to Loki, ignoring the hesitant opening of doors and curious, frightened faces poking out from them in either direction of the hallway within which they now sat.

"You're as big a fool as your Master." Raziel muttered as she scooped Loki's unconscious, broken body into her arms to hold him tight at her chest.

Standing, she willed them both to Zamyael's room and dragged the weight of Loki with great effort to her demon's bed. She pulled the youngling upon it, flinching at the loud cracking and popping of bones as she forced Loki's body to lay flat so it could heal itself.

She ran her hand gently along each limb, realizing the entire left side of Loki's body had been shattered.

She mended what she could with her magic and then lowered herself onto the bed so she could sit beside him. A feeling of utter dread overwhelmed her as her eyes trailed from Loki's broken face to the toe of his battered leather boot. She reached forward to take the boot off of the broken foot which it housed within it and thought better of it. No sense in causing any more unnecessary pain than Loki would already, no doubt, feel.

It was then, as Raziel's eyes trailed over the youngling, that Loki's words finally struck her.

What had it been he had said?

If you would have cared then you would have asked about the baby.

That wasn't right. But it was close enough.

"Oh, Noliminan." Raziel muttered to herself. "You damn fool."

Given that Lucias had made it clear he would never, under any circumstances, supplicate sexually as a female, Raziel understood if he had—after all of these many, many years—extended such a courtesy to Noliminan, it had been offered as a final bridge toward the uneasy peace which had ever existed between the pair of them.

If Noliminan had, thereafter, disavowed Lucias' attempts, then the writing was on the wall.

The end, Raziel understood all too well, was here.

Part Three:
Love and War

-1-

Noliminan stood outside of Raziel's door wearing an impatient frown. When my mother answered, it was with a scowl. "Your Grace."

"How is he?"

"Still unconscious." Raziel replied, her gaze slightly lowered. "Was it truly necessary to strike the lad?"

"Yes." Noliminan frowned at her. He clearly felt no need to explain himself to Raziel.

Given Lord Loki was under my mother's care when he misbehaved, I knew—from Noliminan's conversation with Raphael—that Noliminan was just as angry with her for allowing such blatant disobedience as he was with Lord Loki for exhibiting it.

Had Raziel not found it necessary to laugh at Lord Loki's quips, perhaps Noliminan's rage would have boiled at a much slower rate. That she failed to recognize her part in Lord Loki's fate was, to him, a disconcerting display of disobedience.

"Regardless of Luke's orders that he not disclose his location, Loki had no call to speak to me as he did."

Raziel sighed and shook her head. "I know, but—"

"I will not discuss this matter with you, Raziel." Noliminan warned her in a tone which chilled me to the bones. "Where is Loki that I might heal him?"

Raziel swallowed. "In Zamyael's bedchamber."

Noliminan's brow furrowed. He had juxtaposed to Raphael that Zamyael must be staying with Lucias if Lord Loki was staying with Raziel. That the two had decided to switch their servants up, he complained to Raphael, made absolutely no sense to him. He supposed the only reason this could have come to be was because Luci must need the care of a woman to see her through the end stages of her pregnancy.

He opened Zamyael's door and frowned as his eyes danced over Lord Loki's battered body.

"Perhaps I have pushed things a bit too far, Azrael." He muttered to the room at large.

I, who am not used to being addressed directly when I am not in my corporeal form, started. I supposed Noliminan must know that—because Lord Loki was in the room with him—I was about. I will remember, in future, he had told Lucias that he had sensed me in the room after the pregnancy came to light.

Most likely, I finally understood, I was being pulled into the room when the baby growing inside Lucias was awake. It certainly explained my sudden undesirable ability to see the two of them in their privacy together.

"But you must concede the youngling had it coming to him."

Though I do not share this with Raziel, the immediate response which formulated in my mind was that I did not have to concede to anything of the sort.

Yes, Lord Loki had baited him. But he had done so only because he believed this is what Lucias wanted. He never would have spoken thusly to Noliminan otherwise. And, when he had done so, it was in a private setting. The only other souls, in his mind, who heard him were Raziel and Raphael.

I watched as Noliminan stepped forward and laid his hand on Lord Loki's forehead to will his body to heal. He studied Lord Loki with keen interest as the bones reshaped themselves to their right.

His hand hovered over Lord Loki's ankle, which was still slightly bent, but he made no move to correct the issue. I suspect he believed it would do Lord Loki well to bear at least one scar which would remind him of what could happen to him when he disobeyed Noliminan's direct orders.

He has a distasteful habit of leaving just that one mindful scar.

After examining Lord Loki's ankle, his hand returned to his forehead. He laid it upon his brow and then muttered ancient words I shall not even attempt to slaughter with my pronunciation—and which I did not understand—under his breath. Whatever the words meant, they caused Lord Loki's breath to become deep and regular.

It was almost as if he were putting him in a deep, comforting sleep.

Satisfied that Lord Loki was righted, Noliminan turned abruptly around, stopping short after realizing he had nearly run down Raziel. He frowned at her, obviously put off that she had followed him so closely. "If he awakens, send me word at once. I shall be by to speak with him as swiftly as I can."

"To apologize?" Raziel asked, her fiery eyes burning with curiosity.

"I have nothing to apologize for." Noliminan snapped at her.

Raziel's lips parted as if she wanted to say something, but then snapped immediately shut. She shook her head and forced herself to smile. "Of course not."

"You and I still have business." He muttered. "It can wait until tomorrow. I will be by to speak with you first thing in the morning."

"Yes, your Grace."

Noliminan nodded at her and made his way out of Raziel's living quarters and into the hall. From there he stormed toward Lucias' abode, frowning at the demons he passed—it was their perspective from which I was able to watch him—in the hallways who sat in their waiting stances outside of their Masters' doors to guard them.

News had clearly reached their ears because they were all staring up at him with wide eyed fear and thoughts of understanding in regard to what, exactly, he could do to them.

If Lord Regent Lucias' apprentice wasn't safe, Noliminan wouldn't think twice about destroying any one of them.

Noliminan, as he ever did, ignored them.

When he reached Lucias' apartment, he let himself in without knocking. He made his way to the library, stopping short as he opened the door to find Sappharon sitting behind Lucias' desk and shuffling papers. Frowning at the irreverent creature he said, "I suppose you aren't going to tell me where your Master is hiding out, either."

"You would suppose right, your Grace." Sappharon didn't bother to raise her gaze. She never had been able to look

Noliminan in the eye. I know by his complaints to Raphael that this is just one of the many things he loathes about her.

What neither of them understand, but which I see all too clearly when I read the turn of her thoughts, is that her refusal to look at him has nothing to do with her fear of him. She doesn't fear him. She despises him.

And—this, too, must be said—with damned good and justifiable reason.

Sappharon, I must admit, is another one of those souls who I shall never pass judgment upon when the time for judging arrives.

"But I will deliver whatever message you may have for Lucias should I see her."

Noliminan's lips pursed at Sappharon's mention of Lucias' feminine essence. She, like Lord Loki, had amended her thoughts toward Lucias the moment that Lucias had admitted to her the preference to live in the female form. Clearly, this did not please the King of Lords. "I'd rather just write her a note."

"As you will, your Grace." She stood, her gaze still averted, and made her way around the desk. "If you'll leave it here, I'll see that she gets it this evening."

Noliminan nodded and watched with guarded curiosity as the strange little demon darted out of the room. Because Sappharon hovered on the opposite side of the door, spying upon him, I wasn't forced out of the room with her.

Rolling his eyes at the door, Noliminan shook his head and made his way to the other side of the desk. As he lowered himself into Lucias' chair, his eyes began darting over the paperwork Sappharon had been rifling through.

Buried beneath a document of no consequence he saw the blue print to his castle on Anticata. He froze for a moment before reaching for it and pulling it out from under the other papers. Reading the notes which were scribbled in various corners, his eyes widened.

The notes were cryptic. They were written in what was obviously a code. It was no code I know. If Noliminan knows it or not I have no idea. But, if not, then he could not—in the limited time he had before Sappharon would return—decipher it.

"What are you up to, tukte lolo?" He muttered to himself as he smoothed the parchment over the desk.

He shivered as he ran his finger over the square which represented Lucias' apartment. I suspect that he has many fond, and not so fond, memories associated with those rooms.

He raised his gaze and fell back into his chair.

"Whatever she's up to, Az, it will play out in its own time." He muttered, addressing me directly for the second time that evening. "In the meantime, how about we give the devil her space?"

He folded the blueprint and shoved it under the papers where it had originally been hidden.

Sappharon, who realized there was nothing worthwhile to spy on, made her way to her own room.

With her, I was forced to leave as well.

-2-

Lucias—very female and clearly pregnant—stared at the letter Noliminan had sent with a concerned, irritated frown. Seeing her so, despite the fact that Lucias is my father, I immediately amended my reference to her essence.

She was, very clearly, at peace wearing this form.

Given that, who am I to force her into corners which Noliminan has put her in for the majority of her life and from which she has momentarily found her freedom? She was, at the end of it all, victim to the same painful prison as was Zamyael.

This is not to say that anyone else understood that this was her preferred form. So it is that, even though she was living as *she* during the next few parts of my telling, others will think of her as *he*. Though the reality of the child growing in her womb was unknown to the majority, those few who were told of her state by either Lucias, herself, or Noliminan were under the belief that this was a planned pregnancy and that she had taken this form only for the purpose of the birth.

The only two she told that she prefers this form were Lord Loki and Sappharon. Her motivation for sharing this with Lord Loki has already been discussed. With Sappharon, she had felt that, given Lord Loki had been told, the one who had been longest in her servitude deserved the same courtesy.

The reason I am clarifying this for you now is so that you do not, later, become confused by the manner in which people consider her. Remember that my tale is told from their points of view. Not my own. So it is that when Zamyael sees her in her female essence, Zamyael is under the belief that she will revert to being a male after the child is born of her own volition. Therefore, when she thinks of Lucias, in her mind Lucias is still very much *he*.

But enough of this distraction for you, my dear mortal witness. It is time for me to return to the story itself.

The majority of the letter was filled with questions regarding their child. Yet, at the end of the letter, after the apologies and sentiments of concern, was troubling news regarding Lord Loki's misbehavior and the subsequent punishment that he faced.

"Sappharon." Lucias muttered as she raised her gaze to meet her brat's. "Are you certain Noliminan wrote this letter?"

"Ta, my Lady." She nodded, her long black hair—desperately in need of a wash and brushing—danced about her slender face.

Now is not the time to chastise the child about her grooming habits.

"He ordered me from your library and then wrote it. He told me to deliver it to you with no ado."

Lucias shook her head and lowered her gaze back to the parchment. I suspect she doubted very much that Noliminan had ordered anything of Sappharon. Everyone knew that Noliminan refused to talk with the demon unless talking was what was required. He wouldn't have wasted his words. "What exactly did he do to Loki?"

"Struck him." Sappharon shrugged. Lucias didn't miss the ghost of a smile which danced at the corners of her thick lips. I could tell by her expression that she didn't much care for that smile.

When she didn't expound, Lucias let out an irritated sigh through her teeth. "Struck him?"

"Yes, my Lady." Sappharon replied. Her expression hardened slightly. It was a good thing for her that it did. When Lucias heard the rest of it she was looking for anyone or anything to pay for Noliminan's temper tantrum.

Had Sappharon still been wearing her self-satisfied smirk, I know it would have been her face which took the brunt of Lucias' rage.

"He refused to tell Noliminan where you were. He hit Loki so hard that he flew through the door and into the hallway. By all accounts, he crumpled into a broken mass on the floor. Metatron told me that Noliminan healed him, but he hasn't awoken yet from the blow."

"When, exactly, did this take place?"

"Yesterday." Sappharon replied, her eyes now wide.

"And it took you until today to tell me?" Lucias raged at her. "What on which moon is the matter with you Sappharon? Loki is akin to being your brother! You should have come to me the barest shift of the shadows that you knew he was in trouble!"

"I did!" She cried. "My Lady, I swear! The moment after I read Noliminan's letter to you—"

"You read my letter?" She sprang forward, her hand flying. Though I know she regretted hitting Sappharon the moment that she heard the crack of her bone against the back of her hand, her rage made her helpless to do otherwise. "And then resealed it? To hide your treachery from me?"

"My Lady, I . . ."

Sappharon fell to her knees in immediate supplication. I could feel Lucias' guilt raging through her like a forest fire. She stepped backward, forcing herself to gain her composure lest she kick the brat.

"As soon as I knew I sought out one of your children to see if Raphael had shared the details of the news."

Lucias shook her head and spun away. I suspect she wanted nothing more than to destroy the demon for not coming to her straight away. "Leave me, Sappharon."

"Yes, my Lady."

When the brat left the room, Lucias raised her gaze to meet Zamyael's. She was watching her from the bed they shared wearing a tired, concerned frown. I watched Lucias' eyes narrow as she looked upon her, but she bit back any anger she might have shared. Lord Loki's punishment was not her fault. It was Lucias'. For having told him to disobey Noliminan should he be given a direct order.

When Zamyael spoke, her tones were docile. "You must calm yourself, Lucias."

Lucias looked swiftly away, biting back the words which rose to her tongue.

"Your responsibility right now is to the child in your belly." Her tones were reasonable. This only served to infuriate Lucias all the more. "Loki is in the best of hands. Raziel will take care of him."

"That may be." Lucias conceded. "But I must go see him."

"In your current state?" Zamyael asked, her raven brow rising over her coal black eye. "What will Raziel say when she sees you are truly a woman and not a man?"

Lucias shook her head. "Loki's wellbeing is far more important to me than Raziel's pride."

"My Lord," Zamyael sighed. "Forgive me, but it isn't. If you must visit Loki, at least cloak yourself in your other form. Even if you do not become it." She looked away, her expression taut. "Make no mistake. I love Raziel. But if she were to learn that you have supplicated to Noliminan by becoming male and you are now living as a woman—even just for the purpose of your pregnancy—she will use these facts against you should the time ever come when she must."

"Surely not." Lucias shook her head. Though I did not tell Raziel this as I relayed the story, I find it strange that Lucias seemed to be unwilling to believe that Raziel was as petty as all of that.

"Take my counsel, my Lord." Zamyael replied, still in docile tones. "Whether you believe my words or you do not. I beg it of you. Do not give her the upper hand. Not right now. Not while you are not in control of her."

Lucias thought about this for a moment and then nodded.

Zamyael blushed prettily at having her opinion—for once—be heard and respected.

Pregnancy, I thought as I looked upon the demon with a strange adoration which I did not recognize because it was foreign to me at the time, suited Zamyael just fine.

-3-

Raziel was conflicted in regard to her feelings as she opened the door to find Lucias standing on the other side. But, in keeping up her pretenses that her loyalties still lay with her Ruler rather than the ultimate King, she sprang forward, wrapped her arms around his neck and pressed her lips against Luke's own.

Lucias reciprocated the kiss, but began chuckling as he placed his hands upon Raziel's shoulders to push her gently away.

"I thought you left us!"

"Never think it." Lucias replied, smiling cautiously at her. "Where is Loki?"

"Sleeping." Raziel muttered. "In Zamyael's bedchamber."

Lucias nodded, kissed her forehead, and then pushed past her. Raziel followed on his heel, stopping at the door as Lucias slipped within and lowered himself into a chair at Loki's bedside. He reached toward the sleeping God, grasped his hand and squeezed it tightly.

"Oh Loki." Lucias sighed. "Forgive me."

"What have *you* done which begs forgiveness?" Raziel asked, very tentatively, not breeching the door frame. She wanted to know if there was something more to the argument between Lucias and Noliminan than what she already suspected existed.

She also wanted to know, if there was, how she could use this to her advantage.

"I told him to deny Noliminan's orders should he ask where I was." Lucias sighed. He raised his dark eyes and met Raziel's gaze. He looked much older than his years. Raziel wasn't exactly saddened by this. "I take it he obeyed me."

"He did." Raziel sighed and crossed her arms over her full breasts. "Did you really tell him to advise Noliminan to shove his orders up his ass?"

Lucias froze for a moment and met Raziel's gaze with a puzzled expression. "He didn't."

"He did." Raziel chuckled.

Lucias shook his head and let out the strange little whistle through his teeth which he is so damn fond of. "I was joking when I told him to do that."

"He obviously didn't think you were."

Raziel grinned at him. She couldn't help herself. If Lucias ordered Loki to respond to Noliminan in this way then it was, indeed, very much Lucias' fault that Loki was struck as he had been.

Which relieved Raziel of any explanation regarding her own part in the ballyhoo.

"You would have been proud of him, Luke. He was very brave."

"I'm sure he was." Lucias sighed as he ran his hand over Loki's troubled brow. "And I am."

Raziel nodded. As she did so, she felt her own brow furrow. Because, she realized, despite herself, she did care about the answer to this next question. "How is Zam?"

"She's well." Lucias muttered. "She's been a great help to me."

"Has he?" Raziel asked, somewhat distantly.

Zamyael wore a male body now. Constantly referring to him as a woman did none of them any good and only served to annoy Raziel beyond all telling.

"Ta." Lucias muttered. He raised his gaze and gave Raziel a warm smile. "*You* would be proud of *her*."

Raziel nodded and sighed. "If he has been helpful to you than I am." Her gaze darted to Loki, who lay lifeless in his bed. "Though you've left me without a servant. It is most troublesome."

Lucias chuckled and shook his head. "I'm sure Lady Martiam will grant you temporary aide if you ask it of her."

"I cannot replace Zam." Raziel snapped at him. "And nor do I wish to." Here was a bit of truth. "Our pairing may have been made of my twinning instincts to protect him. Yet I have come to love him in my own way."

"I know you have." Lucias nodded.

Raziel sighed. Now was the time to dig the wedge in ever deeper. "Noliminan has been by to see Loki several times."

Lucias' jaw clenched. "Has he, now?"

"I really do think he regrets having overreacted."

"You make your peace with his behavior in whatever regard you find it necessary, Raz." Lucias replied. His tone brokered no hint to his true feelings. Nor did his dark brown eyes, which were trailing over Raziel's face as he tried to ken Raziel's position on the matter. "I shan't forgive him for this matter any time soon."

Raziel nodded. She wouldn't try to justify either Noliminan's actions or Lucias' response to them.

She saw no reason, nor found any desire, to so.

She wanted them at war with one another. And the best way for her to remain unscathed when they chose to do so was to remain neutral so that whomever won the argument would abdicate the other's crown to her.

This thought made her smile.

She did covet Lucias' crown.

Yet, how would it be to be known as the Queen of Lords?

"How is everything else going?" Lucias asked, sighing and falling against his chair. He raised his hand to the bridge of his nose and began to rub it. Raziel wondered if he realized how very much he looked like Noliminan when he mimicked his mannerisms. It was disconcerting. "Is everyone behaving?"

"Everyone is asking where you are." Raziel shrugged. "But for the most part, life proceeds as it does."

"As it ever shall." Lucias smiled at her, lowering his hand to the arm of the chair.

"Our children miss you." Raziel offered. "Near to every one of them has asked me where you are."

"Upon Noliminan's orders I am certain." Lucias replied, frowning.

"I don't believe that's true." Raziel admonished. "You're their father, Luke. They love you. All of them. In their own ways."

"In their own ways." Lucias agreed as he crossed one long leg over the other. "How angry would you be with me if I asked if I might sit by Loki's side on my own for a bit?"

"I wouldn't be." Raziel smiled. "If you have need of me—"

"Then I shall seek you out." Lucias gave her a guarded smile. "Thank you for understanding."

Raziel responded with a tight smile of her own and nodded. "Goodnight, Luke."

"Goodnight, met paken."

-4-

Tristan watched Lasterian with cold fascination as he dipped a brush into a bucket of hot, soapy water and then began scrubbing the marble tile of Tristan's bedroom floor. The hour was late and the last thing in the world the child should have on his mind was scrubbing Tristan's floor.

All of his behaviors had been queer lately, however.

Yet, when Tristan approached the child to ask him what was the matter with him, Lasterian only shook his head and stared at him with haunted blue eyes.

"Nothing." He insisted when Tristan pressed the point. "I'm just as right as rain."

Sure you are, Tristan thought as he scratched absentmindedly at his left cheek. *You and Evanbourough both. Just as right as the fucking rain.*

He snorted and shook his head. Lasterian either didn't hear him or chose to ignore him. He suspected it might have been the latter. Lasterian's once overpowering devotion toward Tristan had fizzled into something which felt forced and false.

"Las?"

He stopped scrubbing. But he didn't turn to face Tristan.

Why in the name of the Thirty Heavens are you behaving so fucking odd?

"I'm going to go out for a bit." Tristan advised him. "Why don't you go on to bed?"

"Spots." Lasterian muttered as he sat upward, resting his bottom on the heels of his feet. He didn't turn to face Tristan, the God noticed. Rather, he simply stared at the floor. "Everywhere."

Tristan sighed.

Yes, there were spots on the floor. But they were the veins of the marble. Not dirt. And Lasterian would never scrub them out, no matter how violently he tried.

Tristan shook his head, threw the blanket off of himself and pushed himself off of the bed. "Whatever you say, Las."

Lasterian didn't respond. Rather, he dipped his brush back into his bucket so he might began scrubbing again.

It was sadly pathetic and it was more than Tristan could bear.

He stormed out of his apartment and made his way, angrily, through the Halls of the Heavens to Lady Theasis' door.

He raised his hand, hesitating. He didn't know if Theasis knew what was wrong with his angel and his lover any more than he did. But he thought that if Evanbourough had spoken to anyone it would have been the Lady.

Gritting his teeth, Tristan knocked. Then he waited.

When she opened it was with an irritated smile. When she realized it was Tristan on the other side of the door, she grasped at her robe and pulled it tight, almost as though she were embarrassed at having him found her in a state of near undress.

"Lord Tristan." She forced a smile. "What a . . . surprise."

"I apologize for intruding, my Lady." Tristan said, sighing. This had been a mistake of the most fundamental proportions. "I should have realized you were entertaining."

She gave him a cold glare. "As it so happens, I am not."

He smiled apologetically. "I'm sorry. It's been a long day."

"How may I assist you?" She asked, her eyes trailing nervously over his face.

"I wonder if you've had the opportunity to speak with Evanbourough as of late."

Her eyes narrowed slightly. "No. I can't say that I have."

He nodded, sighed and forced himself to smile.

"I see." He stepped back. "Forgive me, Lady."

"It's no matter." She said, her expression softening. "Is something wrong with Evan?"

"Yes." He said the word before he could stop himself.

She frowned slightly at him, looked over her shoulder, and then stepped back, opening the door to him. "Come in, Tristan."

"No, I—"

"I'm concerned about him too." She replied, her tone soft. "Please. Come in."

He sighed his relief and rolled his eyes closed.

Given Evanbourough's unrequited devotion toward her, Theasis' quarter was the last that Tristan ever wanted to seek. Yet, if she could enlighten him as to what was wrong with Evanbourough, he thought he might forgive the covetous current which so obviously passed between the two.

"May I offer you a drink?"

"No." Tristan shook his head. "Thank you."

She nodded, stepped toward a delicately made chair which was covered in crushed black velvet and lowered herself within. Tristan noted that she raised her long legs beneath her well-made bottom as she toyed with the neck of her robe with her long, elegant fingers. "I'm not certain what help I can be to you, my Lord. He's been acting strange for several months now."

"I know that he has." Tristan muttered as he lowered himself into a chair which was obviously meant more for its esthetics than for its comfort. He found himself amused by this fact as he shifted his weight upon its seat. Though he understood that women liked esthetically pleasing things, he didn't understand why they were willing to give up function for form. "So has Lasterian."

"Lasterian?" She blinked at him. "Your pretty?"

"My angel." Tristen seethed through his teeth. He was tired of the assumption that—just because Lasterian served him—Tristan forced Lasterian into his bed. "Not my pretty."

Attempting to calm himself from his sudden flare of anger, Tristan forced himself to look around and take marked notice of the delicately made tapestries hanging upon her pastel colored walls.

"Whatever happened, they both started acting strange on the same day."

She sighed. When he looked at her, he realized she was regretful in regard to her insinuation. "I wish I could help, my Lord. But Evanbourough has remained ever distant from me for some time."

He nodded. "Me too."

She bit at her bottom lip and lowered her gaze. "But, you know, I believe he has been spending quite a bit of time with Raphael lately."

"Raphael?" Tristan felt an unexpected sting from this slap. "Are you certain?"

She nodded, not meeting his gaze. "So I'm told."

"Told by whom?"

She cleared her throat. "I'd rather not say."

"My Lady, please." Tristan sighed. "If he has found confidence in someone then I should very much like to talk with this individual. Perhaps I can help him—both of them."

"Yes." She sighed. "Mayhap."

She raised her gaze and gave him a tired smile.

"Metatron and I . . ." She cleared her throat. "We play storming stones from time to time."

He felt his eyes narrow at what he assumed to be her lie. He couldn't picture Metatron being content with playing such a mindless game.

Especially whilst a beautiful woman sat across the storm board.

"He mentioned his own concern for Raphael. From what I understand, the King of Lords is less than aware of Raphael's relationship with Evanbourough. Metatron is concerned because he has seen Evanbourough leaving the King of Lords' apartment quite a lot as of late and he is worried Raphael will be punished for—"

"Don't."

Tristan had once overheard Camael telling Lasterian he was severely punished at Michael's hand for having broken the King of Lords' law that, as his property, Camael was to remain virgin so his loyalties weren't split.

Tristan didn't hear exactly what had befallen the archangel. What he was certain of was that whatever happened to him had been, in Camael's mind, brutal.

"Please. Don't voice the thought. I understand his concerns perfectly. I share them."

Theasis gave him a tired, apologetic smile. "He meant no ill will toward Evanbourough by sharing this with me."

"No." Tristan agreed.

He knew Metatron well. He was a powerful archangel. And he was one of the rare few inhabitants of the Sixty Realms who had the King of Lords' near to total confidence. But he wouldn't purposely place anyone in harm's way unless it was absolutely necessary to his duty to protect the King. "I know he didn't."

"You might try speaking with Raphael." Theasis sighed. "This is all I am trying to tell you."

"I might." He agreed.

But he wouldn't.

Raphael would never talk to him about what was wrong with Evanbourough. He knew this as surely as he knew Apollo would ride the sky with his Gods be damned morning star strapped to his chariot once the silver rooster crowed that it was time to do so.

She nodded, almost as if she understood the run of his thoughts. "I'm sorry that I cannot be of more aid to you than this."

He shook his head and forced a smile in her direction. "No, my Lady. You were a great help."

"I wasn't." She said as she stood. He followed her lead by finding his own feet. "Tristan, you know I care a great deal about

Evan. If I knew anything which would help him, I would tell you."

"I know." He didn't like it, but he did know it. "Thank you for your candor, my Lady."

"Always." She sighed. "If you hear anything . . ."

He gave her a tired smile but made her no promise.

Coming to her for help the first time had been difficult enough on his pride. He wouldn't be seeking her assistance a second time unless he saw no other solution.

"Good night, my Lady."

"May Moira bless you." She replied with a slight nod of her head.

There's a queer parting, he thought, shivering at the idea that Moira should have any part in his future.

But he didn't voice this. Rather, he merely nodded at her and took his leave.

-5-

As you must understand by now, unless I am specifically summoned by Noliminan or Lucias, my punishment for my constant interference in the fate of my brothers when they are unjustly punished for infractions, large or small, prevents me from appearing before anyone who calls my name simply at their whim.

On the rare occasion where I believe the situation is dire enough that I am willing to risk the consequences to form myself and speak with someone, I do so. Though, for the most part, I follow the rules which were set out for me when I was given my tasks and my magic.

There is one other way for a person to see and speak with me. But such a meeting is a tricky thing.

The person needing my attention is required to be with a dying mortal at the precise moment in time between the mortal's actual death and my removal of the soul from the mortal body.

I refer to this moment as the moment of aether.

The chance encounter is so rare a thing that a horrible practice has been developed by many of the Gods needing to speak with me. I speak of the practice of sacrificing one of their kind so they might be present during aether.

Such sacrifices are typically made on the cusp of the Guf, which, as I earlier told you, is located on the Seventh level of the Heavens. The sacrifices are often violent and the result of them has been that a river of blood has formed, flowing around the Guf and making entrance to the Hall of Souls nearly impossible for anyone other than Gabriel, myself or one of the two ruling Gods.

I have named the river the Lethe, which literally translates from ancient angelic text to the river of forgetfulness. I have so named the river due to the tragic fact that, even if I might be seen and converse with the person making the sacrifice during aether, the person making the sacrifice tends to forget that my tongue is still bound and that I cannot answer any of their questions without facing dire consequences.

In short, the sacrifices are generally unproductive and are always, in my opinion, brutally unnecessary.

Given all of this, I was disappointed, though not surprised, as I watched Lord Tristan snatch one of his fairies from one of the forest tribes, drag her to the Lethe, and place a knife to her throat.

To his credit he did hesitate before slicing her neck. And he began to cry as he pulled her body toward himself as the moment of aether approached her.

Distracted by his obvious grief for his own actions, Lord Tristan was late in calling my name. Though I was hopeful that Raziel would leave this part of my tale out of her Tome, I must admit that, understanding I may be punished for it, I ignored the rule which would have forced me to discount Lord Tristan's plea and formed myself at Lord Tristan's side.

At the time I thought no one but he and I would ever know of this very slight disobedience.

When Lord Tristan looked upward, meeting my gaze with his own, his blue eyes were dark and haunted. Given all of that, I made no judgment against him for his misinterpretation of the rules which bind my tongue.

"She will find a place of stature in Lady Martiam's halls." I assured Lord Tristan. "She was a pure and honest soul. She has earned her right to serve whatever God chooses her."

Lord Tristan gave me a fleeting smile and nodded. "Thank you for telling me this."

"I cannot speak to that which befell your friends." I warned him.

"You can." Lord Tristan held the lifeless body of the fairy toward me. "I made sacrifice so that you would."

I sighed and shook my head.

Why does discontentment make such fools of men who should know otherwise?

"The sacrifice allows you to see me and to speak what words you will to me. It doesn't allow me to speak free words with you."

Tristan's moan was guttural. His haunted eyes flew to the lifeless body of the fairy in his arms. The sound he made was mournful and painful to my ears.

Here was a man who had sacrificed his own virtues for the sake of another; a man who was unprepared for his sacrifice to mean naught.

"Sir Azrael, I beseech you." He gently laid the lifeless body of the fairy to the ground and forced himself to his feet. I tried to ignore the buzzing of her fear as her soul danced with disquiet impatience behind me. "Lasterian is a broken creature who I can no longer bear to look upon. Evanbourough has done something to him—or knows what has been done to him—and carries the burden with excruciating guilt. I must know what has happened so I might fix them both."

"You cannot fix them." I sighed. "Either one of them."

He lowered his face into his hands and shook his head. I knew he would begin to cry if I weren't standing before him.

I felt my eyes narrow. I couldn't tell Lord Tristan what had happened outright. But, perhaps, I could allude to a cure.

"Lasterian needs know only that whatever has befallen him was not his fault and that you love him yet." Tristan gave me a strange frown. "And Lord Evanbourough needs to understand that his loyalty to, and fear of, his betters, while generally well served, is inappropriate where Lasterian is concerned. He isn't protecting Camael's son. And nor is it, if this is his intent, appropriate."

As I spoke, I lowered my eyes and prayed silently to Lady Moira that my words and actions would never be retold.

"Tell Lord Evanbourough we have spoken. Tell him I have advised you that my nephew did not lie to him regarding what befell him and he should not be the one who Lord Evanbourough punishes with his admonishment and fear." I raised my gaze. "Perhaps, understanding that Camael is not being served by his perceived protection for Lasterian, Evanbourough will forgive himself for his confliction and feel comfortable in sharing with you what he knows."

"Why wouldn't he tell me what he knows anyway?" Tristan asked, obviously hurt by the mistrust that both Lord Evanbourough and Lasterian were thrusting upon him.

"Lord Tristan, I can tell you not." I sighed. "Take heart in the fact that Lord Evanbourough loves you—and Lasterian—enough that he has shared the matter with no one." With a knowing smile I added something I should not have. "Including Raphael."

Lord Tristan's brow furrowed momentarily. And then he smiled. "Thank you, Sir Azrael. For your candor."

"I wish only that I might be of more help." I meant this. There are times I loathe the binds upon my magic. I understand them. This does not mean that I do not loath them. "We are, all of us, bound by the rules of our own gifts."

The buzzing cries of the fairy were beginning to pound through my head. Frowning, I looked over my shoulder as I reached backward to calm her. Lord Tristan, who couldn't see or hear her, watched my movement with palpable interest.

"I must leave you now." I muttered, returning my attention to Lord Tristan. "I have said too much and you have given me a task that I must complete before I go mad."

Lord Tristan gave me a tired smile and nodded. "Isn't there some other way to call upon you if one needs to speak with you?"

"No." I advised him. "Not without us both facing the ire of our betters." I felt a genuine tinge of anger then. "I am to be neither seen nor heard. This is my punishment for once interjecting my face and my opinion into a matter where neither belonged."

"I am sorry." Lord Tristan said, his tone soft.

"Don't be." I smiled at him. "It is a mistake I would make a second time."

-6-

Evanbourough stared at his plate, less than amused with Tristan and the actions that he had taken to curry a word from me.

Yet, he found himself relieved at the end of the conversation, after Tristan explained to him that I refused to tell him what I had bore witness to. He was relieved I hadn't advised Tristan that Evanbourough had blamed Lasterian for something which was not his fault.

He really had been trying to protect Lasterian by forcing him into silence with his accusations that the young angel was lying. True or not, Lady Raziel really would have destroyed Lasterian for making the mere suggestion of it.

"Will you tell me what did happen?" Tristan asked after Evanbourough allowed he may have had the wrong of things where Lasterian was concerned.

"No." He sighed.

He supposed Lasterian was due an apology. When he gave it to him, he would ask the angel if or not he wanted to share his troubles with Tristan.

"If he wants you to know then he shall tell you himself." He felt his lips purse. "I'll speak with him. And explain that I miscalculated your potential reaction."

"My potential reaction?" Tristan asked, his tone flat. "How, exactly, did you tell him I would react?"

"I told him you would be angry with him." Evanbourough replied, meeting Tristan's gaze. "And you would have been if my suppositions that he was being untruthful with me had been accurate."

"No, I—" As Evanbourough passed him a guarded, knowing smile, Tristan stopped himself. "Alright. Without knowing what occurred, I can't say one way or the other how I would have reacted."

"I'll speak with him in the morning."

"Thank you." Tristan sighed. "Now. About what's been going on between you and I?"

"Past." Evanbourough smiled at him. "With my apologies."

"Your apologies are accepted." He returned Evanbourough's smile and Evan was glad for it. "I want you back."

"I am yours." Evanbourough assured him. "I have always been yours."

"I'm glad to hear this." He gave Evan a tight smile. "I thought I'd lost you to Raphael."

"No." Evanbourough shook his head and lowered his gaze. His cheeks were flaming with his embarrassment. His time with Raphael had been innocently passed. Yet, he understood how Tristan might believe otherwise. "Raphael has other concerns aside me these days."

"Such as?"

"A demanding master." Evanbourough raised his gaze, his embarrassment passed. "Between the King of Lords and Queen of Ladies, Raphael is being ridden hard."

Tristan chuckled as he lifted his fork and toyed with it. "Is that so?"

Evanbourough was helpless but to smile in response. "Not literally, you dirty old man."

Tristan's laugh was loud and true. It wrapped around Evan like the arms of a dear and long missed friend.

Evan vowed to himself, as he watched Tristan, that, no matter the circumstances, he would never risk the loss of his beloved again.

- 7 -

Lasterian stood between Lords Tristan and Evanbourough, dwarfed by the size of them, biting back his sheer terror as Lord Tristan pounded upon Sovereign Lady Raziel's door.

At Lord Evanbourough's encouragement, Lasterian revealed what had happened to him. Lord Tristan all but exploded with his anger, flinging anything and everything he could get his hands on against his wall. Against Lord Evanbourough's advice, and Lasterian's desires, he insisted on raising the matter with Lady Raziel directly and demanding Zamyael be punished for having violated his property.

Lasterian understood that, by law, he *was* Lord Tristan's property.

But Lord Tristan had never treated him as such before. That he did so now pained the angel more greatly than the fear and self-loathing which he had endured since Zamyael had attacked him.

Later, after Lord Tristan calmed down, he apologized to Lasterian for his reference to the angel as his plaything. And Lasterian forgave him.

But the damage was done.

He knew, now, exactly what value Lord Tristan placed upon him and his service.

And he realized that, although Lord Evanbourough was wrong about Lord Tristan blaming him for what happened, he had been right about the depth of Lord Tristan's anger that he was now damaged goods.

As Lord Tristan's knocking was ignored, he became angrier and his pounding became more insistent. By the time the door did open, Lord Tristan's face was, once again, a stone cold mass of rage.

Realizing, however, that it was Lord Regent Lucias who answered, and not Lady Raziel, he had the good sense to bite his cheek and let Lord Evanbourough do the talking.

"My Lord Regent." Lord Evanbourough said, his tone carrying the same surprise Lord Tristan's expression embodied. "We must speak with Lady Raziel."

"She isn't here, Evan." Lord Lucias' dark eyes danced over Lord Tristan's face, never once looking at either Lord Evanbourough or Lasterian. "May I aide you in her stead?"

"No." Lord Tristan snapped, his hand flying to Lasterian's shoulder and squeezing it so tightly that Lasterian flinched under the pain. He bit his tongue lest he cry out. He noted that Lord Lucias' dark brown eyes were now dancing over his face. He wished desperately the floor would open beneath him and swallow him whole. "My Lord, my matter with Lady Raziel is personal in nature. I must speak with her at once. Do you know where she—?"

"Step into this apartment, Tristan." Lord Lucias said, his tone gentle and inviting. "And tell me, right here and now, what this is all about."

His jaw clenched, Lord Tristan gave one shake of his head. Again, it was Lord Evanbourough who spoke. "My Lord, it would be best if we discussed the matter directly with Lady Raziel."

"Who answers to me." Lord Lucias responded, still gently; still in inviting tones. "You had the good sense to seek me out when my brat was in danger." His eyes were still dancing over Lasterian's face. "Let me grant you the same courtesy."

"Lasterian has done nothing wrong!" Lord Tristan's tone was thick with his anger. "It was the Gods be damned demon who—"

Lord Lucias reached forward and grasped Lord Tristan by the collar of his shirt. He pulled him roughly forward, spinning around with him as though he weighed no more than a rag doll and then pushing him deep into the warmth of Lady Raziel's sitting room.

"Say another word whilst standing in the hallway and I'll take your tongue." He seethed. He turned swiftly around and glared at Lord Evanbourough and Lasterian. "Get you in here now, Evanbourough. And let us speak about this with reason."

Lord Evanbourough placed his hand gently upon the small of Lasterian's back. The angel felt himself begin to scoot backward, not wanting to face Lord Lucias, who was obviously angry with him for having coupled with Lady Raziel's demon. Yet, there was no choice but to move forward as Lord Evanbourough was firmly pushing him in, reaching behind himself to close the door.

"My Lord," Tristan groused at Lord Lucias. "You fail to understand the severity of what has—"

"I understand the severity perfectly." He replied, his tone still reasonable and calm. "Zamyael violated my grandson against his will and you want her punished for it."

"I . . ." Lord Tristan stammered. Lasterian, himself, was staring up at Lord Lucias in terrified surprise. "How do you know?"

"Zamyael told me as much." He sighed, his gaze returning to Lasterian. "She didn't tell me who it was." He admitted. "But I assume, given the expression on this boy's face, and your justifiable rage toward her, it must have been him."

"It was, my Lord." Lord Evanbourough said, his eyes lowered to the ground. "I must admit I bore witness to the aftermath. I disbelieved the child was not involved in the fracas and I have made matters worse than they necessarily ought to have been."

"Do you know this child—or his father for that matter—to have ever have lied to anyone before?" Lucias asked with a raised brow. To this, Lord Evanbourough shook his head. "Your behavior is disappointing, Evan."

Lord Evanbourough flinched, his dark eyes darting to Lasterian and then returning swiftly to his feet. "Yes, my Lord."

Lasterian, confused by the quarter from Lord Regent Lucias, swallowed and forced himself to continue to stare at the ground.

"I assure you, Tristan," Lord Lucias said, his tone stern, "Zamyael is paying dearly for her mistake."

"I'd like to throttle her pretty little neck." Lord Tristan seethed through his teeth.

"Yes." Lord Lucias sighed. "I understand this." Lasterian braved to look upward and swallowed the lump in his throat as he marked the quiet patience in Lord Regent Lucias' eyes. "But the matter has been taken care of. So I would ask that you please refrain from bothering Raziel about it."

"But she—"

"Tristan." Lord Lucias' tone was flat. "I am dealing with the problem of Zamyael. You will say nothing to anybody about this matter. Do you understand me?"

"I . . ." He shook his head. Upon seeing the seriousness of Lord Lucias' request, however, he gave a small nod. "As you will me, my Lord."

"Good." He sighed, almost as though relieved.

As he did so, he raised his hand and set it upon Lord Tristan's shoulder.

"You told me that you believe the children have just as much right to their free will as do the mortals." Lord Tristan nodded. "With free will sometimes come poor choices." Lasterian felt his brow furrow at this sentiment. "We must protect the children's right to make poor choices, just as much as we must fight for their right to make good ones."

Lord Tristan sighed, met his gaze and nodded. "Of course, my Lord."

Lord Regent Lucias turned his gaze to Lasterian then. "I cannot take your pain away from you, child. I wish I could. But I can assure you this: Zamyael has been punished and is filled with more regret than you shall ever know for what she has done to you."

Lasterian found himself stepping backward and toward Lord Evanbourough. He had no reply to give Lord Lucias aside the one which had been bred within him by his father since his childhood. "Yes, my Lord."

"Then the matter is closed." He sighed. "And Raziel is never to hear the first word about it."

Having no other choice, they, all three, agreed.

-8-

"Welcome back." Zamyael smiled at Lucias as he entered their shared bedchamber. His eyes darted upward. She noticed they were dark and filled with deep shadows.

"I met your angel, Zam." He said, running his hand through his hair. "Did it have to be Camael's boy?"

Zamyael felt the heat of a blush creep into her cheeks. "I told you. It could have been anyone who darkened my doorway that day."

"Yes." He muttered, his eyes darting over her face. "And I understand perfectly well why. But my grandson? And Tristan agreed to stand beside me should it come to a fight." Lucias sighed. "Never mind the fact that you violated my flesh and blood," His dark expression at this sentiment terrified her, "I need Tristan's loyalty. And you may have lost it for me."

"Did he tell you as much?"

"No." Lucias muttered. "But wounds cut ties." He sighed again and shrugged. "Past is past. I told them that you have been punished." His eyes narrowed slightly. "Have you been?"

"You know that I have." She whispered as her hand fell to the swell of her belly.

She was to give away the only child she would ever in her miserable life birth. If this wasn't punishment enough for her treatment toward the pathetic little, pie eyed angel, she didn't know what was.

Never mind the raging guilt she had been feeling over her ill begot actions. She had come to realize, over time, that she was no better than Nollminan in her violation of Lasterian.

And what did this make her?

Treating someone who was vulnerable to her powers in the same manner as she had been treated when she, herself, was vulnerable?

Lucias nodded, stepped toward the bed and crawled toward her. As he did so, he lost the cloak of masculinity he shrouded himself in and showed her the face he had been born with.

She smiled at him. He made a beautiful woman.

"Raziel misses you." He muttered as he crawled under their covers. "Asks about you."

"Does she?"

"She does." He gave her a tired, crooked smile. "I told her that you miss her as well."

"Liar." She grinned. It wasn't a lie. Not really.

But she was happier, here with Lucias, than she had been in more years than she could remember.

"I thought I might take my liberties." He chuckled.

"How is Loki?"

His brow furrowed. He let out the endearing little whistle through his teeth and he looked swiftly away. "Healed. Physically, by any road. I sat with him through two Seventh Moons and he didn't so much as flutter an eye open." He sighed. "I couldn't stay at his bedside forever."

"Too much work to do here." She offered.

"Ta." He agreed, rubbing his belly. "Too much work to do here."

"Sappharon thinks you ar angry with her." She curled her nose at the thought of Sappharon. She held no ill will toward the brat, but she did wish she would take a Gods be damned bath. "For reading Noliminan's letter."

"Good." Lucias snorted. "I am."

"She doesn't mean to be troublesome." She sighed.

"I know." He agreed with a small chuckle. "It's just her way."

"Just so."

"I suppose I owe her an apology." Lucias offered, very tentatively. "For hitting her."

"I suppose that she doesn't expect one."

"All the more reason to give her one." Lucias muttered. "Don't you think?"

Zamyael felt her brow furrow. And then she shivered. He was telling her in his own way that she should apologize to Lasterian. She didn't know if she would be able to do this.

Not because she didn't want to. In fact, having kindled his child and reflecting on the pain she had caused him, she wanted more than anything in the world to speak with him and to explain her motivation.

But she didn't know how to go about doing so. And she feared if she made even the slightest attempt it would only serve to wound Lasterian more than help him.

What would he say when he learned of her pregnancy? What would he think of her willingness to let it live, abomination that it might become? What if he demanded to bring the child's existence to light, resulting in the damnation of them both and the destruction of the baby?

Never mind the very real possibility that her apology would fall on deaf ears.

Would she, herself, forgive Noliminan if he were to approach her today and apologize for mistreating her?

No. She sighed. *You wouldn't. Not now. Not after everything.*

There were too many variables to consider. And she knew she must think these things through before she could face Lasterian.

With all of these thoughts running through her mind, she gave a true hearted answer but made no promises as to how she would, ultimately, deal with Lasterian. "Yes. All the more reason."

He leaned over and kissed her forehead. In his female form, his lips were soft and wet and enticing.

She would let him take her in this form, she realized as she closed her eyes to the pleasure of his embrace as he wrapped his arms around her.

Come to that, she would, she knew as she snuggled against him, let him take her in any form.

-9-

Raphael hesitated at the door to the library. King Noliminan had been in a sour mood for Countenance alone knew how long. But he held in his hand the response to a letter King Noliminan had written to Lucias several waning moons before.

He hadn't read it, knowing it wasn't his place, but he suspected it answered some—if not all—of King Noliminan's questions.

Raphael heard enough rumors in the kitchens and the wash houses to suspect that half of what Lucias might say to King Noliminan would anger Raphael's Master rather than please him. There was a growing rift amongst the angels and the demons in regard to the Divine Plan. Many of them didn't understand why the mortals were entitled to the gift of free will while they, themselves, were meant to remain enslaved.

Raphael supposed that he understood why some of the angels and demons were discontent with their lot. He, himself, harbored no such complaints. King Noliminan could be a hard Master, he supposed. But, generally, if Raphael were punished then the punishment was well deserved.

Yet, he had friends where he knew this wasn't the case.

His brother's lover, Raystlyn, was such a beautiful creature that even Narcissus—the vainest and most beautiful of all of the Gods—was jealous of him. As such, Raystlyn was bartered for pleasure or punished for the mere turn of his preternaturally beautiful silver eyes. Raphael had seen Haniel poultice Raystlyn on so many occasions after a brutal beating that he now loathed to visit his brother lest he find Raystlyn at Haniel's cottage, whiling away this shifts of the shadows.

"Don't lurk, Raphael."

Raphael, who hadn't seen Queen Raguel approaching, started. "No, your Grace. Of course not."

She gave him a strange smile. "Did you finish my laundry?"

He sighed and shook his head. No. He hadn't the time. After King Noliminan was finished with him, he had asked Raphael to sit at Apprentice Lord Loki's bedside in the event there were any changes to Lord Loki's well being.

That the young God had yet to awaken was troubling to King Noliminan and he wanted to be available to speak with him to discuss his behavior and subsequent punishment for his disobedience the moment Lord Loki opened his eyes.

Though Raphael admired Lord Loki, he didn't understand what all the fuss was about. He had been in the room when Lord Loki had disobeyed King Noliminan and, by Raphael's estimation, King Noliminan had been far more patient with him than he deserved. Raphael had seen King Noliminan punish a person for far less than Lord Loki's quip about making him a hat. That he held his anger at bay until Lord Loki brazenly offended him with his vulgarity was troubling to Raphael at best.

Raphael knew he was in a unique situation in so far as understanding King Noliminan's methods. His Master frequently talked through events which took place with him—more to work his thoughts out in his own mind than out of any need for Raphael's input on the matter—and so Raphael understood why it was necessary to punish those who disobeyed. King Noliminan was the ultimate ruler of both the Heavens and the Hells. Thus, it was required that he temper his patience.

Which, in Raphael's estimation, was immeasurable based on what he had witnessed throughout the years.

"Why must you defy me?" The Queen of Ladies was asking. Raphael realized he had barely heard what she was saying to him. It had been a long night followed by an even longer day.

"I apologize, your Grace." Raphael bowed to her. "I was on task for King Noliminan last night. My time was not at all my own."

"My tasks are equally as important."

"Yes, your Grace." He could hear the impatience in his own tone and he bit it back as swiftly as possible. The cleanliness of Queen Raguel's illimitable supply of garments was the least important thing in the world in Raphael's estimation. "I shall see to them before I bed for the night. It is a promise."

She gave him a strange, cold frown and then nodded. "See that you do, Raphael."

Knowing he would be spending the majority of the evening at the washing pools, he plucked up his courage to enter King Noliminan's library. There was no time for reverie.

"Your Grace?"

King Noliminan looked up from his desk, frowning. His wore a strained expression and used a rather irritable tone. "What is it, min 'lasupita?"

"I've news from Lucias." Raphael sauntered forward and held out his father's letter. "It arrived an hour ago. I apologize for my delay in its delivery. I—"

"No excuses." He grumbled, reaching for the letter.

"Yes, your Grace." He sighed and lowered his gaze.

He turned to take his leave, but King Noliminan stopped him. "Wait. I may have a response."

Thinking of Queen Raguel's piles of laundry, Raphael clenched his teeth. He had no time to wait for King Noliminan to read and then ponder his response to Lucias. However, he returned his attention to him and gave him an obedient bow. "Yes, your Grace."

King Noliminan must have sensed his hesitation because his brow furrowed slightly. Raphael watched as his eyes narrowed and then darted to the envelope in his hands. Whatever Raphael's complaints, he held no interest in them.

He slid his finger under Lucias' seal and popped it open. Deftly, he pulled the parchment from the envelope, flicked it, brought it to his nose to breathe in the scent of it, smiled and then set to studying it. Raphael watched all of this with silent amusement from the corner of King Noliminan's desk.

"Huh." He grunted when he finished reading the letter. Raphael knew he wasn't brokering questions so he kept those which were buzzing through his mind in his own head. "Good." He raised his gaze and gave Raphael a tired smile. "Mother and child both fare well."

"I am pleased to know this, your Grace."

"She wants to place the child in the Guf with Gabriel until he's old enough for his training." Raphael felt his brow furrow. Gabriel had no time whatsoever to add mothering to his growing list of already overwhelming duties.

King Noliminan chuckled at his expression and granted him a tired smile. "I agree. Other arrangements must be considered."

Raphael bit his lip, lowered his gaze and said, "I would be pleased to see to your child in Gabriel's stead." He looked upward, finding a strange smile dancing on King Noliminan's lips. "If it would please you."

"It *would* please me, Raphael." He answered, his expression still strange. "But I do not find you a likely candidate given your current duties. Do you?"

"I would make the time, your Grace." He replied greedily.

King Noliminan sighed, "It isn't practical that I should add child rearing to your already full days."

Disappointment flooded through Raphael's soul. "As you say, your Grace."

"Don't look thusly." He muttered. "You will necessarily be critically involved in the boy's life."

This placated Raphael. He very much wanted to be a part of the life of any children King Noliminan sired. But more so this one as he understood profoundly that this child would forever be his favorite. He smiled softly at his benevolent Master. "Yes, your Grace. Of course you are right."

"I am loathe to admit it but I believe, given the tasks the boy is meant to be set to, Zadkiel should see to the child's rearing." King Noliminan muttered.

Raphael, surprised by this announcement, felt his mouth slack open. "Zadkiel, your Grace?"

"Zadkiel," King Noliminan said, sighing

Raphael doubted that this was the right choice. His brother was, just lately, extremely discontent. And his anger toward his betters was palpable. How would he treat the very child of the man responsible for having crippled him?

This is what he said, "Given his ailments "

"His limitations are physical." King Noliminan snapped at Raphael. "And justly deserved."

Raphael bit his tongue and gave his Master a supplicating nod of agreement. Zadkiel, he well knew, was not long a safe topic of conversation. "Would you speak to him of this matter yourself?"

King Noliminan frowned at the question, looked away and nodded his head. "On this occasion, I believe that would be for the best."

Raphael was relieved that he had grasped the delicacy of the situation. "Yes, your Grace."

"See to Raguel's domestic issues." King Noliminan gave him a patient, amused smile. "My response to Luci must wait until after my conversation with Zadkiel."

"Yes, your Grace." Raphael sighed.

Bowing, he took his leave.

-10-

King Noliminan's system for summoning a member of his Quorum is ingeniously simple. Each of the twelve archangels wears a chain around his ankle with a bell attached to it. King Noliminan keeps a box in his library which houses twelve larger corresponding bells. If he has need of one of us, he reaches into the box in his library and rings the corresponding bell which represents the angel he requires. The bell on the angel's ankle will then ring and the angel will make his way to King Noliminan's library to discuss what is needed of him without a moment's hesitation.

It had been so long since Zadkiel's bell had rung, however, that he found himself staring at it with wide eyed curiosity which was tempered with disbelief. He raised his foot, shook it to make sure the bell wasn't broken and then waited, his eyes glued to the thing, until it started ringing again.

Zadkiel knew if he answered the call and it had been made in error, he would be humiliated for thinking, after so much time had passed, King Noliminan had found a need for him. Yet, he also understood, if the call was legitimate and he didn't show, his punishment would be necessarily harsh. If King Noliminan needed him enough to drop his pride to call on him, he'd best make sure he didn't keep his Master waiting.

He stumbled to the mirror, brushed his hair and threw on the gold robes King Noliminan preferred him to wear to court. The hem of his skirt was far too short, but he understood this was to give others a good view of his damaged leg. He had long ago given up his protests that they failed to protect his modesty because they always fell on deaf ears.

When he was ready, he made what run he could and then jumped upward into the clouds. At flight, he knew, he was as beautiful as any one of his brothers. He was swift and graceful on the wing.

By the time he reached King Noliminan's library the bell on his ankle had become insistent. He smoothed his skirt as low as it would go, swallowed his fear and stepped into the room.

King Noliminan sat behind his desk, his eyes narrowed and an irritated expression crossing his fair face. Zadkiel, who never felt comfortable meeting King Noliminan's gaze directly, averted his eyes. "You're late, Zadkiel."

"Forgive me, your Grace." He secured his staff so he could bend over it and avoid tumbling to the floor and embarrassing himself any further. "I was still abed."

"Abed with whom?" He asked. His tone was almost accusing.

"No one, your Grace." Zadkiel felt his cheeks flush. The only lovers he had ever had were forced upon him by the King of Lords in the propagation of the bronzie race. And, now, he understood, he was too ugly to dare claim anyone's desire. "I am merely slower on my feet these days than I once was."

King Noliminan's eyes danced the length of him and the taut expression vanished. It was replaced by smug satisfaction at having wounded Zadkiel.

He nodded and gave Zadkiel a guarded smile.

"Of course you are." He raised a hand to indicate one of the chairs on the opposite side of his desk. "You may sit."

Given it was painful to stand for any length of time, Zadkiel was grateful and so complied. As he settled into his chair, he smoothed his skirt over his damaged leg again and forced himself to give King Noliminan what he hoped was an adulating smile.

"It is not common knowledge and so it must not be said," King Noliminan sighed as he sat back in his chair, "but Lucias and I have created a child with one and another. It is Lucias who bears the babe."

If he would have said Lucias had decided to live out the rest of his life as a turtle then Zadkiel wouldn't have been any more surprised. He let out a gasp and then immediately slammed his mouth shut.

"Yes." King Noliminan chuckled. "I imagine this will be the common reaction when the announcement is eventually made."

"Forgive me, your Grace." Zadkiel shook his head. "You have taken me by surprise."

King Noliminan acknowledged this with a downward turn of his eyes and a patient smile. "Given our constraints with time, neither Lucias nor I are in any position to raise a child."

Zadkiel felt his brow furrow. It was true that his father had little involvement in his own rearing. Lucias left the raising of his children to their mothers. It was also true that King Noliminan was less than participatory in the raising of his own children. Yet, Zadkiel was left to wonder why they would choose to birth a child together if neither one of them had the inclination to rear it.

It wasn't his place to voice his thoughts on the subject, however. "Of course not, your Grace."

He braved to raise his gaze to meet King Noliminan's own. There was some emotion buried deep within his light brown eyes which terrified Zadkiel. He flushed again and turned his attention to the hands folded on his lap.

He waited. And when King Noliminan didn't continue, he leaned slightly forward on his chair.

"Please forgive me. But what have I to do with any of this?"

King Noliminan didn't immediately respond. Zadkiel could feel his eyes trailing over the curves of his face, almost as though he were assessing Zadkiel.

Finally, he said, "I trust you will never disobey me again."

Zadkiel swallowed and shook his head. Did he mean to set him free of the imprisonment of his broken body? Could he dare hope that this new, clearly favorite son, granted King Noliminan the ability to see Zadkiel's true regret and, thus, finally forgive him?

"Never in life."

"Look at me, Zadkiel."

Hesitantly, his fear consuming him, Zadkiel raised his gaze and met King Noliminan's own.

"I am going to entrust you with the rarest of all gifts." Zadkiel licked his lips and nodded. His heart was beating so fast and hard he thought it might thrum right out of his chest. "When Lucias' son is born, he will become, for some time, your responsibility."

Zadkiel could hardly conceive King Noliminan's intent. He had been so certain the words King Noliminan was trying to say were to be words of forgiveness that he couldn't, at first, appreciate the magnitude of the faith King Noliminan was placing in him. He shook his head, trying to focus on the words which had actually been said. "Your Grace, I don't understand."

"Raphael offered." He shrugged. "But I think you and I both know that he is less than suited for such a task."

"No." Zadkiel replied. "He is patient and kind and—"

"Has more important things to do." King Noliminan's tone was almost angry. "Are you denying my request?"

"No, your Grace." Zadkiel assured him, his gold eyes widening. "I am flattered by your request. I merely thought you have forgiven me and you might heal—"

King Noliminan's impatient sigh enveloped Zadkiel with all of the disapproval the archangel imagined could be mustered in all of the worlds.

He snapped his mouth shut, readying himself for a blow. It never came. But the anger which consumed King Noliminan over the fact that Zadkiel would sully his confidence with his ill begot pride was palpable.

"If you are not prepared to assist me with this child, then I shall find someone who is." King Noliminan's tone was colder than ice.

"No, your Grace, please!" Zadkiel flew to his feet. His cane fell at his side, leaving him to stand awkwardly on his good leg. His hands circled comically around him, catching the desk in front of him as he fell forward. "I beseech you! Forgive me! I wish more than anything to find your good graces again. I will do anything you ask of me!"

"Sit down!"

Zadkiel, less than gracefully, complied.

"You try my patience every time that I look at you." King Noliminan spat at him as he crossed his arms over his chest. "When I am ready to forgive you then I shall. Not a moment before. Do you understand me, Zadkiel?"

"I do." Zadkiel swallowed and lowered his gaze. He could feel his eyes stinging and he blinked them to stay whatever tears meant to fall.

"Good." He sighed, heavily.

"Your Grace, please forgive—"

"I am finished with this conversation." King Noliminan snapped. He raised his hand to the bridge of his nose and began to rub there. It was a gesture he had long made when he was frustrated or angry. Zadkiel, knowing he was the cause of his Master's frustration, wished he could flee. "Let us return to the task for which I have called you."

"Yes, your Grace." His voice was shaking and his mind was spinning.

"I need my son to learn compassion, mercy, responsibility and perseverance." He lowered his hand, then, and gave Zadkiel a tired, angry smile. "Will you be able to teach him these things?"

"I will, your Grace." Zadkiel whispered.

"Good." He nodded and flicked his hand at Zadkiel. "Leave me."

Zadkiel swallowed and nodded. He leaned over to grasp his staff and realized, as his fingers caught nothing but cold marble and empty air, it was gone. He looked upward and met King Noliminan's eyes.

They were swimming with his amusement.

"I think, Zadkiel," he said with a harsh frown, "that you must carry your own burdens for a time."

Zadkiel blinked at him, his mind reeling with pain.

"In a week, or mayhap two, I will give you back your staff. Until then," his eyes narrowed, "it really is about time you learn how to just make do."

-11-

King Noliminan waited for Raphael to return from the washroom and then handed him the letter he had written to Lucias. Once Raphael left him, he made his way to the balcony and, now being alone, out of my line of view.

Until, that was, Gabriel slipped from the room where Raphael generally slept and stood in the archway of Raphael's balcony door.

"Zadkiel, Zadkiel." King Noliminan sighed now, raising his thumb and forefinger to the bridge of his nose and rubbing there. And then he chuckled. "Lucias, Lucias."

"Your Grace?"

He started and looked upward. It was in this moment that he realized Gabriel stood before him, hovering in the doorway, his dark eyes trailing over his face. He blinked, cleared his throat and lowered his hand from his face. "Gabriel."

"I'm sorry for disturbing you."

King Noliminan shook his head, blinked again and cleared his throat. Gabriel had caught him in a rare moment of reflection and I sensed he suddenly felt embarrassed by his contemplation. "How might I help you?"

"Raphael isn't feeling well." He said, his brow furrowed. Having been watching Raphael and Evanbourough coupling, I rolled my eyes at the lie. "He asked me to stay with you tonight. I've only come to let you know he's staying at the Gut and I'll be in his room."

"Oh." King Noliminan forced himself to smile at my brother. "Did he finish Raguel's domestic tasks first?"

I had the distinct impression he was well aware of Lady Raguel's recent play for Raphael's attentions. But what he didn't know was her reasoning behind them. I, however, did.

250

Both she and Michael had fallen into a state of despair after her rejection of him. And, though Michael had tried on two additional and separate occasions to beg her to see reason, she had spurned him and finally told him to leave her alone.

Michael, being the gentleman he is, had. In her grief, she would approach Raphael whenever she could simply because she was seeking news about Michael or trying to overhear King Noliminan speaking about him with Raphael.

To this day I find great sorrow in my heart for them both.

"He did."

"Fine."

"Good night, your Grace."

"Yes." He nodded, his eyes dancing over Gabriel's face. "Good night."

Gabriel gave him a faint smile and turned away. Before the door closed, however, King Noliminan called him back.

"Yes, your Grace."

"Come sit with me, Gabe."

Gabriel's smile was blinding in its familiarity. Even though I could not read King Noliminan's turn of thoughts, I kenned what they must have been. In that moment, and in his current state of grief, it wasn't Gabriel who King Noliminan was seeing. It was Lucias. "Of course, your Grace."

"Do you know kings' castles?"

"Yes, your Grace." Gabriel nodded, his smile spreading. "My fath—" He shook his head. "I mean, Lucias, taught me when I was very small."

King Noliminan smiled at him, somewhat haughtily. "Do you prefer to take your opponent from behind as well?"

Gabriel's brow furrowed. "No. I prefer a straight on advance."

King Noliminan laughed at my brother. His question had been innocently meant, but I know, now, that his mind was suddenly filled with a separate connotation. He shook his head and stood. Then he walked to the table where his kings' board sat and lowered himself into one of the two chairs on either side of the board.

"Come, then, Gabe." He said, smiling wickedly at Gabriel, still teasing. "And let us see if you can manage to hold in your hands what I intend to put there."

-12-

Gabriel crawled into Raphael's bed, elated. He had spent near to the full of the night with King Noliminan. They had played three games of kings' castles and Gabriel even bested King Noliminan during one round. Afterward, they sat by the fire, simply biding the night, talking in detail about King Noliminan's Divine Plan and why King Noliminan believed it was an important improvement to the management of the mortal races. After a few malted whiskeys, King Noliminan even engaged Gabriel in a friendly debate regarding why he believed the Divine Plan should only be extended to the mortals. At the end of the conversation, Gabriel understood King Noliminan's reasoning and found it sound on principal. Though, he privately agreed that Lucias had the right of things.

The only thing which troubled Gabriel, as he pulled the warm blanket to his chin and buried his head in Raphael's far too soft pillows, was the manner in which King Noliminan and he had parted.

Though Gabriel couldn't be sure—he had matched King Noliminan glass for glass and wasn't as used to the spirits as was his Master—he thought when they parted that King Noliminan bid his good night to Lucias.

Not to Gabriel.

He played the parting over and over in his mind to the point of madness.

"Good night, Luke." He muttered, shivering. "Good night, Gabe."

He shook his head. There was no mistaking one for the other. Their names weren't similar in any way, shape or form.

Yet, he must have misheard.

King Noliminan would never make the mistake of confusing Gabriel for his father. Even after five malted whiskeys.

Would he?

-13-

Zamyael held the bundle in her hands, laughing through her tears as she raised it to her face and planted a kiss on the forehead of the strange little being in her arms. It had no form, no corporeal body. It was simply a strange, buzzing mass of energy which appeared in the shape of a child's body but held no real form.

She had never seen anything like it in her life.

And she thought, as she looked upon it now, she had never seen anything more beautiful.

"Dathanorna." She whispered as Lucias lowered himself on the bed at her side. He was smiling quizzically at her, waiting quietly to see what her reaction would be to the abomination she had just birthed.

"Dathanorna." He agreed. "Strong and healthy."

She nodded and kissed the child's forehead again. "When will it take a form?"

His brow furrowed. Before he spoke, he cleared his throat. "Soon."

She smiled. "What form will it take, do you think?"

"Mine." He muttered. "Until it learns the benefit of controlling its magic, it will emulate the most powerful entity it can see."

"Yours?" She was confused. "When you were a child?"

"No." He replied, now frowning. "Looking at us you won't be able to tell one from the other." He looked swiftly away. "This is why I cannot allow you to mother it overlong. I must hide it as soon as possible."

"But I thought . . . ?" She felt as though he had reached into her chest and ripped out her heart. She knew she would have to relinquish her child. But she thought she would have more time.

"I'm sorry, Zam." Lucias sighed and brushed a grouping of braids behind her ear. "The risks of allowing you to keep the child, for even sixty shifts, are great. I must take it where I mean to hide it before it awakens."

"Can't I go with you?" She begged. It was useless and she knew it. "Will you let me know where you hide it so I might visit it from time to time."

"No, Zamyael." He replied patiently. "I have found a family which is willing to adopt it as one of their own. The child must take on the form of this family lest it draw attention to itself." He sighed, his patience ebbing. "You know I am right."

She did. But that didn't make this any easier.

"Please . . ." She begged, "Can I not even show the babe to Lasterian? Can I not let him look, just once, upon the face of his child?"

"There is too much at risk, Zam." Lucias reminded her. "For all three of you." He sighed and shook his head. "You cannot tell him about the babe. No matter your pain or regret of your actions toward him."

"Please, Luke!" She desperately begged.

"No."

Now his tone was stern.

He leaned toward her, placed his hands around the form of the child, and ripped it from her arms.

She sprang forward, grasping at the bundle, but it did her no good. He was much stronger and far swifter than she could ever hope to be. By the time she reached the spot on the bed where he had been sitting, Lucias, and her babe, were gone.

Zamyael's grieving for the loss of her child was anything but graceful or silent.

-14-

The child hung from Lucias' jaws as she (being fully able to read her thoughts now that the child was close to birthing, I knew she thought of herself as female) carried it deep into the forest. The moment she left Zamyael's side she took on the form of a wolf pup. When the child awoke, a wolf pup was what the child saw and, so, a wolf pup is what the child became. Once the babe fell to sleep again, Lucias aged herself so she could carry it.

The forest was chilling. Here is a place where mortal spirits dwell which have escaped my grasp. Some through cunning and trickery; others because they refused to allow me to take their hands and lead them forward to the next path they must take in life. Some are good. Some are evil. Every one of them, as a result of their unnecessary, self-imposed exile, have run mad.

Living, thinking mortals are afraid of this forest and, as a result, will stay away. Gods have no pity for them, except, by necessity, Hades, who rules them, and will ignore them as they would anything which failed to hold their interest. The only living beings which now inhabit the forest are the animals.

Lucias had been visiting the wolf pack which dwelled here throughout the course of Zamyael's pregnancy. They never accepted her as one of their own, by any means, but they behaved in such a manner to suggest that if she were to leave the pup here the pack would accept it. In fact, one of the she-wolves had, at Lucias' hand, lost an entire litter. Given the nature of the beasts, Lucias knew she would be more than willing to replace her lost children with another and protect it as her own.

When she reached the den, she dropped the sleeping pup at its mouth.

Relieved of her burden, she jumped upward, assuming her own form, and made herself comfortable on a high branch in one of the nearer trees. She watched the pup as it awoke and began mewling. And she smiled as the she-wolf who recently lost her litter craned her neck out of the den and toward the crying baby.

Lucias' fear had been that, upon seeing the she-wolf, the pup would transform itself into her image. But it didn't. Its sense of self-preservation—and hunger—overrode its desire for power. It remained a pup. And it remained mewling.

The she-wolf, still all mother, circled around the pup twice and then fell on her side.

When the pup found the warmth of her belly and began to feed, she made no move to push it away.

Knowing it was now out of her hands, Lucias returned to Zamyael to comfort her.

Lucias vowed to return every day thereafter in the form of the wolf until she was certain the child was safe.

Really, this was all there was left that she could do.

-15-

Though it was against all of the rules, I formed himself by Lucias' side and held her hand during the birthing process. I was willing to face any retribution for my disobedience should it come. I wanted, with all of my heart, to be remembered as having bore witness to this rare—and probably exclusive—event.

As I took Lucias' hand in my own, I knew there would be no repercussions. I saw only gratitude and love in her dark brown eyes.

And perhaps understanding. It was almost as though she knew I had overheard her conversation with Noliminan in regard to the fact that I must now assist Zadkiel in raising the babe.

"Do you want to catch him, Azrael?" Zamyael asked, her black eyes somewhat distant. She was still hurting from the loss of her own child.

"May I?" I asked her, wanting nothing more in the world. She nodded and I turned my gaze to Lucias. "My Lady?"

"Yes." She nodded and smiled at me. I realized almost at once that Zamyael's asking the question was Lucias' doing. "The first hands to touch him upon his mortal death should indeed be the ones which bring him into these worlds."

My heart exploded with joy at those words. I stood and walked to the end of the bed, taking Zamyael's place as she walked to the head of the bed and took mine.

The birthing was swift and painless. One minute I was looking at my bare hands and the next the baby was slipping into them. Having witnessed many Gods giving birth, I hadn't expected anything less. The bearing of a God is done at the birthing God's will. Yet, having bore witness to the agonizing pain the mortals endured when they birthed their children, the ease with which this birthing occurred still amazed me.

The moment the baby slipped into my hands, my tears came, accompanied by a joyful laugh.

The child was—is—the most beautiful creature I have ever seen. He has Lucias' face and Noliminan's light brown hair and eyes. Though his face, at the time, was still chubby and new, I rightly predicted it would become a mirror to that of his mother's in her male form.

Having no patience for my adulation, the babe began kicking and let out its first, angry cry. I laughed again and leaned over Lucias, who sat upward and was reaching for the boy with hungry, motherly greed. I handed him over and let out another tearful laugh as Lucias brought the bawling babe first to her lips so she might kiss his head and then to her breast so he might feed.

When the child eagerly latched on, I slipped around the bed to sit on the opposite side of Zamyael and laced my arm around Lucias' well made shoulders. She looked up at me and gave me a peaceful, joyful smile.

"What shall you call him, my Lady?" I realized, as the babe slipped into my hands, that I lost the ability to invade Lucias' thoughts.

"Ishitar." She replied with a tired, amused grin. "My Prince of Providence."

I was helpless but to laugh.

Ishitar, literally translated from the ancient texts, represents a cataclysm of the most devastating magnitude. "For the tasks you mean to give him, his name more than suits."

She smiled her agreement and the three of us fell silent as the babe fed. When he was finished, Lucias, hesitantly, handed the child to me. As she did so, she took on her male form. "Clean him up. And then take him to his father."

I felt my brow rise. Though I understood she meant I was to give little Ishitar to Noliminan, I hadn't realized she meant to hand the child over to Zadkiel so swiftly.

She must have sensed my run of thoughts, however, because she clarified, "Only for a visit. And then I want him back. I mean to keep him in Zamyael's care for a while yet."

Zamyael, who had been staring at the child with silent aching, raised her black eyes and gave Lucias a hopeful smile. "You do?"

"Yes." She nodded. "Until the time comes to return you to Raziel, I see no reason to revert you to your male form. And since you are equipped to do so in your current state, you'll make as good a wet nurse as any Zadkiel can procure."

Zamyael beamed at her. "Thank you."

"But you are to see to your chores, Zamyael." Lucias warned her. "If the child becomes burdensome then we must make other arrangements."

"I will, Lucias." She assured her. "I promise."

"Good." Lucias smiled at her and returned her attention to me. "See to your task, lad."

"Yes, my Lady." Holding the babe close to my chest, I bowed and left them.

As I walked away I heard Zamyael ask the question that had been preying upon her mind for months. "He calls you Lady. Is that the form you prefer, then?"

"Yes." Lucias' answer was hesitant. "It is the form I was born with. Same as you."

"Why did you never tell me?" Zamyael's tone was painful to hear.

"Because it is a secret I cannot reveal." Lucias replied. "Please, Zam. Understand. I am a prisoner of Noliminan's will the same as you."

"My Lady," she replied, causing me to smile. "I assure you that I do."

Still smiling at Zamyael and her immediate ability to amend her thoughts toward Lucias, I allowed the door to close behind my corporeal body so that I might see to my task.

When I reached the bathing pools, I stripped off my robes and slid into the tepid pool with the child in hand. I washed the baby thoroughly, dried him off and then swaddled him in a blanket

Lucias had left on a table beside the pool for just such a purpose. When he was properly wrapped, and I was appropriately clothed, I raised him upward, kissed his soft forehead and lost my form, reappearing outside of Noliminan's bedchamber.

Funnily enough, before then I had never transferred my corporeal body while holding another and I was skeptical that the babe would transfer with me. I was slightly amused to find that he did.

I smiled and then lightly rapped on the door.

"Your Grace," I said, still nuzzling the baby's forehead. "'Tis Azrael. I bear a gift."

"Oh?" He replied in a somewhat irritated tone. "Can it wait?"

"It can." I replied, grinning. "But I think you would rather receive it now."

"Very well." He grunted.

Still grinning, I opened the door and stepped through. Noliminan, seeing the bundle of blanket I carried, sat abruptly forward, his face now the perfect picture of joyful surprise and anticipation. "Is that . . . ?"

"Prince Ishitar. The Prince of Providence." I agreed, stepping forward and handing King Noliminan his son.

He snorted at the name, and the title, but held his hands toward me with jubilant greed. I stepped forward and allowed him to take the child from my arms.

Noliminan nestled the babe and then pulled the blanket away from his face. As he looked down upon his son for the first time, he smiled a smile so beautiful that I was nearly blinded by its glory.

"My son." He replied, looking proudly up at me. "My perfect, magnificent, radiant son!"

"Yes, your Grace." I laughed at him and braved stepping forward to sit upon his bed. "Is he not simply breathtaking?"

"Yes." Noliminan nodded his smile widening. He returned his attention to the babe. I was relieved he chose not to admonish me for taking my liberty. "He is the most breathtaking of all of my creations!"

I smiled, not reminding my Lord and Master he had help with the molding of this particular gob of clay. "Indeed he is."

"Ishitar." He laughed and nuzzled his lips against his son's forehead. "Perfect little Ishitar." Then, very cautiously, he raised his eyes. "I assume you saw Luci?"

I allowed him a guarded smile. "Yes, your Grace."

"Is she well?"

"She is." I smiled. "She's asked if I might take the babe back to her when you are finished with him. You need only call me and I shall come and retrieve him."

Noliminan gave me a long, searching gaze. "Then she isn't returning any time soon?"

"I cannot say, your Grace."

"This is not to say that you do not know." He snorted.

I merely continued to smile.

"Very well." He sighed. "Let the devil play her games." His smile returned as he held the babe upward. His hand was so large that it literally swallowed the back of Ishitar's tiny head. "I shall call you when I a tire of playing."

"Yes, your Grace." I stood, bowed and took my leave through the door.

Once on the other side, I returned, with a somewhat lighter heart, to my duties.

-16-

When Loki finally awoke, some two weeks after Ishitar's birth, it was to find the King of Lords sitting at his bedside wearing a dour expression.

His brow was furrowed. His lips were curled into a tired frown. And his light brown eyes were tracing the length of Loki as though trying to gain a measure of the young God.

When he realized that Loki was awake, and watching him, he snapped his eyes upward to meet his gaze and forced himself to smile. "So. You're finally awake."

Loki didn't respond. He didn't know *how* to respond. He wasn't sure how he felt, in that moment, about the King of Lords sitting at his bedside. He was both angry and exalted at the same time. And he had a feeling that anything he did say would convey neither.

"You've been unconscious for a very long time." Loki watched him, suddenly certain of an undeniable truism: The King of Lords didn't like him.

In fact, given the light burning in his eyes, Loki had no choice but to believe that he loathed him.

"I am relieved that you have finally come around."

Though his expression, and the dark shadows in his eyes, belied his words, this was as close as he would come to making an apology. Loki wisely chose not to respond.

"You shouldn't have defied me."

There it was. And, to this, Loki did respond. His voice, hoarse and cracking from lack of use, didn't hide the irritation which lay on the surface of all other emotions.

Though he acknowledged the fact that Lucias was a Lady in his own mind, he knew that she would never stand for him addressing her as such to others. She didn't want anyone— probably not even the King of Lords—to know how she felt about her true essence. Thus, he respected her enough to refer to her as male when speaking of her with another.

"I didn't defy you, your Grace. I obeyed Lord Regent Lucias."

"My orders supersede his." His tone was sharp, angry. "In the future you will remember this."

"In the future I will respond exactly the same way." Loki braved.

His entire body was thrumming with fear as he spoke. He knew, given his current state, the King of Lords was not a God whose patience should be exploited.

"I beseech your forgiveness, your Grace. But it isn't you I have to live with day in and day out. If I'm meant to face the wrath of either of you, I'd as soon it not be him."

A strange expression crossed the King of Lords' face. Loki didn't much care for it. "You truly are well suited."

Loki, swallowing his fear, shrugged.

"When you see him, will you please tell him I was here?" His tone was tight. "I really do need to speak with him."

"I will tell him, your Grace." Loki promised. What Lady Lucias would chose to do with the information was none of his.

Frowning, he nodded. "If he refuses then you are to tell him that Raguel has given Adam his Eve. I've asked Countenance to interfere with the matter and she is now a grown woman." He lowered his gaze as his features flooded with a somewhat fond expression. "I expect nothing less than that he'll snake his way amongst them and convince her to steal my fruit."

"I will, your Grace." Loki promised. Knowing what he did of Adam, and having already played games with the human, he suspected it wouldn't be Eve that would be the one to eat the damned fruit.

The truth of the matter was that Loki cared not a wit about what happened in regard to the barter over Adam and Eve. His pursuit had ever been the protection of his goatee. He hoped desperately that Sappharon had seen to Adam while he had been unconscious and that the time wasn't wasted due to his inability to participate in Lady Lucias' game.

"I'll come and see you tomorrow." The King of Lords stood.

"Yes, your Grace."

He nodded at Loki, gave him a strange sneer and then left the room.

Loki watched him leave with a sense of relief. He didn't like the conflicting emotions of worship and fear that enveloped him in the King of Lords' presence. It was too damn unsettling.

He understood, a bit, how Lady Lucias must feel about him. And he was sorry for his Mistress.

Not long after, the door opened and the Sovereign Lady stepped in. Loki forced himself to smile.

"Noliminan told me that you are awake." She smiled softly in return. "I'm sorry. I didn't realize he'd snuck in."

"It's okay." Loki replied, not believing that for even a single shift of the shadows. He wouldn't be surprised to find that Raziel had put the bastard up to his visit. "He was amiable enough."

She lowered herself into the chair where the King of Lords had recently been seated. "How are you feeling?"

"Well enough." Loki replied, taking assessment for the first time of his physical condition. "My ankle hurts. But I think I'll try and get up in a little while all the same."

"I'm not surprised." The Lady nodded. "Noliminan visited you directly after you were hurt and healed your wounds. But he failed to mend your ankle." She looked swiftly—guiltily—away. Loki conned, at once, that his broken ankle was meant to be a reminder to hold his tongue. "I hope you don't have a limp."

"I assure you that I won't have." Even if it cut him to the quick every time he took a step, he wouldn't give the King of Lords the smug satisfaction of knowing that his point had been made.

"He was worried you wouldn't wake up." Lady Raziel's voice was distant. Her expression was soft, but her eyes had the vacant stare of someone looking inward.

What game are you playing?

"Lucias, I should mean. He's paid you a visit nearly every day. He'll be sore that he wasn't here when you came to."

"I'm not sure why I didn't." Loki muttered. "I didn't mean to scare him."

"He cares about you." Still in that muttering, distant tone. "A great deal, actually."

"I care about him."

To this she smiled. She seemed to come back a little bit and Loki was glad of that. He didn't like the not there expression that she had worn. "I know that you do."

"He's not taking me back into his service. Is he?"

"No." Lady Raziel was frowning. "He and Zamyael have been assisting the angels and the demons who wish to go to war over their right to free will." Her brow furrowed slightly. "He means to make his strike soon and he doesn't want you to be caught in the middle of it."

Loki ignored his surprise over this news. He knew that Lady Lucias was fighting for the rights of the children. But he had no idea that she meant to fight alongside of them should they rebel.

Lady Raziel didn't need to be told of his ignorance, however, and so he asked a question that he was truly curious to know the answer to. "Are you going to warn the King of Lords?"

She hesitated for a long moment.

Finally, she said, "No."

Loki wanted to ask her why but he held his tongue. He supposed that he already knew the answer to that and he didn't much care for it. With Lady Lucias out of the way, Lady Raziel would be raised to her throne. She would be in complete management of all Thirty of the Hells except the Thirteenth level, which was to become Loki's domain.

"Can he win such a war?" Was the question he asked instead. He was curious about this too. He wasn't certain which was stronger of the two, or if they were equally matched. Though he would never dare voice the words aloud, he suspected the latter to be true.

"If he has enough support on his side." Lady Raziel frowned at him. "But I fear . . ." She shook her head. "No. I don't believe that he will win."

"Can't you stop him?" Loki heard the pleading in his own voice. He already knew the answer to that—the greed in Lady Raziel's eyes to sit at the King of Lords' side as his equal rather than his subordinate was palpable—so it was fruitless to ask.

"I don't want to stop him." Loki hadn't been expecting that honest response. He felt his brow raise as anger burned slowly in his gut. "It needs to be done and he's the only one with enough power to do it."

Liar, he thought. *Selfish, greedy liar.*

"But if you believe that he can't win—"

"At least the point will be made." She smiled coldly at Loki. "I don't like it any more than you do."

Liar!

The word was a screaming echo through his head.

"But it has to be done."

"I want to fight at his side." Loki growled.

"So do I." Lady Raziel continued her attempts to dissuade Loki from his knowledge of the truth. "But he's ordered us both to stay out of it. He has his reasons for that and I must assume they are sound and follow them."

"Then he has given up the fight before it has truly begun." Loki sighed his exasperation.

"No." She corrected him. "He's merely preparing for all eventualities."

Though Loki had always been very leery of Lady Raziel, he now didn't trust her a wit. Nothing else that she might ever say would be taken at its face by the youngling. Yet, if Lady Lucias did fail in her mission—as Lady Raziel so clearly hoped that she would—he would need her on his side.

He'd already lost his favor with the King of Lords. He couldn't afford to ostracize himself from both of the reigning Gods.

"I'm tired."

Lady Raziel, believing she had bamboozled Loki, smiled at him and stood. "I'll leave you to your rest."

"Thank you." Loki sighed as he rolled his eyes closed.

"You're welcome." She replied as she slipped out of the door.

Loki, watching her back as she left him, shuddered.

-17- ·

I watched as Lucias glared at Raziel with quiet anger. Lord Loki had awoken three days before and Raziel had failed to call for her or to even advise her it was so. If she didn't still need Zamyael to help her with the spell work which was required to secure the castle, I sensed Lucias would have backhanded Raziel so hard that Lord Countenance might have only found her five thousand cycles of the sun past Fifth Moon.

As it was, she held her rage at bay.

"You should have called for me the moment he opened his eyes."

"Noliminan was here." Raziel said, her tone soft and filled with pleading for understanding. Lucias, I suspect, knew her better than she knew herself. I am certain she saw the lie of the tone for what it was.

Games were afoot.

And they were games being played at Lucias' expense.

I suddenly remembered Zamyael's warning to Lucias to not give Raziel the upper hand by showing herself to Raziel as a female. I wondered if she was grateful for the counsel and for the fact that she had, for once in her life, listened to Zamyael's well meant advice.

"Then you should have summoned me the moment Noliminan was gone." Lucias' head cocked slightly to the side. Yet she managed, somehow, to hold her patient tone.

"Loki wanted to rest."

"While this might be true," Lucias allowed, "I would have sat at his bed side whilst he slept."

"Luke," Raziel sighed, holding her hands innocently apart at her side, "I apologize. But since you left me with the management of these Thirty Hells—"

"Twenty Nine." Lucias corrected her with narrowed eyes. "Loki, if you remember, is now awake."

Raziel's attempt to give her a warm smile was a failed one. "Of course. Forgive me." To avoid snapping, Lucias appeared to bite the inside of her cheek. "I only meant to remind you that my time has not, necessarily, been my own."

Lucias swallowed and gave Raziel a false smile. It looked real enough on her lips, and the relief which flooded Raziel's eyes proved that Lucias was the master of her true emotions. "Very well. Let it not happen again."

"Never, my Lord." Raziel replied, lowering her gaze.

She wasn't fast enough. By her expression, I kenned Lucias saw the smug satisfaction glimmering in those fiery orbs before they were turned away.

"I must now see to Loki."

"Of course, my Lord."

Lucias turned away from her, allowing whatever games Raziel was playing to wait. Lucias' duty was to Lord Loki in that moment. Not to the protection of her throne. I was pleased by her ability to separate what she wanted to do from what she must do.

If I have the right of things, Lucias would have reflected, as she walked toward Zamyael's bedchamber, that this struggle for power between herself and Raziel had been brewing for some time. If she had missed it, it would have been to her own folly.

She entered the bedchamber and, as her eyes fell upon Lord Loki's face—his still bearded face—Lucias smiled.

Here was one person who would never, under any circumstances, betray her.

I believe the obvious fact of this gave her a minute bit of relief. Lord Loki had no desire to take over the management of the Hells. He found it distasteful enough managing the Thirteenth level. His complete obedience must have pleased Lucias in a manner she would never be able to put into words.

Lucias lowered herself into the chair at Lord Loki's bedside and rubbed the heel of her hand against her tired eye. It was apparent that the routine over the past cycle of the sun had become exhausting.

I, who remained corporeal at the palace on Anticata, bore witness to the fact that the added responsibility Prince Ishitar had presented only served to increase this fatigue. Not to mention that there was still quite a lot of work to be done before Lucias could release Zamyael and call the angels and the demons to the first meeting that would propagate the rebellion which loomed on the horizon.

She turned her gaze to Lord Loki and sighed.

"Damn it, Loki." She muttered, dropping her hand to her lap. "I can't keep up this pace much longer. The spells are almost done and the time has almost come. But I can't pay you, or any of the children, until I know you will survive this."

It was clear to me that, once she made the first strike, there would be no coming back. Lucias would be unable to visit Lord Loki.

There was a knock on the door. Raziel didn't wait for Lucias to respond. She stuck her head in, her fiery eyes blazing and her lips set to a frown. "He's asking for you again."

"Tell him I have no desire to speak with him right now." Lucias growled at her.

Raziel sighed. "I have. Numerous times." She forced a smile. "He really wants to see you. He said it's very important."

"Loki is more important than anything he has to speak with me about." I noticed Lucias was biting her cheek again. I didn't know who she was angrier with: Raziel or Noliminan.

I reasoned that at least Noliminan had the sense to realize he had made a mistake and apologize—if only in his letters to Lucias. Raziel, it would seem, was so consumed with her greed for power she had forgotten everything Lucias had ever done to protect and care for her.

"I cannot hold him at bay forever."

Lucias met Raziel's gaze. "At this juncture, I must keep my distance from him lest I say something we shall both, later, regret."

"Lucias . . ." Raziel sighed. She pushed the door open and stepped in. "Please. Luke. You and I both know he is sorry for his behavior. So you must at least allow him to apologize to you."

"Apologize?" Lucias growled, her voice booming throughout the room. I suspect she knew that Noliminan, waiting for her in the sitting room, had heard her too.

But she didn't seem to care.

"He owes me far more than an apology! And he owes Loki worlds more than that!"

"I know, but—"

"Bwuet Va!" Lucias cut her off. She was still screaming. She appeared to be so wrapped up in her rage that she missed the moment she had been waiting for.

Lord Loki's eyes had sprung open and they were trailing Lucias' enraged profile with unguarded adoration.

"He's going to pay for hurting Loki. He's going to pay dearly." Lucias opened the door and screamed down the hall. "And you can tell him that!"

Raziel sighed. She ran her hand along Lucias' arm. Lucias bore this false display of adoration without verbal complaint. "I'll tell him you are in no mood for guests."

Lucias let out a long, exasperated breath through her teeth. The whistle she is so damned fond of came with it. "Tell him whatever on whichever moon makes *you* feel better."

This earned no response. Raziel merely frowned at her and then slipped out of the room. Lucias watched her go, her anger compounding tenfold.

"I'm not looking forward to granting my fealty to *her* at this juncture."

Lucias started at the sound of Lord Loki's tired voice. It was cracked and dry from lack of use, but she had no care for that. She turned swiftly and fell to her knees so she could grasp Lord Loki's hand desperately in her own.

"You're awake." She whispered, smiling. "When did you open your eyes?"

"Somewhere around the time you promised revenge for my purity." Lord Loki chuckled. Even his chuckle was dry and cracked. The sound of it broke my heart.

Lucias ran her hand over Lord Loki's brow. She smiled adoringly at him. I hope beyond all hopes that Lord Loki could see and understand the true extent of her regard for him.

"Let him apologize to you, my Lady."

Lucias blinked at this. I wasn't certain if she was more surprised by Lord Loki's choice of title or by his willingness to understand that she loved Noliminan and wanted more than anything in the world to hear his apology.

"He doesn't deserve to feel better." Lucias replied, her tone soft.

"No." Lord Loki sighed his agreement. "But you do. And watching him squirm will make you smile."

At those words, she did smile. "I shan't forgive him immediately."

"I wouldn't ask so much of you." Lord Loki muttered. He rolled his eyes closed and laid his head back upon the pillow. "I'm tired, my Lady." Lucias nodded. "Go speak to him." And then in a tone which rang with the truth of his emotions. "If for no other reason than to make him go away. I do not wish to look upon his face again." And then with a blush. "Yet."

"Very well." She smiled at him, seeming to be understanding of his ambivalence. "I shall allow him to apologize to me if it will make you feel better."

"Thank you, my Lady." Lord Loki whispered.

By the time she reached the sitting room, Noliminan had gone.

Lucias didn't seem to feel like trailing after him. She muttered a promise under her breath that she would speak with Noliminan later.

Not knowing, of course, at that time, that circumstances would make it so that later would never come.

-18-

Sappharon, who had stayed in contact with the angels and demons who meant to revolt, had hidden herself in her bedchamber for five days after Raystlyn last visited her. Fifty eight angels, at Raystlyn's last estimation, had been discharged from their services and sold to various brothels against their will.

Sappharon shuddered as she ran her fingers through her unkempt hair.

When the first brothel had been created in the Hells it had been the design of a demon named Sooka, who had been discharged and—at Lady Lucias' mercy—been given the choice of exile or of finding work in the Hells where she could support her own needs.

Grateful to Lucias, Sooka made her way to the public kitchens on the Sixth level of the Hells.

A true beauty, she found herself the subject of unwanted advances by both Gods and demons. Fearful she would be raped, she sought Sappharon's wisdom. Sappharon's advise was that, while Sooka would be defiled one way or the other given she had no God to protect her, she could take control of her own fate. If she were Sooka, Sappharon had advised, she would give what the Gods and demons wanted only if they were willing to pay a price.

Sooka had taken to the task with gusto. In a single year's time, she had gathered all of the disgraced demons on the Sixth level and turned enough of a profit that she was able to advertise her protection to demons without Gods on other levels.

And they had answered.

After yet another year, Lucias found it necessary—due to complaints from the Gods—to call Sooka to her counsel. She talked to her, sympathized with her plight, and granted her the rare advantage—as a demon or angel—to become the Mistress of all fallen, but not yet exiled, demons and angels who were willing to work in her employment rather than any one of the kitchens.

Sooka, of course, accepted. As a result, she was now considered the third most powerful demon in all of the levels of the Hells.

The first, of course, was Zamyael. And the second was Sappharon, herself.

Over time, the Gods became incensed with the idea that a demon—let alone a woman—would have control over the only royally approved pleasure house within any of the Realms. In retaliation, they established unauthorized brothels of their own. Though, in these brothels, the angels and demons who were employed were not necessarily there voluntarily.

It was to these brothels that the fifty eight angels Raystlyn had come to speak with Sappharon about were bartered.

And treated cruelly, by Raystlyn's accounts to Sappharon.

When she heard the door to the apartment opening for the first time in Lord Countenance alone knew how long, she stared at her own door in fear. Then, when she heard Lady Lucias calling out to her, she sprang from her bed, her indignation raging, through her bedchamber door, down the hall and into Lucias' arms.

Lucias, who wore her female form whenever she was near her son, hadn't been expecting Sappharon to fly at her and she, at first, froze. Upon sensing Sappharon's grief, however, her arms wrapped around the demon and she held her tight, kissed the crown of her head and muttered, "What's wrong with you, child?"

Sappharon pulled away.

"My Lady . . ." She closed her eyes tightly, trying to stay her tears. She didn't want to cry in front of Lady Lucias. And she hated herself for not being able to stave her pain.

"Sappharon . . ." Lady Lucias' tone was filled with her overwhelming concern for Sappharon's feelings. This served to only make her feel worse. "Met paken? What troubles?"

Sappharon shook her head and buried her face against Lady Lucias' soft bosom. She let out a single sob, her own sensibilities burning. "I'm sorry, my Lady."

"Sorry?" Lady Lucias' hand stroked the back of her head. Her tone was warm, but very tentative. "What has happened?"

She raised her gaze and met Lucias'. The concern she found in her Mistresses dark brown eyes was not feigned. "My Lady, we must act now."

"Now?" She replied, frowning.

"I know you told me not to meet with the others, but—"

Lady Lucias pushed her away. Sappharon stumbled over her robes and onto the floor. She stared up at her Lady with pained indignation.

"I gave you a direct order." Lady Lucias groused. "With the intent to help you out of the prison you have trapped yourself within!"

"I know." Sappharon forced herself to her knees and held her hands out in supplication. "You don't understand. They come to me. And they tell me what is happening. We haven't been meeting as a group. And—"

She swallowed and lowered her gaze. She raised her hands to her face as she did so, not wanting Lady Lucias to see the pain radiating through her soul.

"Everything is escalating. Not improving. And I'm running out of excuses as to why you refuse to help them."

"Refuse?" Lucias' expression was as pained as her tone. "Do they believe I refuse?"

"I tell them you do not." Sappharon assured her, terrified of her Mistresses reaction. "But they are starting to not believe me."

She lowered her gaze and bit back her discontentment.

"They need you, my Lady." She whispered. "And, if not you, then someone." She raised her gaze, terrified of the repercussions of her next word. "Now."

Lady Lucias raised her slender hands to cover her face. Hidden from Sappharon's regard, she shook her head.

When she spoke, her voice was a pained whisper. "I'm not ready."

"If not you," Sappharon swallowed, "then whom?"

Lucias' hands lowered, though her eyes remained closed. She stood in silence, her expression one of excruciating pain. When she spoke, her voice was a whisper.

"Ask them to give me one more cycle of the sun." She opened her eyes and met Sappharon's gaze. "Ishitar . . ."

"I understand, my Lady." Sappharon sighed. "But a year with your babe is a luxury your other children cannot afford."

As if struck, Lady Lucias paled.

And then she nodded.

"Tell Zadkiel that I need him." She muttered. "But tomorrow. Zamyael will not easily give up another child. Especially one she's actually held at her breast and bonded with."

Relieved that Lucias understood the magnitude of the situation, Sappharon closed her eyes, nodded and promised to do what she could.

Though Lucias' desires should circumvent those of the angels and demons seeking Sappharon's help, Sappharon couldn't, after all of this time of promising Lucias would protect them, betray them.

She wished with all of her soul that she could.

-19-

Zadkiel watched the door of his cottage bathed in anticipation.

Sappharon had told him that Lucias meant to deliver Prince Ishitar to him that day.

It was something he wanted so badly that his entire soul sang with joy. It was his one chance for redemption, true. But his joy had more to do with his anticipation than that.

273

This was to be one of the most powerful Gods ever created. And this child was to be raised by *him.*

Despite all of their disappointments in him, Zadkiel was the one they had entrusted this responsibility to. And he would not fail them. No matter the personal consequences. He would prove to them both that they had made the right decision.

It was well past dawn when he heard the knock. He made his way—still without his staff—painfully to the door and opened it. When he saw me standing on the other side, babe and staff in my hands, Zadkiel grinned. "Come in, Az."

"You know I am not allowed." I smiled at him as I handed Zadkiel his long lost staff. "Why must you anger him?"

"I suppose it's my nature." Zadkiel shrugged. He grinned as he positioned the staff under his arm and reached for the beautiful child in my arms. Still smiling, I handed the baby over. Zadkiel brought the boy toward himself and laughed, joyfully, as Ishitar pulled at his long, gold hair. "Thank you, Azrael."

I gave him a guarded smile and nodded.

"Take very good care, Zad." I cautioned. "Any step you make out of right will propagate destruction."

"Yes." He agreed with a sigh. "It will."

"Just so." I laid my brown skinned hand upon Zadkiel's golden shoulder. "Good luck, brother."

"And to you." Zadkiel returned.

Terrified of what the future might hold, I replied, "And to us all."

-20-

Zamyael shook the bars until she was satisfied that they would not budge. She lifted her gaze and shot Lucias—wearing her male form now that Ishitar was gone—a grand smile. "I think we've finally done it."

Lucias smiled in response and nodded to her.

"Good. My fingers are itching." She walked over to the cell and tried the door herself. It flew easily open upon her touch. "And Raziel wants you back."

"Is she angry with me?"

Lucias shook her head, stepped behind her and wrapped her arm around her waist. It felt good to stand beside her, cradled in her arms. Though she now thought of Lucias as female given she knew that was the face Lucias preferred to wear, she blushed slightly when she felt the hard column of Lucias' lust—given she wore her male face—pressed against her.

It meant that Lucias coveted her still. As she still coveted Lucias.

Zamyael would miss her sorely.

"With me."

"I'll miss you."

"I shall miss you too." Her voice was soft to Zamyael's ear. "But it is well over time you return. The dathanorna is hidden, Ishitar has been placed with Zadkiel and our work here is done. I have no excuse to keep you from her any longer."

Zamyael nodded. She didn't know where her child had been hidden. Lucias refused to tell her. But she knew it was in good care and, though her grief cut her to the quick, this was all that mattered.

"I know you must return me to my male form." She said, her gaze lowering.

"I must." Lucias agreed. "For your own protection."

"Can you delay it?" She asked, braving to look at Lucias once more.

"To what purpose?"

She sighed. "I must seek out Lasterian."

"You cannot tell him about—"

"No." She agreed. "I know." Then with a tired sigh. "But I can show him my true face. And I can give him the apology he desperately deserves."

Lucias considered her. Her dark eyes danced over Zamyael's face. Finally, she nodded. "You have sixty shifts of Countenance's shadow. Upon the end of those shifts, I will cast the spell."

"It is long enough." She agreed.

"And you cannot be seen."

"No." She agreed to this too. "Not by anyone but Lasterian and, if necessary, Tristan."

"You're doing the right thing." Lucias acknowledged.

"Yes." She agreed.

She bid Lucias goodbye, willing herself after she had done so to stand before Tristan's door. She hesitantly raised her hand—she was terrified—and knocked.

("You actually went to your pathetic little angel before you came to me?" Raziel snaps.

("My Lady," Zamyael's voice is small and her gaze lowered. "I owed him an—"

(Raziel spins violently in her chair, striking Zamyael. I feel myself flying forward, wanting to interfere but knowing any move I make to protect her will result in the punishment of us both.

("This is the worst of it!" She cries. "The infidelity and the baby I could bear! But not immediately coming to me after—"

("My Lady?" I force my tone to be respectful. "We're running out of time."

(Her angry gaze flies in my direction. She spits, "This does not concern you, Azrael."

("You're right, my Lady." I agree, my gaze lowered. "It doesn't." I force a smile. "So I beg you wait until I've finished and punish Zamyael then."

(Zamyael's eyes are burning with gratitude. I allow myself to send her thoughts of my affection. She seems to hear them. She relaxes slightly as she lowers her gaze to her hands.

("Fine." Raziel spits. "Finish it then."

("Yes, my Lady."

(I close my eyes and nod in supplication, returning, somewhat relieved, to my tale.)

The door was answered almost immediately.

Not by Lasterian, however. It was answered by Tristen.

He stared at her, his eyes dancing over her face as if trying to determine who she was. Finally he realized—marking that she was wearing her scooped skirt and braids as she did—there could only be one female demon who would brave to knock upon his Heavens' bound door.

His greeting was a tight bark. "Zamyael."

She swallowed back her fear as his rage consumed him. "My Lord, I must speak with Lasterian."

His blue eyes narrowed and his expression became cold. "To say what to him, exactly?"

"To . . ." She swallowed. "To apologize." She lowered her gaze. "Please, my Lord. If he sees my true face . . . If I tell him my story . . . Perhaps he will understand why I hurt him as I did."

She could feel his eyes darting over her. Over her face and over her breasts, which were bare because she wore only her skirt.

And she could feel his rage dissipating as his desire to touch her—to take her—consumed him.

"Only if I may hear your story as well." He finally said.

It was a small price to pay. She let out a long, deep breath which swallowed a sob and nodded her head vigorously. "Yes, my Lord."

She followed him into his apartment, her gaze lowered in supplication. She could feel his eyes upon her as he looked over his shoulder, stealing glances at her, his mood calming with every step.

When they reached Lasterian's room, Tristan reached for the handle of the door, not bothering to knock. He pushed the door open and stepped in before her. When he spoke, his tone was gentle. And it was kind.

"Lasterian." He muttered. "Zamyael has come to speak with you."

She braved to raise her gaze then. When her eyes fell upon Lasterian, she let out a surprised and horrified gasp.

His features were gaunt and his hair unkempt. His eyes—his beautiful navy blue eyes—were round and haunted.

He said nothing to her. He only watched as she stepped forward and gave him a curtsy.

Swallowing, she licked her lips. And then, after apologizing to him, she told him her tale.

He listened—they both listened—and he came back to himself toward the end. Enough so that, though she promised Lucias she wouldn't, she shared with him her news about their child.

"A baby?" He asked, his voice low and weak. "My child?"

Tristan shifted uncomfortably at Zamyael's side. But he said nothing. She knew by the sorrowful expression upon his face that he had no intention of betraying either one of them.

"Are you angry I did not come to you?" She asked. "That I went to Lucias instead?"

"No." He shook his head, his eyes—still haunted—swept over her face before finding the fold of his hands. "I wouldn't have listened to you then. I wouldn't have believed you if you had come to me in your male form."

Biting her lip, she nodded. "I'm desperately sorry, Lasterian."

He was silent for a moment. When he finally spoke, it was to ask Tristan to leave them alone. With great hesitation, the God complied.

When he was gone, Lasterian let out a long, tired sigh. "It isn't you I am angry with at this juncture."

Zamyael swallowed and raised her gaze.

"I was." He admitted. "But I would have eventually recovered from your ill actions toward me."

"Why, then?" She asked, raising her hand and indicating his current state.

"Evanbourough, at first." He muttered. "And then my father."

"Your father?" She started. She couldn't imagine Camael doing or saying anything which would harm his one and only child.

"Aye." He sighed. "When I told him I strayed from Tristan's service—I didn't tell him about what really happened because I was embarrassed by it at the time—he explained to me exactly what it was the King of Lords did to him upon learning of my siring."

He shook his head, obviously grieved by Camael's plight. As she had always been.

"It wasn't exactly a surprise that he'd been punished. He'd told me that before. It was the severity of the punishment which concerned me." He sighed. "Though he told me such would not be the case if I spoke with Tristan, I became afraid that if—"

He swallowed. And then he went on.

"I became afraid that if Tristan were to learn what had happened to me then the same might befall me. Especially after Evanbourough told me he would be angry with me." He lowered his gaze. "And when he did learn, he treated me as damaged goods rather than someone who was hurting and in need of his comfort and counsel."

Zamyael felt her eyes stinging with her tears. Her pain for him was physically palpable to her. She lowered her gaze and shook her head. "Evanbourough and Tristan have both behaved abhorrently."

"They have." Lasterian agreed. His tone was flat. "But Evenbourough isn't my keeper. Tristan is. And it is Tristan's betrayal I shall never forgive."

"I'm so sorry."

He was silent for a moment. When he finally spoke, his tone was soft. "I forgive you, Zamyael."

Biting her lower lip, she nodded. "Thank you."

He reached for her hand. She let him take it.

Zamyael wasn't certain how long they sat together in silence. Long enough that she returned to her male form and Tristan, finally unable to stay his curiosity, returned to check on the pair.

It was then, as he slipped into the room, that she knew it was time to take her leave.

"Goodbye." She whispered before leaning forward and kissing Lasterian's forehead.

She gave Tristan a curtsy and then left them both, using her limited magic to will herself home.

As Raziel's sitting room appeared around her, her smile faded. Now it was time to see if Raziel had become aware of the true reasons she had, necessarily, been gone.

She found her Lady in her library pouring over a new Tome. Seeing her so, with a look of such utter concentration, gave her time to force the smile she was required to grant her Mistress to her lips. She wasn't certain, at the moment, how she felt about Raziel. And, more importantly, she knew it didn't matter because Raziel wouldn't care. She expected Zamyael to behave a certain way and Zamyael knew it was in her best interest to give Raziel what she wanted.

"Looks important." She said when she was ready.

Raziel started and looked upward. The intense concentration was replaced by a slow brewing, somewhat sloppy grin. "I'm writing it for Adam."

"Noliminan won't be pleased."

"*That's* unfortunate." The smile grew wider. "Welcome home."

"It's good to be home."

"Loki is staying with us." Raziel's voice was gentle. It held a touch of desire to it which Zamyael recognized all too well. "Just until he's on his feet."

"Okay." What else could she say?

"He's staying in your room." The smile granted to her was apologetic. "Will you stay with me in mine?"

"It shall be torturous but somehow I think I can bide."

Raziel chuckled at this. Her words echoed Zamyael's own. "Noliminan won't be pleased."

"*That's* unfortunate." She smiled around the words. Cock blocking Noliminan suited Zamyael just fine.

"When does he plan to make his first strike?" The fullness of Lady Raziel's curiosity was only partially recognizable in the tone of her voice. Anyone else would have missed it, thinking the question was born out of courtesy. But Zamyael knew her far too well for her trickery to work on her.

"I would imagine soon." Zamyael replied. Then with some honesty, "He didn't to tell me. He thought it best I not know in case . . ."

She let her voice trail off. Everyone knew where she had been for the past while and if a certain someone was angry enough after the first strike was made, torturing Zamyael for information would not be at the bottom of the to do list.

Raziel's nostrils flared. "He'd best keep his distance from you. After Loki—he wouldn't dare."

What Noliminan would or wouldn't dare do was one of those questions whose response was always up for grabs. Zamyael had been the brunt of his frustrations where Lucias was concerned on far too many occasions. She—better than anyone else—knew exactly what the Bwuet Va was capable of.

"By any road, I don't know."

"It's a shame." Raziel sighed. "I'd like to be ready."

Zamyael didn't respond. Whatever Lucias had planned there would be no 'being ready' for it. She'd refused to tell Zamyael what even the cages in the cellar were meant for. Zamyael thought now, as she was looking at Raziel, she might know.

But she couldn't tell Raziel her suspicions. Her discretion had been the only thing Lucias had asked of her after hiding her child.

"Do you mind if I bathe before I resume my duties?"

"Do you mind if I join you?" Raziel asked with a playful, hungry grin. Zamyael smiled and shook her head. She did mind. She loathed placating Raziel with her disgusting male parts. But she wasn't stupid enough to let her mistress know this. "Go to it. I need to finish up a paragraph and then I'll join you."

Zamyael, relieved that she had managed to escape Raziel's wrath over her absence, happily obeyed.

-21-

It was one of those very rare occasions when Raguel knew she wouldn't be seeing Noliminan that day and so allowed herself to wear her natural form. She had come to loathe this form. But sometimes she chose to wear it so she could walk about without being recognized.

Especially when her intent was to sit by Loki's bedside to bring him comfort because she knew Raziel wasn't at home.

As she was walking, she became suddenly aware that someone was watching her. Irritated by this, she turned her gaze southward to find out who it was. When she saw that it was Lucias she froze in her tracks.

Her fear didn't stem only from the fact that he was one of the few people who would recognize her face. Also, there was something about his expression which was troublesome, if not frightening.

She raised her hand in greeting and turned to face him. As she did so, the strange smile Lucias was wearing grew cold and his generally bronzed face grew pale. She meant to ask him if he was okay, but there wasn't the opportunity to do so. Too swiftly he was advancing upon her, his hands curled into claws and his eyes burning with insanity.

"I'm sorry." He said.

The question as to what he was sorry about began forming in Raguel's mind but never had the opportunity to materialize.

In a flash, he was upon her, his fingers digging into her eye sockets. She screamed from both surprise and pain and began bucking her body, trying to get him off of her.

It was no use. Lucias, fully made from Noliminan, was far stronger than Raguel.

She heard the sickening *plop, plop* beneath the cries of her own painful scream and understood with lightning clarity that Lucias had ripped out her eyes.

She raised her own clawing, angry hands to his face, but this gave Lucias a greater grip on her. She felt strong hands grasp at the very base of the bone of her wings, which she only wore in this form, and heard the crack of them as Lucias pulled violently upward, ripping them off of her back.

She screamed from the agony of this and began kicking at Lucias, though this gained her no advantage. She felt Lucias' arms wrapping around her waist; she felt herself lurching as Lucias transported them to some sort of room which was vast and cold.

The ground struck her hard when Lucias dropped her. She sprang up, grateful to be out of the death grip that Lucias had held her in and screamed in frustration as she heard the unmistakable clang of heavy metal and the much quieter click of a lock as a door latched closed.

She flung herself in this direction—blind and so unable to even guess the distance—and cried out with pain as her already battered body hit the cold metal of bars.

She understood in that moment that she had been locked in some sort of cage. That she was now Lucias' prisoner. And if she didn't figure out the spell work around the cage—and fast— she was to be the subject of Azrael only knew what manner of torture and humiliation.

"He shouldn't have attacked Loki." Lucias' voice was calm. There was not even the smallest ounce of apology within his words. "It's his fault you are here. So, if you're going to be angry with anyone, be angry with him."

Panic seized Raguel as she grasped the bars holding her captive and began shaking them.

He's gone mad!

"I'm not responsible for Loki." Raguel cried. "Please—you can't do this to me."

"Forgive me." Lucias did not sound sorry at all. "But that means little and less to me. This is about Noliminan and his treatment toward the children. It is not about you, personally."

"Lucias, please—!"

"I'm not any fonder of you than you are of me so let's not make this any harder than it has to be on either of us." Lucias growled, cutting her off. "I've got a present I must deliver to Noliminan now." He chuckled. "Lovely jewels of emerald and soft feathers of white."

"Lucias—!"

"You're going to be here a while." He advised her. "You might as well become comfortable with the idea."

Raguel heard the crackle in the air which told her Lucias had gone and her panic overwhelmed her. She began screaming; she was helpless not to.

She wondered in some distant portion of her mind if anyone could hear her. Knowing Lucias, she supposed they probably could not.

Yet she was helpless to stop herself. So she went on screaming with every ounce of pain and fear that coursed through her until her throat hurt and her voice failed her. And, she went on pulling at the bars until she fell in a heap to the floor, exhausted.

She understood very clearly she was trapped; no amount of spell work was going to free her.

Even more clear was that she was at the mercy of a God who loathed her. A God who had done untold things to those he was charged to punish.

If he could do those untold things to beings he cared about, he would feel no compunctions as he carried about whatever pains he intended to inflict on Raguel.

"Dear Gods . . ." She muttered to the empty room. "Zadkiel . . . please just claim me now."

-22-

Michael put his book aside, angry by Raphael's sudden burst through his cottage door. His anger dissipated, however, when he saw the ashen expression on his brother's face. He flew to his feet and stepped swiftly toward him. "What on which moon is the matter with you, Raphael?"

"Everything." His brother's voice was shaking and his body was trembling. His arms were hidden behind his back. Michael tried to look around him, but Raphael was having none of it.

Nor was it required.

Raphael thrust his shaking hands forward, showing Michael what he was holding. At first, it didn't register. The wings did, but not the round pieces of jelly he held in his other palm. "What—?"

"Lucias gave them to me." Raphael swallowed. Hard. Michael shook his head, still not comprehending. "They belong to Queen Raguel, Michael."

Michael recoiled. He stared down at the broken and battered wings and the jelly like objects with sudden, horrific comprehension. Those bits of jelly were *eyes*.

Raguel's eyes!

Raguel's beautiful, emerald green eyes.

Eyes which had looked upon me with such devastation of the soul in her pain of my rejection of her.

And with so much love for me as she bid me away for my own protection when I, thereafter, sought her favor.

"The Gods . . ." He hit Raphael's hand, forcing him to drop the horrific items to the ground. He was used to the brutality of war. He had seen severed body parts before and it never phased him. But, loving Raguel as he did, he couldn't bear the sight of them. "The Queen of Ladies . . . ?"

What a fool I am . . . What a Gods be damned fool.

"He has her captive." Raphael shook his head. "He said he's going to hold her captive until King Noliminan agrees to a list of his terms."

"Loki's beard . . ."

"We're damned." Raphael cried. "All of us damned."

"Not all of us." Michael closed his eyes for a moment.

He had to regain his senses.

Now was not the time for grieving or self pity. There would be plenty of that later.

He forced the soldier in him to push aside the lover and opened his eyes to look upon Raguel's bits and pieces. "You have to give those things to King Noliminan. He has to understand what is going on."

"I cannot." Raphael whispered. "He'll send me to Zadkiel!"

"He'll send you to Zadkiel if you don't tell him." Michael warned him.

"I cannot do it, Michael." He shook his head vigorously. "I cannot bear the thought—I don't want to see his face."

"There's no help for it, Raph." Michael sighed, frustrated with him.

"Will you not give them to him in my stead?" His voice was shaking and his face went ashen again. "He likes you best."

This was a lie and they both knew it. Obviously, King Noliminan liked Raphael best or Raphael wouldn't have been chosen to be his right hand.

Michael was his warrior. Not his friend, as he suspected Raphael was. He'd never even spent a single day in King Noliminan's personal service.

"Raphael, I cannot." Not being able to look at them, how was he to touch them? And how could he look King Noliminan in the eye without being overcome with rage and loathing because King Noliminan had failed to protect Queen Raguel?

"Please, Michael." Raphael cried. "I beseech you!"

Michael sighed. His eyes darted to the bits of Queen Raguel's body lying on the floor. He knew that, even though his love for his Queen haunted him, he was stronger of spirit than Raphael. He also knew that if King Noliminan was to be told Lucias had finally lost his tether that it would have to be him doing the telling.

And—he understood this, too—it would be Michael who would be asked to bring their father to justice.

"Damn it, Raphael." Michael sighed again.

It isn't his fault. He doesn't know about your love for the Queen.

"I'm sorry . . ." Raphael's eyes, so alike to King Noliminan's, shimmered with his tears. "I just . . . I cannot bear to . . ."

"What about Raziel?" Michael wanted to know the full extent of the thing before he sullied King Noliminan with the news. It was better to think through all of the corners than to be taken by surprise. "Is she safe?"

"Yes." Raphael swallowed. "For now."

Michael nodded. He understood well enough. If King Noliminan would give into the demands that Lucias' had made upon him this day, everything would go away and peace would be restored.

If he didn't . . .

Well. If he doesn't, then Lucias will go as far as destroying everything King Noliminan loves a piece at a time. And damn the consequences.

Michael couldn't let that happen. He had to find Lucias and bring him to justice before anyone aside from the Queen of Ladies could get hurt.

"Stay here." He demanded of Raphael. "If you aren't going to be brave enough to face him then it's best I see to this task alone." He didn't mean to be cruel and he was sorry when Raphael flinched. "He'll take one look at you and panic."

"I'm sorry, Michael."

Michael believed that he was.

He nodded at him and used his more godly magic—which, being the sons of Lucias and Raziel, the twelve of us are all blessed with but rarely ever use—to will himself to King Noliminan's rooms. Once there, he made his way through and, eventually, found King Noliminan in the back on the open veranda, halfway through a bottle of whiskey.

"Your Grace." He bowed, his eyes never leaving King Noliminan's profile. "I seek your audience."

King Noliminan looked upward and Michael was struck, yet again, by how alike to Raphael he looked. He found a smile for Michael. It was a smile which infuriated Michael deep to the soul given what he must tell him.

Where were you? Rutting with one of your damn whores? You should have been protecting her!

"Of course, Michael."

Michael flashed him a false smile in response which was all teeth. King Noliminan must have sensed the doom in such a smile because his expression grew immediately serious. "Thank you, your Grace."

"What ill news?" He asked, his brow high over his left eye. "You look as though the devil has trapped your heart."

Near enough to the point, Michael thought, unable to pull back his gruesome grin.

He gave a curt nod and stepped forward, lowering himself to one knee before King Noliminan so he was looking up at him rather than down. He knew King Noliminan preferred his head to be higher than those of his servants and he had ever complied with such requests when the conversation between them must be formal.

There was nothing for it. The time had come. He swallowed back his fear and loathing and did what he had ever done in moments such as this by raising his hand to his chest and performing his duty. "Lord Regent Lucias has made a strike for war."

King Noliminan frowned. His expression was that of a man who did not look at all surprised. "Surely not."

"Surely so." Michael nodded at him. "He's captured the Queen of Ladies." Here he forced himself to use an even tone lest his emotions betray him. "He's cut out her eyes and pulled the wings off of her back. I have them at my cottage."

King Noliminan's expression would have been horrifically comic to Michael in another situation. His eyes were wide and his nostrils were flaring. He looked like a wild horse gone mad.

When he spoke, his voice was deep and troubled. "Just Raguel?"

"As far as we know." Michael returned, honestly. "He'll take what you love from you a soul at a time."

The King of Lords nodded his understanding. But Michael knew him well. He knew his pride well. He wouldn't understand the full measure of Lucias' intent until everyone that King Noliminan held dear fell into his trap.

"What would you have me do, your Grace?" Michael asked.

"First, bring Raziel to me." Michael nodded. He would have tried to do so even if he hadn't been asked. "And none of her games or excuses."

-23-

Raziel listened to every word Michael said, her heart growing heavier by the moment. She held no true regard for Raguel anymore, but she couldn't show that. Raguel was, after all, her daughter. Now was not the time to be glad she was out of the way.

What she said was, "I'm not going anywhere."

"My Lady, you have no choice." Michael growled at her. "The King of Lords has issued you a direct order."

"An order I will defy." She shrugged. She didn't believe she was in any real danger from Lucias and, so, she didn't see a need for the dramatics.

"Now is not the time to try his patience." Michael warned. "You are to come with me and you are to come with me now. Or he will come after you himself and he will punish you for your disobedience."

She allowed her eyes to dance over Michael's face for a long moment. Finally, she acknowledged within herself that her son was right. If Lucias had taken Raguel, then Noliminan's patience would be pushed to its limits.

Now was, indeed, not the time to press the issue.

"Very well." She muttered. "I'll go. But find Zamyael and tell him to pack my things."

"I will, my Lady." Michael agreed, his lips pursed.

Not waiting to see if Michael would do as he was bid—there was no need to; Michael always did as he was bid—Raziel willed herself to Noliminan's apartment. She stepped to the veranda, where Noliminan was sitting and, with her arms crossed over her chest, growled, "Well?"

Noliminan turned his eyes in her direction. They were blazing with fury. Raziel had the better sense to suddenly be frightened.

"To the Hells with you, Raziel." He said as he raised his finger and pointed it at her. "To the Hells with you and Lucias, both."

The world spun swiftly around her and she began to stagger with her disorientation. Finally, darkness consumed her and she fell in a heap on the floor.

When she awoke, some several days later, it was to the crying, screaming agony of the souls trapped on the Thirteenth level of the Hells.

Noliminan, it would seem, had damned her.

-24-

The court was called quickly. Theasis sat by herself this time. Evanbourough had secured a seat by his beloved Tristan.

She was happy for them both that they had reconciled.

Not wanting to sit alone, however, she was relieved when she saw Loki, still bearded but walking with a slight limp, approaching her. The handsome God smiled, bowed and then asked for a seat. "If I won't be intruding."

"As long as your gaggle remains a safe distance away, then you shan't be." Theasis replied with a smile, standing and pointing to the chair beside her. "How are you?"

"Well enough." Loki replied, leaving out all detail. "Though I'll be better with the promise of your soft company."

"It is granted." Theasis replied, her grin widening. She was coming to care for Loki and she had no intention of tempering such emotions. "I shall even make your supper."

Loki chuckled at this. "You're an abhorrent cook."

Theasis smiled, not offended. "Then you shall make my supper."

"Better." Loki grinned at her.

There was no more time for pleasantries.

The King of Lords stood. Gabriel blew his horn. All was still.

Loki and Theasis also fell still. The three vacant thrones at the head of the room put off an ominous, angry glow which could not be denied. Theasis reached for Loki's hand and squeezed it tight. She knew Loki cared for his God and that his absence must weigh very heavy on Loki's mind.

Matters were not helped any when the King of Lords' angry, tired gaze fell straight upon the pair of them. "Where is he, Loki?"

"I'm not at liberty to say, your Grace." Loki replied to this. Though his tone was proud, he had the common sense to keep it low and respectful

"I am ordering you to say." The King of Lords' voice was silky in its direction.

"I understand, your Grace." Loki shrugged as he gave over to the King of Lords his fealty. "But Lucias issued me his order to keep his location a secret first."

There was a collective moan in the room. Everyone was catching their breath and waiting for the King of Lords' to rage.

Theasis sensed that he was about to explode when he, suddenly, spun around to glare in the direction of the Quorum.

"Azrael!" Terrified, I rose and stepped forward. "Where is he?"

"My Lord." My voice shook and my eyes were darting around the room. "My tongue is bound. I cannot let it loose. The consequences for me would be dire."

"I *order* you to tell me!" The King of Lords said in a calm tone as he stepped toward me with his hand raised. I cried out and flinched back. He stopped the blow but an inch from my face. Then he added, through gritted teeth, "Where is he, Azrael?"

I swallowed and forced my back to straighten. Theasis felt Loki's hand clamp tight around her own. "Your Grace, I am bound . . ."

He flew at me in a rage, his eyes bulging wide and his nostrils flaring. He picked me up with one deft hand and hurled me across the room. Loki flinched. Everyone else sat watching in stunned horror.

Everyone that was, except Evanbourough.

To Theasis' dismay, Evanbourough flew from his seat, jumped upward and outward and flung himself between my hurtling body and the wall. Evanbourough grabbed me and quickly spun himself around so it was his back which took the brunt of the blow rather than my spinning body.

Theasis cried out and stood—ready to bolt. Loki grabbed her hand and forced her to bide.

The silence in the room following this fracas was deafening.

Every pair of eyes was turned to the heap on the floor that was myself and Evanbourough. I began to stir. I stood upright, shaking my head, and then began staggering in a strange circle which spoke volumes as to my disorientation.

Evanbourough continued to lie, unconscious, on the ground.

After recovering from his surprise, Tristan ran to Evan, scooped him up in his arms and began rocking him back and forth. As he did so he let out a long, low and guttural scream.

The King of Lords, enraged beyond all telling, screamed over it, advancing on me with such speed that he was little more than a blur. As blindingly fast as my Master, Metatron flew from his waiting stance to place himself before me in an attempt to protect me.

The King of Lords, blind in his rage, stopped dead before Metatron. A look of utter confusion that the archangel would defy him crossed every line of his brow.

"Your Grace, it is enough." Metatron pleaded, the flames which made up his body dancing wildly around him. He was clearly as terrified of the King of Lords as I was. "You cannot force Azrael to loosen his tongue. There are far too many consequences should he do so." His fiery eyes darted around the room. "Aside what might happen to him, personally, you shall never have the trust of this Council again if they know you can force him to tell you what you want to know at your whim."

"This is not a whim!" He raged as his hand flew, striking Metatron across his cheek. "Lucias has Raguel! Azrael alone knows what he is doing to her! I must know where he is so I can reclaim her!"

"You aren't going to be able to reclaim her." Zamyael's gentle voice danced through the silence. Theasis felt Loki tug at her hand and she very slowly sat down. "He's spelled the place so you can't get near it."

The King of Lords turned on his heel and glared at Zamyael. "Do you know where he is?"

"Yes, your Grace." Zamyael replied. "But knowing isn't going to help you. His magic is powerful."

"Tell me anyway." The King of Lords stormed toward her, his hand raised again.

Zamyael merely laughed at him. "Aren't you strong and brave? Nearly killing two of your court before all eyes of the Gods. And now you're after me?"

"Zamyael . . ." Michael begged her.

It did no good.

"Well go on, then." Zamyael stood, threw her head back and glared upward at the King of Lords. "You can't possibly do anything to me that's any worse than what you've done to me before." She snapped. "So go on."

"I am losing my patience with you and your complaints, Zam." He growled down at her through gritted teeth. "Tell me where Lucias is hiding."

Zamyael stood her ground. The King of Lords was just about to strike her when Tristan called across the room in an angry, growling voice. "For the love of the Gods. He's at your earthly palace on Anticata. Just . . . Please, your Grace. Leave her be."

Theasis felt her brow rise. Evanbourough had told her what Zamyael had done to Lasterian. That it would be Tristan who rose to the demon's defense was puzzling to her on many levels.

The King of Lords swung around on his heels. "What do *you* know about it?"

Tristan pulled Evanbourough closer to his chest. His blue eyes were burning. "I stand with him. As do others in your court."

Another collective gasp flew around the room. Theasis flew her gaze to Loki and the two exchanged a silent, woeful look. Loki nodded at the truth of Tristan's words and looked swiftly back to the fray unraveling before them.

"Who dares?"

"I do." Theasis snapped her gaze to the back of the room. An angel stood—a single, solitary angel—defiant of his God, who was glaring at him with wide, angry eyes. "I've been mistreated and abused since the day I took my post." He swung his strange, silver eyes to the God beside him. "And I will stand for it no more."

The King of Lords began walking toward the stairs so he could reach him, probably to throttle him, but Metatron, knowing he would be punished for his insolence, stopped him. He grasped the King of Lords' shoulder with one hand and turned his gaze up to the defiant angel.

Her eyes on the pair of them, Theasis didn't miss the strange reaction of the rest of the Quorum, who were sitting upon their pillows behind them. Haniel began rising to his feet. Camael and Uriel, both on either side of him, grasped his hand and pulled him violently down. Uriel, was whispering desperately in his ear. As he did so, Haniel paled and fell, very limply, to the floor.

"Raystlyn," Metatron begged, "be certain of your words. There is no turning back."

"I have no desire to turn back." The angel replied, his gaze flying to Theasis. Theasis gave him a tired smile and nodded at him. She would take care of the angel, when all was said and done, if he were to be exiled. He nodded and returned his gaze to Metatron. "I am already damned at the hand of the one who should protect me. I may as well be damned to the hand which actually does."

"Get you both out of my court." The King of Lords groused. "And never let me see either face again."

Tristan buried his face in Evanbourough's hair, kissed him and then gently set him down. He held out his hand as he stood and he waited. The angel, Raystlyn, began walking down the stairs toward him. So, too, did Lasterian, whose hair was brushed and cleaned, and who was not, for a change, cloaked in the deep despair that had enveloped him for the past sun cycle or so.

Once he'd gripped both hands in his, Tristan bowed slightly to the King of Lords, turned and walked gracefully and with head held high out of the room.

All waited in silence.

Theasis' mind was racing as her eyes darted around the room.

Which members of the Council stood on Lord Lucias' side of the argument, she wanted to know. Who braved such damnation as most assuredly would come? How could she aide them in what ways she, given her task to protect them at the end of it all, was able to do?

"And may the rest of you be damned by your cowardice." The King of Lords growled, his eyes also darting around the room. "Traitors those three may be, but at least they were brave enough to face me. Where are the rest of you? If your cause is so noble and good?"

"Please, your Grace." Metatron's voice was gentle. "You've learned what you wanted to know."

The King of Lords grunted and began storming away. He stopped as he passed me, his eyes wide and wild. "You will show yourself to me in sixty shifts."

Lowering my face, I nodded. "Yes, your Grace."

Then rounding upon Metatron, "And after I have finished with him, I will then deal with you."

"Yes, your Grace." Metatron, whose flames were still dancing with the fear he had the better sense to feel, lowered his head in fealty.

With that, I lost my form.

The King of Lords nodded to the place where I had been standing and continued his angry gait out of the room.

Theasis turned to Loki. "Do you know how many?"

"No." Loki shook his head. "But enough that Lord Regent Lucias believes he can win the fight."

-25-

I was trembling as I knocked upon Noliminan's door. I knew what was coming and it terrified me.

Raphael opened the door with a tired, somewhat consoling grin. "He's calmed down a little bit."

"For all the good it will do me." I muttered. "He's liable to take one look at me and flare up again."

"He cannot be *that* angry with you." Raphael, who had rarely ever been on the wrong side of Noliminan's hand, sighed. "You just did what you were supposed to do."

"I defied a direct order, Raphael." I corrected him. "In front of the entire Council of the Gods. He's not angry with me. He wants to prove a point. The entire theatrical performance had been to prove a point."

I hated myself for speaking too much. I hoped Raphael would not share with anyone that I braved his counsel.

"He already knew where Lucias is. And he knows who in the Council is against him." I advised him. "He doesn't care! He's playing a damned game of kings' castles."

Raphael, who didn't entirely believe me, glared at me. "But you just did what you were first ordered to do."

"As did Zadkiel." I tried to make my brother see reason. This was a fruitless proposition but I understood, for Raphael's future sanity, I had to try. "And you see how that bodes for him."

"Yes, but he needs you more than he needs Zad." Raphael blushed slightly. "I didn't mean that to come out the way it did." He smiled. It was a smile which was very definitely laced with sorrow. "I meant he relies on you every day and Zadkiel only when he has need of him."

"As our father always tells us, you must never forget, Raphael, that any one of us can be replaced at Noliminan's whim." Raphael flinched. I felt bad for my words. Yet, I know all too well, after having been thrown into private conversations between the two ruling Gods, that they are true. "Even you."

Raphael's bronze skin paled at this. "Might Lucias help me."

"I have a feeling that he would try." I found a smile for him at this. If given the opportunity, I would have sided with Lucias in this war. But I am one of the Quorum. This loans me very little room for such luxuries as choice or opinion.

"You'd best get it over with." Raphael replied, still pale.

I sighed. Yes. There was nothing for it but to get it over with.

I knew Noliminan was in his bedchamber and so it was there that we walked. I hesitated for a moment, knocked and then opened the door when I heard him bid I should come in. I was not surprised to be met with an expression of pure displeasure. "Your Grace."

"You are timely." Noliminan growled at me. "I'll give you that."

"Yes, your Grace." It is difficult not to be timely when you are everywhere at once. There is simply no excuse for tardiness.

"Raphael believes I should be lenient with you." His brow raised high over his left eye. "What do you think?"

"I think it doesn't matter what I think."

Which is the point, isn't it?

Noliminan snorted at this. "You're as catty as your mother."

"No, your Grace. I wasn't being catty." I tried to keep my tone even.

"May I ask you something?"

I nodded. It wouldn't do me any good to say no. Noliminan would ask me anyway. But, then, it would be asked in anger rather than in the mildly curious tones it was being asked now.

"Are you and Evanbourough?" He chuckled as if he were amused. Given Camael's fate, I found it distasteful. "Is he your lover?"

"No." I snapped, trying to keep the depth of my irritation out of my tone.

He knew better. Upon his order, and for the sole purposes of keeping us in our places and under his control, the entire Quorum was chaste. And I, out of all of them, bore witness to what had happened to Camael—and Metatron—when Noliminan learned of the existence of Lasterian.

Poor Camael had been castrated. Though no one else knows this truth, he has even been denied the re-growth of his male parts. And his female parts, though he never has had a taste for it, have been sealed closed lest he try and find his pleasure that way. As for Metatron, who had lied to protect Lasterian's true mother by telling everyone he had been the one to birth the child, he'd spent the past two thousand years in a very restrictive prison when he wasn't seeing to Noliminan's duties.

He will be whipped by Michael for his insolence today, I rightly prophesized.

I loathed thinking of what would happen to poor Raphael when Noliminan inevitably realized it was he who was the member of the Quorum which tarried with Lord Evanbourough. And that Lord Evanbourough's protection of me had stemmed out of his loyalty and love for Raphael.

"I have no lovers."

Noliminan smiled at this. "I find that hard to believe. You're fair enough."

"I frighten people." I frowned.

What trap are you trying to trip me into?

"Surly there must be someone." Noliminan barked at me.

"No." I continued to frown. I didn't like this conversation. Aside from the fact that I knew Noliminan was baiting me, it reminded me all too potently that I was, and always will be, alone.

Mayhap, I reflected, *that is the point.*

Noliminan finally looked away. "Then why did he protect you?"

"Because he is honorable, your Grace." I did something I rarely ever do. In order to protect Raphael, I misdirected my response. "He would have protected any one of the Quorum in the same situation."

"I don't think so." Noliminan replied. His expression softened slightly.

"Yes." I insisted. "He would have, your Grace. He's very kind in his heart."

He shook his head at this but dropped the line of questioning. I was relieved. If he would have pursued the issue regarding the Quorum then I couldn't have lied. He hadn't, and I will count my good fortune for this turn of events for many days to come. "So what am I to do with you, Azrael?"

"Whatever you please, your Grace." I muttered in response.

In the end, this is what it always came to.

So why should I play at cat and mouse?

Noliminan sighed and gave me an exasperated look. "What would you do to you?"

"It doesn't matter what I would do to me." I repeated my earlier sentiment. "I disobeyed you. And publicly. I deserve whatever I get."

"Why must you always placate me?" He snorted.

"Because this is what you require, your Grace." I returned honestly.

"Maybe." Noliminan's eyes narrowed as they trailed over the lines of my face. I realized with growing disdain that he was amused. I, however, was not. "But your brothers show their fire now and again. Why don't you?"

"Because it never does them any good, your Grace." I replied to this honestly, too. "It only serves to make you angry and give you the upper hand. You humiliate them into their supplication. I'd just as soon avoid all of that if it's all the same to you."

A strange expression crossed his features upon hearing these words. "You must not think much of me to say such a thing."

"I think all of the worlds of you, your Grace." I countered. "But you require my honesty in all matters. So honesty is what you shall be given."

"You should have just told me where Lucias is hiding."

I sighed at this. Every part of my soul wanted to scream out at him.

He had already known where Lucias was hiding!

"No, my Lord, I shouldn't have. As I suspect you agree."

"You have no right or call to defy me." Noliminan snapped. His curiosity and his patience were gone and his anger had returned. I braced myself for anything. "Or to throw conversations you should never even have been privy to in my face." Here he looked away, almost as if he were embarrassed. "What you see and hear which is meant to be private is not for others to know."

I was infuriated with that response! This was the exact point I had been trying to make!

"Is that what this is about then?" I asked, understanding the issue all too clearly in that moment. "My knowledge of certain aspects of your relationship with Lady Lucias? Which came about due to her pregnancy?"

He didn't return his gaze to me. And his expression hardened. He didn't respond to my direct question. This served to confirm I had been right in posing it.

"I gave you a direct order, Azrael. And in public. You have seen enough of how I react to the world to understand that the one time you cannot defy me without forcing my hand toward retribution is when I give you a direct order before others."

"Even when you bait me a purpose simply to bring about my punishment to make this very point."

The blow came then. It wasn't as hard as the initial one had been, but I did stagger backward and had to catch myself with my wings. When it was over I lifted my hand to my mouth and realized that my lip had been cut. I pulled my hand away to look at the blood upon my fingers and raised my gaze to meet Noliminan's.

Dark fury burned within his eyes.

I understood the fury was not directed, entirely, at me. But enough of it was that I would do well to bite my tongue. I waited, and I watched, as he began to calm himself down again.

"Very well." He finally said. "Since you won't discuss this with me without a bite to your tongue, I have no choice but to dole out your punishment on my own." I lowered my gaze, waiting. "You're to hang the corporeal form you currently keep in your cottage in the gallows until I decide it is time that you may come down. Be that tomorrow or be that in five thousand sun cycles."

Sighing, I rolled my eyes upward. Of course it would be something humiliating. And of course it would be something to test my sanity.

I'd have rather received another blow.

A million other blows!

Until my body had been broken beyond repair!

Gods!

I felt a string of hate for him in that moment. I forced myself to push it down, deep into my gut.

"Yes, your Grace." I hissed, trying to keep the bite out of my tone. "As you wish."

"Get out of here, then." Noliminan barked at me. "And tell Michael and Metatron that I am ready to deal with the pair of them."

I turned and made my way out of his room. I shot a glance to Raphael, who had been hovering just outside of Noliminan's door, eavesdropping on our conversation. Raphael gave me a weak, apologetic smile for having been caught.

I let it go.

I had other matters on my mind aside from Raphael's constant snooping and prying. It is part of who Raphael is. And it is what makes him so valuable to Noliminan.

Also, I understood—all too well—it was Noliminan's knowledge that Raphael was snooping and prying which added to his anger. This discussion regarding privacy of conversations had as much to do in teaching Raphael to hold his tongue as it had to do with me refusing to release mine.

"It's the gallows for me." I groused.

"I heard." Raphael gave another apologetic smile. "It won't be so bad."

"Yes it will." I snapped at him. "I'm not vain like you." Now it was my turn to smile apologetically. "Not that you don't have good reason to be."

"I am sorry." I believe that he was.

"Thank you."

I took my leave. I knew I'd best get at it. Noliminan would be visiting the Courtyard soon to make sure that I had.

-26-

When Evanbourough came to, Theasis explained to him everything that happened after he jumped into the middle of the fray between me and the King of Lords. None of it surprised Evan. Tristan had been very candid with him regarding his involvement in Lord Regent Lucias' war. And, honestly, Evan supported him and loved him for it.

Despite the fact that their relationship, by Tristan's exile, was to be inexorably strained.

Now he sat in the shadows of the Courtyard, waiting for the last grouping to leave so he could speak with me. He wanted to be certain I was unharmed. But he didn't want to draw unnecessary attention to me, given I was about as humiliated as Evanbourough had ever seen anyone be.

When we were alone, Evanbourough stood up and approached me. He stopped a foot or two away and gave me a small, tired smile. "Good Moon, Azrael."

"My Lord." I smiled slightly in return. My eyes were downcast now, however, and my cheeks suddenly grew warm. I wasn't used to people studying me. Let alone when I wore not the first stitch of clothing.

"Are you alright?" Evanbourough asked me. He chuckled slightly. "Apart from the obvious I should mean?"

"Yes, my Lord." I nodded. "Thank you. For your interference."

"It didn't get you into more trouble did it?" Evan asked. "You aren't here because of me are you?"

"No, my Lord." I finally raised my gaze to meet Evanbourough's. "I'm here because Noliminan requires everyone to forget about me again." Evan felt his brow furrow at this. I smiled at his confusion. "My magic is rarely called into the public eye. He believes that, if I am seen hanging here, everyone will forget that I am also watching them."

"Ah." Evanbourough nodded. "I see."

"And you, my Lord? Did you fare well?"

"Yes." He nodded. "I bruised my shoulder. Nothing more. I had time to brace for the impact so it really wasn't such of a much other than the force of it knocked me cold for a while." He smiled to himself then. "Theasis saw to me."

I chuckled at this.

Evanbourough felt himself blushing. It maddened him to no end to know I had watched their first coupling. What he said was, "He split your lip."

"Yes, my Lord." I shrugged. "It will heal."

Evan nodded. "Do you mind if I help it along?"

I assessed him with cold appraisal. "No."

Evan nodded again and stepped slowly forward. He hesitated for a moment and then raised his finger to press it against my lip. When the cut healed he stepped away.

"Better?" He asked, smiling.

"Much." I agreed. "Thank you, my Lord."

"Do you need anything?" Evan asked. "A drink of water or something for dinner?"

"No, my Lord." I shook my head. "But thank you for the offer. Part of this is that I'm meant to go without."

Evanbourough let out a long, tired sigh. I wouldn't expire by not eating, but I would certainly grow miserable. "Carvetek mouk."

I smiled in response but didn't comment.

"And you don't mean to cheat, either." It wasn't a question. "Though, you very easily could do so and he would never know."

"I would have to live with myself if I did." I explained. "I do not do well with deception."

Evan smiled at this. "I see."

"Now you won't have to lie about Lady Theasis." My voice was gentle. "This must be a relief to you."

Evanbourough started as he realized I knew about his lie. Yet, how could he have been so stupid? Of course I knew about it. "Part of it is still a lie."

"It's inconsequential." I shrugged my shoulders. "Besides, it is Lady Theasis' lie. Not yours."

"Does she truly prefer living as a female?" He asked, suddenly curious. "Or is it a ruse?"

"I am not the one to ask such a question, my Lord." I replied, narrowing my eyes slightly. "What has she told you?"

"That she does." Evan frowned at me.

"The Lady has never lied to you." I said gently. "I can tell you this much."

Evanbourough nodded. He knew this in the darkest parts of his heart. "Thank you."

"You are most welcome, my Lord." I replied, my smile returned.

Evanbourough realized that beneath my smile were two very sharply pointed teeth. He also realized that he had never been close enough to me to have seen them before. He wondered what their purpose was and thought to himself that they would come in handy if I had to pin someone down and bite at their neck.

I clamped my lips immediately shut as my smile faded away. I didn't like the ideas that were forming in his mind as he cast it toward the creation of a new race of creatures who sustained themselves by drinking the life blood of others.

Evanbourough, not realizing that I had read the turn of his thoughts, looked upward and smiled apologetically for staring. He quickly changed the subject. "Do you think he will punish me?"

I sighed and looked swiftly away. "Of course he is going to punish you."

Evanbourough nodded at this. He hadn't, honestly, expected otherwise.

"He doesn't understand why you did it. He thinks it was defiance. He even asked me if I were your lover."

Evanbourough smiled at this, despite himself. It wasn't entirely an ill begot thought to him. "It was pure instinct."

"This is what I told him." I allowed myself to study his face. "He did not believe me though. Not entirely."

"Everyone knows I'm with Tristan." Evanbourough sighed, exasperated.

"Noliminan does not understand monogamy." I shrugged, not pointing out that Evan was also with Raphael and, now, Theasis and, therefore, a hypocrite. "And he does not understand self restraint." Evanbourough felt his brow furrow. "If he wants something then he claims it. He assumes the same is done by the rest of you as well."

"For the most part it is."

"For the most part."

"Will you get in trouble for speaking with me?" The thought had just occurred to him. If I wasn't meant to eat or drink, and I wasn't allowed the courtesy of my clothing, was I allowed to talk with others when they approached me?

"Probably."

"You don't seem overly concerned about it."

"What else can he do to me?" My voice was hard, angry. And, then, I was suddenly sad. "I guess that's a stupid question, isn't it? He can do whatever he wants to do with me."

"Maybe Lord Regent Lucias will win through."

I stared at him with a strained, tired expression. Finally, I muttered, "That's Moira's business."

Evanbourough nodded his agreement. "She's a fickle Goddess."

"More fickle than you know." My voice was distant. Evanbourough found himself wondering what I was remembering but knew it wise not to ask. He probably didn't really want to know.

"I should take my leave lest I get you in trouble."

"Thank you for seeking me out."

"Certainly. If you do decide you need or want something . . . ?"

"I most definitely will let you know."

Evanbourough nodded and turned away, unsettled. He liked me. But he knew he would never, under any circumstances, be comfortable under my gaze.

Understanding this, I knew, was part of my punishment too.

-27-

Given Zamyael had advised the Council that the place was sealed by magic, Loki was surprised to find that he was allowed to enter the castle where Lady Lucias and her rebels had taken up residence. Walking through what he assumed to have once been a peaceful courtyard, he saw hundreds upon hundreds of angels and demons, swords in hand, practicing hand to hand combat.

In the center of them, giving them their instructions, stood Sappharon.

Seeing her there caused him to stop for a moment and take his measure of her. He had never seen her doing anything which might actually be considered as useful. Yet, here she stood, her back straight, her head held high and her hair, for a wonder, brushed until it shone and braided into a tight plait down her back.

She wore a breastplate which was form fitting enough to her body that he got his first good look at the curve of her. Looking upon her, he thought, *My Gods, Sappharon has a bosom?*

He shook his head at his realization and made his way past them and to the castle proper. He and Sappharon were like water and oil when mixed with one another. He couldn't afford to be drawn to the swell of her small, girlish tits.

The halls within were thrumming with activity. Every fire pit was being used as a forge; every free surface that was stable enough was being used as an anvil.

Though Lady Lucias had told him about the sheer number on her side, until he walked through the castle and saw the preparations with his own two eyes he hadn't, entirely, believed her.

When he reached the Lady's rooms he found her standing in council with Raystlyn and Tristan. They were telling her, no doubt, about the ruckus at Court.

Judging by her expression, she was infuriated.

"My Lord." Loki stepped toward the trio and gave Lady Lucias the fealty of his bow. As he rose, he passed Tristan a guarded smile. "Tristan."

"What became of Azrael?" Lady Lucias asked, getting right to the point. "And no more of your fealty, Loki. I am Lucias to you now. Mind me."

"The gallows." Loki muttered as he swallowed at her command. That she was allowing him to be familiar with her meant that she was uncomfortable with him calling her a Lord now that he knew she preferred to be a Lady.

Or that she's afraid I'll slip.

He nodded and said, "As for Metatron, he was the subject of a public scourging at Michael's hand. He lasted forty lashes before he fell unconscious."

"Damn Noliminan." She spat. "Not a one of the three of them did anything wrong!"

Loki shrugged. He didn't agree with the King of Lords' behavior, either, but thought Lucias oughtn't be surprised. He was coming to understand what motivated him. She must have had an even greater understanding, still. "What orders do you have for me?"

"Tell my sons to stay out of the bridging Courtyard." She muttered. "All of them, that is, but for Zadkiel."

"Why not Zadkiel, my Lord?" Raystlyn braved to ask.

"Never mind." She shook her head and returned her attention entirely to Loki. "I need you to go to Countenance. Have him see to the aging of the mischief fairy to take over Tristan's place in Council."

"Aiken Darklief?" Loki asked.

"Yes." She nodded. "You're going to need him." Then with a tight smile. "And pick out your demon. Make certain it will be someone who will be loyal to you."

"As you will." Loki sighed. He wasn't certain he was ready for the responsibility of owning a demon.

"Once you see to the aging of the mischief fairy," Lucias continued, "then I want you to visit the basement." Loki blinked. "See which of them you can trust and that are willing to trade their damnation for their aide. Tell them if they will join our war then you will free them upon the end of this fracas."

Loki frowned, "Is that wise?"

"We need a reserve. An army Michael and Metatron won't see coming. And we have an innumerable number of souls which we can bring to our aide." Then she snapped, "Make no mistake about it, Loki. He'll be raiding the Guf for the same purpose. Martiam's Halls as well."

"But the purpose of the Guf—"

"Their infallible duty is to Noliminan." She snapped. "Do you think, given that, they will care?"

"No." Loki agreed, swallowing under the weight of her regard. "They won't care."

She nodded, pleased that Loki understood the severity of the situation. "Also, I need the business with the speaking ape resolved. Immediately."

"My Lord, with Sappharon here—"

"I don't have time to worry about Adam. If we mean to win our barter, and keep your Gods be damned goatee, then you need to wrap up this loose end."

"Really, my goatee is the last thing—"

"See to it Loki. But deal with the fairy first. The aging of Aiken Darklief will take several waning moons of our time at best. So be swift about seeking your request from Countenance."

Loki, finally understanding just how far she meant to go, bowed, and took his leave.

-28-

Countenance rarely, if ever, had guests.

Thus, he was surprised to hear a knock upon his open library door.

When he saw Loki, however, his face split into a grin. Here was a God he respected. "Apprentice Lord Loki."

"Lord Countenance." Loki bowed.

Countenance gave him a small smile with his not quite there lips and tried to meet his gaze with his equally not quite there eyes. He knew he was a horrific thing to look upon and so he did not take Loki's strange, tight smile personally.

"How nice to see you." Countenance allowed his smile to grow. "And still wearing your beard."

"It's a goatee." Loki chuckled as he stroked it. "But thank all of the Gods."

Countenance laughed in response. "Thank Lord Regent Lucias." Loki's smile grew as he nodded his agreement. "How might I assist you?"

"I come regarding Aiken Darklief of the Oakland Grove."

"He is a comely baby." Countenance admitted.

"He is at that." Loki agreed. "But I need him to grow up. I haven't time to wait for him to come into his manhood. The fairies need protection and I can't give them as much as they require. With Tristan gone . . ." He cleared his throat and shook his head. "They need an Emissary God to be their King."

"You're messing with Moira." Countenance warned with a raised, not quite there brow.

"This may be, but I don't have a choice."

"She can be nasty when she's not on your side."

"This may also be." Loki conceded, his purple gaze lowered. "Will you meddle with Aiken Darklief's time?"

"I can." Countenance nodded. "If you insist."

"Thank you." Loki visibly relaxed. He pulled out the chair across Countenance's desk and lowered himself into it. "What's your price?"

"Don't worry about it." Countenance shrugged.

"No." Loki smiled at him. "Really. I wouldn't feel right."

Countenance shook his head. "I truly don't have need of anything from you, Apprentice Lord Loki."

"Surly a favor from Lucias then?"

"Heavens no." Countenance chuckled. He had never heard anyone other than those close to the members of the Small Council say any one of their names without granting them the fealty of their title. It spoke to the close relationship that Lord Regent Lucias and Loki shared. And it sealed his understanding that he owed this God—apprentice or no—fealty in his own right. "I'll stay out of his way if it's all the same to you."

"There has to be something you want." Loki sighed. "Please? I don't like open ended favors."

Countenance felt his brow furrow. There was something he wanted. He simply loathed putting Loki in such a position as to ask for it.

"There we go." Loki chuckled at his expression. "I knew it. What is it?"

"Can you arrange a dinner date for me?" He asked, looking down to his hands.

"Of course I can." Loki's voice was gentle but amused. "With whom?"

Countenance felt his smile dancing over his lips. It was a nervous smile. "Lady Martiam."

Loki started at this. Martiam hardly ever offered the favor of her company to the most handsome of men. This is why Countenance, who wasn't truly handsome, and who had never been able to form well enough to consider himself a man, was terrified to ask her on his own. "I can try."

"That's all I ask." Countenance shrugged.

He knew right then and there that Loki would fail and, thus, his request was not a condition. He understood all too well that

Loki would replace Lord Regent Lucias regarding the punishment of the damned ones when the time came.

He had lived long enough to learn that, sometimes, free favors bought more than those which were paid for.

"If she doesn't want to see me, I understand." He forced himself to smile as he met Loki's gaze. "I certainly wouldn't blame her."

"Stop that." Loki frowned at him. "You're . . ." He struggled for whatever word he wanted to say. "Comely. In your own way."

Countenance grinned and lowered his gaze at this. "Yes I am." He bit back his laugh. "In my own way."

Loki's frown grew. "I think she just doesn't date, Lord Countenance." He tried. "I've never seen her with anyone and from what I hear she's extremely chaste."

Countenance smiled at this. He'd heard otherwise and he'd made the God who'd spread the false rumors pay dearly.

The magic of time, he reflected as he tried to repress his grin, could cause great angst on those rare occasions when he chose to use it to ill aims.

"Well." He said, holding his smile. "I know you work with her in the disposition of the souls, so, I thought I would ask you to try given she knows you better than me."

He reached across the table, but pulled his hand back swiftly. He suddenly remembered that he had heard that Loki didn't like affection from other males in any form and he didn't want to offend him.

"I'll see to the matter of Aiken Darklief of the Oakland Grove."

"Thank you," Loki nodded at him. "Would you like to join me in one of the courtyards for a drink?"

"Yes." Countenance answered him, surprised. "If your offer is a true one, then I would."

"I'm not a false God." Loki assured him. "And I could use an evening of no stress." He shook his head. "You obviously understand my boundaries." He glanced at the hand which had reached for him and then retreated. "And I'm tired of fighting off roaming hands."

Countenance nodded. He supposed he understood.

Though, to himself, he thought, *I wish I had half your problems.*

He settled on a lie. "Yeah. Me too."

"Good." Loki stood. "I'll go dress for it. See you in sixty shifts?"

"Sure." Countenance nodded, grinning at the reference of his shadow under the sun. "Sixty shifts it is. And afterward I shall see to the matter of your fairy."

-29-

Loki stood at Martiam's door, his lips drawn thin.

This was a waste of his time and he knew it.

Countenance was a nice enough fellow—after drinking with him and getting to know him, Loki genuinely *did* like him—but he was a horrendously ugly thing and Martiam, it had been said, had turned down even Narcissus when he had asked for her company.

The door opened and Loki smiled. Martiam was nothing if not beautiful. "Apprentice Lord Loki?"

"Lady Martiam." Loki bowed to her.

"Do you come for your servant?" Martiam asked, her pale blue eyes wide. "Because I have a soul for you who would suit you very well if you are ready."

Loki felt his brow furrow at this. Lucias had told him to select his servant, but this wasn't why he was here tonight. "I suppose that I'm overdue. But the reason I actually came is to ask you a favor."

Martiam smiled. It was a very lovely thing.

"Intriguing." She stepped back, pulling the door open as she did so. "Please. Come in."

Loki nodded and stepped within. As his eyes drank in the room he felt himself smile. The rooms were very delicately decorated. "Very pretty."

"Oh, thank you." Martiam nodded. "I do like pretty things."

"Me too." He answered, giving Martiam one of his most charming smiles. He wondered, as his eyes darted around her room, if he were unable to convince her to meet with Countenance if he could, perhaps, convince her to meet with him.

Variety is the spice of life, he grinned at the thought of his ever growing gaggle.

Martiam blushed prettily and turned away. "Take a seat. May I offer you a drink?"

"Scotch if you have it."

"I always keep a supply." Martiam replied, walking to the bar. "I don't touch the stuff myself. But Lord Lucias seems very fond of it." Martiam chuckled. "And I am *very* fond of Lord Regent Lucias."

Loki felt his brow rise at this. Maybe Martiam wasn't as chaste as rumor suggested her to be. "Me too."

Martiam looked over her shoulder wearing a strange smile. Loki smiled in return, not correcting whatever thoughts were running through her mind. "You must miss him."

"So must you."

"Yes." Martiam turned to face him. Her smile was easier now. "Very much." She handed Loki a glass of spirits and then lowered herself, very gracefully, into a delicately made high back chair. She pulled her feet upward and tucked them beneath her generously swelling bottom. "How may I help you, my Lord?"

Loki looked at his glass, swirled the scotch and then raised his gaze. "Someone asked me if I would be willing to see if you would join them for a dinner date."

A strange expression crossed her beautiful features. "Whom?"

"Well." Loki frowned and looked down at his scotch again. "Lord Countenance, actually."

Martiam was silent for a long while. Finally, however, she spoke. Her tone was strange. "I see."

"Should I tell him no?" Loki asked, raising his gaze to meet Martiam's.

"I don't honestly think he would like me." Martiam answered. Loki felt his brow furrow.

"Why would you say this?" Loki asked. "He finds you very appealing."

"He doesn't know me." Martiam shook her head. Her long, dark brown hair danced over her full bosom. "And, anyway, I don't date. It's a waste of my time."

"Why would you say this?" Loki repeated the question.

"Because, as you know, few of us live full time in our female essence." She shrugged. "It's all very flattering, Loki. But I tire of everyone assuming that, because I refuse to supplicate to the male politic, I owe them something." She sighed. "I'd just as soon be by myself."

"I don't believe this is true." Loki used a gentle tone. "Theasis lives happily enough as a female."

"Yes." Martiam nodded. She looked troubled, though. Not relieved. And this troubled Loki. "When it suits her. And I am no one's whore like Theasis is."

"Theasis is no one's whore." Loki felt his eyes narrow with his anger at the insult.

"I'm sorry, Loki." Martiam sighed. "But she is. She uses sex for barter. Its prostitution no matter how you look at it. And I want nothing to do with it."

Loki, frowning, shook his head. He couldn't argue against her logic. But he didn't agree with it, either. "Do not ever call Lady Theasis a whore in my presence. I will not stand for it. Not from anybody."

Martiam contemplated him with great interest. Then she nodded and looked, very swiftly, away. "I apologize. Given your gaggle, I assumed she was just one of your many geese."

"Never in life."

Though he, himself, thought of his woman as his gaggle, the assumptions that everyone he slept with was merely for pleasure rather than because he genuinely cared for the women was becoming as tiresome to him as was the joke over his goatee.

Especially where Theasis, who had seen to teaching him the arts of being a man, was concerned.

"She is very dear to me."

"I understand." She was still looking away. "I won't call her a whore again." A distracted smile played on her full, feminine lips. "In your presence."

"Thank you." Loki nodded. He found himself grinning at the cattiness. "Shall I tell Countenance no?"

Martiam sighed and returned her gaze to Loki. "Is it truly just dinner? Or is he after something from me?"

"Really, dinner is all he asked for." Loki assured her

"Very well. Tell Countenance I will be in the bridging Courtyard at sundown." She sighed. "I am not interested in a date. However, if he should happen to find my table, then he is welcome to join me."

"Thank you." Loki smiled softly at her. And then, grinning, "May I join you tomorrow?"

Martiam frowned. Loki immediately regretted the request.

"I'm sorry." He shook his head. "I didn't mean to offend you."

Martiam sighed. "Please do not be offended, yourself, if I tell you that I must pass on your request."

"I'm not." Loki assured her. He found his smile again. Martiam's expression softened. "I understand."

"Thank you." Martiam returned. "Are you certain I cannot talk you into taking a look at Samyael? He'll be very loyal to you."

Loki sighed, then shrugged his shoulders.

Why not? He'd been ordered to do so anyway.

"Alright." Loki agreed. "I'll take a look. But no promises."

Martiam gave him such a knowing smile that he shivered.

-30-

Aiken, terrified, turned his violet gaze to Lord Countenance. He was to meet his Lord and Master. And he wasn't sure that he was ready to do so.

Aiken had become a strangely beautiful man. He was extremely tall with long white hair—which he littered with wildflowers—that danced to his hip bone. His large wings were iridescent. They shimmered in the light of the sun. As did his pale skin. And his canine teeth, hidden behind thick and strangely sensual lips, were sharply pointed fangs.

In the custom of his people, he wore no clothing. Lord Countenance warned him that this would be something that the King of Lords would require be corrected.

"Settle down, child." Lord Countenance, sensing his anxiety, muttered to him. "Loki is a kind God. And you will please him."

Aiken, who was unsure about this, merely nodded.

It was Lord Loki's demon, Samyael, who opened what had once been Lord Regent Lucias' door. Aiken stepped closer to Lord Countenance, his entire body trembling with his fear. He had never seen a demon before. As such, he hadn't expected them to be so stunningly made.

He had expected that a demon, by its very name and nature, would be a monster.

"Samyael." Lord Countenance bowed to the demon. Aiken marked that the demon bowed even lower in response. "I've an appointment with Loki."

"Right this way, my Lord." Samyael opened the door to them and backed within a sitting room that was decorated in a very masculine fashion. Aiken looked around it with more than just a minute bit of curiosity.

Fairies, who loved nature and all other beautiful things, were far more delicate in their tastes.

"He hasn't changed anything." Lord Countenance muttered in surprised tones. "It's as though Lord Regent Lucias still graces these very halls."

"Yes, my Lord." Aiken didn't know how else to respond.

"No matter." Lord Countenance counseled him. "Lord Lucias *doesn't* live here anymore. It is merely Loki who you must please today."

"Yes, my Lord." Aiken swallowed. With all of the regard that Countenance had paid Lord Loki over the course of Aiken's years this was a frightening enough prospect.

What if Lord Loki didn't like him? What if he sent him back to the Oakland Grove and bid Lord Regent Lucias best try again? Where would Aiken be then?

Aside scorned by his people for being a despised king and a false God?

You'll be turned out. He thought, knowing the truth of it. *After being stoned, that is.*

Though Lord Countenance walked bravely into Lord Loki's library, Aiken hung back, walking forward only after Lord Countenance gave him a frowning, impatient glare. He stepped through the door and stopped short.

The man behind the desk was probably the most masculine, yet beautiful, creature Aiken could have ever hoped to see. Aiken knew, upon meeting his dark purple eyes, that he believed in love at first sight. The kind that would span the ages.

Lord Loki was not delicate, like Aiken himself, but broad and muscular.

And he wears a beard, by the Gods.

A beard Aiken recognized. It was the beard centaurs wore after succeeding with their rites of passage.

Lord Loki's depthless eyes turned immediately from Lord Countenance to Aiken and a small, troubled smile played upon his lips. His eyes flicked to Aiken's nether regions and then immediately back to Aiken's unguarded gaze. "The King of Lords will never stand for *this*."

Lord Countenance shrugged at Aiken's side. "He's a mischief fairy. Mischief fairies do not, traditionally, wear clothes."

Lord Loki chuckled as his grin grew. "This I know."

"Leave it to the King of Lords." Lord Countenance warned. "He's proud."

Lord Loki tittered in response as his gaze danced over Aiken and then returned to Lord Countenance's not quite there smile.

"Indeed." Lord Loki stood and walked around his desk.

Aiken pushed his left leg behind himself and bent, his hand curled at his forehead in a fairy's fealty. "My Lord Loki."

"*My* Lord Aiken." Lord Loki replied. His expression was as gentle as his voice. And twice as beautiful in its deep tones. "Welcome to the Halls of the Hells."

"It is my honor." Aiken swallowed his fear. He hoped Lord Loki didn't see it. He thought, perhaps, he had not. "As it is my honor to serve you."

"Well," Loki sighed. "That's a bit of nonsense, really. You'll govern the races of the fairies on your own. And it is still Lucias who you shall answer to. Not me. I am still, after all, no more than an Apprentice Lord. Whilst you are to become an Emissary and, thus, my superior."

"Then it is my honor to be your friend."

To this Lord Loki made no reply for a moment. His purple eyes narrowed, however, and then widened before his lips parted into a smile which was worlds more than pleasing.

"Time will tell." He chuckled as he met Lord Countenance's gaze. "Countenance shall tell."

"That's Moira's business." Lord Countenance murmured. "Not mine. And she's one goose whose feathers you have more than merely ruffled. So watch your back."

Lord Loki, obviously tired, nodded. "I know how to deal with Moira when she's angry."

Lord Countenance grinned. "Do you, now?"

"As you say, she's a goose whose feather's I've ruffled." His grin was both haughty and naughty as he raised his hand to his face, ran two of his fingers over his goatee and stuck out his tongue.

Aiken burst into laughter.

Lord Countenance, who seemed to understand that his action bore a sexual connotation but couldn't, quite, grasp what, exactly, it was, shrugged his shoulders and turned to Aiken to bow. "Good luck, Emissary Lord Darklief. You're on your own now."

"Good luck to you." Aiken returned, still grinning at Lord Loki's joke.

When he was gone, Aiken returned his attention to Lord Loki. "I always wondered what was so famous about your goatee."

Grinning, he nodded, "The ladies do seem to like it."

Aiken couldn't stop grinning at him. "For a wonder."

He shrugged. "I come by my talents naturally." He winked. "What can I say."

"Piss on the Gods!" Aiken cried, understanding everything.

"What?" Lord Loki started. Though, he smiled slightly at Aiken's blasphemy. Aiken was glad to see this.

"You're a Gods be damned nymph!"

Lord Loki's brow furrowed. His eyes darted away. "I prefer to think of myself as a centaur."

"Perhaps." Aiken replied. "But if you aren't a nymph then I'll eat your left foot."

"You *are* a mischief fairy." Lord Loki replied. He was smiling. But his eyes were dark and brooding. "So I wouldn't put that past you."

It was Aiken's turn to shrug. It was no secret that his people were cannibals.

Lord Loki's eyes examined his face as his lips thinned. "I have to take you to the King of Lords."

Aiken, embarrassed, lowered his gaze. "I'm sorry, my Lord. I have a problem holding my tongue."

"I don't care about that. But other's might. So be wary."

"Yes, my Lord." Aiken nodded.

"Given Lucias is no longer here, the King of Lords, alone, can remove the veil of your mortality and grant you the powers that are rightfully yours as a God."

"If I please you." Aiken bowed to him.

"Oh yes." He smiled. It was an extremely guarded smile in Aiken's estimation. "You are rude and impertinent. As am I. So, yes. You do please me."

Aiken, blushing, and more than merely pleased by Lord Loki, turned away. He waited while Lord Loki rose and walked toward him.

"I suppose Countenance warned you that the King of Lords shall order you to wear clothes."

"I must, then, politely decline."

Lord Loki grinned at him—finally a true grin—and shook his head. "No you won't. But you can concede without giving in. Tell him you'll cover your cock and he'll be placated."

"If I have to." Aiken curled his nose in distaste at the idea of covering any part of himself.

"It's better than clothes." Lord Loki's voice was filled with understanding. Aiken, who desired his Lord and who needed his Lord's approval, was grateful for it. "Tell him you'll wear a loin cloth or a cod piece and be done with it. You don't want to fight with him. Not in these days and with his mood. Concede, or you will be forced to wear full dress."

"I shall take your counsel, my Lord." Aiken bowed to him.

"I thought you meant for us to be friends." Loki smiled.

"Yes." Aiken nodded. "I should like that very well."

"Then how about we go?" Lord Loki asked him, a brow rising.

"Yes, my Lo—" Aiken shook his head and his smile grew. "My friend."

Lord Loki nodded and waited. Friends this God may want to be, but Aiken was in his fealty all the same. He would never forget that. Not in all of his days.

He followed Lord Loki, silently, and caught his breath as they entered the very halls of the Heavens. When they stood before the King of Lords' door, Aiken reached forward, tentatively, and grasped Loki's hand. He was relieved when the God accepted it, squeezed it, and then let it go.

A handsome angel with black eyes and hair opened the door. He was a warrior, Aiken kenned. And if he were not a General or Commander then Aiken would eat one of the angel's wings.

"General Michael." Lord Loki bowed to him. "I must see the King of Lords. Is he free?"

Michael's black eyes danced to Aiken. His expression hardened as his eyes trailed over Aiken's naked body. "He's free." He growled, his eyes glued to Aiken's, though he was pointing in the direction of Aiken's nether region. "But he won't like *that*."

"That's Moira's business." Lord Loki muttered. "Not yours."

Michael recoiled. But he seemed to smile secretly to himself, as if amused. "Of course, my Lord. Come."

They entered and followed Michael down a long hall to the very edge of the apartment. There, they stepped outside and onto a patio.

And for the first time in his life, Aiken saw the glory of his maker.

It was all too much. He fell to his knees and brought his fingertips to his chin in supplication.

Lord Loki sighed, clearly irritated. Yet, he did not admonish Aiken. Nor did he reach for him to force him to his feet. Rather, he seemed to understand.

"Your Grace," Lord Loki's deep voice was another sigh. "I bring before you Emissary Lord Aiken Darklief, first of his name, son of Lord Regent Lucias, King of the Oakland Grove and ruler of the all other races which cross his borders. I beg you release him his mortal veil and grant him his father's rights."

The King of Lords, his attention interested but not compelled, suddenly sat forward.

"That?" He asked. Curiously, Aiken noted, not rudely. "But Aiken Darklief is only a child!"

"Lord Countenance has seen otherwise." Lord Loki bowed to him. "I beg you, again, to grant him his Godly form."

Aiken felt the King of Lords' eyes dancing over him, assessing him. "Lucias' son."

"Ta." Lord Loki bowed to him. And then he smiled wryly. "Not his fault."

The King of Lords snorted.

"Will you grant him his Godly form?" Lord Loki inquired.

"Leave us." The King of Lords waved a hand at Lord Loki. He turned to Aiken, his purple eyes questioning. Despite Aiken's silent plea that he stay, he turned and left the room, close on Michael's heels.

Aiken rose, turned to the King of Lords, and bowed. When he spoke, his words were a whisper. "Your Grace."

"Why do you dare meet me in your flesh?" He asked irritably. "It's not seemly."

"I am a mischief fairy, your Grace." Aiken bowed again. "We see no need in such trivialities as clothing."

"It won't do." The King of Lords replied, looking away from him. "You'll wear clothes in my court."

"I can't." Aiken swallowed his fear as he watched the King of Lords stiffen. "But perhaps a consolation?"

"What consolation?" He snapped, returning his attention to Aiken. He was clearly very annoyed with the fairy.

"I shall cover my most offending parts." Aiken waved a hand before himself before bowing. "Will it suit?"

"It suits me." The King of Lords growled and turned his gaze away. "Though it's your purity if baser Gods rape you."

"I have a sharp bite, your Grace." Aiken assured him. "And I dare anyone to bend me over without my accord."

This earned him a strange, clearly disapproving frown. "Of course you do." He snapped. "You are, as I said, Lucias' son."

"I've never met that worthy." Aiken assured him. "My self respect is my own."

"Good." The King of Lords nodded and returned his gaze to Aiken's. "Do not let me see you undressed again in a public setting if you know what's good for you."

"I assure you, your Grace, that I do." He bowed, his mind dancing with amusement. The order had been 'in a public setting'. This meant Aiken was free to do what he wished in his private abode.

"Under this concession, I will lift your veil after your vows are made." He muttered. "The formalities of your vow will be seen to by Michael. Speak with him before you leave. Understanding that the vows you make to him, you make to me."

"Thank you, your Grace."

"Good day to you." The King of Lords dismissed him.

"And to you."

Fearful of what promises must be made, Aiken left the King of Lords to seek out the warrior, Michael.

-31-

Haniel sat on the swing which hung from the porch roof of his cottage. Raystlyn, who had been visiting his cottage for the past ten or more sun cycles, sat beside him. He desperately clutched at Raystlyn's hand. Haniel wanted more than anything in the world to ask him to stand down.

But he could not.

He, better than anyone, understood Raystlyn's plight. He had been making stews and potions for as long as they had been friends in an effort for his healing to advance after having been beaten or prostituted by his Lord.

"Will I see you again?" Haniel asked. He couldn't keep the pain that he was feeling out of his tone. Nor did he try.

"I shall always be around." Raystlyn cleared his throat. "Theasis will take me into her care eventually."

"Ta." Haniel sighed. "If you are exiled. Even then, I will not be allowed to seek you out." He shook his head. "And you will not be able to reach me here."

"If I had another option, I would take it."

"I know this." Haniel barked, not wanting to hear this.

"I love you." Raystlyn squeezed his hand tighter. "And I am sorrowful that I may have put you in a precarious position by taking care of me these past years."

Haniel nodded, raised Raystlyn's hand to his lips and kissed it.

"When is it supposed to happen?" He finally asked the question which had been preying upon him all day.

"Sunset." Raystlyn muttered.

"When it's most crowded." Haniel shivered.

He knew he should do something to stop it, but he had promised Raystlyn that he would not. Given everything between them was at its end, he couldn't break his promise to Raystlyn. No matter the consequences.

"Yes." Raystlyn sighed. "If there were any other way . . ."

Haniel didn't want to hear this either. He'd heard all of the speeches he had needed to hear about his father's cause from

Lucias himself. There was nothing Raystlyn could add that would make any difference.

"You could join us." Raystlyn begged half heartedly.

"None of the Quorum can be part of this." Haniel frowned. "More is demanded of us. We are held to a higher standard."

"You are nothing more than higher priced slaves." Raystlyn spat.

Haniel knew he was right. But what was he to do about it? He shrugged his shoulders and shook his head. "Mayhap. But I cannot turn against my brothers. Even if my father is right in his cause."

"Yet, all twelve of you would. If you could."

Haniel shook his head. He didn't think this was true.

"Not Michael. Never in life." He frowned. "And definitely not Metatron."

"Mayhap not." Raystlyn conceded.

They fell into silence and waited. The sun arched through the sky, finally setting in the west. They exchanged a tired, fearful glance and then looked over the edge of patio and down into the bridging Courtyard of the Gods.

Bright red and orange light exploded upward and outward in a cloud which reminded Haniel of one of the healing mushrooms he used in his stews. He cried out, turned to Raystlyn and buried his face in the angel's shoulder.

He didn't want to watch this after all.

Raystlyn, understanding, laced his arm around Haniel, pulling him closer. He buried his face in the crown of Haniel's head and gently kissed him.

Finally, after a long bout of silence between the two, Raystlyn announced in a tired, husky voice, "Well . . . I guess that's that." Haniel shook his head, his tears falling freely onto Raystlyn's silk shirt. "I must go now, Haniel."

"No." Haniel clutched at him, desperate to keep him. "You can hide here! They shall never find you here!"

"I cannot hide." Raystlyn whispered. "Nor do I wish to. Lord Regent Lucias needs me. And I will stand at his side. Let it be the death of me if it must be. But I will stand at his side."

"Go then." Haniel's voice was cracked and desperate to his own ears. "And damn us both for it."

-32-

After I collected Ishitar for a visit with Noliminan, Zadkiel sought out the bustle of the bridging Courtyard, where he now sat in the center at a table, by himself of course, watching the coming and goings of the Gods.

So it was that, when the explosion hit, it was not less than three feet from where he sat.

One minute he was sipping wine and the next he was laying on his back, staring with distracted interest at his arm.

It had been ripped off of him and lay some ten feet away. Its fingers were still twitching as though they were still under Zadkiel's command.

Feeling an itch upon his nose he stared at those fingers and thought distractedly, *Stop it fingers. You cannot scratch that itch.*

Then he thought no more.

-33-

Uriel darted here and there with Cassiel on his heels. For the most part he knew everyone would, eventually, be okay.

And then he came upon Zadkiel.

"Loki's beard." Cassiel muttered behind him. "Is that . . . ?"

"Get Evanbourough." Uriel snapped over his shoulder. He became incensed when Cassiel, frozen in horror where he stood, failed to move. "Now, Cassiel!"

Cassiel, as though slapped, nodded and then turned tail to find Lord Evanbourough. Uriel lowered himself to his hunkers, reached behind Zadkiel's neck and pulled him upward.

Thank all of the Gods that are or ever were, he thought, *that you didn't bring Prince Ishitar with you.*

Panicking, Uriel looked around himself to make certain this run of thoughts was true. When he was satisfied that it was, he returned his full attention to his brother.

There would be time to worry about who was in care of the babe later.

Zadkiel's slender chest bore a caved in look that Uriel didn't much care for. Blood was flowing from his lips. And both arms and legs had been severed; his left arm at the elbow, his right at his shoulder and both legs midway down his thighs. "Oh, Zadkiel."

As he stared down upon his brother, Zadkiel's golden eyes opened. Uriel forced himself to smile down at him as he muttered, "Uriel . . . ?"

"Heil." Uriel smoothed back his golden, sweat soaked hair from his handsome face. "All shall be well. We shall get you fixed up."

Zadkiel nodded. His eyes were growing distant. "The light burned my eyes."

"Can you see?" Uriel asked him, gently.

"Ta." He nodded.

"What were you doing here?" Uriel whispered. "Loki warned all twelve of us not to come here!"

"I was hungry." Zadkiel's brow furrowed. "And I was lonely. Ishitar is spending the night with Noliminan . . . I wished for company so I sought Azrael." His brow furrowed. "But Azrael is not here. Noliminan will be most displeased with him."

Uriel frowned. No one except the Quorum were supposed to know about Ishitar. He looked swiftly around to see if anyone overheard Zadkiel speak his name. When he was confident they had not, he forced himself to return his attention to his brother to give him a smile.

Evanbourough stepped beside him and lowered himself to his hunkers. He gave Zadkiel a small, dark smile. "Heil, Zadkiel."

"My Lord." Zadkiel's brow furrowed. "Is that a new shirt?"

Evanbourough looked swiftly down at his blood soaked shirt, forced a smile, and then nodded. "Yes. It is."

"It is very comely."

"Thank you." Evanbourough reached forward and ran his hand gently over Zadkiel's brow. He turned his gaze swiftly to

Uriel. It was a gaze which asked him what, exactly, Uriel expected him to do.

"Evanbourough shall take you to his apartment." Uriel announced his plans gently. "You will stay with him until you are well healed. But I must now seek King Noliminan." He forced himself to smile at Zadkiel. "He shall come to you. He shall mend you right as rain."

"No he shan't." Zadkiel said, his eyes blazing.

The Gods love him but he was so distracted from what was happening in that moment he was holding on to old arguments.

"He shall." Uriel promised him. "Be a good lad. Go with Evanbourough. I shall be there shortly."

"I shall return swift, Zadkiel." Evanbourough assured him. "I must palaver with your brother."

"Yes, my Lord." Zadkiel said in a tone which spoke volumes regarding the fact that he cared not a wit for the outcome of this situation.

Uriel stepped away, his forced smile fluttering from his womanly lips as he turned his back to Zadkiel so he might face Evanbourough. "There is no time for palaver, my Lord."

"What are you thinking, Uriel?" Evanbourough asked, his tone exasperated and his hands spread wide at his sides. "I cannot care for him."

"You are the only one without a servant aside Theasis and she has agreed to take in other wounded." Uriel, forgetting his place, snapped. "You have a room in your apartment in which Lasterian no longer graces."

"Yes, but—!"

"Zadkiel is Raphael's brother!" Uriel seethed at him. "Given the risk you put Raphael in every time that you lay with him for your self-serving pleasures, does this mean nothing to you?"

Evanbourough's black eyes danced over Uriel's face. Finally he gave his head one shake. "No. But for the sake of prosperity, you must understand he would fare better with another."

"I disagree." Uriel replied, understanding Evanbourough's point all too well. He'd mastered servants before but they'd never worked out. Many a demon had been subjected to—and not survived—his tantrums. "You have already protected one of my brothers." Evanbourough blushed and looked away. "And there is not any room anywhere else. He shall need constant care. You will be the one to give it to him."

Grunting, Evanbourough turned away from him and returned to Zadkiel. Uriel looked swiftly around, realized Zadkiel was the last of them, and sought out King Noliminan.

The King of Lords stood, his hands on his hips, in the center of the courtyard. His expression was one of deep sorrow and exploding anger. Uriel swallowed and stepped toward him. "I require your aide, your Grace."

"Everyone requires my aide." He snapped. Then, seeing Uriel's expression, his tone softened. "What is it, min 'lasupita?"

"Zadkiel took the brunt of the explosion, your Grace." Uriel explained swiftly.

King Noliminan's expression softened slightly. "Is he okay?"

"No." Uriel shook his head. "He is in a bad way. I beseech you to heal him."

"His state is that poor?" Uriel nodded. King Noliminan let out a long, tired sigh. "Where is he?"

"I bound the care of him to Lord Evanbourough."

King Noliminan glared at Uriel. He was still angry with Evanbourough for interfering with his argument with me while every God of the Council was looking on. Thank all the Gods that he hadn't yet noticed that Apprentice Lord Loki had moved me to the Great Hall of the Gods. This wasn't a conversation Uriel wanted to be forced to navigate. "Why?"

"He has no servants." Uriel sighed. "He can spare the room and his time, your Grace."

"Evanbourough is too busy worrying about *my* servants to take care of his own." The King of Lords snapped at Uriel. "Zadkiel should stay with me."

"That will not work, your Grace, and we both know it." Uriel responded, irritable. "You do not have the time nor the patience for his care and Queen Raguel is not there to see to him. He would be left to Raphael."

He instantly regretted this statement. Raphael was standing beside King Noliminan. Uriel's brother flinched and then looked swiftly away. Uriel wondered, again, who was seeing to the care of Prince Ishitar, but then reasoned that it must be another one of their brothers.

"He needs the care of a God. Not an angel. Even one of Raphael's stature. This is all that I meant."

"Then let Lucias—" King Noliminan stopped midsentence. Lucias was responsible for this mess. He was not an option. "Evanbourough will do."

"Thank you, your Grace." Uriel sighed. "May we seek him?"

They didn't waste time on formalities. King Noliminan willed all four of them—Raphael and Cassiel included—to Lord Evanbourough's sitting room. It was King Noliminan who called out. "Evanbourough? Where are you?"

"Here, your Grace." Evan's voice echoed from the room at the very end of the hallway.

King Noliminan nodded and the four of them walked swiftly toward him. Once there, the servants stayed outside and King Noliminan stepped in. Evanbourough, making room for him, slipped out into the hall with Raphael, Cassiel and Uriel. Uriel noted that he'd laced his arm around Raphael's waist and kissed him softly on his cheek.

He flinched, hoping King Noliminan would not realize the show of affection for exactly what it was. When the time came that he realized Raphael and Evanbourough were having an affair they would both pay.

And dearly.

No one knows that truth better than I. Aside my beloved Camael, that is.

He shook his head. Now was not the time to pine lost lovers.

"Such a performance merely to gain my audience." King Noliminan said in gentle tones as he lowered himself to Zadkiel's side.

"Your Grace." Zadkiel's voice was shaking.

"It shall do no good to tie your old limbs back on." King Noliminan purred at him. "You must grow them back."

"Yes, your Grace." He said. He wore such a brave expression on his face that it was heartbreaking. Uriel hoped such brevity would remain during the excruciating pain he was about to endure.

"And what is this?" King Noliminan ran his hand over the sunken, buried ribs of his chest. "Oh. Dear."

"What is it, your Grace?" Cassiel asked.

"Trouble." King Noliminan nodded at him. He turned his smile to Zadkiel then. "But not too much trouble."

"No, your Gra . . ." Zadkiel's thin whisper trailed into nothingness.

"Evanbourough." King Noliminan turned his gaze toward the God standing at Raphael's side. An odd expression crossed his brow as he looked from Raphael to Evanbourough and then back again. He didn't miss a beat, however, and Uriel was glad for it.

"I need you to find Haniel. I'll need him to make a stew. Tell him Zadkiel's rib has punctured both his lung and his heart. He'll know what to do."

Lord Evanbourough bowed and then was simply gone.

"See?" King Noliminan smiled down at Zadkiel. "Everything shall be taken care of."

Zadkiel wheezed as he attempted to finish the 'your Grace' he was not able to complete, but he failed.

Then he turned his gaze to Uriel. His gold eyes were blazing. Uriel braced himself for whatever would come as Zadkiel turned his gaze back to King Noliminan.

"My leg . . ." King Noliminan furrowed his brow. "Will be . . . straight?"

King Noliminan cleared his throat and forced a smile.

Of all the damned and foolish questions to have asked in this moment, Uriel thought, *when the Bwuet Va is angrier with Lucias than he ever in life has been.*

"Well, now." King Noliminan said. "I don't think that is necessary." And then with a commanding tone which brokered no argument, "Do you?"

"No." Whatever fight was left went out of Zadkiel then. "Never again."

"I am pleased you understand." King Noliminan said sharply. He'd seen Zadkiel's expression as well. He was angry that Zadkiel had the audacity to try and worm out of an old punishment given his current predicament. Especially given the haste with which he had appeared at Zadkiel's side.

"Now lie back." He ran his hand over Zadkiel's brow, blessedly putting him to sleep. "And let me get to work."

-34-

When Lucias asked me if I would procure Ishitar from Zadkiel and deliver him to Noliminan for a visit, I realized, almost at once, what she wanted of me and that I was helpless to stop her from doing what she meant to do.

Sitting on the floor of Zadkiel's cottage, I rolled the ball to Ishitar, who giggled the sweet, soul touching melody which only a very young child can manage, and then rolled it back.

I forced myself to smile at the baby, not wanting him to feed off of the negative energy which was beating from me as I watched the drama unfold between Zadkiel and Noliminan.

I think he sensed my discontentment all the same.

Ishitar crawled toward me and climbed into my lap.

"Azy." He muttered as he reached for my curly black hair. "Azy Rapy."

He was a strangely perceptive child. He is, now, a strangely perceptive man. It shouldn't have been any surprise to me that he knew something was wrong. Yet, I wondered how he could have known that in this moment I was also watching Lady Eir step behind Raphael and place him in a chokehold.

"Yes." I replied, running my hand over his silky hair. "Azy is sad for Raphie."

"Rapy Lulu."

I shook my head, closed my eyes and buried my face against his soft curls.

"That's right." I muttered. "Raphie is with your Mima."

He giggled again and pulled away.

"Rapy fiys," he spread his hands wide and began pumping them up and down.

I didn't understand what he was doing.

Until, that was, I looked up and, with sudden horror, understood more than I cared to.

My most tangible corporeal self was in the gallows of the Great Hall of the Gods watching as Raphael's mangled, beaten and bruised body manifested above Noliminan's throne.

He was naked with his arms spread wide and his head lolling forward because he was unconscious. His arms had been nailed to the wall at the wrist and his feet at the ankle. As for his wings, they had been stretched wide behind him, the bones of them nailed at the place in the middle where they joined so they could bend as if he was in flight.

As abhorrent as the image was to me, there was no denying what Ishitar, with his child's eyes, must have seen.

"Rapy fiys," he spread his hands wide and began spinning with his attempt to imitate what appeared to him to be an angel in flight.

"Dear Gods," I gasped at the sad irony of these innocents caught up in Noliminan and Lucias' game before pulling Ishitar, not at all gently, into my arms.

Frightened by my sudden outburst, Ishitar's small bottom lip curled very slowly into a pout before he began to wail.

-35-

"Get him down!" King Noliminan roared at Michael.

Michael, who was standing beneath Raphael, looking up at him with wide eyed horror, could only shake his head.

He had spent the last one hundred and eighty shifts trying to get Raphael down. But he couldn't. Whatever magic was holding him there was more powerful than any that Michael possessed.

The Gods pray, he thought. *It's more powerful than any magic* you *possess! So how can you expect me to obey you?*

"There's nothing I can do, your Grace."

King Noliminan flipped away from Michael and toward me, I was hanging on the opposite wall from Raphael where the rows of tables upon stairs ended. "Who brought him here!"

"He isn't really here." My voice was shaking. "This is just an image of him."

"Where is he?" King Noliminan demanded.

"At your castle in Anticata." I replied. "He's hung in the center of the Courtyard so that everyone fighting on Lucias' side can . . ."

"Can what?" He growled impatiently.

"Humiliate you." I muttered and lowered my gaze.

His teeth clamping shut and his nostril's flaring, King Noliminan spun on his heel and stormed out of the Great Hall.

When he was gone, Michael raised his gaze to meet mine. "Dear Gods, Azrael."

I rolled my eyes closed, giving Michael a perfunctory nod.

Knowing I would not answer the questions which thundered through his mind, Michael shook his head, turned away from me, and followed after our Lord and Master.

-36-

Raguel turned her face to the door when she heard it opening. She could smell Lucias' scent permeate the room. She was glad it wasn't the other one. While Lucias at least pretended to be kind to her, Sappharon couldn't be bothered.

"Noliminan says hello." Raguel snorted. She knew better than that Lucias had spoken with Noliminan after having taken her and she wasn't falling for the jibe. "Are you hungry?"

"Yes." Raguel answered him honestly. "And I smell. May I take a bath?"

Lucias sighed. "Maybe later."

"Luke." Raguel sighed. It was the first time she had ever called Lucias by either of his familiar names in the full of her life. It felt like sour fire on her tongue. "Please. Noliminan isn't going to know if I am miserable or comfortable. Your point is being made either way."

"You're probably right." Lucias lowered himself onto what Raguel assumed was a chair. He often spent his time there, watching over her. She wasn't certain what his motivation was, but she didn't trust that it was for her benefit. "Mayhap later."

"Thank you." It was the best she would get for now. She would push the issue, as he suggested, later.

They sat in silence for a while. Raguel was about to ask him if he meant to get her something to eat when the door opened and someone new walked in. The unmistakable scent of freshly made bread overwhelmed her senses.

She was suddenly ravenous.

"Thank you, Raystlyn." Lucias stood and walked across the room. He grabbed the basket of food and made his way to Raguel. She reached her arms through the bars, desperate for anything to eat. Lucias pushed her hands away and lowered himself to his hunkers, placing the basket on the floor just outside of the cell so she could reach through and grab as much of the food as she needed to.

Which turned out to be quite a lot of it.

It had, after all, been near to a full waning moon since he had fed her.

"Slow down." Lucias cautioned, rather irritably, from his chair after Raguel had eaten three pieces of chicken and two large biscuits. "You'll make yourself sick."

"I didn't realize how hungry I was." She admitted. "And this is very good. Thank you."

"Feeding you was Raystlyn's idea." He sounded amused. But Raguel didn't care. Let him be amused. He was far more pleasant this way. "Not mine."

"Thank you all the same."

He fell into silence again as she finished her meal. When she was done she heard him walking toward her to grab the basket. He carried it to where she assumed the door to be and placed it on the other side. When he returned to his chair it was with a heavy sigh.

"Tell me what is happening." She pleaded.

333

"No." He muttered. "I have no care to placate your boredom."

"Then talk to me about other things." She begged.

"I'm in no mood for palaver with you." He snapped.

"Luke, please." She sighed. "There must be something you wish to speak with me about. We haven't passed words in as long as I can remember."

He let out a long, exasperated sigh. "I honestly have nothing to say to you, Raguel. And, anything I would say, I doubt very much you would like to hear."

"Tell me anyway."

"Fine." He snapped. "I do have a question."

"What?"

"Has Noliminan seen you in this form?" He asked. "Since he forced your change, I mean."

"No." Raguel shook her head. "He doesn't allow it." She felt her brow furrow. "He caught me once in this form after my change. I was in my own bedroom—and fully clothed—so I didn't think anything of it. I've never seen him so angry in all of my days."

"What did he say?"

"He didn't *say* anything." Raguel confessed.

It wasn't one of her happiest memories but she didn't see any reason not to share it with Lucias. He knew who Noliminan was as well as anyone did. And she wanted to keep him talking in case he said something she could later use to her advantage.

"But after he was done with me I couldn't walk for days."

"He beat you for it." His tone was filled with righteous indignation.

"Yes." Raguel nodded.

"Carvetek mouk." Lucias muttered. "I always wondered why you put up with it."

"I put up with it because I love him." It was more complicated than this. But telling him she was frightened of Noliminan wouldn't keep him talking.

"I love him, too. But I'm not about to let him dictate my essence." Lucias snorted.

"I am." Raguel chose not to call him out on that particular lie. Not yet, by any road. But she would when the time came that she must. "It doesn't bother me. And it makes him happy. So why not?"

To this Lucias made no reply. Raguel could feel him assessing her, however. She knew there was much he would like to say. She was surprised he was tempering his tongue.

"Has anyone else ever seen you in this form since your promise?"

Raguel felt her brow furrow. "No. At least, not anyone who would recognize me for who I am." And then as an afterthought. "I suppose Azrael has. Why?"

"Because you've grown to be very handsome." He said simply.

Raguel felt herself blush from head to toe at the unexpected compliment. "Thank you."

She didn't know if it was true or not. She never spent any large amount of time examining herself or comparing herself to others in her male form. She was a beautiful woman and her knowledge of this had always been enough to sate her vanity.

"Would it be easier for you if I were I to wear my other form?"

"Probably." This was said by Lucias reluctantly and under his breath. "But it's safer for you if you stay in this form."

"Why?"

"Because I don't like you in your other form." Lucias answered her honestly. "You infuriate me."

"Why?" Raguel truly wanted to know if her suspicions were accurate.

"Because I loathe your supplication toward him." He snapped.

She knew at once he was lying. The reason Lucias loathed her in her female form was because it was a painful reminder to him that she was Noliminan's wife. A position of status which Lucias—when Lucias thought of himself as Luci—coveted.

"You should defy him now and again."

"That's all well and good for you, Lord Lucias." Raguel smiled cruelly around the word 'Lord'. "You came by his heart and his regard naturally. You and Raziel both." She shook her head. "I have had to earn it. And it hasn't been the easiest of all things to hold on to."

Lucias fell silent again.

"He's bedding Raziel again." Raguel said calmly in an attempt to reengage him in the conversation. "Isn't he?"

"Yes." Lucias didn't lie. Though he did sound surprised. "I didn't think you knew."

"He smells like her sometimes." Raguel shrugged. Then in cold tones. "Sometimes he smells like you, too."

"I can assure you, I sleep in mine own bed." Lucias scoffed.

"I'm aware of that." Raguel snapped at him.

Aware of the fact that, when you are in Noliminan's bed, sleeping is the last thing on either one of your agendas.

And then she told him something she didn't believe he knew but which would anger him beyond telling.

"But sometimes he invites Gabriel over. To sleep with him, I think. Nothing more. But every now and again when he's talking to Gabe he starts talking about once days and he starts calling him Luci."

"Luci?" Lucias' tone was taut.

She realized almost at once that he was unaware of the fact that she knew about his affair with Noliminan. Given she slept in the room next to her Lord and Master, she wondered how he thought that could be.

It didn't matter. She would use this knowledge to her advantage.

"Luci." She muttered. "Luci or Luke. It depends on which version of you he prefers to be with in that particular moment."

Lucias was silent for a long, long time.

Finally he pronounced, "He told you about me, did he?"

"No." She sighed. "But really, Lucias, how stupid must you think me to be? I sleep in the room next to his. And neither one of you are particularly quiet when you go about it." Lucias cleared his throat. "My point is that he is pretending Gabriel is you."

"He is not."

"Yes." Raguel frowned. "He is. And Gabriel never corrects him. Just goes on pretending to be you." She felt her brow furrow and then shared another truth. "It troubles me."

Lucias let out a low breath between his teeth. It whistled slightly. Raguel couldn't tell if it was made from irritation or anger or, maybe, regret.

Finally, "Why are you telling me this?"

"Because you love Noliminan." Raguel snapped. "And he loves you. And I am nothing more than his trophy."

"That isn't true." Lucias replied, though his tone was softer now.

"It is true." Her temper was rising and she was beginning to lose control of her tongue. "He will never love me. I will always just be the one who agreed to be a woman for him when you and Raziel refused."

"My being male was initially his idea." Lucias muttered. "Not mine." That whistle again. "By any road, he loves you for this if for nothing else."

"No." Raguel shook her head. She was tired and this conversation was painful. "He loves me because when you refused his bed I did not. And that, my Lord Lucias, is the extent of his regard for me."

"I don't believe you."

"Believe it or don't." Raguel snapped at him, frustrated. "I do not care."

"You had best *start* caring." He was standing, she realized. And he had walked toward her. She could feel him hovering outside of her cage. "I didn't refuse his bed. I never refused his bed!"

"Yet you were ousted from it all the same." She sneered at him.

The tenor of his voice was pure venom. "I was never ousted from his bed. It was he who was ousted from mine. As for his, I will claim it whenever I please."

"Then claim it." She snapped at him. "I care not anymore. I found someone else to warm mine when you sneak into his."

When he spoke, his tone was icy. "With whom are you passing your time?"

She gave him a tight, cold smile. The smug satisfaction she felt for claiming the one prize which would never be his resonated with every word.

"Why, my Lord Lucias," she grinned, "when you slip into my husband's bed for a roll and a tumble, it is Lord *Loki's* beard that I ride."

Lucias sprang forward, his hands out and his expression a twisting mass of rage. When he reached her he used, for the first time, the magic he had stolen from Zadkiel when he had destroyed the courtyard.

Knowing the gate to every level of the Hells was about to open upon us all, it was Raguel's male body that my father ordered me to claim.

-37-

Barkiel heard the guttural scream of his Master, forcing him out of his reverie to find his feet and run from Raphael's bedchamber to the library down the hall.

Seeing Raguel, in her male and angel form, laying upon King Noliminan's massive desk with Michael bent over her openly weeping and King Noliminan pacing back and forth across the room in an angry storm, he stopped short.

He stared at the scene—so completely wrong, yet somehow so *utterly* right—with his lightning bolt eyes wide with panic.

"Queen Raguel . . ." He managed.

"*Lord* Raguel!" King Noliminan screamed. "This is as much as she has ever thought of me! Of our marriage! That she would expire herself whilst in this form and not her other!"

Michael spun on him. His generally handsome features were chiseled ugly with the horrified lines of his grief and his teeth were bared as his mouth curled into a snarl.

"No matter the form!" He seethed, unreasonable in his sorrow, not considering the price he was about to pay for grieving for the wife whose actions King Noliminan had been offended by. "She *is* dead!"

King Noliminan's eyes went wild with his fury. Michael would pay for his outburst. And he would pay dearly.

"Since you value this corpse so much more than you value me," he seethed at his General at Arms, "I shall send you to see to its Gods be damned grave."

He flicked his fingers at Michael and the corpse which had once been the Queen of Ladies. As he did so, they both disappeared.

"Do you have something to say about this as well?" King Noliminan rounded on Barkiel.

"No, your Grace." Barkiel, who knew better than to voice any kind of opinion, lowered his gaze.

He, himself, had never been the subject of King Noliminan's rage. Yet, as a middle child of the Quorum, he had watched it explode around him on every side.

Given he preferred to be forgotten about, he was not going to give his Master a reason to raise his ire today.

"Lucky damn thing for you." King Noliminan growled before he was simply gone.

-38-

Aiken was leaning on Loki's desk with his arms crossed over his chest, listening to Loki as he went through the list of the souls in the basement whom he believed were willing to fight on Lord Regent Lucias' side in exchange for their freedom.

He wasn't certain about what he thought of the idea. But he supposed it was really not his concern.

His purpose for having been aged before his time, he understood, was to assist Loki where he could in Lord Lucias' war. If the place where he was needed was directly at Loki's side, who was he to complain about that?

Complain, indeed. Such a chore to be forced to look upon his handsome face at every shift of the shadows during the day.

He felt himself smiling at this thought as he shook his head.

"What?" Loki smiled in return. Loki was always smiling it seemed.

"Nothing." Aiken shrugged. He knew better than to share his desire for his friend with him. "Just considering the politics of war."

"We've both certainly been thrown into the—"

A crackle of energy exploded behind him. Aiken had time to mark only one thing as it did so.

The King of Lords stood behind Loki with a scythe in his hands wearing an expression of twisted rage. He spun it fiercely in Loki's direction, ripping through the flesh of his neck.

As if Countenance was frozen by winter, Loki's head flipped off of his neck and flew up into the air.

The spray of his blood exploded around him, toward Aiken.

Instinctively, Aiken tried to scramble backward over the desk. He was unable to do so before he was blinded by the gore of Loki's lifeblood.

The King of Lords, still spinning, reached upward and grabbed the head from the air. Beneath the whistle of the scythe Sam cried out, ducking to miss its swing.

He wasn't fast enough.

His left wing was severed midway down the bone and his arm, which he had thrown up in his surprise to shield himself, was cut off at the shoulder before the blade sliced through Loki's torso, splitting it in half.

The King of Lords reached forward and grasped the beating heart from Loki's chest before Loki's body fell lifeless to the ground. He stuffed it into his robes and then bent over Loki to grasp the lower half of what used to be Loki's body.

There was another crackle of energy and then, quite suddenly, the King of Lords was simply gone.

Aiken, ashamed of himself for not rushing to protect his best friend, flew off of the desk, scrambling on his knees to crawl to the upper half of Loki's body, which was all that was left. He pulled it into his arms and began rocking it back and forth, his tears flowing unabashedly down his cheeks in violent rivers.

He didn't know how long he sat there, cradling what was left of Loki, before he realized Sam was laying at his side, moaning in pain.

He wrapped his other arm around Samyael and, not knowing how to reach the castle on Anticata so Lord Lucias could fix them, took them to the basement where he knew he could lock them away until such time as their bodies could be healed.

-39-

Having watched the entire drama play itself out, I was less than surprised when I was summoned by Noliminan to his library. He handed me a wooden box and demanded I deliver it to Lucias at once.

I complied.

Of course I complied.

But I loathed Noliminan in a way I had never loathed him before for forcing me to see to this task.

Not that I had been any more pleased to do Lucias' bidding when I had been asked to deliver Queen Raguel to Noliminan. But for some reason unknown to me at the time, I felt the level of betrayal more acutely this time around.

I knocked on the door to Lucias' library and I waited to be granted entry. She looked up at me with quiet concern, not realizing the package that I held in my hands was intended for her.

"Azrael." She smiled gently at me. "You shouldn't be here, met paken."

"I come at Noliminan's bidding." My tone was flat to my own ears. I know she understood at once by the fact I had given Noliminan no fealty—and I never would again—that I wasn't there for pleasantries. Just as she understood that I wasn't there under my own accord.

Swallowing, I raised the box in my hand.

"He sent me with . . ."

I couldn't face her; couldn't meet her gaze.

But I didn't need to. She came to me and grabbed the box from my hands, spinning away from me at once with the intention of walking toward her desk.

I steeled myself for her reaction.

As if I could have.

The moment she took the box out of my hands the bottom of it fell open and Lord Loki's severed head fell out and rolled across the floor to land grotesquely facing in our direction.

Every scrap of hair had been removed, the all too famous goatee and his eyebrows included. His mouth was open and his genitals—which Noliminan had obviously severed from his lifeless body—were shoved into his open mouth.

But the most disturbing thing of all, at least in my opinion, was that, staked to the top of the head, with a note pinned grotesquely upon it, was Lord Loki's still beating heart.

As Lucias reached for the note it burst into flames and Noliminan's voice boomed around us.

"You coveted the love of this heart and this traitorous mind." I shivered upon hearing these words. "Let us see if you can recover your beloved Loki of old from either one of them."

Lucias threw her hooked hands to her own face and screamed.

Terrified that she meant to claw her own eyes out to devoid herself of the image before her, I flew forward and wrapped my arms around her waist. I lifted her up, pulling her away from the severed head. She began kicking wildly to get away from me so she could claim it.

Not knowing what else to do, I formed a second corporeal body over Lord Loki's head and lifted it, holding it desperately to my chest. While this form of me ran with the head to somewhere I could separate the different sections so that Lord Loki might grow back together, the other fought Lucias, who was, literally, raving.

"Loki!" Lucias cried, her voice shrill and not her own with her arms and legs still flailing. "Oh dear Gods no! Not my beloved Loki!"

"He'll be okay." I tried to remain calm. It was an impossible thing to do. Never in my life had I seen Lucias lose control of her senses to this degree. Never again in my life, I understood, would I be able to survive it.

It took everything within me to do so now.

"My Lady, I know that he will be okay." I swallowed my tears, knowing she needed me in a way that she had never needed me before. "I'll send Haniel to you . . . I'll send whomever you want to you."

"Haniel can't save him." She sobbed. "He took his head and his heart." She pulled away from me then and fell to her knees. "Either one or the other will never be the same."

"They will be."

"No." She sobbed as she fell over her knees. "Oh, Gods! My beloved Loki . . . You are forever gone from me now!"

-40-

Zadkiel looked distractedly from his bed to Ishitar, who was playing on the floor. He was reaching upward to the wall, crying at the top of his lungs. "Azy Kiki! Azy Kiki!"

"Ishitar."

Zadkiel forced himself to lean forward. It took every ounce of his strength. He swallowed and licked his lips.

This wasn't the first time Zadkiel had seen the baby act strangely.

"Come here, min 'lasupita!"

"Da!" He looked over his shoulder and shook his head. After doing so, he spun around and raised his hands to the air again. "Azy Kiki! Azy Kiki!"

"Ishitar, please." Zadkiel shivered. He grasped his legs with his hands and lifted them, trying to spin on the bed.

"Azy Kiki!" Ishitar cried again, now in a desperate tone which brokered on madness before, for no discernible reason, he buried his small hands in his hair and began to pull desperately upon it, almost as if he were trying to tear it from his own head.

"Ishitar!" Zadkiel screamed. "No!"

No longer caring about his damned and useless legs, he pushed himself off of the bed and fell onto the floor with a painful crash so he could crawl to the boy.

"Azy Kiki!" Ishitar screamed.

Ishitar pulled violently, succeeding in tugging fistfuls of hair as he did so.

"Dear Gods . . ." Zadkiel cried as he tried to pull himself along the floor with his useless arms, forcing himself to ignore the pain. "Ishitar, please!"

"Azy Kiki." Ishitar replied as he turned to face Zadkiel.

Then, as if this had been his intent all along, wearing a strange smile, he threw the hair into the air.

Zadkiel watched in silent fascination as it slowly drifted side to side, almost as if it were the weight of a feather, to the ground, where Ishitar was sitting.

"Kiki he go bye bye."

"Ishitar." Zadkiel swallowed.

Kiki he go bye bye?

"Kiki." The boy said as he fell upon his hands and began crawling toward Zadkiel. "Da. Nolo. Kiki he go bye bye."

The Gods pray . . .

Zadkiel involuntarily shuddered.

He didn't know who Kiki was. But he had heard Ishitar say Nolo before.

Nolo was Noliminan. If whomever Kiki was went bye bye at Nolo's hand, then the poor sod would soon be paying Zadkiel a visit.

When Ishitar reached Zadkiel, who was now laying spent upon the floor with his mind reeling in horror, he wrapped his arms around the archangel's neck, opened his lips into a round 'O' and then leaned forward to give him a sloppy baby kiss on the forehead.

"Da." He said as Zadkiel allowed his head to fall upon the floor. "Da Da Da Da Da."

"Da." Zadkiel agreed as he closed his eyes.

To this, Ishitar had no response but his sweet baby's laugh.

-41-

Michael sat beside her open grave, staring at the palms of his hands.

They were dirty from his task and crusted with blood from the rocks within the earth which had scraped them. Though he knew it was past time for him return to face his punishment, he couldn't bear the thought of leaving her on this uninhabited world.

As alone dead as you had ever been during your life.

After he dug into the clay and stone of the ground, he gently wrapped her in his clothes, laid her body into the soil and covered her with the earth.

He then allowed himself to weep before casting himself out to find a grave marker. After her epitaph was chiseled into the stone by his sword, he sought a weed which bore a small white flower upon it that would grow over her to tell all creatures of any world where she lay.

Naked but for his small clothes, Michael rolled his eyes closed and then opened them so he could look up to the sky.

Another night at his Lady's side, he decided.

And who, honestly, would miss him?

-42-

I held Lucias in my arms all that night as she wept against my chest, and I listened to the hitching sobs which did not dissipate even after she had fallen asleep.

When morning came, she awoke to the realization that there was no time to grieve for Loki if there was to be any chance in saving him. She sought out Sappharon and Zamyael and then, wearing her true female form, ducked into a hidden passage way which was located in her room that led underground and to the stables.

I followed—I had no choice given she was bringing the demons with her—taking notice of the fact that she dismissed the small cottage which had been built behind the stables and the small face of the youngest inhabitant looking down upon them and watching them pass through what he considered to be his yard.

Once out of the confines of the castle proper, and the spells which had been cast to keep its inhabitants from using their magic within, Lucias willed all three of them to her apartment in the Hells Realm. There, she began searching for Samyael, who she knew would have been at Loki's side when the attack occurred.

She didn't find Samyael. But she did find Emissary Lord Aiken Darklief.

She chose to let Zamyael, who knew Aiken, explain to the mischief fairy that Lucias was one of the Loki's many geese and that she desperately needed to see him to give him news.

Aiken refused. He wasn't about to put the remains of Loki or Samyael, who was in agonizing pain and who was all too aware of what had taken place, in even a minute bit of danger.

Zamyael, as manipulative as any creature I have ever known when to be so is to her benefit, encouraged Aiken to step into what had once been Sappharon's bedchamber so they might speak in private. The minute the door shut, Lucias called to me, asking me to take my corporeal form.

"Azrael," she reached for my hand when I stood before her, "I'm not asking for you to betray anyone. So I beg you answer my question."

"My Lady," I swallowed. Hard. Being the only one who was aware of the true depths of her grief I would give her whatever information she asked for. Consequences be damned. "If I can."

She nodded. "I only need to know where Loki's body is."

As she said, there was no betrayal here if I were to provide her with the information she sought. Aiken's intent, after all, was that Lord Loki be healed as much to his rights as was possible.

"He and Sam are in the basement." I didn't hesitate to respond. "In the apartment where the Gods will reside."

"Thank you, met paken." She kissed me on the cheek, her woman's lips soft against my skin, and then willed herself to stand at Loki's bed side.

346

When she entered the room where Lord Loki rested, she looked around, confused. Samyael was nowhere to be found.

Another part of me, the part which had been watching Samyael grieve, had convinced the demon that it would be best if he stayed in a room of his own rather than hover over what was left of Lord Loki's lifeless form. I did this because I knew that Lucias needed to be alone with Lord Loki so that she might fawn over him and help him to heal.

Deciding she would send Zamyael back for Sam later, Lucias wrapped her arms around Lord Loki's torso and willed them back to the edge of the castle grounds.

This time she wasn't seen.

For the sake of the young boy who lived within the cottage, I was more than grateful for this small wonder.

-43-

Aiken was furious with Zamyael when he learned from Samyael that Lord Regent Lucias had come to claim Loki's remains from the basement where he had placed Loki and Samyael to heal.

Not because he didn't think his friend was in better hands under Lord Lucias' care. Rather, because Zamyael had felt it necessary to lie to him about the fact that she was distracting him so Lord Lucias could take Loki's body parts.

If he would have known that it was his father looking for Loki, Aiken would have just sent Zamyael to collect him.

In an effort to ward off his anger, Aiken found himself wandering the bridging areas which joined the Heavens to the Hells.

The first place he went was the bridging Courtyard. He ordered himself a drink and watched with great curiosity as the demons and angels bustled around him, visiting each table and serving the Gods and Goddesses who were making merry with their dinner or their drinks.

At first he couldn't figure out what it was that troubled him about the scene. But then, suddenly, as the demon who was assigned to his table brought him his glass of vodka, it became all too clear.

While there were demons in the Courtyard, not a one of them were sitting at any one of the tables. Not even those where Gods who served the Hells bound Realms were seated. Yet, angels were scattered everywhere, laughing and making merry with one another.

Their Gods being present or not.

What is this all about? Where are the demons?

He smiled up at what he, for the nonce, considered to be *his* demon, handing him one of the rare gems which were mined in a cave not far from the Oakland Grove. The demon stared down at his fingers, his hazel eyes wide, and shook his head.

"No, Emissary Darklief." He said. "You aren't to pay for your drinks."

"This isn't in payment of my drink." Aiken gave him a tired smile. "It's for you. A pretty in thanks for your care of me. You might trade it for something you desire."

"Thank you, Emissary Darklief." He replied. "But I'm not allowed to accept it."

Aiken felt his brow furrow at that. "But the angels who serve me take my pretties all the time."

"Yes." He was starting to look frightened. "But I'm a demon. Not an angel. And demons aren't allowed to take any type of payment for our services."

"Why not?"

"We just are not." He replied, lowering his gaze. "But thank you all the same."

Before Aiken could ask him any more questions, the demon darted away. Shaking his head, he let out a long, deep sigh before throwing back his drink.

Though he hadn't thought it possible, he was now angrier than he had been before. So he simply let his feet wander until, without realizing this is what he meant to do, he found himself standing outside of the Great Hall where the Gods came when the King of Lords called Council.

As he looked upon the arched doors, he blinked.

They were very large and extremely ornate.

Made of marble, they were decorated with a carving of every race of mortal Aiken had ever heard of. And, he would admit, some he had never before seen.

Stepping toward them, he found his eyes widening as he searched for the carving which represented the fairies. When he found them, he let out a surprised gasp.

The fairy carving was the very likeness of him! And wearing his lately come by loin cloth, no less.

"Loki's beard . . ." He muttered under his breath.

As he did so, he realized another truism which made his head spin.

In the carving his hand was raised, palm to the sky. Standing upon it were ten small pixies in various stages of making ready to take flight.

He shook his head and crossed his arms over his chest.

Though very few knew this—including the fairies themselves—the reason that a fairy's skin shimmered in the sunlight was because when a pixie died their soul took up residence on the closest fairy's flesh in much the same way as a barnacle did upon a whale. They stayed until there were enough of them to merge together to create a single soul that was large enough to become worthy of entering Martiam's halls.

Aiken, who had always been aware of the fact that his body laid host to these far too small pixie souls, had long used them to his advantage. Knowing pixies wanted nothing more than to be useful, he had learned to tap into his ability to call on them when he had need for spies or to seek out one of the inhabitants of the Oakland Grove if he needed to speak with them.

Thus, whomever carved his image had been able to represent fairy and pixie as one by putting them together in this pose.

He made a mental note to find out who this person was.

Reaching for the handle so he could open one of the doors brought about another unexpected smile. One was carved in the image of an angel and the other a demon. The only reason he knew this is because the demon had wings made of onyx while the angel's wings were of white marble. Both, aside from this, were exactly the same in face and form.

Shaking his head yet again, he grasped the demon—he supposed this was the only right thing to do given he was a Hells bound God—and pushed the door open.

After seeing the door, he had no right to be surprised.

Yet, it was impossible for him to react otherwise.

Whenever Loki talked about being called to Council, he always spoke of 'finding a seat'. Because of this, Aiken had assumed the room was antiseptic. He had envisioned the tables where the Gods sat were non-descript with hard, uncomfortable chairs stationed behind them.

This was far from the case.

There were twenty steps, upon which were at least forty tables per step. Each table had its own personality, many of which he immediately associated with stories Loki had told him about individual Gods or Goddesses.

There was one which was decorated femininely to the extreme. Though he had never met Lady Moira, given the table cloth was literally made of intricately interwoven tapestries, he associated it with her almost at once.

Another, very near the front, he believed belonged to the sea people. Aegir and Triton immediately came to mind, though the bowl in the center, which was carved into the shape of a most handsome and masculine merman, very definitely bore the face of Poseidon.

"They group themselves to their tasks." He muttered under his breath.

And then he saw the table which could belong to no one but Loki.

It was decorated completely to his tastes with a high backed leather chair surrounded by about twenty smaller seats which were, without question, meant for the comfort of Goddesses rather than Gods.

Realization made him start. "They're meant for his gaggle!"

Laughing, he, once again, shook his head.

As he did so, he allowed himself to turn his attention to the front of the room.

Where his eyes landed upon the thrones.

How could they not?

Four ornate thrones, each as different from the next as they could possibly be.

The King of Lords and Lord Regent Lucias' were the easiest to identify. They sat close together, one made of solid gold and the other of pure silver. The King of Lords'—the gold one—was decorated with jewels. It's padding was cream colored leather.

Lord Regent Lucias'—the silver one—was far more simple in nature. Yet, somehow, more beautiful. The silver of it was carved into the arcs of flames which had been lightly hued so that it actually appeared to be on fire. There were no jewels to speak of and the padding was covered with simple brown leather.

"And they say vanity is a sin." Aiken chuckled to himself.

He assumed the throne beside Lord Lucias' was the Sovereign Lady's. And the Queen of Ladies', to the left of the King of Lords', was, like Lord Lucias', simple, yet soft.

Far to the left of all of the thrones was a long silken runner. It was the azure blue color of a summer sky. Upon it were eleven pillows, each and every one of them different from the next.

"The Quorum?" Aiken asked himself. "But if so, why only eleven?"

Yes. As he stepped toward the pillows, he knew this to be the case.

First was Raphael's, tawny in color. Next came Michael's, which was black, like his hair. Zadkiel's was a brilliant gold and far smaller than the rest of them. He supposed that the smallness of it was to cause Zadkiel discomfort.

Aiken had to stop his assessment as his eyes fell upon Metatron's. Like the archangel, it was entirely made up of flames. He found himself walking toward it and lowering himself to his hunkers to run his fingers over it.

The flames don't burn!

After Metatron's, there was no pillow at all. Aiken found himself frowning at that because he understood this was

Camael's place and he was meant to sit on the hard ground on his knees.

Shivering at the meaning which might be behind this, he forced his gaze to fall to the next pillow over, which appeared to be made of leaves and herbs. This had to be Haniel's. And next to his, a femininely delicate pillow that could only belong to one of the two archangels that Loki had juxtaposed should have been born female rather than male—Uriel and Mihr.

Given Mihr was the youngest, and belonged at the end of the line, this one had to belong to Uriel.

After Uriel's came Gabriel's. Aiken knew this because it matched the simple brown leather of Lucias' chair and because a trumpet—which Gabriel was purported to blow to call the Council to order—lay across it.

Next was mine, which is crimson in color. Crimson, and not entirely formed. It looks more like a pool of blood than it does a pillow. This caused Aiken to shiver.

The next pillow, like Metatron's, caused Aiken to actually step forward and touch it. It was Barkiel's pillow. And it was a buzzing ball of electricity, as was the archangel, himself.

"Damn." Aiken swallowed as he touched it and was not shocked. "These creatures are passing queer."

The last two were very simple. Another black one which could only be Cassiel's and then another delicately feminine one made of grass which could only be Mihr's.

"Forgive me, Emissary Darklief."

Aiken cried out, spinning around. He thought that he was alone.

His eyes danced the back of the Hall, searching for the source of the voice. It didn't take long for them to fall upon me as I was hanging naked from the gallows at the back of the room, my wings stretched wide so that they appeared to him as though they were made from rivers of blood rather than flowing red feathers.

How could I have forgotten that you were there? And how is it that I didn't see you when I was looking at the audience before?

352

"Sir Azrael." Aiken flew his hand to his chest. "You frightened me."

"I apologize, Emissary Darklief." I smiled at him, attempting to grant him a comforting tone. "I only mean to warn you: It isn't safe to caress the pillows."

Aiken felt his brow furrow. He stepped away from the line of pillows and toward the bottom row of tables. "Why?"

"It is too intimate a gesture." I lowered my gaze. "I know you are curious. Which is why I didn't say anything before. But I beg you, now that your curiosity is sated, please don't touch them ever again."

Aiken licked his lips and then nodded. "Of course not. I didn't mean to offend you. I'm sorry if I did."

"You didn't." I replied, returning my gaze to meet Aiken's. "And nor would it offend my brothers." I looked away again. "Which is not to say that it wouldn't offend our Master."

Understanding dawned on Aiken like Apollo's morning star.

"Dear Gods." He sighed, understanding the repercussions that might come if the King of Lords believed he had molested his slaves. "Forgive me. I wasn't thinking."

"It can be forgiven." I replied, grinning at the thought that he considered us to be slaves—given he loathed the thought—and returning my gaze in his direction. "Which is why I didn't, as I say, stop you before."

Aiken nodded. He licked his lips again—he always did this when he was nervous—and then he braved, "I know you can't talk to me." I nodded my agreement. "But can you tell me if Loki will be okay?"

"No."

Aiken was overcome with disappointment by my answer.

"You misunderstand, Emissary Darklief." I tried to explain. "I can't tell you because I don't know. He is in Lucias' hands, as you are aware. Which is where he must be to have any hope of recovering."

"What are the chances that he won't?" Aiken's voice was a whisper to his own ears.

"Lucias claimed him swiftly." I used the most soothing of tones. "If anyone can heal him, then it is Lucias."

"I wish I could talk with him."

After considering, I said, "Maybe you can."

"What?" Aiken started. "How?"

"Not directly." I sighed. As I did so, I raised my arm and pointed a finger toward the wall above the thrones. "But you can tell *him* what you want to say to Lord Loki. And he'll tell Sappharon, who has been given Lord Loki's care whilst Lucias sees to other tasks."

"Sappharon?" Aiken started. "She loathes him."

"No." I corrected him. "She's jealous of him."

Sighing, Aiken looked in the direction in which I had been pointing.

And, for the second time, he felt like an unobservant fool.

How had he not seen the archangel crucified to the wall when he had been looking upon the thrones?

There was no question who the archangel was. His face was identical to the King of Lords. This archangel could be no one other than Raphael.

"Dear Gods." Aiken swallowed. "Why would the King of Lords do this to Raphael?"

"No." I replied, hopefully gently. "This is a projection of Raphael. And Lucias' doing rather than Noliminan's. But he can hear you. And you can hear him if he will speak with you." Then, with a tone laced with pain because I emphasized with the devastation that Raphael felt, "He won't, however."

Aiken, understanding more than he wanted to, stepped before the thrones, looked upward to meet Raphael's guarded, mistrustful gaze, and gave him what message he thought Loki would receive without finding offense by Aiken's concern for him.

-44-

Sappharon gave Raystlyn a guarded smile as he raised his bow and pulled the string.

The Gods love him because he is beautiful. But as far as skills as a warrior goes, he is sorely lacking.

"No." She shook her head and stepped toward him. Swallowing as she breathed in the scent of him, she raised her hand to set it upon the small of his back as she stood behind him. She reached her arm upward and grasped the string with her own fingers, forcing his to re-grasp it when he let go thinking she meant to take over. "Feel the draw."

He gave her a cautious smile and nodded.

"Here." She pulled slightly. And then she raised the tip of the arrow to where she estimated his eye should fall firmly upon his target. Given she was shorter than he was it was a guess. Yet, she was extremely skilled at archery, so it was a very educated guess which she felt she could rely upon. "Now. If you shoot straight like this, what do you think will happen?"

"I'll hit the target." He shrugged.

"No." She shook her head. As she did so, she tilted the bow so its aim was slightly upward. "The arrow will curve as it flies through the air. If the distance is short you aim right for the target. But if it is long, as this target is, you have to raise your aim above it and estimate the arc the arrow will take after you let it fly."

She released the string and wrapped her fingers around his own. He shifted uncomfortably before her as she did.

"Now." She muttered, ignoring his distaste that she would stand so close to him. "When I count to three."

He nodded.

"One . . ." She forced him to pull very slightly so there was more tension, "two . . ." She raised the aim where it needed to be, "and . . . three."

They released their fingers in unison. The arrow flew through the air, whistling its song as it fought against the wind.

And, for the first time since Raystlyn had picked up a bow, the mark was perfect.

"I did it!" He cried, spinning around in her arms and looking down at her with wide, excited eyes. "I hit the mark!"

"You did." She nodded and released him, stepping away. Attractive though he may be, he held no fascination for her. "Now try it on your own."

"I can't do it on my own." He shook his head, suddenly much more interested in her.

"Yes." She raised her hand and set it, very hesitantly, upon his shoulder. "You can."

He gave her a very doubtful smile, but he pulled another arrow from his quiver and he strung it.

He took his time finding his mark, but Sappharon didn't admonish him. There would not be time in battle for such nonsense, but this was irrelevant here. He was strong enough with his split sword that the need for him to ever use his bow for anything more than a silent attack where he would have time to levy his aim would be near to non-existent.

When he was sure enough of his aim, he pulled taut on the string. He swallowed, clearly uncertain of himself, and then, after counting to three, let the arrow fly.

It didn't hit its mark. But it was the closest he'd ever come on his own.

He threw the bow to the ground and, spinning toward her, wrapped his arms around her waist.

"You did it, brat! You taught me how to aim my bow." He pulled away, grinning.

She blushed and looked away. "You always had the skill within you, Raystlyn. You just needed the right instruction."

He spun then. Her legs flew behind her as he did so and her black wings caught the air.

"Whatever." He said before setting her gently upon her bare feet. "What's next."

She laughed and shook her head. "Stay here. Hit the mark without my instruction. And then we'll talk about what's next."

"Sappharon!"

She turned away from Raystlyn at the sound of Zamyael's voice. Though irritated, she could see Zamyael was regretful for having interrupted the lesson.

"I'm sorry." She shook her head. "But Lucias wants to speak with us." Her eyes flicked from Sappharon to Raystlyn. Finally she grinned. "You too, Rayst."

"Did he say why?" Raystlyn asked.

"No." She sighed. "But given his state over what happened to Loki, it can't be anything good."

"No." Sappharon, who had watched over Lucias as she grieved her unrequited love, knew this better than anyone. She had laid abed for almost the full cycle of the sun before finally rousing to start formulating her response.

In the end this had been a good thing.

Sappharon had needed the time to train her army, which was honestly made of soft handed angels and demons who had never once raised blade or bow. Though she wasn't one hundred percent confident in their skills now, she at least thought they might enter into a battle and not be totally decimated.

Not to mention the fact that it had taken time to bring Aiken around to convince him that more than just his love for Loki was required to stand against Noliminan. He had been frightened, rather than inspired, after Loki had lost his head.

And he had only, just this morning, agreed to take up Loki's duties with the damned ones where Loki had left them before he had been decapitated.

She didn't admonish Aiken. He was so new to the politics of the Gods. And the wars he had always waged amongst his mortals held far less consequences than this particular battle.

Sappharon stepped toward Zamyael and laced her arm around her waist. She grinned at her as she lay her head upon her shoulder. "How's Lasterian?"

Zamyael, blushing, lowered her gaze. "He's fine."

"Just fine?" Sappharon winked.

"We're taking it slow." Zamyael shrugged. "We have a lot of water to put under our bridge."

"I hope you let it flow freely."

"Countenance will tell." She shrugged. "Raziel has been imprisoned but she is still my Goddess. I must remain faithful to her until she releases me from my binds."

Sappharon sighed, but nodded.

"Believe me," she said, "I understand."

Zamyael gave her a knowing smile. "I know you do."

They made their way to Lucias in silence after that, with Raystlyn watching the pair of them with guarded curiosity.

Lucias, wearing a male face given Raystlyn would see her, sat behind her desk, her expression dour and her eyes still burning with pain. Sappharon loathed Noliminan for causing her Mistress such discord.

"Brat, I need you to look over Loki for the short time." She muttered as she tapped her fingers on her table. "I have to go and I need to take Zamyael with me."

"Where are you going?" Raystlyn braved.

"To talk to Raziel." Lucias muttered. "To tell her what has happened."

"Can you do that?" Sappharon asked, surprised.

"Noliminan sent her to my basement." Lucias shrugged. "I haven't, yet, been banned from my home."

"What do you intend to tell her?" Zamyael asked, her eyes lowered.

"The truth." Lucias shrugged. "What else?"

"What truth?" Zamyael asked, surprised.

Sappharon, grinning, lowered her gaze.

The manner in which an answer could be formed to this particular question was innumerable.

-45-

For the first time since she had been imprisoned, Raziel heard the sound of someone approaching the grouping of cells in which she had been forced to live. Though she wasn't certain why, neither Lucias nor Loki had bothered before.

She raised her gaze and started.

Before her stood a fairy.

And what a breathtakingly beautiful fairy he was.

"Hello." She braved.

"My Lady." The fairy put his leg back and bowed to her in the manner that fairies do. He looked over his shoulder and then returned his gaze to Raziel. "Lord Regent Lucias is here to speak with you. Will you receive him?"

"Yes." Raziel flew to the bars of her cages and grasped them desperately. "Please."

The fairy nodded and stepped away.

Lucias stepped forward, keeping back and in the shadows. Raziel wasn't certain what this was about until Zamyael appeared.

That worthy flew forward, his hands grasping Raziel's and pressing his forehead against Raziel's own.

"My Lady." Zamyael said, his strong fingers bringing Raziel comfort.

"Zam." Raziel whispered. "What news?"

"Raguel's soul has been expired." Lucias said this in flat, hard tones. "I sent her body to Noliminan and he disparaged over the fact that I forced her to be male when I rid myself of her."

Raziel froze. Terror over came her. "But you forced her!"

"And yet he was angry." Lucias shrugged. "I thought that you have the right to know."

"But you forced her!"

"Still angry." Lucias replied, his eyes narrowing. "In response, he beheaded and emasculated Loki."

"Loki?" Raziel felt her eyes grow even wider than they already were.

"Ta." Lucias leaned against the cage across from Raziel's. It was empty. "He damned you for nothing, Raz. What do you think he's going to do to you when you return to him after this thing is over?"

"Nothing!" Raziel cried. "He loves me!"

"He *loved* you." Lucias agreed as he stepped forward. "When you were his wife." His lips split into a cynical, hateful grin. "Think about that why don't you."

"He loves me yet!"

"He loved Raguel." Lucias shrugged. "And she *did* agree to be his woman." He chuckled, almost cruelly, under his breath.

"Just what in the name of my Thirty Hells do you think he'll do to *you* for not only denying him such pleasure but for forcing your ability to do so in his face?"

Raziel, immediately understanding what Lucias was telling her, fell to the floor of her cage as her fear as to what would become of her overwhelmed her.

It was no surprise to anyone that she never, thereafter, wore her male form again. Her woman's form was, after all, the only form she had which would give her any hope of saving her own skin.

-46-

Sappharon lowered herself at Loki's bedside.

Oh, how she loathed him.

"Lucias' favorite." She muttered. "Ha."

She let her eyes trail over his useless body. "You have no heart and you have no head. Leastwise that aren't black and rotting."

This made her grin.

Yes, the parts of him not associated with his heart stank. But she didn't care. As long as they weren't attached to his heart there was still the barest of chances that Loki wouldn't return as the Loki whom Lucias was so enamored with.

And then, maybe, Lucias would realize, once and for all, that she, Sappharon, was the only one who had ever really stood unwaveringly by her side.

-47-

Lasterian stood behind Tristan, his entire body trembling.

This was it. The first true battle of the war. And though he had been trained at blade and bow by Sappharon, he still wasn't certain he could appropriately wield them.

Not that there was time to question the matter within his own mind.

As soon as they stepped upon the battlefield, Lord Regent Lucias paced before them, reminding them of why they were here and assuring them whatever price they might pay in facing Michael's army would be well worth it if even one of their brothers or sisters were given the free will that they, themselves, had long been denied.

Free will? Lasterian thought abstractly through his terror. *Is that what we're fighting for? Even now, when I'm treated more as an object than I ever have been before?*

He held his tongue as the fire of the cannon burst over his head, signaling the first defense. The sound was foreign to him. And terrifying.

He covered his ears.

As far as perspective went, his was irrevocably lost.

There was nothing left of Lord Tristan that he knew in that moment. He was a soldier and relished this role with an unhealthy gusto.

Angel, demon, Tristan didn't care. This wasn't about the color of the wings. This was about whose side people were on. He looked for the color of the sigil on a man or woman's breastplate and then swung his broad sword based upon this alone.

Arms, legs, heads, torsos . . . Lasterian followed Tristan's wake and tried to fend off those his God was unable to deploy. So it was that he stood directly behind Tristan when they finally came upon Michael.

"Lower your sword," Michael grunted under his breath as steel met steel and sparks flew between them, "lest I be forced to destroy you."

"Lower your sword and join what is right!" Tristan yelled, drunk with lust from taking the blood of those he had felled. "Damn you Michael! You are my brother in heart and mind."

"No, Tristan." Michael said, teeth clenched as his body spun in an arch which brokered no further argument. "If you stand against King Noliminan, then no bonds will bind us!"

Lasterian sprang forward, intending to gut Michael with his sword, but it was too late. Tristan's head was severed from his neck in one swift blow. It landed upon the ground and rolled ten feet before it came to an end, blood and sinew trailing behind it, where another warrior inadvertently kicked it into the fray.

Lasterian fell to his knees on the field and scurried after his Master's head praying between tears that he might find it and that, if he couldn't, his own would be the next one severed.

-48-

"We won this battle." Michael stood before King Noliminan, fatigued, his hair matted with gore and his face caked in the blood and entrails of his enemies. "What orders, now?"

"Given all of this," King Noliminan growled, "it is time for you to bring Lucias before me so I might decide if I shall send him to Zadkiel."

"Your Grace." Michael raised his gaze. His eyes darted over his Master. "This is extreme."

"Extreme or not," King Noliminan barked, "this is my order!"

"Very well." Michael replied, turning away. "As you ever command me, then I shall make it so and order Zadkiel to be at the ready."

-49-

Zamyael watched Lucias carefully after the battle.

She hadn't expected to lose. Her heart was breaking and she was pacing back and forth across the floor of her library.

"My Lady?" She tried.

"Do you know where Tristan is?" She stopped her pacing and turned to Zam. They hadn't been able to find Tristen's head and this troubled Lucias. She knew that by being forced to grow it back irreparable damage would be inevitable. "Did Noliminan imprison him?"

"No." Zamyael sighed. "He's in the care of one of the Gods."

Though it was out of character that he would do so, Noliminan had actually placed Tristan with Evanbourough until his head grew back. Zamyael had reasoned, when she first learned this, that it must be because Tristan could do no harm until he was healed.   Otherwise he would have been locked away in the Thirteenth level.

Also, given Zadkiel and Ishitar were there, Noliminan knew Evan would understand that any turn he made out of rights would bring about dire consequences.   To betray Ishitar would be to betray Noliminan.

Thus, where else would Tristan, who was not exactly Tristan at this juncture, be more secure?

"Will you take me to him?"

"Of course."

As if she had any other choice.

<h1 style="text-align:center">-50-</h1>

Looking with grave irritation at Prince Ishitar, who lay sprawled out on the floor with his arms and legs swinging back and forth at his sides, Zadkiel ceased his sweeping and put his weight on the broom.

"Come, come, you little brat. Up now so your Da can sweep."

Ishitar laughed and shook his head. "No."

Zadkiel sighed. "If you don't move I'll clobber you over the head with my staff!"

This only made him laugh all the more. He knew that Zadkiel would do no such thing.

"Ishitar, please." He tried. "Get out of my damn way."

"No." He laughed again, raised himself up on his hands and stuck out his tongue.

"Fine, then." He shrugged. "I'll just sweep you up with the rest of the dirt."

Putting his broom to the ground, Zadkiel began sweeping toward him as if to make good on the threat. As he did so, Ishitar rose into the air, giggling, his neck and knees bending backward and his hair falling in a silky river toward the floor.

"Azy makes Ishy fly."

Zadkiel snorted. "Thank you, Azrael."

Though he couldn't see me, he heard my low, deep laughter. This made him smile.

He swiftly swept the area where Ishitar had been laying and then watched with fascination as the boy was lowered onto the floor.

He decided he was becoming all too comfortable with his knowledge that I was always in the room with him. It had become apparent to him that, even though I wasn't in my corporeal form, Ishitar could see me as clearly as he could see Zadkiel.

Often Zadkiel pondered upon this fact. But, often he pondered upon much about the child. He had a feeling that he would never understand the true depths of the power which resided within him.

But, then, what did he know? He had been raised with his archangel brothers. Never a child God.

All of this could be normal.

Couldn't it?

Pondering this, he walked toward the wall and propped the broom against it. Tired, he stepped toward his favorite chair. When he found his comfort he held out his arms, smiling as Ishitar stood and stumbled clumsily toward him.

He let the boy crawl into his lap and grinned as he threw his arms around his neck to hug him. "Ishy wuvs Da."

"Da loves Ishitar." Zadkiel replied, turning his face so that he could kiss the boy's cheek. "But you must mind me, lad. And not always rely on Azrael lifting you out of my way."

Ishitar nodded against his lips and turned to face the door. "Lulu."

"Lulu?" Zadkiel asked him, confused.

He knew that Ishitar called Lucias by that name. But he hadn't spoken of Lucias for long and long. Because of this, Zadkiel wondered what he was up to that would have brought about Ishitar's sudden attention to him.

And then came a knock on the door.

Zadkiel blinked his surprise.

"Very well." He muttered before kissing the boy's cheek again. "Lulu."

Not wanting to get up, he called out to whomever had knocked that they might come in. As he did so, Evanbourough stepped out of the kitchen with Lasterian—who looked thoroughly chastised—on his heel.

Zadkiel took a moment to ponder Evanbourough's treatment of the angel since Lasterian's return with Tristan's battered body and sighed. Though Evanbourough was nothing but kind to Zadkiel, he understood all too clearly why Evanbourough fared better without the service of a demon of his own.

When the door opened, Zadkiel froze.

As he had suspected when he had heard the knock, Lucias stood on the other side, his expression tight and drawn. Zamyael stood beside him, her gaze lowered to the floor. While Lucias' attention fixed immediately upon Evanbourough and Lasterian, Zamyael's rose and fell upon Zadkiel.

"Ishitar!" She cried and flew forward.

Lucias, startled by the sound of his son's name, snapped his head in Zadkiel's direction.

"Ishitar." He whispered as Zamyael fell upon her knees at Zadkiel's side.

The baby let out a squeal of laughter and immediately plunged his chubby hands into the braids making up Zamyael's hair. "Zamy!"

"Zamy." She nodded, laughing as he began tugging on her braids. She raised her hand to wrap around his and gently pulled his fingers away.

"Oh, Ishitar." Lucias began walking toward them.

Zadkiel, seeing this, swallowed. His heart exploded with his grief.

He had been given an order; an order he could not defy.

If he did so, he would risk losing Ishitar.

And nothing was worth that risk. Not even the promise of being permanently healed would entice him.

Especially not for the father who is responsible for my current state of health.

Not only was it Lucias' fault that he had been flung from the Heavens to begin with, it was also his bomb which had blown

Zadkiel apart. Whether he had done so on purpose or not meant nothing to Zadkiel at this point.

Lucias fell upon his knees before Zadkiel and held his hands out for his son. Zadkiel wrapped one arm around the boy and moved the other forward, seemingly meaning to grab Ishitar with it so that he could lift him into Lucias' arms.

What he did, instead, was lean forward.

The barest moment after it was clear that Zadkiel could not be stopped from doing what he meant to do, Lucias' eyes grew wide with understanding. Panic seized him and he began to pull away.

Too late.

Zadkiel's fingers swiped his brow and he fell in a crumpled mass on the floor at his feet.

-51-

I watched in horror as Zadkiel leaned forward, knowing his intent even before he did and understanding that he had misunderstood Michael's directive that he be at the ready. Not that he actually make good on utilizing his gifts.

And, this must also be said, I watched in fascination as Zamyael flew toward Lucias, knocking her body over so that it fell upon the ground.

Zadkiel's eyes, which had been dull and nearly lifeless since the explosion in the courtyard, suddenly gleaned in such a way as I had never seen them do before. I understood at once that this was because the power that Lucias had taken away from him in the courtyard explosion was now returned to him.

He fell back in his chair, shaking his head. It was almost as if he were trying to rid himself of whatever it was that came over him.

"Lucias!" Zamyael cried as she flew forward.

She wrapped her arms around Lucias and, with her face pressed against Lucias' cheek, Zamyael realized that she was still alive.

"Thank the Gods." She cried.

And then they were gone.

Zadkiel blinked at the spot where they had been sitting and said, rather flatly, "I didn't kill him."

"Da made Lulu go night night."

With wild fascination, I watched as Lord Evanbourough swung around to glare at Lasterian.

"That," he growled, "is how a servant behaves when their Master is in danger. They throw themselves in front of them to protect them! They don't snivel on the ground and let their Master lose his Gods be damned head!"

"I didn't snivel on the ground!" Lasterian cried.

Oh, Evanbourough. Haven't you caused the child enough pain?

Ignoring him, Lord Evanbourough pushed him out of the way and stormed down the hall to Tristan's room.

Lasterian, battered and broken as he was, fell to his knees and wept.

"Take me, Zadkiel." He whispered. "I can't live this way anymore. I need it all to end."

Zadkiel, who was still dazed, merely looked upon him.

"I beg you." Lasterian held his hands to Zadkiel, palms up, to entreat him.

"No." He said, his voice calm and alien, yet forcefully strong.

"Please!" Lasterian cried.

"No." He repeated, shaking his head again. "Not today. If you still want this tomorrow, then come to me. And I will see that it is done."

Lasterian looked up at him with haunted eyes. Understanding that he wasn't going to bend, however, he nodded.

Ishitar's eyes followed him with quiet interest as he stood, turned away from them and left the room.

-52-

"What are we going to do?" Zamyael asked, her voice shaking.

Sappharon, sitting at Lucias' side, cooling her forehead with a wet towel, sighed. The solution seemed simple enough to her.

"We don't tell anyone." She muttered. "We run the war as if our orders continue to come from Lady Lucias."

"Are you mad?" Zamyael sat upward. "How are we to do that?"

"Lucias gave you and I the power to allow others to come and go." She reminded the woman whom she thought of as her only true sister. This affection was born out of the fact that it was Sappharon and Zamyael alone who had been pulled from Lucias' soul rather than birthed or sired. Yet, it was also born out of the fact that Zamyael had, ever, been the only one to ever have truly understand her. Even Lucias couldn't, really, make that claim. "We can manage the magic without anyone else knowing."

"Well and good." Zamyael's voice shook with every word. She was terrified. "But what about our strategy?"

"You return to the Hells and continue to go about your spying upon Noliminan." Sappharon advised. "Placate him in whatever manner that you can. Convince Evanbourough that Lucias has woken up and is still running the show. I'll bark the orders to the army, the same as I have been doing all along."

"This isn't a game of kings' castles, Sappharon." Zamyael reminded her.

"You're right." Sappharon snapped. "It isn't. And the time for tit for tat is over."

"What do you mean to do?"

"What Lucias should have already done." Sappharon snapped, leveling her gaze upon Zamyael. "Give the Bwuet Va an all out war."

She grinned, then. It felt good upon her lips.
"And this time," she promised, "there will be no retreat. No matter *who* loses his Gods be damned head."

-53-

Theasis lowered herself into the chair next to Aiken's, her eyes wide as she looked around the room.

The sheer number of empty seats surrounding them maddened her. Between the deserters and the wounded, only a third of the Council remained for this meeting of the Court.

"I must go pick out my demon today." Aiken muttered under his breath. "Lucias sent me a direct order."

"Is it such a bad thing?" Theasis asked him as she watched the Quorum filter in.

"It's abhorrent to me." He replied. "It's immoral. I can't bide it."

"Then don't look at it as slavery." She sighed. "You see how Loki treats Sam. Like his equal."

"No." Aiken shook his head. "He treats him better than most. But not as an equal."

"That's not to say that you can't." Theasis frowned at him. "Really, Aiken. Why don't you look at this as an opportunity to save someone? To protect them from one of these other idiots who will be scavenging Martiam's halls to replace the demon or angel that they lost in battle to wounds or imprisonment?"

Aiken's brow furrowed at the sentiment. "I hadn't thought of that."

"If it will make you feel better," she offered, "I'll go with you."

"It would." He reached for her hand and squeezed it. "Thanks."

"By Loki's beard!" A childish voice intoned behind them. "It's a fairy!"

"By Loki's beard it is." Aiken agreed, looking over his shoulder and granting Armand, who had been damned to wear the face of an adolescent boy, a friendly smile. He stood and held out his hand. Armand, realizing that his nakedness extended its curtsey to the majority of his body, accepted it with a blush. "Aiken Darklief of the Oakland Grove."

"Armand." He replied, releasing Aiken's hand. "Of nowhere in particular worth mentioning."

Aiken smiled at that. Theasis thought it a lovely smile.

"I believe I know one of your kinsmen." He said. "Puck Flightail of the Fauns. He and his people live in the Oakland Grove with my fairies."

"So he does." Armand smiled. "He's my son."

"He's a fair friend." Aiken acknowledged with a nod.

"Thank you." Armand's smile grew.

"Will you join us, Armand?" Thea offered.

"If my presence won't embarrass you." He looked surprised.

Theasis understood why. Armand was one of those Gods that others didn't like because of the magic that he yielded. Given that he was responsible for the damnation of those with a taste for young children, Thea had often wondered what that said about those other Gods.

"Never in life." Aiken answered for her, offended at the very idea.

Grinning, Armand took his seat.

As he did so, Raphael, who had been hanging over the King of Lords' throne since the beginning of the rebellion, began screaming and writhing in agony.

Theasis, crying out in surprise, spun around and looked in that direction. The King of Lords, sitting in the throne beneath him, twisted to look up at him.

The expression on the King of Lords' face was one of horrified condemnation.

Zamyael walked in then, stopping short just inside the door. Her expression took on a startled quality which held no sense of surprise. After a brief moment of contemplation, she flew forward and grasped at the King of Lords' hand. He kept trying to push her away until something she said convinced him to stand.

The moment he did, Raphael let out a final, weeping wail and then fell still.

"Piss on the Gods!" Aiken cried out.

It was a mistake.

Every eye in the Council turned in his direction.

And then the unwanted chatter began.

"A fairy?"

"Who is that?"

"Loki's beard!"

"Silence!" The King of Lords roared at them all. "This is not a bronzie carnival and Aiken is not a freak that you may gawk at!" He turned around to look up at Raphael. Then he returned his attention to the Council. "This will be short. Much has happened in the past few years; not a lick of it good."

"That's an understatement." Someone behind Theasis muttered.

She looked over her shoulder to see Zuko, a God she had never liked, who appeared in age to be only slightly older than Armand. His face, which would have been handsome, rather than merely pleasing, given a few more years to mature, had a deep abrasion from the battle they had all been forced to fight. It ran from the right corner of his forehead, over his nose and ended just beneath his left ear.

Looking at him with such a hideous wound caused her to shiver.

"Raguel's soul has been expired." The murmur through the room was deafening. "Seen to by Lucias' hand. In retaliation I sent him Loki's head. His response was the battle that ensued last week which has temporarily seen to the reduction of our numbers."

Theasis felt Aiken reach for her hand. She let him take it.

"Michael!" He snapped his gaze in the direction of the Quorum. "Give your report."

Michael, who had been sitting in his waiting stance—as was his place—staked his sword to the ground and used it as leverage to pull himself to his feet.

As he did so, Theasis felt her heart tug. His eyes were puffy and his face was slightly red. If she didn't know him better, she would have guessed that he had been crying

Michael turned on his sword and bowed his head to the King of Lords. "My plan is to work with Gabriel in the Guf to round up those with mortal experience at battle. We must regroup our numbers given the fallen, but I do not believe that we will have an issue doing so if we pardon menial sins."

The King of Lords nodded. "Then do so."

"Yes, your Grace." Michael bowed his head to him. "Metatron and I will meet this afternoon to discuss strategy. We know not when Lucias will next strike. But we will be ready for him and we will, once again, prevail."

The King of Lords let out a long sigh. As he did so, he fell into his throne. Raphael immediately began screaming so he forced himself to his feet with his hands.

"Damn his hide!" The King of Lords cried. He turned his gaze to Zadkiel, who was looking up at him with an extremely strange expression. "The moment—the barest moment—that Metatron or Michael brings him to you, you are to run you finger across his brow."

"It will be done." Zadkiel, who was normally docile, was staring up at the King of Lords with uncustomary anger. "I assure you."

"Very well." The King of Lords snapped. "If there is nothing further—"

"One small thing." Lady Moira said, rising and turning toward Aiken. "This matter with the fairy . . . it's troublesome to me."

"It's troublesome to me as well." The King of Lords groused. "But done, I assume, at Lucias' orders." His eyes flicked to Countenance. "What have you to say for yourself?"

Countenance, who rarely was called into conversation, flinched. He looked toward Aiken and licked his lips. When he was standing he said, "As you say. I was given a direct order."

"Then the matter will be dealt with upon Lucias' damnation." He advised Moira. "It is a high enough price to pay."

"Loki's hand is all over this." Moira shook her head. "And now I must unstring and restring my tapestry." She glared with clear distaste at Aiken. Theasis wondered why she felt such disdain for the mischief fairy. "And all for the sake of this insignificant creature."

"If I am that damned insignificant then your stupidly ridiculous fucking tapestry shouldn't require restringing." Aiken growled at her. There was a collective groan that he would use profanity at Council. It was ignored only because this was his first appearance and because circumstances were extremely dire. "Loki lost his head. He isn't ever going to *be* Loki again. What more, in the name of all that is right, do you wish to take from him, you stupid, *worthless* twat?!"

Hanging in the gallows, I shivered. I knew that he would pay dearly for that last bit.

But that is a story for another day.

For now, suffice it to say that one does not insult Lady Moira without retaliation.

Theasis watched as Moira's mouth opened and then slapped shut. As she did so, all of the women who made up Loki's gaggle began to sigh and whimper as if the thought hadn't occurred to them, until Aiken voiced it, that Loki just wouldn't be quite so Loki anymore.

Frustrated with the lack of foresight of these Goddesses, Theasis shook her head.

Just what part of "I sent Lucias Loki's head" have these stupid geese failed to understand?

As for the King of Lords, he stood at the podium wearing a sardonic grin. He knew, as Theasis did, that Moira had fallen for Loki's charms. In her demand for repayment from Loki, her own infallible magic had worked against her.

His expression wasn't the only one which was smug. Many of the other Gods were pleased to learn that Loki had been put permanently in his place.

"Enough." The King of Lords muttered. "This meeting is called to a close."

Theasis watched him leave the room. She turned to Aiken and gave him a weak smile.

"Aiken, I'm sorry. I know I said I would go with you to Martiam's, but . . ." She flicked her gaze to the Quorum, who were all surrounding Michael, bent over him and whispering their questions to him. "Michael is dear to me and he seems to be upset. I'd really like to speak with him."

"Go." Aiken laid his hand upon her shoulder and squeezed it. He seemed to truly understand.

She was grateful to him for his seemingly unswayable friendship. Upon first sight of him, she hadn't believed him to be the steadfast creature that Loki had claimed him to be. She had expected flightiness from him. Mischievousness.

Which came in spades, of course, given he was a mischief fairy.

But she hadn't expected his infallible sense of right and wrong or his unwillingness to bend when it came to his protection over those he held dear.

"Bring him peace if you can."

-54-

Jamiason sat upon a rock, looking up to the sky. It wasn't that he would rather be anywhere else. It was beautiful here. It was just that he was bored.

Mostly, because he had no friends here.

Nor, did he want friends here.

He knew that this was a state of transition for him. Once a God chose him—*if* a God chose him—then he would make friends. But he had heard the rumors which suggested making friends here might not be wise.

Angels and demons were not to interact with one another once they'd been chosen by their God. The consequences were apparently dire. As such, Jamiason, not wanting to be damned before he'd found his glory, had decided he'd wait to make friends until he knew which color his wings would turn out to be.

He heard someone coming and he looked in their direction; he was interested. He quickly realized that it was Martiam and, with her, was another God.

He was not a very masculine looking God. He was extremely tall and very pale with skin which sparkled iridescently in the sunlight. As for his hair, it was long, white and littered with wild flowers.

He wore wings at his back which were as beautifully iridescent as his skin.

A fairy, Jamiason thought.

As they drew closer, Jamiason realized this was a fairy he knew. It was the mortal king, Aiken Darklief of the Oakland Grove of Anticata.

He stood, forced a smile, and stepped forward. They'd never met formally and Jamiason doubted he would be recognized, but they had shared the meadow. Given this, Jamiason owed him the courtesy of his regard. "Your Majesty."

King Aiken's violet eyes immediately turned toward him. He hesitated before he bowed in return. "I'm afraid that I'm at the disadvantage."

Jamiason smiled softly up at him. He was, indeed, a very tall creature. "My people share your Oakland meadow."

"Ah." King Aiken smiled at him. His sharp fangs danced against his lips. It was disconcerting. "Of course. You're . . ." He shook his head. "I'm sorry. I know your face. But I don't remember your name."

"Jamiason Scrountentine." Jamiason replied, lowering his gaze. "I'm of the nymphs upon your field." His smile was fleeting. "Or, in the least, I was."

Understanding dawned upon King Aiken's face.

"Of course you are." He seemed suddenly alarmed. "Forgive me. I should know the few nymph males living in my own grove."

"It's no matter." Jamiason smiled. "I died my mortal death. And we never got the chance to officially meet."

His brow furrowed as he remembered his own reckoning. He had been dragged from his bed, beaten mercilessly, raped by every one of the fauns and then pissed and shat upon before he had been tied to a stake and burned alive.

"The fauns were not overly fond of having a male nymph in their meadow."

"I'm sorry." King Aiken replied, his expression dour. "Had Puck known . . . He would have stopped your death."

"He didn't know until it was too late." Jamiason shrugged. "I hold no ill will against him." As an afterthought he added, "Nor against your people or you."

"I did hear about it." King Aiken said, not meeting Jamiason's gaze. "But it was afterward. Your body was burnt beyond all recognition before I laid eyes upon you." His voice was deep with regret. "I must apologize that I did not immediately know you upon sight."

"I understand, your Majesty." Jamiason assured him.

"I'll take him." King Aiken said and turned toward Martiam. "If he's free. I'd like him." And then, as if offended by his own action, he turned toward Jamiason. "If you will it, that is. If you'd like me to be your Lord God protector."

"I would." Jamiason whispered.

How has Moira favored me so?

"I knew of you before and I . . ." He shook his head. The fairies had ever only spoken of his fair treatment toward them. Jamiason knew he could do far worse than King Aiken. "Yes. I should like to serve you in whatever manner you will it."

Though neither of them knew it, in that moment Moira, who had discovered the manner in which she would repay Aiken his verbal insults against her at Council, had thread the future into her tapestry, binding one to the other.

Tying off the knot, she laughed.

-55-

After spending the full of the night writing a letter to Zamyael, Lasterian determined he had no desire to change his mind. If anything, writing down his reasons for Zamyael merely confirmed that he had no other option available to him.

He explained to her that she wasn't the cause. That he had come to love her in his own way. That he saw her as a woman and not a man. And that, more than anything, he didn't begrudge her that dark day from which light had come.

Given Lasterian was generally rather simple in his manner of thinking, I found him to be extremely clever, in his final moments, to stop short of directly referencing their ill begot child.

And in his devotion.

At the end of the letter, he asked Zamyael to protect Saristia who, in retrospect, had made them a family, from Lord Aegir. Unfortunately, it was a protection that poor Saristia would, eventually, require.

After finishing the letter, Lasterian went to Tristan and he explained to him why he could not face the dawn of another day. He didn't know if Tristan heard him or not. And, if he were honest with himself, nor did he care. He had gone to Tristan only because it was his duty to go to Tristan. His love for his God, at this point, did not extend its courtesy beyond that simple truth.

Perhaps this was what drove his despair more than the rest of it.

What angel worth his salt no longer desired to serve his benevolent God?

He went to Zadkiel. And he repeated his question from the day before. "Will you please end it for me?"

Zadkiel's golden eyes danced over his face. He flicked them swiftly to the toddler who was constantly in his care and said, "Ishitar, why don't you find Evanbourough? I believe he may be picking fruit so that I might make you a pie."

Ishitar looked up at him, grinning. Then he looked to his left and raised his hand. Lasterian, who was always baffled when in the presence of Zadkiel and the toddler, ignored the strange turn of this particular event.

When he was gone, Zadkiel returned his attention to Lasterian.

"Lasterian . . ." The archangel sighed. "This is a heavy choice. And one which neither your father nor mother will understand."

"This is my only choice." Lasterian whispered. "And not my father's. Nor my mother's, whomever *she* is. I am finished."

"There is life yet left to be lived."

Lasterian shook his head. He hadn't told Zadkiel why he had come to him. He didn't need to. All that was required of him was that he ask his question. And he had.

"No." He sighed. "Not for me."

Zadkiel gave him a tired, distracted smile. "I won't sway you?"

"No." He agreed.

"Very well." Zadkiel said.

He leaned forward and laid his fingers upon Lasterian's brow. With the swiftest of movements he slid them over the angel's forehead.

Thus was the end of Lasterian's pain.

(Zamyael begins to weep.

(Raziel turns her fiery eyes in her direction, her brow furrowed.

(She realizes, I understand as I read her thoughts, the extent of Zamyael's regard for Lasterian in that moment. And the extent of her grief that the father of her child is forever gone from her.

(I think she will strike her again. She raises her hand to do so. But, at the last moment before her fist would fly, reason overcomes her and, instead, she lays her hand upon Zamyael's shoulder.)

-56-

Camael swallowed as he raised his hand to knock. The bell on his ankle was ringing insistently.

When the door opened, he froze. Michael stood before him wearing an expression he'd seen only one other time. An expression which Camael now associated with his own personal doom.

"Michael." He mumbled.

"Camael." He held out his hand. Camael looked down at it, his brow furrowing. The extended hand told him everything he needed to know. "What have I done wrong *this* time?"

"You haven't." Michael muttered as he grasped Camael's hand in his own and forced the handshake. When he was finished, he brought Camael's hand upward and pressed it against his cheek. After closing his eyes and shaking his head against Camael's palm, he sighed, "It's about Lasterian."

Camael felt his eyes widen. His voice was a whisper. "What has he done?"

"Best you let King Noliminan tell you himself." Michael whispered, opening his coal black eyes and searching Camael's face with his haunted, horrified gaze.

Ever since Queen Raguel had died, Michael's eyes had been soulless. In Camael's estimation, however, the worst of it had been that King Noliminan had forced Michael to discard her things immediately prior to the last Council. Michael, at Council, grieving over Lady Raguel, had been an unbearable sight for the remaining members of the Quorum to behold.

"He's in the library."

"Michael . . . ?"

"He isn't angry with you, Camael." Michael whispered. "He never really has been."

His eyes darted away swiftly. Camael suspected he had done so to hide the lie. Michael, out of every person who Camael had ever known, despised a lie.

Remembering that Michael had once offered to lie on Camael's behalf, rather than mutilate him, Camael forced himself to smile. He let the hand at Michael's face cup his cheek. "Promise me that—if nothing else of me might remain intact— my ass will not become my cap."

"Just . . . Go to the library. And talk with him." Michael's face paled at the reminder of what he had been forced to do to Camael. "Without worry from me about your precious ass."

Camael chuckled at him, nodded and then stepped past Michael.

Despite the clearly dark reasons that he was here, he was helpless but to find himself amused by his brother. Because, truly, Michael was very much a source of great humor when he took himself so Gods be damned seriously.

Which, must be said, is with every shift of every shadow.

When he reached the library, Camael raised his hand and knocked. King Noliminan beckoned him in almost immediately. His tone, much as Michael's expression had done, brokered only doom and gloom.

Camael slipped into the room and forced a smile as he gave King Noliminan his fealty. "Your Grace?"

King Noliminan's strange, caramel colored eyes danced over Camael's face. His expression was stony and unyielding. "I need you to sit, child."

Camael pulled out one of King Noliminan's chairs and lowered himself within it. "Your Grace? Michael told me that my son has caused you distress?"

"Per say." King Noliminan muttered. He let out a long, tired sigh as he raised his hand to his nose and rubbed the bridge of it with his thumb and forefinger. "Are you and Metatron still pretending that Metatron birthed the child?"

Camael froze. This lie had been told to protect Uriel. And protect Uriel—whom Camael ever only thought of as female—it had. Who knew otherwise? Who would have told?

"My Lord," Camael tried. "Metatron is—"

"Not now, Camael." He lowered his hand and met Camael's gaze. "I understand what you and Metatron were doing when you raised the issue."

"How long have you known?" Camael whispered.

King Noliminan gave him a long, searching gaze. Finally he looked away and said, "There truly is little that goes on which I do not hear about."

"But then why did you—?"

"If you and Metatron love Uriel enough to lie for him," King Noliminan muttered, "then it is not my concern. The parents of the child needed to be punished and as far as everyone else knows the parents of the child were. As for you and Uriel, I only needed one of you to make my point."

"Your Grace, I—"

"Not now, Camael." He snapped. "I must tell you something which will pain you. But before I do, I must advise you that, in order to protect all three of you, I need Metatron to go on playing his part. And I need you to convince Uriel to do the same. Otherwise, my hand will be forced and Uriel *will* be punished." His eyes flicked upward and met Camael's own. "And I will have Michael take the tongue from all three of you for propagating the lie and making me out to be the fool."

Camael shook his head and lowered his gaze. He knew that King Noliminan would make good on this threat. "Yes, your Grace."

"Lasterian has chosen to meet his end with Zadkiel." His tone was as harsh as his words.

Camael felt himself slump backward in his chair. His eyes grew wide and his mouth slacked open. The only thing which he could compare this pain to was the few times when he had been kicked in the groin by a mortal during a struggle. Before, of course, he had been castrated.

"It would seem he was unable to live with his failure in protecting Tristan during the battle."

Camael rolled his eyes closed and shook his head.

This makes no sense!

He and Lasterian had talked about Tristan and his behavior and Lasterian had seemed to come to an understanding of it. Lately, he had told Camael, he had even fallen in love with some unknown beauty.

At the moment he was unable to ponder it. His grief was too acute.

Nor was he able to stay the tears that first stung, then welled and, finally, flowed in two rivers down his cheeks. He swallowed. Hard. Shaking his head again, he opened his eyes and met King Noliminan's gaze.

His Master's eyes were swimming with his disappointment that Camael would be weak in his presence.

Camael swallowed his grief, raised his hands and wiped his face. "Forgive me, your Grace."

"I have nothing more to say to you." He muttered and looked down to his paperwork. "You may leave me now."

Camael, knowing all too well what was good for him, did as he was bid.

-57-

The more Camael ruminated upon Lasterian's death, the more furious he became. Listening to the buzz of his thoughts, there was only one person he blamed.

Zadkiel.

My only recourse as I sat in the corner of the room with Ishitar on my lap was to watch as the door to Evanbourough's apartment flew open and Camael came charging in.

He didn't see me. And he didn't see Ishitar.

The only person he could see was Zadkiel.

He stormed toward him, his eyes wide and wild, and he reached for the staff upon which Zadkiel supported himself.

Had Zadkiel not been standing beside one of Evanbourough's high back chairs, the violence with which his staff was removed from beneath him would have been enough to cause him to tumble.

Perhaps if he *had* tumbled, Camael would have come to his senses.

But he didn't.

Pulling back his arm, the fist which had been balled since the moment Camael left Noliminan's library flew and connected squarely against Zadkiel's jaw.

Zadkiel flew off of his feet with the force of the blow—any man who *wasn't* crippled would have lost his purchase under the force of that particular blow—and sprawled gracelessly on the ground at Camael's feet.

"To the Hells with you Zadkiel!" Camael screamed down at him. He pulled his foot back and kicked Zadkiel right between the legs. Zadkiel screamed with pain and doubled over himself, exposing his kidneys, which Camael also kicked. "You expired my son, you carvetek mouk!"

Ishitar, having been confused up until this point, began wailing. Though he didn't understand what was taking place, he did know that the man that he thought of as his father was under attack. Even at such a young age, Ishitar's instinct was to protect what he loved.

He flew off of my lap and ran to Zadkiel. I tried to catch him, but he was too fast. Camael's foot flew backward and the heel of his boot struck Ishitar right in the center of his forehead.

The wail became a mortified scream.

Never in life had Ishitar experienced of any type of pain which wasn't self inflicted. He didn't understand how he had become subjected to it now.

What he did understand was the cause of it. And his young child's mind couldn't reason that Camael's kicking him had been an accident.

As Camael spun around, his expression horrified by what he had done, Ishitar grit his teeth, put his hands on his small hips and seethed, "Bad Camy! Bad Camy! Camy go fly with Raphie!"

Upon Ishitar's command, Camael did.

-58-

Zadkiel held Ishitar's small hand in his own as he stood outside of Noliminan's door. He raised his other hand, knocked, and he waited to be granted entry.

It was Gabriel who answered.

And with hair which was touched at its roots with grey and eyes that were tired and wrinkled at their corners.

Zadkiel, who had never seen any God, angel or demon age, swallowed. "Gabriel . . . My Gods. You look—"

"Horrific is the word I believe you are searching for." He chuckled and bent at the knee. His lips split into a grin as he opened his arms wide to Ishitar.

Ishitar flew into them, wrapping his arms around Gabriel's neck. As he did so, Gabriel kissed his cheek and then looked up at Zadkiel. He mouthed the words, "What happened?"

To which Zadkiel shook his head and mouthed, "An accident. He'll be alright."

Gabriel, frowning, mouthed, "Noliminan isn't going to like it."

"Moira's business."

Gabriel gave him a look which spoke volumes about the truth of that sentiment. As he did so, Zadkiel realized the grey hair and wrinkles were suddenly gone.

"Ishitar." Zadkiel chuckled. "Gabe, tell the child thank you."

"Thank you?"

Gabriel meant it as a question, but Ishitar didn't take it that way. "Welcome Lulu."

Gabriel, who understood that Noliminan sometimes called Lucias his lolo—because Noliminan sometimes called Gabriel his lolo—flinched. But he smiled and forced himself to lean forward and kiss Ishitar's forehead again.

Given that the only time he'd ever actually met his mother was the day Zadkiel had put her in a coma, it wasn't Ishitar's fault that he confused the face of the two.

Though Zadkiel did, suddenly, have a thought.

He bent to Gabriel's level and reached for Ishitar's cheek. "Ishitar? Can you do your Da a favor?"

Ishitar grinned and shook his head.

"Then do you want to play a game?" He tried. "With Noliminan?"

"Ishy play with Nolo?"

"Yes." Zadkiel beamed at him. "Let's play a game with Nolo."

Ishitar laughed and nodded.

"Heal the bruise on your face like you healed Gabriel." Zadkiel forced himself to laugh. It was as false as anything he had ever done but he knew, if he were to protect Camael, it was required. "And then he won't understand why Camy flies."

Ishitar giggled and clapped his hands. "Camy and Raphie fly!"

Gabriel's eyes grew wide. He mouthed, "What did Camael do to him?"

Zadkiel shook his head. He'd tell him later. Right now, he needed to convince Ishitar that this was little more than a game.

"Wouldn't it be fun to play with Nolo?" Zadkiel tried.

Ishitar, giggling again, nodded. As he did so, the bruise on his forehead disappeared altogether.

Zadkiel, free of the burden of the child given that Gabriel held him, fell back on his hands, relieved.

But he laughed for the sake of prosperity. "Nolo will be so surprised when he sees Camy flying!"

Ishitar laughed again and returned his face so that he could bury it in Gabriel's hair.

Zadkiel knew their time was limited. "Take me to him."

"Of course." Gabriel stood, still holding the boy in his arms, and turned to lead them to Noliminan's library.

Once there, Gabriel did a strange thing as far as Zadkiel was concerned, but a smart thing in my mind given he was trying to convince Ishitar, and Noliminan, that he was the boy's mother.

He pushed through the door and announced, almost rudely, "Zad and Ishitar are here."

Noliminan, startled, looked up. His eyes narrowed upon Gabriel for a moment—not that it was Gabriel that he saw—but then seemed to brighten with his understanding.

He stood and stepped forward, holding out his arms.

Gabriel lowered the boy to the ground and allowed Ishitar to run toward him. As he did so, he cried, "Nolo, Nolo, Lulu went night night."

Noliminan was clearly more interested in the fact that his son—who he hadn't bothered to visit since he had been a babe in arms—was able to run to him than he was in whatever words Ishitar had to share. He laughed and lowered himself to his hunkers, his arms wide to wrap around Ishitar when he flew into them.

So this is what he looks like when he is a true hearted father.

Zadkiel shook his head, banishing the thought from his mind.

He didn't want to have any regard for Noliminan. Not anymore.

"Really?" Noliminan grinned at his son.

"Ta." Ishitar grinned in response.

"Well that's an interesting turn of events."

Zadkiel steeled himself. He hadn't told Noliminan what had taken place with Lucias. And he was terrified, now, that he would be punished.

"Your Grace." He forced himself to give Noliminan fealty. It burned his tongue given everything that had passed between them. "I can no longer stay in the Halls of the Hells with Lord Evanbourough."

Noliminan snapped his gaze upward, surprised. "No?"

"No." He swallowed. "Even if no one else knows about Ishitar, my father does. And he's proven he has no scruples."

Noliminan let out a long, tired sigh. "That he has."

"You bid that no one enter my cottage." Zadkiel reminded him. "Even Lucias."

"I did." He nodded.

"Then there is no safer place for your son."

Noliminan turned to the babe, buried his lips into his curls, and then nodded. "No." He agreed. "There is no safer place."

"Please let me take him there."

Noliminan closed his eyes and nodded. Given his war with Lucias was in full swing, what other choice did he have?

"Thank you." My brother lowered himself to his knees as best as he could and held out his arms. "Come Ishitar. It's time to go home."

Ishitar, giggling, pulled himself out of Noliminan's arms so he could fly into Zadkiel's embrace. As he did so, he turned to Noliminan and laughed.

"Nolo!" He said as his hands danced around him. "Da made Lulu go night night!"

Zadkiel, needing to get them the Hells out of there before Noliminan could figure out what in the name of the Sixty Realms Ishitar was telling him, used his more Godlike magic and willed them home.

Standing in his own kitchen he shook his head and cocked his neck so that he was glaring at the child.

"What are you trying to do, boy?" He growled. "Get your Da expired?"

Ishitar, laughing, flew toward him and pressed his lips against Zadkiel's cheek.

Loving the child with all of his heart, Zadkiel shook his head and lowered Ishitar to the ground with no further thought, or care, about Noliminan's potential admonishment.

-59-

A few days after Zadkiel put Lucias into a coma, Sappharon had laid her body next to Loki's, knowing this is what Lucias would have wanted. Strangely enough, as she lowered herself into a chair beside their bed, she realized it seemed to calm them to be together.

In those early days, she wasn't kind to Loki. Not even with Lucias laying by his side. She hated him and made no bones about telling him so on a daily basis.

She also found great sport in moving his head around his body to see if it might reattach itself to an arm or a leg rather than to his neck. Though, this had stopped after Zamyael chastised her and told her that, if Lucias were to wake up and find Loki's head with his still opened mouth pressed against his crotch, Lucias would be less than pleased by the joke of it and Sappharon would be punished.

After that, though she didn't find herself necessarily kind to Loki, the insults stopped. She still refused to bathe or tend to him—she left these chores to Zamyael when she visited. She merely no longer tried to interfere with his healing process.

Which was a good thing for him.

Within two waning moons the head had attached itself to Loki's neck and the smell of rot began to subside. Several waning moons later, other than his hair, which had yet to grow, he looked almost like the Loki of old.

She realized almost at once that his quick healing had quite a lot to do with her putting his head where it belonged, but even more by the fact that Lucias was laying at his side and willing him to heal.

Even unconscious, it would seem that Lucias' thoughts were clearly centered upon Loki and Loki alone.

This caused her loathing for him to explode exponentially.

One night she was bent over him, staring at the marvel of his physical beauty despite herself, and she realized his nose was crooked. She assumed it must have broken when his head had fallen to the ground after dropping out of the box. She wasn't certain what made her do so, but she reached forward and re-broke it so that she could set and straighten it. When she did, Loki let out a strange, guttural scream that was both chilling and terrifying.

He was coming back to himself, she decided. Though, clearly, still out of it enough that he didn't understand a wit of what was taking place around him.

Perhaps a sun cycle went by when, one night, she came in after a particularly hard battle to find that his hair had finally restored itself. She realized, by the thickness of his damn beard, that she must not have visited the pair of them for some time and she felt, strangely enough, guilty about that.

Lucias' appearance never seemed to change. Her hair didn't grow and her expression remained as surprised and afraid as it had been the moment Zadkiel had touched her.

Sappharon wasn't able to bear to look at Lucias overly much. As a result, she gave all of her attention to Loki. And, seeing Loki's transformation, she gave him her first kindness by shaving his beard into the goatee style that he preferred.

As for the words she spoke to him, they didn't soften.

"Where is your gaggle now, you carvetek mouk?" She seethed as she shaved him. "Where is Moira or Sooka or Elzbeth? Hmm? Not even your precious Theasis has been to visit you. No. It's me that's left to see to the trimming of your Gods be damned beard."

He made no response to this. But, then, she didn't expect him to. He hadn't even heard her. Which was fine with her. She'd said what she wanted to say to him.

Life proceeds as it does, even when those that you love are frozen in their own minds. So on and on the war went. Though, now, she returned every night to the pair to mourn over Lucias and to shave Loki's beard so she might sling insults his way.

About half way through the war, everything changed.

Raystlyn sullied her with a rumor that the bronzies—which were a race which had been propagated by Zadkiel at Noliminan's order before he was crippled—had captured a dathanorna and caged it up to put on display in their travelling circus.

She would later learn that the rumor was unfounded and untrue. The bronzies had found a changeling, not a dathanorna. At the time, however, she panicked.

Not because she was worried about Zamyael's babe. She knew where that particular creature was hiding and it wasn't amongst the bronzies.

It was her own daughter, the one whom she had never told anyone existed, who she was concerned about.

It was a rare thing for Sappharon to cry. Yet, as she shaved Loki's beard whilst Zamyael had taken Lucias' body to bathe on this particular night, she couldn't stop herself from sobbing. Before long, she had laid her head upon his chest and was telling him about the babe, and its father, and every other horrid thing that had ever happened to her in her overly long life.

She told him about her great love for Lucias. She admitted to him that her hate for him had always stemmed from her jealousy over Lucias' attentions toward him. And, over the fact that, while Lucias respected Loki, she had always considered Sappharon to be a burden.

It was as she spoke this final admission that she felt strong fingers stroke her hair. Startled, she sat abruptly upward and realized Loki had opened his eyes and was looking at her.

There was no pity in his dark, purple eyes. Nor was there any smug satisfaction over her pain. Rather, there was kindness. And warmth. And—what astonished her the most—acute understanding.

She swallowed and swiftly wiped the tears off of her face. He merely laid there and watched her, his eyes drinking her in, taking measure of her.

Then, as if it took every force of will he had in him, he said two hoarse, almost indistinguishable words.

"I understand."

That was all. Simply, I understand.

After that, everything between them changed.

-60-

Witnessing the war wage on, I understood the price more than anyone. So it might seem strange to you that I let antiquity take its course.

But what else was I supposed to do?

This is who I am. What I am. I have no choice but to accept that I must watch what I do not agree with without interface lest I go mad.

So, hate me if you must for not sharing the gruesome details of the rebellion, which I, myself, was forced to witness. And bear with me, if you will, that I focus on the love which grew in Zadkiel's heart toward Ishitar.

Though, trust, in your heart, watching the war play out has destroyed my sensibilities in a manner that no man must ever know. The destruction of brother fighting brother became all too painful for me to bear.

In reflection, I cannot deny that I believe Noliminan's decision to allow Zadkiel to raise the boy was the right one. He grew from babe to young man understanding the difference between right from wrong. And knowledgeable in the fact that, even if what he wanted was important, if it wasn't right then he should refrain from wishing it should be so.

The interestingly wonderful thing about Zadkiel was his understanding that, in order to temper Ishitar, he must mask his knowledge from the boy that he suspected he had greater powers than he probably should. He had to grow into a man not deluded by his power, but measured by his restraint when he learned the sheer expanse of his abilities.

Thus, it was that, as a pre-adolescent boy, Ishitar questioned himself and his worth. Just as every one of us pre-adolescent boys have done.

He thought he was ugly. He thought he was gangly. He thought he would never amount to anything and would disappoint his father when the day came that he must not.

Yet, at the same time, he learned he was gentle. He understood he was thoughtful. And he learned the value of his forethought before an action might be made.

My fondest memory of Zadkiel and Ishitar is when Zadkiel brought the young boy to the Great Hall to show him where Raphael and Camael were crucified above the Great Thrones of the Small Council.

Zadkiel indicated them both and said simply, "Raphael is a prisoner of your parents' stupid war and you cannot help him. Camael, however, is a prisoner of your hate for an accident against you that he immediately regretted. Would you continue to make him pay for something that is lost from your mind?"

Ishitar didn't remember hanging Camael beside Raphael. Let alone the reason why he had done so. Thus, as he looked upon them, he became contemplative and thoughtful. Shaking his head, he agreed with Zadkiel and Camael, who at that point was lost in his own mind, was set free.

I can attest that Camael sought the one true love of his life. And I can further attest that Uriel returned Camael to something which was a shadow of the man he once had been.

But even this small miracle, for poor, broken Camael, was a long wrought and less than simple process.

As for Noliminan, he raged when he learned Camael had been set free. He had assumed, the entire time, that it was Lucias who had crucified my brother. As such, he didn't understand why Camael was set free whilst Raphael—who, it must be said, is Noliminan's favorite of we twelve—was forced to remain imprisoned.

I was relieved that, when he demanded answers from Camael, he understood the archangel was too broken and afraid to give them. He assumed, I know, that he would get his answers when Lucias was finally presented to him at the end of the rebellion.

"Love, Ishitar." Zadkiel whispered as he set his hand upon the boy's shoulders as the pair of them stood beneath Raphael. "This is my advice to you. If you make every decision out of love, then you can never go wrong."

-61-

Though Tristan recovered long before Loki, Evanbourough refused to let him leave his apartment. The reason for this was simple: Tristan had run mad.

With each passing sun cycle, his reason deteriorated. He kept insisting that he be returned to Lucias so he could rejoin the war. But Evanbourough, rightfully, was afraid that his actions—which seemed self destructive at best—would result in chaotic consequences.

Also, it would seem the King of Lords had forgotten that he'd placed Tristan in Evanbourough's care. If he were to make himself known, or the fact he was physically healed, he would be immediately placed on the Thirteenth level. Given Evan and Moira shared an enmity between them, he saw no reason to tempt her into reminding the King of Lords that Tristan still ran free.

After some time, Tristan asked for Lasterian. Evanbourough, no longer able to placate him by merely telling him that Lasterian was not at home, was forced to explain to Tristan what had happened.

The consequences for Evenbourough were dire.

Tristan, who had once been gentle and forgiving of Evanbourough's sometimes hard ways, exploded in a rage upon him. He raved at Evanbourough that he had forgiven every little thing Evan had done in disrespect of their love of one another because Evan had never lied to him. That he had done so now was the irrevocable last straw in Tristan's mind.

His physical reaction to Evanbourough's lie to him—which honestly had been told to protect him—was something I would never have expected. He beat Evanbourough until he was unconscious and broken. No longer loving the oft times hypocritical God, he then left Evanbourough for good.

In Tristan's mind, the only reasonable thing for him to do was to seek out Lasterian's child and raise him or her as his own. Then, all the mistakes he had made with Lasterian would be corrected.

So it was that he eventually found himself standing in the center of the forest, listening to the sound of the souls who had fled me at the time of aether from fear of where I would take them. No soul being allowed to wander aimlessly for long, they all, eventually, gravitate toward the Realm on their inhabited world which is ruled by Hades.

His purpose for being there was simple. He had overheard Hades speaking with Evanbourough when the pair of them thought he was sleeping about a strange presence in this particular forest. Though Hades didn't know what the presence was, Tristan thought that he might.

He wandered from lost soul to lost soul, asking each of the spirits if they knew what Hades was referring to and, if so, where he might find it.

Himself insane, he didn't realize that these poor creatures were all equally mad.

Eventually, he came across one who was new to the forest and so had, for the time being, retained her sanity.

"It wanders the full of the forest," the ghost of a young child told Tristan. "But it keeps itself in the cave beside the lake on the far west side."

Tristan thanked her and began wandering in that direction.

Having never met a dathanorna, he wasn't certain what he expected to find. He did have the better sense to be fearful. Even if the thing were an adolescent, as it must still be, it could take on the form of any creature it wanted and could, in the very least, wound Tristan so he might be forced back to his bed to recover.

He most definitely didn't want that.

Yet, he had come this far and he wanted Lasterian's child desperately. Zamyael might have abandoned it. But Lasterian, given the choice, never would have. It was his duty, in

Lasterian's stead, to convince it that it must come home with him.

He stepped into the shadows of the cave and looked around.

Sure enough, there were signs that someone—something—had made this cave its home.

There was a small pit where the ruins of many fires lay. There were hides of every type, stripped clean and made into blankets and rugs. And, most surprising to Tristan of all, there were rows and rows of books, stacked from the floor to the ceiling. More books than any creature could have read in the span of even Tristan's lifetime.

Frowning, he shook his head.

Books?

How would a young child, who had been forced to raise itself alone in the forest, know how to read?

He licked his lips and then called out to the creature.

"Dathanorna?" He kept his tone gentle and unassuming. He didn't want to frighten Lasterian's son or daughter. "I come to you in peace. Will you not remove yourself from the shadows to speak with me?"

There was movement to the left of him. He darted his eyes in that direction but was unable to see anything other than the glistening wall of the cave.

"I'm a friend of your father's." Tristan said softly. "I mean you no harm."

"You know my father?"

Tristan started. It was a woman's voice. Not the voice of a child.

Remember. It can take on any form that it chooses.

He turned toward her. When his eyes fell upon her, he gasped. Her face was virtually identical to Lucias' demon, Sappharon. As for her figure, there was no mistaking the two. While Sappharon was slender and girlish, this creature was full figured and voluptuous.

How can that be?

"What is my father's name?"

"Lasterian." Tristan told her. Then he smiled. "And your mother is the demon Zamyael."

Her eyes narrowed and her lips pursed.

"You know nothing." She spat. "That pathetic little Goddess who once was is not my mother."

"But she is!" Tristan started walking toward her. She stepped away from him.

"No." She shook her head. "She isn't."

"But I know that she is!" Tristan cried. "She gave birth to the only dathanorna in existence!"

"Perhaps, then," the creature said, shifting uncomfortably from one foot to the other, "there are two of us. Or perhaps Zamyael lied."

"That can't be . . ."

"I know my mother." She growled at him. "And her name is not Zamyael."

"But you have to be . . ." He heard the hitch in his voice. "You must be Lasterian's child!"

She sighed. "I do not know who my father is. But my mother is not Zamyael. So I cannot be the one who you are seeking." And then angrily. "And now I must move. Lest you tell that I am here and I am destroyed."

Tristan swallowed and shook his head. "I won't tell."

"I will not take that risk." She spat turning away from him so that she could begin gathering her things. "For myself or for my mother."

"Please!" He cried. "I know you are Lasterian's child. You are the only dathanorna in existence!"

"Did you actually see this child with your own two glams?" She rounded on him.

"No, I—"

"Then perhaps, as I said earlier, Zamyael lied." She seethed through her teeth. "Perhaps this angel of yours lied to you as well."

"Why would they lie about something that could get them both expired?"

"Ask them yourself." She spat.

And then, quite simply, she was gone.

He knew she didn't have the power to transport herself. But that was irrelevant. She could turn herself into the smallest of bugs if she wanted. Or any other creature which was so insignificant it wouldn't catch his eye.

With a hitching sigh, Tristan understood what he must now do.

He must find Zamyael. And he must do whatever was required to her until she revealed the location of Lasterian's child.

-62-

"Loki!"

Aiken ran forward, throwing his arms around his friend's neck and holding him tight.

Loki froze in Aiken's arms but then, slowly, raised his hand to pat him on the back. When he spoke, it was with his general sense of good humor. "Not home two seconds and I've already been molested by a Gods be damned fairy."

"I'm sorry." Aiken swallowed and released him. "I didn't mean to—But you're home! And you're . . . ?"

"Not quite myself." Loki admitted. "But well enough." He looked around himself. "How goes everything here?"

"Good." Aiken assured him. "Sam, Jami and I have been working with the damned in your stead. I think we've raised a very good defense which Michael won't see coming."

"Jami?"

"Jamiason." Aiken grinned as he thought of his demon. He had come to love Jamiason as he had never loved anyone before in his life. He was coming to believe that Jamiason was his Shitva. "He's my demon."

"Is he now?" Loki chuckled. "Mr. You'll Never Catch *Me* Enslaving a Demon!"

("Azrael?"

("My Lady?" I look up at Raziel and give her a patient smile.

("Exactly how is it that Loki retained his sanity? Tristan didn't."

("Lucias was able to get to him in time. She had his head and his heart whereas Lasterian was never able to find Tristan's head."

("And having both pieces of him allowed Lucias to heal him?"

("Not entirely." I shrug. "As he told Aiken. He's close enough that no one has been able to mark the differences in him aside Lucias and Aiken."

(She nods at me and I proceed as though she had never interrupted.)

Aiken laughed at that and shook his head. "Thea made me see the sense in it and, upon looking at him, I was smitten."

"So I see." His purple eyes danced with his amusement.

"He was a nymph." He lowered his gaze. "Like you."

"Ah." Loki's lips danced. "Then he must truly be irresistible given that he reminds you of me."

Aiken felt his cheeks flush with heat. "How is Lucias?"

Loki blinked at him. "I don't know. I haven't seen him. It was Sappharon who told me it was time to come home."

("But I thought Sappharon put him to sleep next to Loki."

("She had Zamyael keep Lucias away from Loki from the moment that Loki came to." I tell Raziel. I'm starting to get irritated with her constant interruptions. "She didn't want him to realize that Lucias was in a coma."

("Oh." Raziel seems confused by this. I ignore the questions in her mind and continue.)

Aiken's brow furrowed. "None of us have seen him for some time. We assumed he was taking care of you."

Loki shook his head. "He's probably just busy running the war."

"Yes." Aiken smiled. "That's probably so."

"What about Adam?" Loki sighed. "I was supposed to see to his fall but that task was inadvertently set to the side."

"It's been taken care of." Aiken assured him. "Sappharon convinced him to eat the forbidden fruit." He chuckled. "Then he blamed Eve for it."

Loki snorted at that. "Of course he did."

"She has been telling everyone it was you." Aiken advised, his eyes dancing over Loki's face, waiting to see how he would react to this. "It's almost as if she wanted everyone to think you were up and about this entire time."

"She is the most confounding creature!"

"Said in loving tones." Aiken turned his head slightly to the side and gave Loki a questioning grin.

Surely she hasn't joined the gaggle!

"Let me just say that she and I have come to an understanding of one another and leave it at that." He shrugged. "Things should go smoother between us in future."

"Good to know."

"But there will be time for pleasantries later." Loki said as he raised his hand and squeezed Aiken's shoulder. "Why don't you take me to the basement and show me what you've been able to accomplish."

-63-

Sappharon spun swiftly, the dagger in her hand flying through the air and catching its mark in the forehead of a God that she did not recognize before her feet even hit the ground. It shivered violently in the bare moment that it took for the God to raise his hands upward, reaching for it to pluck it from his head. He was on his back, unconscious, before he had the opportunity to do so.

Spinning in the other direction, she was just ready to let the dagger in her other hand fly when she saw Lord Regan standing behind her, ready to thrust his sword into her gut.

He didn't have the opportunity. One of Sappharon's allies had come up behind him, swung his strong arm around Regan's chest and pulled his sword across his neck. Where flesh had once been now there was a gaping hole. Blood flowed from it in rivers as Regan, his eyes wide with confusion, stumbled toward her and then fell to the ground.

Sappharon watched him fall and then raised her gaze to give her ally a nod of thanks.

The moment she realized who it was, she froze.

And then her anger consumed her. "I don't need help from the likes of *you*, thank you very much."

"Then, in future, I shan't bother with the waste of my time." Metatron seethed and spun away, turning toward his next opponent.

She sneered at him, debating if she should kill him where he stood, and, then, spun away as well.

He had just saved her life. Never mind that he was the father of her only child.

Dispatching of him—which she must eventually do given he was one of Noliminan's pawns—could wait for another battle on another day.

-64-

Zamyael flew away from Tristan, her sword flailing off every blow that he advanced upon her.

"What in the name of the Thirty Hells is wrong with you?" She cried at him. "We're on the same side!"

"Lasterian has been expired because of you." He roared as he, very clumsily, swung his sword to meet hers. "And I mean to send you to join him."

Dear Gods. One of the finest swordsman I've ever known and he's stumbling around me like a child. The reports of his insanity have not at all been exaggerated.

"No!" She replied, swinging as hard as she could at his wrist.

She struck her mark. He cried out in pain and dropped the sword he had been wielding. Knowing he intended to advance upon her with his hands, she fell to the ground and spun with her leg out to trip him. When he stumbled forward, onto his hands and knees, she sprang up behind him and put the point of her sword to the back of his neck.

"He was in love with me, Tristan!" She growled through her teeth. "And I was in love with him. He wrote me a Gods be damned letter explaining why he expired himself. And his reasons had nothing to do with me."

"Centaur dung." He growled, though he didn't move. Having trained with her, he knew she wouldn't hesitate to drive the sword into the back of his neck if she thought he might be a threat.

Frustrated, she reached into her breastplate and pulled the letter from where she had tucked it between the metal of her armor and her flesh. "I have it right here. Read it, why don't you, and see for yourself."

She bent forward and waved it in his face. He raised his head slightly, lowering it again as the sword pricked his skin, and then lifted his hand to snatch the letter from hers.

He read it three times before acknowledging that she was telling the truth. When he did, he fell forward and rested his forehead upon his arm.

"My fault?" His voice was weak; his tone was defeated.

"Noliminan's fault." She seethed. "If Lasterian had had the free will to stand up to you and Evanbourough then he never would have allowed himself to fall into that state." And then, understanding the truth of her own words more poignantly than she would ever admit, "And, if I were a woman rather than a man, he would have fought you both to stand at my side as my husband."

She realized then that he was weeping. She shivered. The Tristan of old would never have let her see him cry. He would never have let anyone see him cry. Yet now, being the broken creature that he had become, he didn't care that she was witnessing his weakness and his pain.

She withdrew her sword, threw it to the ground and fell to his side on her knees. "I love him, too, Tristan. I love him as I have never loved anyone before. As I will never, in life, love anyone else, ever again."

(Raziel flies to her feet and grabs Zamyael by the hair. The demon cries out from the pain of it, screaming as Raziel lifts her and flings her across the room.

("This is the last of it, Zamyael." Raziel roars at her. "I am done with you. Let me never see your pathetic traitor's face again."

("My Lady—!"

("Stay out of it, Azrael!" She turns on me. "I mean to deal with you as well after you finish your tale."

("Deal with me as well?" I start. "I've done nothing to you!"

("Except allow this disgrace to take place!" She seethes. "And demand that I not allow Noliminan to learn of it!"

("I demand nothing of you!" I stand and hold out my hands to her, palms up in supplication. "My request was meant to protect you! What will he say when he learns that you allowed her to bed an angel whilst you were sitting in the next room?"

(She pales. She knows what I am saying to her is right. Zamyael won't be the only one to be punished if it comes out about the dathanorna given that the coupling occurred right under her nose.

(I raise my gaze to Zamyael, who is standing by the wall where she had fallen, rubbing her head where it had hit. I nod at her and send her a thought that she should go, at once, to Zadkiel's cottage. If she is expelled by Raziel then there is no other place where she will be safe. Given that no one is allowed to enter Zadkiel's cottage, she can easily hide should anyone come to call on Ishitar.

(I do this because Noliminan, who has always coveted Zamyael, will seek her and take her into his own service the moment that he knows that Raziel has released her. I know Zamyael well enough to understand that she will never be able to survive his brand of care toward her.

(She licks her lips, her eyes darting to Raziel, and then swiftly takes my advice.

("May I proceed, my Lady?" I manage, somehow, to keep my tone calm and reasonable.

(Raziel, lowering herself in a less than graceful manner to her chair, nods.)

"What are we to do?" He finally whispered.

"Work together." She suggested. "End this war."

He raised his gaze upward, meeting and holding hers. "I mean, what do we do to make it so you can be a woman again?"

"Nothing." She sighed. "There's nothing that you can do. As long as it is Noliminan and Lucias who are in charge of determining our sexes, we have no choice but to be who they want us to be."

"What if we were to take that power away from them?" Tristan asked, his eyes dancing over her face. "What if we were to come up with a spell that is more powerful than theirs? That will allow everyone—including your kind—the choice?"

"It can't be done, Tristan."

What madness! To believe that you can overturn a spell cast by Noliminan and Lucias!

He meant well, she knew, but he was not thinking this through.

"The word 'can't' only applies after one says 'I won't try'."

She glared at him. In his insanity, he was somehow easier to believe when he came up with wild ideas than he ever had been when he was himself. "It isn't that I'm not willing to try."

"Can you get me into the cellar of the castle without anyone seeing me?"

"Yes." She nodded. "Now that Raguel isn't being imprisoned in the cages Lucias never goes down there."

I'm sure as the Hells not letting you know that Lucias is in a coma. No telling what you will do to her thinking you are being helpful if you are to learn that!

"Isn't that where he and Noliminan set up their laboratory when they were young and learning the extent of their magic?"

"Yes . . ." She shivered.

How do you know that?

"Perhaps," he suggested, "they have left something behind that I can use."

"Perhaps they have," she muttered.

And perhaps locking you up in the basement is the most logical thing in all of the worlds for me to do. If you're busy working on spells that will never amount to anything, you can't very well be bumbling around causing more harm than good.

To her response, his thick lips flattened out into a treacherous smile.

-65-

Raystlyn was sitting in the courtyard at a table near Raphael, trying to converse with the archangel to lift his spirits, when Sappharon suddenly appeared in the center of the courtyard and flung Lord Regan's body without thought or care onto the cobblestones.

"This God has gone through sixteen angels. All of whom he has cut apart and sold in pieces to the mortals until the only recourse they perceived they had was to seek Zadkiel's end." She stood tall and proud, her foot upon his chest and her flaming eyes dancing. The wind had caught her long black hair so that it billowed around her in silky waves. Raystlyn thought, as he looked upon her wearing her warrior's brevity, that she was, for once, a pretty thing to look at. "Upon Lucias' orders, I will repay him in like kind."

Her sword flew, cutting through the few tendrils of flesh that remained which held Lord Ragen's head to his neck.

Raystlyn, who had never had a strong constitution, screamed.

-66-

Sappharon realized she had lost any hope of winning Raystlyn's respect the moment she heard him scream. But she had made a promise to another friend she cared about before she had ever even laid eyes upon him. And she meant to make good on that promise.

Her first step was to cut out his beating heart. When she had it in her hand, she turned toward the angel who had sought Lucias' succor before the war—she had come to know his name was Elemiah—and went to him. His blue eyes, which were wide and full of wonder, trailed over her face. His lips were curled into an exalted smile.

She held the beating heart out to him, offering it to him. "Eat it."

"Eat it?" Elemiah asked.

"Eat it." She grinned. "If he is able to piece himself together after I scatter him throughout the worlds, he will always know that the only way he was able to reform is because you ate his life force and then shat it back out."

Elemiah threw back his head and laughed.

Sappharon never found any peace to equal that which she felt as he took that first hungry, and far too delicious, bite.

-67-

Zadkiel started at the knock on the door. Rarely, if ever, did he have visitors. Irritated because he was busy making one of Ishitar's damned pies, he snapped, "Answer the door, boy."

Ishitar, who had been drawing pictures of some of the animals he had seen in the forest so Zadkiel could tell him their names, grinned. "I thought I'm not *supposed* to answer the door."

Zadkiel raised his dough covered hands and shook them in the lad's direction. "How about today we make an exception?"

"As you will me." Ishitar shrugged, set the brush that was caked in the paint that Zadkiel had made him by crushing flowers and berries upon the table, and stood.

Zadkiel shook his head at Ishitar and then returned his attention to the pie.

No one ever visited them. No one aside Zad's brothers that was. And I was chained at Ishitar's side. So what, really, could happen to the boy?

These were his thoughts until he heard Ishitar scream.

Throwing the dough aside, Zadkiel pushed himself upward with his hands and spread his wings so he could fly through his cottage toward the front door. Though he would later wish he'd grabbed his staff for when he landed, his pain was the furthest thing from his mind.

Once in the sitting room, he fell on his knees at Ishitar's side. The boy appeared to be fine, though he had pressed his hand to his head and was now openly crying—though no longer screaming—as if he were in great pain.

"Ishy!" Zadkiel cried. "What happened?"

"He pulled my hair!" Ishitar cried.

He lowered his hand from his head and Zadkiel began to panic. His hair hadn't been pulled. It had literally been ripped from his head!

"The Gods pray!" Zadkiel cried. "Who did this to you?"

"I know not." Ishitar replied, tears running down his boyish cheeks and his thick lips trembling. "He was tall and blonde and he disappeared before I knew what had happened!"

"Tall and blonde?"

That could describe any number of people!

Yet, in his mind, he heard me whisper, "It was Tristan. You know he's run mad. He meant Ishitar no harm."

"No harm." Zadkiel swallowed, grabbing onto this thought. He forced himself to smile as he grasped Ishitar's hand. "He only took your hair. He meant you no harm."

"No!" Ishitar rounded on him. "He stole it!"

"You can grow your hair." Zadkiel smiled tightly at him. "Calm yourself, child."

"I won't!" Ishitar spat at him. "I'm tired of you always telling me what to do. You're my brother! Not my father!" This was like a hard slap to Zadkiel's face. "You and Azrael both. Always ordering me about." He turned and stormed away. "I'm tired of looking upon you both!"

"He doesn't mean it." I formed myself at Zadkiel's side. "You know he doesn't. He's just angry with his parents."

"I take it his visit with Noliminan didn't go well today?" Zadkiel asked, his brow raised.

"Not at all well." Azrael sighed.

"Bwuet Va." Though calling Noliminan by this particular insult was punishable enough, Zadkiel bit back the words he really wanted to say as they would get him into greater trouble still.

I read his thoughts, however, and gave him a weary smile. "Best you go calm him down."

"Best I do." Zadkiel agreed.

Frowning, he forced himself to his feet and limped through the cottage to Ishitar's room. He didn't knock. Rather, he just opened the door and stepped in.

"Ishitar. For the love of the Gods." He groused. "You have to understand. That was Tristan who took your hair."

"Why?" His arms were crossed over his chest and he was glaring at his brother. He wasn't pleased that Zadkiel had entered his room without permission.

"I don't know, child." Zadkiel admitted. "From what Azrael tells me he's gone insane. His head was cut off in your parents war and when it grew back he was no longer himself. He does things that are unreasonable now. He thinks he's trying to help win my brothers and I free will."

"But if he's only trying to help then he should have just asked me for my hair!" Ishitar admonished. "I would have cut a lock of it and given it to him!"

"I know that boy." Zadkiel dragged himself across the floor and sat on the bed at Ishitar's side. "But he doesn't. Not only is he insane, he knows nothing about you other than that you are your parents' child. You may not remember this, but when you and I were in Evanbourough's care, so was he."

Ishitar let out a deep sigh through his teeth which bore Lucias' whistle. Caught off guard by this, Zadkiel involuntarily laughed.

Ishitar ignored him.

"I'm not my father." He snapped. "Or my mother."

"You're right." Zadkiel, still smiling at how very much he had looked and sounded like Lucias, agreed. "You're better than both of them."

His light brown eyes danced over Zadkiel's face. After a moment of reflection, he raised his hand to touch the wound on his head where his hair used to be.

"Will it really grow back."

"Certainly it will." Zadkiel tried not to smile as he lowered his hand. By the time it was on the bed, the hair had, indeed, grown back. "Why not take a nap? I'll finish up the pie and set it to cool on the window."

"What kind of pie?" He asked, grinning.

Zadkiel, chuckling, reached forward to pinch his cheek. He curled his tongue and used a voice that had always made Ishitar laugh. "Shaweet potato, shaweet heart!"

Ishitar, braying his laughter, flew forward, wrapped his arms around Zadkiel's neck and held him tight.

Zadkiel was relieved that he had been able to make the lad smile.

-68-

Zamyael stared at Lord Parsiphany, her eyes trailing over his thick, masculine features. That he had agreed so easily to hand over one of his brews left her not only surprised, but also extremely confused.

"Hand me the hair." He muttered.

Zamyael, shaking her head, did as she was bid. "Noliminan won't be angry that you're giving me a brew?"

"I fail to see how he will find out." Parsiphany advised her. "But even if he does, I have no choice. Before the war, Lord Lucias was clear to me that if anyone from his side ever came and begged my aide that I was to give it." He shrugged. "I am a Hells bound God. I must follow his orders until such time as I am told to do otherwise."

"Yes." She agreed. "But you haven't joined his cause."

Parsiphany raised his wolfishly yellow eyes and gave her a guarded smile. "Haven't I?"

She let out an unexpected gasp that was half laugh and half relief. Parsiphany was an ally they could most definitely use to their advantage. Especially if he was an underground ally.

"Okay." He muttered. "Tristan said you'd hand me two more things that I need."

This, Zamyael couldn't directly do. Instead, she handed him the bag that Tristan had told her contained the testes of a male angel and the ovaries of a female demon.

Parsiphany, seeming to understand, took the bag from Zamyael's hands. He then opened it and dumped the contents into the brew.

"Does everyone have to drink it or . . . ?"

"No." Parsiphany muttered. "I merely need to visit the Great Hall and pour it over the stairs. The next time Council convenes, everyone will be forced to revert to the bodies they were born with."

"But won't the angels and demons charged with keeping the Great Hall clean—?"

"It doesn't matter." Parsiphany shrugged. "Once I pour it, it will seep into the ground and the podium. No one will even know that I poured it. The minute the King of Lords touches the podium he will, albeit inadvertently, make my will so."

Zamyael found herself grinning. "Clever."

Parsiphany nodded and gave her a tired smile in response. "The brew will take exactly one waning moon of the world known as Earth to boil to the ready. Do we have that long?"

"Ta." Zamyael replied, unable to stay the overwhelming greed rushing through her soul. "Though I would prefer it happens now, we have every day in every world that it must take if your spell will return me to my rightful whole."

"Well then, my Lady." Parsiphany grasped her hand and brought it to his lips to kiss. "May you not regret having orchestrated this farce when my will makes itself known."

-69-

Exactly two waning moons after Parsiphany poured his brew, King Noliminan called his Council.

Knowing what was to take place, I found myself swallowing all of the fear within me that something—anything—might prevent me from, finally, being able to no longer be the hermaphrodite freak that I had been born as to become the man I had always considered myself to be.

Even as I watched the Gods filter in from my place in the gallows, I knew that some immanent, unknown disaster would occur to prevent what I wanted—what I needed—to become so.

When it didn't, when Noliminan stepped forward and made to lean against the podium, I cried out.

This called his attention.

I immediately regretted my action as Zamyael, who sat on the floor beside Raziel's now deserted throne, raised her wide eyes in my direction, wildly shaking her head.

To my great relief, Noliminan chose to ignore me. He thought, I suppose, that I was reacting to something else, somewhere else, that I was seeing. My reaction, given my magic, was a common enough occurrence.

As he leaned against the podium it wasn't only my sigh which was heard.

-70-

I cannot even begin to describe the chaos that ensued once everyone was forced to revert to the essence that they had been born with. Realizing that two of his Quorum—Uriel and Mihr— were now women rather than men did not, as I would have assumed given his penchant for preferring females, please Noliminan. Rather, it infuriated him.

And he wasn't the only one who was angry.

Those who had long thought their lovers where the sex they preferred, when they were with one another, were subjected to a rude awakening as they realized that, internally, they had always been deceived.

Even those who should have known better were angry.

I refer, here, to Evanbourough. Though there were many others, Evanbourough is a caustic tale. When he realized that Theasis, who had never even once pretended to be anything but female, was now forced to live that essence, their relationship was immediately and irrevocably ended.

I understand this. Evanbourough is, and ever has been, strictly a homosexual. And though Theasis had, until that day, always supplicated to his desires, she was no longer able to do so.

That he took this as a personal slight and went so far as to berate her for something she had no control over is what is, to me, the part which is most unforgivable.

My heart broke for her. And my loathing for Evan and his constant hypocrisy exploded to an exponential magnitude that I cannot even begin to describe.

But, above all of this pain, what resonated within me was my joy. A joy not directed toward myself, and my own good fortune, but which was directed to my dear Zamyael, who had never, even once in her life, been afforded anything which remotely resembled choice.

Finally, after the span of the ages, Zamyael was simply that. She. Zamyael. The woman she had been born to become.

No matter what pain this magic that she and Tristan had wrought might bring others, Zamyael's joy outweighed it all.

The rest, I knew, I could bide without even the first fallen tear.

-71-

I know you are probably becoming bored at this point because the last few segments of my story have been told from my point of view rather than from that of others. But I beg you bear with me for several segments more. And I beg you remember that this entire tale has been spun from what I have been forced to bear witness to.

For now, it is my own actions upon which I bear reflection.

I knew certain truths at this point, you see. And I had come to a point within my own rumination which made me question if I should raise them to Noliminan and end this damned war.

Not knowing what was right or wrong, I chose to do the only thing I must do. I approached my Lord and Master to pose the question which bore heaviest in my mind.

I knocked on the library door and waited. It wasn't long before he bid me enter, though he called Gabriel's name. When he saw it was me who entered, he hesitantly lowered his quill to his desk. "Azrael."

"Your Grace." I bowed my fealty to him. "I've come to beg a question from you."

"Yes?"

"I have something to tell you." I swallowed. "And yet, I know that if I do so I will be punished by you and cursed by my magic."

A strange, interested expression crossed his handsome features.

"I must ask you what punishment I will receive from you."

"You already hang in the gallows." He shrugged. "Whatever punishment I decree will necessarily be more severe."

"But what if what I have to tell you is important?" I asked him. "What if it involves someone you love?"

"I love everyone."

I didn't believe him. But I understood what he was telling me. It didn't matter who I thought I was helping, I would be betraying someone else.

"My Lord, I beseech you to understand my position."

"What, exactly, is so important to you?" Noliminan leaned forward. "That you would beg me dole your punishment before you loosen your tongue? You've never come to me before to ask to release information."

"Perhaps this, in and of itself, displays the import." I whispered.

He sighed and fell back to his original position in his chair. "Yes." He agreed. "It does."

I granted him a guarded smile.

"Very well." He cleared his throat. "Here is my proposition for you, Azrael. And you decide if it is worth telling me what you obviously believe you must."

"Yes, your Grace?"

"Whomever you are betraying," he advised me, "whomever's secret you wish to divulge. That's who will choose your punishment. And not me. Is it fair?"

Is it fair? No. Does it make sense? Yes. And will it entice me?

Countenance will tell.

"Thank you, your Grace." Is how I responded. "I shall be back with my answer."

"Very well." Noliminan replied, his eyes burning with curiosity. I sensed that this curiosity was more about how I would respond to his negotiation than what it is that I had to say. Strangely, I was at peace with this knowledge. "You are dismissed."

Bowing to him, I took my leave.

-72-

"Your Royal Highness?" I cleared my throat. Ishitar knew I was in my waiting stance on the floor beside him, but I had been quiet for several passing moons. "May I speak with you candidly?"

He raised his adolescent gaze from the academics that Zadkiel insisted he study and gave me a guarded smile. "You know I hate it when you give me title."

"I do." I sigh. "But the time is coming for you to spend more time with others. They will expect Zadkiel and I to show our fealty toward you."

"I know that." He replied, tersely. "Zadkiel never stops harping on it. Don't you start lecturing me as well."

I offered him a tight smile. He'd been drawing away from us. He wanted his real parents to guide him, not we brothers who imposed ourselves upon him as authority figures.

"Forgive me." I bowed my head to him, causing him to glare at me with great irritation. "May I have your counsel?"

"If you must."

He was still so young. I had no business asking him what I intended to. But what choice did I have? This was his parents' war. He was the only one besides the pair of them to have a true stake in its outcome.

"I believe I know how to end the rebellion."

Ishitar started. "Between my mother and father?"

"Ta." I said, not daring to meet his gaze. "But I need your counsel to know if what I propose to do is the right thing to do."

Ishitar's eyes were contemplative. He replied, now frowning. "What do I know about their game of kings' castles?"

"But this isn't a game."

"To my father it is." Ishitar reminded me. "You know it is. Every time I visit him he's contemplating my mother's next move and asking me how I would respond to it."

"I understand, but . . ." I didn't know how to explain to him the true depth of the problem. "What if it's more than that?"

"It isn't more than that. Though, if you perceive that I can aide you, I shall try."

I was grateful to him. "Your mother slumbers. Your father is unaware."

"I know both of these things."

I shivered. He shouldn't have known either of these things. No one had ever told him about either and he was too young when Zadkiel put Lucias to sleep to remember. I reasoned, given his knowledge of events in the past which he shouldn't have known about, that he must hold a small bit of power which is akin to my own.

"I feel as if I should tell your father about your mother's fate." I said. "But if I do, I will be cursed by my magic. I might harm your mother in the long run." And, then, the true point of the matter. "Or I might harm you."

"Why would you tell him?" Ishitar asked, his brow furrowed. "What benefit do you perceive could come by it?"

"I believe he will put an end to the war if he realizes it is not her whom he is fighting." I explained.

"If you believe this, then why do you seek my permission?"

"I don't." Perhaps, I reasoned, I had made a mistake. "Only your opinion."

"My opinion is that you should do whatever it is you think is the right thing to do." He shrugged and returned his attention to the book on the table. "In this situation, I do not believe your magic will curse you."

"You don't?"

I swallowed as I watched him look up at me again. I waited, curious, to see what he would say.

You see, I had a theory at this point about Ishitar. But my theory was being put into question. Did he have the power to prevent my magic from cursing me? And, if he did, would he use it?

Realizing I was waiting for his answer, he let out an irritated sigh. "I have to get back to my studies."

"I understand." I had my answer to my second question and it broke my heart. "Forgive me."

I fell back into my waiting stance, and into silence, so I could consider the course I meant to take on my own.

I am uncertain how long I sat at his feet in my own contemplation. Perhaps sixty shifts. Perhaps many more. What I do know is that, when I finally decided the course I must take, I looked up to find that he was watching me with patient curiosity.

I forced myself to smile at him.

"What did you decide?" He asked.

"To tell him." I muttered. "It's the right thing to do."

He nodded and held his hand toward me. Swallowing, I lowered my gaze to it and raised my own hand to take it. When my eyes fell upon it, however, I froze.

Grasped loosely in his fingers was a small lock of his hair.

I stared at it for a long moment and then raised my gaze to meet his. "What's this?"

"You will need it."

Licking my lips I reached for his hand and took the hair from his grasp. My words to him as I tucked the lock into my satchel were spoken in a frightened whisper. "Thank you."

He studied me for a long moment before shrugging his shoulders and returning his attention to his book.

-73-

"Your Grace?"

"You again." Noliminan muttered as he lowered the glass of wine he had been drinking to the table. Gabriel sat beside him, his eyes wide and haunted. The pair, I knew, had been playing their games.

I loathed Noliminan for it.

"Me again." I swallowed. I flicked my eyes to Gabriel. "Might I speak with you alone?"

He sighed and flicked his hand to Gabriel. The gratitude in my brother's eyes seared my soul.

When he was gone, I said. "I agree to your terms."

Noliminan started. "Do you now?"

"Yes." I agreed. "May I speak freely? Knowing whose punishment I must face?"

"Ta." He snorted. I understood that he didn't realize the serious nature of the facts I wished to share so I forgave him his flippancy. "Our terms are acceptable to me."

This time I lowered my gaze because the words that I had practiced to share with him had escaped me. I was left to improvise, despite my preparation.

What if my theory regarding Ishitar's ability to protect me from the curse of my magic is wrong?

"Lucias is in a coma." I said it quickly and without pause. Whatever would happen to me would happen. I had only to wait. "Zadkiel tried to expire her, but he was unable to master the magic given the strength of her soul."

"Loki's beard." Noliminan sighed. "You are certain?"

"Ta." I swallowed, relieved. I felt no change in myself. My magic, it would seem, held its anger against me at bay. "Very certain."

Noliminan's eyes were burning. "I can end this game now."

"Your Grace," I cried, suddenly understanding my folly. I knew deep within my heart that he meant to finish the job Zadkiel had been unable to do. "While she sleeps?"

"Yes." He smiled.

"But, you Grace—!"

"Bring her to me, Azrael." He commanded me. "Now."

-74-

Ishitar lowered himself upon a log which had recently fallen across the path that he used to travel from Zadkiel's cottage to the lake in the center of the forest where he—and sometimes Zadkiel—would fish.

Today he had wanted to be alone. So, after he had finished his chores for the day, he headed out to make certain that the pair of them would have dinner.

Not that he was alone. He was never alone.

As always, I, who was ever at his side whether Ishitar wanted me there or not, followed him.

There were times this annoyed the living Hells out of him.

Even when he passed water or covered his feet he had to do so with me watching him. Never mind that his body was starting to have certain cravings which he was unable to sate because, every time he had a mind to find his hand, he was forced to stop himself when he realized I was staring at him.

As maddening as it was for me, I imagine it must have been damnation for him. He wanted to be a normal boy. But how can a person be normal when they had not even a single shift of the shadows to themselves?

For most of this particular morning, Ishitar had ignored me. And I, understanding that I was an irritation to him, kept quiet and to myself.

Grateful for my silence, Ishitar eventually turned to me and said, "I hope Zadkiel makes me a pie."

I gave him a guarded smile. "He does every day."

"I know." Ishitar grinned. "I shouldn't eat the whole thing, I suppose."

"You're a growing boy." I shrugged. "You'll slow down with your age."

Ishitar nodded. "What flavor do you think?"

I gave him another guarded smile and flicked my eyes to his hands. Ishitar's fingers, after having spent the entire afternoon the day before picking blackberries, were stained red.

Ishitar laughed. "I suppose you're right."

I nodded and, once again, fell silent.

"Azrael?"

"Hmm?"

"What's wrong?"

I shuddered. Best to tell him the truth. "I took your advice."

"My advice?" Ishitar knew what I was referring to, so his question was actually rhetorical. Still, I answered.

"I told Noliminan that your mother slumbers." I muttered. "Now he is demanding that I bring her to him so he can destroy her."

Ishitar grinned. "What do you intend to do?"

"I have no choice." I replied. "I must take Lucias to him."

"Then its best you not wait." Ishitar turned away from me. "As for me," he said as he stood, "I promised Zadkiel I'd bring fish home for supper."

I opened my mouth, but then closed it again. I didn't understand his lack of concern. I wondered if he had turned into his parents' son despite the pains Zad and I had taken.

One way or the other, I realized, games were afoot.

-75-

When I appeared before Noliminan holding Lucias, he pushed himself out from behind his desk and literally leapt over it to take her from my arms.

"Luci . . ." Noliminan muttered, his lips pressed against her. "Mestok comp et? Glirk tom pe."

Of course I didn't understand a word of this. But I knew it was unnecessary as I watched him carry her to the sofa and lay her gently upon it.

He ran his hand over the top of her head and then turned to look over his shoulder at me. "Bring me Ishitar."

"Yes, your Grace."

I bowed to him, leaving at his command. The version of me sitting at Ishitar's side, watching him fish, turned toward the lad.

"Your father wants me to bring you to him." My voice was shaking. Now that I wasn't mired in fear I had no further control over my reaction to it. "I shall see to delivering your fish to Zadkiel."

"Did he . . . ?" Ishitar began.

"No." The relief was palpable in my tone. "He merely kissed her."

He nodded and stood. When he was on his feet he reached for my hand. I let him take it. I also let him carry us to his father's apartment rather than using my own magic to do so.

He didn't knock on the outer door, which I found odd until I realized there was no reason for him to do so. Given this was his father's house, he could come and go as he pleased without asking Gabriel—or whichever one of my brothers was serving Noliminan today—if he might do so.

He did, I will say, knock on the closed library door.

It opened as if it had a will of its own. Which, under Noliminan's command, I suppose it did. I allowed Ishitar to step in first and then followed. The door slammed shut behind me.

Noliminan was where I'd left him. Though now he had lowered himself to his knees and was muttering to Lucias under his breath. I couldn't hear the words he spoke, though I knew it didn't matter. I wouldn't be able to understand them even if I could hear them.

He kissed her forehead again and then turned to face us both, rising to his feet as he did so. "It needn't be said that neither of you are to make mention of her current condition."

"Of course not, Father." Ishitar replied, his tone low and respectful. "What do you mean to do with her?"

"Care for her." He shrugged. His eyes turned to me. "I must employ you in a manner I never have before, Azrael. Serve me well and I shall bring you down from the gallows."

I blinked at him. My eyes darted to Ishitar and then back to Noliminan.

"I will do what I can for you, your Grace." I assured him. "As long as it isn't to loosen my tongue."

"What I need you to do is hold your damn tongue." He chuckled slightly. As for me, I sighed my relief at the sentiment. "Aside from one small thing."

"Yes, your Grace?"

"How long has she been unconscious?" He asked. "And who has been playing games with me in her stead."

"Your Grace, I—" I swallowed. "I cannot give you an answer."

Ishitar cleared his throat. My eyes darted toward him. He was absentmindedly tugging at his hair as his eyes trailed almost lazily to the ancient satchel I always carried with me. I understood at once that he was telling me that as long as I kept his hair with me he believed I would be safe from any curse resulting from my magic.

Noliminan failed to notice this exchange. When he spoke his tone was harsh. "Do not try my patience, Azrael."

"Perhaps if we made a game of it." Ishitar suggested.

Noliminan, frowning, turned to look at his son. "What kind of game."

"What if we guessed who it was?" He smiled playfully. I found myself startled by his pure guile. "I should say a name—Loki, perhaps—and he will tell me no." He gave me a guarded smile. I knew this game would never play out the way he wanted it if I didn't have his permission and his hair. Noliminan, however, had no way of understanding that. "If it was Loki, you wouldn't say anything at all."

"It wasn't Lord Loki." My tone was one of bitter relief as I turned to look upon Noliminan. "Your Grace, will this game play well for you?"

He considered me for a moment, looked toward Ishitar, who was still smiling playfully, and then returned his attention to me. "It will do."

Grateful he didn't mean to push the issue, I agreed to play the game with him.

"Raziel?"

"She's in prison." I remind him. "And angry that she is now forced to live in her birthed form."

This idea pleased him. His angry scowl turned into a cynical smile. "Too bad for her."

"Too bad for her." For once I agreed with his true sentiment.

"Zamyael hasn't the guile." He muttered as he turned to lower himself into the chair beside the one where Lucias lay sleeping.

Ishitar took the second and I found my waiting stance on the floor at the lad's feet. "Tristan?"

"Has run mad." This was no secret to anyone.

"Raystlyn?"

"Too weak in his constitution."

Ishitar watched us for several passing shifts as we sparred with names. It was almost frightening, the interest he took. And downright eerie when he became bored of Noliminan's seeming ignorance and said softly. "Sappharon."

I started and turned my gaze in his direction. As for Noliminan, he stormed, "She doesn't have the wit!"

"Perhaps not, Father." Ishitar agreed. "But you told me that, since the first battle, Michael and Metatron have been able to pull little more than a draw. Didn't you say she trained under Metatron when my mother insisted she learn combat skills?"

I lowered my gaze. She had done more than merely train under Metatron. It was during the period in which Metatron was her mentor that the pair had fallen in love. Something which follows them to this day, I know. Even if they both deny it.

Noliminan snorted and turned his gaze to me. He realized, as he watched my reaction, that I hadn't denied Sappharon was the culprit.

"Sappharon." He said with a note of distaste in his tone. I raised my gaze to meet his. His eyes searched mine before turning to look at Lucias. He contemplated her for a moment and then returned his gaze to me. "Here is my quandary, Azrael. And what I need your help with."

"Your Grace?"

"Sappharon's games have caused a rift amongst the Council." He advised me. "You've seen for yourself that our numbers have dwindled."

"I have, your Grace."

"We need to convince others that she has the wrong of things." He raised his hand to rub the bridge of his nose. "We need to convince them to come back to my way of thinking."

Ishitar, listening to him, narrowed his eyes. I found myself wondering what, precisely, the boy was thinking. Did he find this calm which Noliminan was exuding in light of the new information he was garnering as forebodingly troublesome as I did?

"Sappharon believes she's a match for me at kings' castles." He lowered his hand and met my gaze again. "What do you think?"

"I think that if she was, you and I wouldn't be having this conversation." I admitted.

He smiled. My response pleased him.

A rare enough thing.

"Well, then." His eyes shimmered. "If it is a game of kings' castles Sappharon wants to play, a game of kings' castles we shall give her."

"Yes, your Grace." I lowered my gaze.

He meant to use me as his pawn. As such, I had no other option but to wait for him to command me my first move.

-76-

Sappharon stepped into the bedchamber where Lady Lucias had been laying since Zadkiel had put her to sleep and flew into a panic. She wasn't laying on her bed. Rather, the spot where she had been sleeping only sixty shifts before was ominously empty.

She rolled her eyes closed and lowered her chin to her chest. There could only be one reason that Lucias wasn't in bed. And this reason was that she had finally awoken.

Sappharon knew that this eventuality must take place. She was only sorry she hadn't been here to explain her position to Lucias. Though she reasoned it probably wasn't necessary. Lucias would understand why she had insisted on keeping her state of health a secret. And she would support her for having done so.

Certain of this fact, Sappharon set about preparing Lucias' bed for her. She would want her sheets tucked and her pillows fluffed when it was time for her to bed down to recover her strength.

Seeing to her tasks, Sappharon, knowing her true place, happily renewed her vow to serve her Mistress thoroughly and completely in every detail from this day forward.

-77-

Loki opened up his cooling cupboard and frowned as his gaze fell upon a pot of stew that Aiken had made the night before. He lifted the lid and sniffed at it, deciding that it smelled rather good. He even pondered, for a moment, dishing himself out a pan to warm over the fire.

Then he remembered that mischief fairies had a penchant for cannibalism and he shivered.

"No thank you." He muttered to himself as he reached, instead, for the goose he had cooked three days prior.

He turned, kicking the cupboard door closed with the heel of his boot and walked toward the table.

As his eyes fell upon the cream colored envelope, he froze.

Scrawled neatly across the parchment in Lady Lucias' hand was Loki's name.

He swallowed and stepped toward the table. Lowering the goose with one hand to set it down, he reached for the envelope with the other. He raised it upward to fan beneath his nose. And he smiled as Lady Lucias' scent of cloves and old spices overwhelmed him.

"Welcome back, my Lady." He mused as, dinner forgotten, he pulled out a chair and turned the envelope over. Her symbol was stamped perfectly into wax at the folds to seal it.

Smelling her, he was overcome with desire. Something he no longer fought. Especially now that he realized everyone had been forced to revert to the form they had been born in. Now, more than finding his desire for her distasteful, he found himself curious.

Exactly what did she look like as a woman?

"Beautiful." He muttered to himself. "Of that you can be certain."

"Why, yes. I am." Aiken's deep voice enveloped him. "I'm pleased that you are finally coming to see my way of things."

Loki chuckled and met his friend's gaze. As he did so, he held out the letter. "From Lord Lucias."

"Lord Lucias." Aiken grinned at him. "Are we still playing that game?"

Blushing, Loki lowered his gaze. He'd thrown back one too many cups one night and had shared more with Aiken than he would, in retrospect, have cared to. Though Aiken rarely ever brought the matter up, he did tease about Loki's unrequited love for his Lady from time to time.

"Fine." He conceded. "It's from the Lady."

"Loki." He sighed impatiently as he found a chair and reached for the goose that Loki had abandoned. "You know I'm never going to tell. I haven't even raised the fact to Jami."

"I appreciate that, Aiken." Loki conceded as he met his friend's gaze. His not sharing this was James—Loki couldn't pronounce his Gods be damned name so called him James—meant much and more to him. "I really do."

He nodded and looked away. "What does she have to tell you? If it isn't too personal?"

Loki shrugged and turned his attention to the letter. He ran his finger carefully beneath the seal, not wanting to break it. He meant to keep all of her letters to him.

As he did so, Aiken pulled meat off of the goose. One bite later and he spat it out.

"Piss on the Gods, Loki." He growled. "This is disgusting."

Loki raised his gaze and gave his friend a patient smile. "Oh, that's right. You prefer ganders."

"I eat geese in equal measure I assure you." Aiken grinned playfully at him. "You just haven't cooked this one properly."

"Didn't have the time." Loki muttered, returning his attention to the letter. "And Sam was out."

"I'll warm up some stew."

Loki snorted at that. "No thanks."

"Honestly, Loki." Aiken grumbled as he put the goose in the trash bin and pulled out his stew. "What must you think of me to believe I'd put mortal meat in your food?"

"That you're a fairy." Loki was beginning to ignore him as his eyes scanned over the letter before him.

"I can assure you, I shall feed you nothing you wouldn't put upon your own table."

Loki heard him but ignored him. He knew Aiken would put a bowl in front of him and he would eat it knowing the meat was animal rather than a thinking mortal.

As he read the letter, he felt his brow furrow.

"What's wrong?" Aiken asked, some shifts later, as he sat a warm bowl of stew in front of Loki.

"She tells me that there is a traitor amongst us." He muttered.

"A traitor?" Aiken pulled his hand away. When Loki looked up at his friend the offense was palpable upon his features. "Who?"

"She doesn't say." He threw the letter aside. "Only that it is the newest member of our little pack."

"But—?" He shook his head. "Loki. I'm the newest member of our pack. Aside Jamiason and Sam. And I swear, if Jami was up to something, he would have told me."

"As far as I know, she doesn't know about James." Loki muttered. He wasn't even about to begin to believe that it was the loyal Samyael was who she was referring to. He raised his eyes to look upon his friend. "But she does know about you."

"On my mother's honor, I would never betray you."

"Your mother had no honor." Loki grinned at him.

"Loki . . . This isn't a joking matter."

"No. It isn't." He sighed. "Aiken, you know I don't believe it's you."

"Yes." He sighed his relief. "Thank you."

"I must ponder what the message truly means." He advised Aiken. And, not wanting to think upon the issue for the nonce, he reached for his stew. "For now, how about you tell me about your day?"

Aiken, granting Loki a guarded, concerned smile, complied.

-78-

The game of kings' castles was now truly begun. Noliminan and Ishitar sat in Noliminan's library, contemplating which moves to make. Sappharon, Zamyael, Emissary Darklief (in attendance but not joining in the discussions) and Loki sat in Loki's library contemplating their moves. Before them lay the instructions they believed to be coming from Lady Lucias.

There I was, in both libraries, witness to all of this and unable to interfere.

It was maddening.

Mostly because, with the shifts of the shadows, Ishitar grew more and more like his father. By the time he was old enough to take a wife, it was clear to me that he believed his father hung the moon—yes, I am aware of the irony in that statement because, when a new world is created, he literally does.

Ishitar watched Noliminan manipulate the other players. He even began suggesting strategies which seemed to both surprise and intrigue Noliminan.

One strange occurrence did temper the young man. On a recognizance mission of sorts—another of Ishitar's strategies—Ishitar began visiting Raziel's apartment to see if she had anything that his father didn't know about that they could use.

There, of course, he met Zamyael.

Their relationship blossomed in such a way that I never would have expected. He found, in her, the mother he had sorely been lacking and she embraced him as her long lost son. So much so that, even when Loki or Sappharon would describe his behavior as odd, she would argue the point and dissuade them from believing something was wrong.

He was clever with her. And he was able to manipulate her to gain information about Sappharon and Loki which he would pass to his father so that they could use it against them.

Now and again I would voice my opinion to him and ask him why he was behaving in the manner that he was. This wasn't how Zadkiel and I had raised him. To which, of course, he always responded with anger.

Until finally . . .

"Zadkiel is not my father and neither are you! You're not even Gods. Mind your damn station or I'll mind it for you!"

That was the last time I ever raised the issue with him. In fact, my heart was so broken by his words that I ceased speaking to him altogether. He either didn't notice or he didn't care.

He was too involved in his father's game of kings' castles to worry about me and Zadkiel.

It was a sun cycle after this conversation occurred when I went to Zadkiel and told him everything that was going on. He sat across the table from me with an angry expression.

"He's turning into his father, is he?"

I nodded, running the lock of Ishitar's hair between my fingers to remind myself that I wouldn't be cursed by my magic for loosening my tongue. As for Zadkiel, I trusted him above all other people. He wouldn't betray me or my counsel. Especially not where Ishitar was concerned. "Yet, somehow, he is worse. Some of his ideas are . . . disturbing to me."

"Damn it." Zadkiel lowered his gaze to his hand. It was sitting upon the table. He held an apple within it which he turned over and over in his fingers. "I had hoped that I'd had some influence on the boy."

"So had I." I admitted. "But the last time I spoke with him he put me in my place. He cares not a wit what guidance I might give him."

"Unacceptable. What are we going to do about this?" Zadkiel asked.

"Do?"

"We can't let him become his father."

"I fear it is too late." I admitted.

"Wait and see. Is that your approach?" Zadkiel muttered. The tone of his voice dripped with sarcasm. "And hope that, eventually, one small bit of influence we've had over him will matter in the end?"

"What other choice do we have?" I asked. "It isn't like we can manipulate the boy to our advantage. He won't listen to a single word we say."

"Precisely." Zadkiel muttered as he twirled the apple over and over in his fingers. "Because we aren't Gods." His eyes rose from the apple in his hand so that his gaze was meeting mine. As they did so, his lips split into a mischievous grin. "Azrael, what is the one thing that our father has always told us is the best way to beat any opponent at kings' castles?"

I shrugged. "Mind the board."

"Mind the board, ta." He nodded. "And concentrate on the face across the board."

"What are you suggesting?"

"That you do as you were ordered, Azrael. Mind your damn station." He winked at me. "And I'll go on minding mine." I felt my brow furrow as his grin broadened. "In the meantime, let's see if we can't teach our boy a thing or two about the proper way to play at kings' castles."

-79-

I had my doubts that my brother's plan to best Noliminan and Ishitar at kings' castles would be a successful one. Yet, understanding that something had to be done, I agreed to do as he bid.

When Noliminan called me to his library to bark his orders at me, I appeared and I obeyed. When Zadkiel called me to his cottage to conspire, I appeared and I followed his instruction.

Though no one else knew this to be so, Zadkiel's kitchen had been transformed into a war room that even Michael and Metatron would be envious of. His table had been turned into a tactical map with every God in every realm represented in their places. His walls had all been painted white and he used them to work out strategies and write down his plans lest they be forgotten when the game was deep in play.

If a plan played itself out, it was as equally wiped away by a new coat of white paint as if a plan had utterly failed. After which, Zadkiel would stay up the full of the night, if necessary, to replace it with his new tactic.

I came to understand something about Zadkiel during these days that I never would have suspected despite my abilities to read his mind: As far as the game of kings' castles is concerned, my brother is a master.

Michael's army made of the Guf and Martiam's halls clashed time and again with Loki's damned. Sometimes they won. But more often, thanks to Zadkiel's planning, they either lost or came to a draw.

Sappharon, who had never really been fond of any of us, began looking at me with an odd shimmer of admiration in her fiery eyes every time I visited to pass Zadkiel's orders. Neither she nor Loki had any idea that Zadkiel was the true puppeteer; they assumed, given my abilities, that their part of the game was being orchestrated by me.

The trickiest part of Zadkiel's plan was trying to convince Loki that Aiken was, indeed, the spy that Lucias had warned them about. His loyalty to Aiken was unwavering. And rightfully so. Even after he conceded verbally that Aiken was the culprit, he did so with the underlying thought that he would tell me whatever he thought I wanted to hear if only to make me shut up about it.

Though I had argued with Zadkiel on the necessity of this point, he made it clear from the beginning that neither side could know that it was actually me who was the double agent.

"If they suspect you, all of our plans will fail." Zadkiel had warned me. "Because if they suspect you, by default, they will suspect me."

"Yes, but—"

"I know you admire Emissary Darklief." Zadkiel's lips pursed. "As do I." I sighed, and nodded my agreement to that statement. "When the board clears, everyone will know what side he's on. For now, he's an important pawn in one of my most critical plans."

"I wish I knew what your plans were." I snapped at him. I didn't like the fact that I suddenly couldn't breach his mind.

Ever since the game had begun, he'd masked his thoughts and feelings in a code he had developed when he and I had first sat across from one another at the kings' board after I'd been granted my ability to read thoughts. That he never dropped his guard and thought outside of the code he'd created in his mind was disconcerting to me at best. "It isn't right that I don't know your move until you command me to make it."

"I can't take the chance that Ishitar isn't paying more attention to you than I believe he is." He shrugged. "Anyway, you're the master at puzzles. That you can't figure it out tells me that you aren't really trying."

I frowned at him. Because he was right.

I didn't want to know his moves before he made them. Otherwise, as he said, I would have long ago deciphered his code. "Fine," I scoffed. "Tell me what Gods be damned game you would have me play now."

-80-

Loki watched Aiken with curious regard as he walked toward the table where Loki sat waiting for Council. He hadn't seen Aiken in almost a sun cycle. Aiken, who Azrael was trying to convince Loki was a traitor, had become uncomfortable in Loki's presence.

He stopped at the table and, lips pursed, tapped on the corner. "Loki."

"Aiken." Loki cocked his head and gave him a tight smile. "Would you care to sit with me today?"

"No, I . . ." His violet eyes were avoiding Loki's at all cost. "I wouldn't want to make you uncomfortable."

"Why would I be uncomfortable?" Loki asked him.

"With everything that's going on." Aiken shrugged. "I . . ." His smile was tight. "I just wanted to say hello."

Loki sighed. "So you've said hello."

Aiken nodded and, finally, raised his gaze. "I'm sorry for . . . If you—"

"Aiken," Loki sighed again. "Sit the fuck down. And let's go get a drink after Council and talk out whatever it is that's troubling you."

"I think you already know what's troubling me."

"No." Loki held his hand toward the chair next to him. "So sit down and tell me before Gabriel blows his Gods be damned horn."

Aiken's brow furrowed. He didn't, Loki noted, sit down. "I overheard you telling Azrael that you believed him that I am the traitor."

Loki blinked at him. "And?"

"I'm not."

"I know you aren't." Loki shrugged.

"Then why did you—?"

"To get him to shut the fuck up about it." Loki snapped. "He was pissing me off." He pointed at the chair again. Aiken, realizing that Loki wasn't lying to him, stepped toward the chair and pulled it out. "I already *told* you that I don't think it's you. Don't you think I'd have retracted that opinion to your face if I'd changed my mind?"

"But I thought—"

"You should know me well enough by now to know that I don't talk out of both sides of my face." Loki replied, rather tersely. "If I have something to say to you, I'm going to say it."

"Why would Azrael be saying that about me?" His voice quavered. Loki realized, all too acutely, that the idea that I would be spreading rumors about him had cut Aiken to the quick. "I genuinely liked him. I don't understand what I could have done to him to make him lie about me."

"I don't know." Loki looked over his shoulder to the back of the room where I was still hanging in the gallows to glare at me. I lowered my gaze, ashamed. "But you can damn well bet that I intend to find out."

-81-

Though I wasn't supposed to, I appeared in the space where Camael's missing pillow belonged and leaned over Metatron's lap to glare at Zadkiel. "You and I need to talk."

"About what?" Zadkiel asked, frowning at me. His eyes flew to our brother, whose own flaming gaze was flicking from one to the other of us with curious interest.

"About Emissary Darklief." I snapped, not caring that Metatron was overhearing us. I had no intention of saying anything that would put our game at risk.

"What about him." Zadkiel shrugged.

"You *know* what about him." I seethed.

Having made my declaration, I allowed that version of myself to disappear.

-82-

Loki and Aiken stood outside of Zadkiel's cottage, passing guarded, curious glances. I hadn't told them what Zadkiel had to say to them on Zadkiel's instruction. I had merely told them that Zadkiel would explain to them why I had been behaving the way I had.

"Meager." Aiken muttered under his breath.

"He *is* in exile." Loki sighed. "What do you think he has to tell us?"

"I know not." Aiken replied, his brow furrowing. His heart had been so heavy for so long that he wasn't certain that he could believe that this conversation could lead to anything good. Still, I had promised him that Zadkiel would give him an explanation as to my behavior. And he desperately wanted to know why I had accused him as I had.

When the door opened, Aiken started. He had only ever seen Zadkiel wearing the short skirt at court that showed off his deformity. Seeing him fully dressed, in his ankle length robes,

Aiken wasn't distracted and, for the first time, realized how utterly breathtaking my brother truly is.

"Lord Loki." Zadkiel hobbled backward, opening the door to them. "Emissary Darklief."

"Will you get in trouble if we come in?" Loki asked.

"Not if you make haste and aren't seen." Zadkiel muttered. "Please. Can I offer either of you a drink?"

"You can offer us the truth." Aiken sighed. "Azrael advised us that you would tell us why he was behaving so abhorrently."

"On my orders." Zadkiel replied as he shut the door behind him. "Let me get you that drink."

Loki nodded. As he did so, Zadkiel held his hand toward the kitchen. The two Gods exchanged another glance and then made their way in that direction.

As Loki looked upon Zadkiel's war room, as he saw the table with the well placed pawns and the walls black with Zadkiel's strategy, words between them were, suddenly, no longer required.

-83-

Zamyael slipped into the chair across the desk from Lord Loki, granting him a guarded smile. He had grown less and less willing to take her counsel since she and Ishitar's relationship had blossomed. She didn't blame him for this. She understood that he thought her overly cautious where the youngling's feelings were concerned.

"Zam," he sighed. "We have a problem."

"What problem?" she asked, her eyes trailing over his face. He wore an extremely serious expression that was completely unlike his general mood.

"My army is depleted." He advised her. "I have no more damned to offer up to Sappharon for war."

She felt her brow furrow. "I don't understand. Lucias has always told me that her basement is always full."

"It is when it isn't being ravaged." Loki shrugged. "And with this new system of free will, the damned are no longer, necessarily, being punished."

"What has that to do with me?"

Loki leveled his gaze upon her. Knowing that she wouldn't like what he had to say, I cringed as he simply told her, "Everything."

-84-

Camael opened the door to the cottage that he and Uriel shared with a rare smile. When he saw a God standing on the other side who was identical in face to his father, aside his hair and eyes, he froze.

He didn't need to be told that this man was Prince Ishitar.

His broad chest was bare and he wore a simple white linen shendyt which fell to his knees. His upper arms each bore gold bracelets in the shape of a serpent. Both had glittering emerald eyes. Around his neck he wore an ancient stone on a thick gold chain which Camael had once seen in King Noliminan's library. He knew it came from some distant world which was no longer in existence because King Noliminan had ruminated upon it one night when he was deep into his cups. As for his feet, these bore simple straps of black leather tied to black leather soles.

He was handsome and commanding. Camael's eyes nearly burned as they looked upon his glory.

He swallowed. "Your Royal Highness."

"Camael." His lips were drawn tight. "I apologize for coming unannounced. Lady Zamyael suggested you wouldn't be offended."

"I'm . . ." He shook his head. "No. I'm not."

"May I come in?"

"Please." He stepped back to open the door. He was at once grateful that Uriel was spending the day in service to King Noliminan. Signs of her were scattered throughout the cottage, but he doubted Prince Ishitar knew enough about her to recognize them as belonging to her. "May I offer you something?"

"A strong glass of wine will suit." He replied as his eyes darted around the small room. "This is very quaint."

"It fits me." Camael muttered as he walked to the tray where he kept his spirits. "I'm grateful to your father for allowing me my respite."

He turned to find Prince Ishtar watching him with guarded interest. His eyes were trailing over Camael's wings, which were the same color of navy blue as his eyes. His lips, which had been drawn tight moments before, were slack.

Forcing a smile, Camael handed the glass to the Prince of Providence.

"I wronged you Camael. I beg your forgiveness."

Camael started. Never in life had any one of his betters apologized to him for anything. He didn't know what to make of it now.

"Your Royal Highness." He swallowed. "It isn't necessary. You were only a babe in arms. You didn't—"

"My ignorance and my youth are no excuse for the humiliation I caused you." His tone was warm and his words were simple. Camael felt his mouth go dry. "I hope that you and I might work together with this behind us."

Camael was shocked by this apology from this particular God. It meant all the worlds to him. "It is accepted, Prince Ishitar."

"Thank you." Prince Ishitar reached forward, grasped his shoulder, and squeezed it. Camael shivered. "I remember your son. Vaguely. But I remember him."

Camael gave him a tight smile. He and Uriel were still grieving over the loss of Lasterian. It had been a devastating blow for them both.

"Will you tell me about him?"

His brow furrowed as he contemplated Prince Ishitar. Finally, he shook his head. "Forgive me, your Royal Highness. The loss of my son is raw to my heart. I cannot . . . Metatron and I have agreed that we will not speak of him with others for the nonce."

"Of course." His lips twitched. "Metatron is mighty. I shouldn't want to risk his wrath."

Camael laughed—actually laughed for the first time since Lasterian had died—at this. "Metatron *is* mighty."

This earned him Prince Ishitar's first honest and open smile. "Do you have a kings' board?"

"I am my father's son." Camael grinned at him. "And very adept at the game."

"It would please me to sit across from you and play." Prince Ishitar's voice was low and gentle. "If you will allow me the courtesy."

"Your Royal Highness," Camael swallowed the sheer joy at having been asked, "Courtesy is nowhere in it. I have ever loved the game."

-85-

My lips twitched as Zadkiel's plan fell into place. Ishitar was distracted, as he sat across from Camael, with plotting how best to extract information about Lasterian from him.

Though it had taken some argument, Loki had convinced Zamyael to plant the story in Ishitar's mind that the late Lasterian had hidden a weapon. This weapon, she told him, could end the war by shifting the balance of magic. Unfortunately, she explained, Tristan had run mad. Thus, she was having a hard time convincing him to betray Lasterian confidence and hand over the weapon for her use.

This ploy worked due to two of Noliminan's greatest failings. And due to Ishitar's youth and ignorance.

The first was that Noliminan had known that Zamyael had taken Ishitar to her breast when he was a babe. He knew Zamyael's nature well enough to believe that, given this, Zamyael would never do anything to betray the young Prince. What he did not realize—and what Lord Loki had eventually used to convince her—was that her loathing for Noliminan, himself, was equal in strength to her love for the boy.

It wasn't Ishitar she was lying to, Lord Loki had convinced her. With Ishitar, they were merely playing at kings' castles. A game that Ishitar loved.

It was Noliminan who they were deceiving. And it was Noliminan whose villages they meant to destroy.

Noliminan's second failing, and Ishitar's ignorance, came into play in regard to Lucias' most important rule of the game: mind the board, mind the moves, but never forget to concentrate on the face of the player opposite you.

Noliminan's undoing was his injustice and his ego. Remember, Lucias' instruction had ever been to keep your eyes on the face of your enemy. Zadkiel's was a face that Noliminan never bothered to take the time to see.

As for Ishitar, who had been taught the game by Zadkiel, he should have known better.

Then again, when Zadkiel and Ishitar sat across one another at the kings' board, Zadkiel almost always let Ishitar win.

-86-

I shared Ishitar's apology with Zadkiel. How could I not?

It was evidence that the pair of us had done something right; that he could be returned to the boy we loved.

A simple afternoon of conversation and games with Ishitar had salved Camael's most profound wounds.

It could not be denied that Ishitar had intended to gain something by this exchange, but bringing someone he had wronged comfort brought about peace in his own heart all the same. I knew that if he could feel guilty over the pain he had caused Camael, then he could be made to see he was also wronging Lord Loki and Sappharon.

"It's time." Zadkiel muttered as he raised his gaze to meet mine. "Are our allies ready?"

"We've all been waiting for you." I shrugged.

"It's a risky move that could leave us all exposed." Zadkiel considered the tiles of his kitchen floor. After a long moment, he raised his gaze to meet mine. "But I believe that it is time we make the final play."

Who was I, as I looked upon a white wall which was black with written strategy, to disagree?

-87-

"He's been . . ." She looked as though she had been slapped. "Sappharon! You lie!"

"Zamyael," Sappharon rolled her eyes. "You know better than this. I caught him sneaking off through the bridging Halls!"

"But he's—"

"A traitor." Sappharon hissed at her, fighting back a grin. "If he would betray Loki, what makes you believe that he would be loyal to the likes of you?"

They were, of course, discussing the supposed turncoat, Emissary Darklief, in their haughty tones.

"He's just young." Zamyael sighed.

"Perhaps. But he's been betraying Loki all the same." I could tell that it pained her not to grin. But Sappharon was made for this game. "And, perhaps, I can concede, he did so only because he believes this to be some cosmic game."

"Damn Noliminan's hide."

I had to turn away from Ishitar, who I was forced to always follow. I couldn't hide my smile. Both women were just too damn good at playing their parts. Their expressions and tones were convincing beyond measure.

"How do we temper the youngling?" Zamyael asked. "He won't listen to any of us. I thought he saw Loki's way of reasoning, but . . ." She appeared to be extremely wounded. "It would seem he doesn't."

"You lecherous traitor!" Lord Loki's voice boomed after Emissary Darklief's body, which came sprawling into the room where the women stood. "You serve the King of Lords? After all I have done for you?"

"I . . . I . . ." Aiken stammered. His body was literally shaking.

"If Sappharon hadn't warned me about you, then you would have delivered the weapon to the King of Lords!"

"Loki, calm yourself." Zamyael begged.

"A weapon that could end us all!" Lord Loki yelled and kicked at Aiken.

Hard.

I cried out from where I stood beside Ishitar, though no one heard me. Except, of course, Ishitar. And my reaction, which I understood at once had been the point, only served to feed into his belief that this drama playing before us was real.

"Loki!" Zamyael cried. "Please! You know that he loves you. Cleary he does! But this rebellion has been draining upon us all! You must remember how heavily burdened he must be right now."

"Then perhaps it's time that we bring an end to that which ails him." Lord Loki snapped.

I blinked. I almost believed the drama that was playing out before me. The other actors were just that good.

"But how? He's . . ."

"Where's Zadkiel?" Lord Loki's eyes blazed. "It's time that we force him to join the war."

"Never!" The cry was issued by Ishitar as he stepped out of the shadows where he had been hiding. "Zadkiel will never betray Noliminan as you cowards have! There is nothing that you could offer him to convince him!"

"And just who the fuck are you, anyway?" Lord Loki seethed. "Another one of Noliminan's Gods be damned spies?" He turned to Aiken and kicked him again. "A spy who thinks you can win?" Lord Loki turned upon Ishitar, ratcheting up his outrage. "You and this piece of dung?"

Emissary Darklief was forced to endure another kick. I frowned at Lord Loki. He seemed to be enjoying kicking Aiken far too much for my tastes. No one was supposed to actually get hurt.

"Take him if you wish. As for Zadkiel, he's already been taken prisoner and is at our base even now to be used for *our* gain!"

The blood drained from Ishitar's face, though I could tell he wasn't certain what to believe. He stepped toward Emissary Darklief, held out his hand and then pulled him to his feet.

I followed them as they disappeared into nothingness and appeared again before Zadkiel's cabin. Ishitar ran from room to room—not that there were many to search—until the truth of Lord Loki's words hit him.

Zadkiel, who was busy with seeing to his part of the plan, was nowhere to be found.

-88-

Aiken had sensed from the moment that he and Prince Ishitar appeared before the sparse cabin that the Price of Providence was a young man about to come undone. He feared, wrongly, that Zadkiel was in danger. Still, there was a plan that they needed to follow. Not to mention that they were acting on the orders of a kings' castles master who had yet to steer them wrong.

Even now, Jami was breaking into the King of Lords' apartment at Loki's request that he play his part in this game. Jamiason, you see, had been ordered to set all of the explosives around the place and to draw my brother, Barkiel, away from his post as guard at the entrance to the passageway that leads to where Lady Lucias slumbered.

Was it the right thing to do? Countenance's shadows would tell.

The only matter which weighed heavy upon Aiken, at the moment, was drawing the King of Lords out so that Jamiason could see to his tasks in peace. Given Jami was at great risk, Aiken put his mind completely to the task at hand.

"Is Zadkiel gone?" He wanted to hear Prince Ishitar confirm it.

Prince Ishitar falling to his knees was confirmation enough.

"If they have him, they will force him to the King of Lords' apartment. They will try to use him to destroy him!" Aiken repeated the script he had practiced forlornly. "Aiming to strike at the heart of the King of Lords by destroying his very home. The King of Lords will never forgive Zadkiel for that. Be it his plan or not."

"This is my fault." Prince Ishitar leveled his gaze upon Aiken. His light brown eyes were blazing with pain. Yet, chillingly, his demeanor was calm. "I could have protected Zadkiel." He swallowed and winced. "I could have protected my father."

"You still have time." Aiken snapped at him, truly frustrated. Countenance's shadows came very swift when the task at hand was of vast importance.

Prince Ishitar stood up, his back immediately straightening as though he had never shown any display at all.

In fact, he seemed far too determined for Aiken's liking.

"I know what I have to do," he proclaimed.

Aiken didn't care for the tone that darkened these words.

-89-

As Aiken was seeing to the task of distracting Prince Ishitar, Jamiason, who had set the necessary explosions where they belonged, began roaming the King of Lords' abode. He opened every door, every cabinet, but disturbed not a single thing.

Until, that was, he was in the King of Lords' bedchamber.

Jamison, who had spent his entire mortal life hiding from others and being wary of his surroundings lest he be murdered, heard the faint sound of a whistle coming from the direction of one of the walls. It was so subtle that it should have been missed.

Jamiason, turned that way to contemplate it. Yet, there was nothing there but a wall.

A wall, he saw, which was covered with one of the tapestries woven by the mischief fairies in the Oakland Grove.

"Coincidence?" He asked himself. "Or a sign?"

Having ever been Lady Moira's puppet, Jamiason didn't believe in coincidence.

He stepped toward the tapestry and reached for its edges. He allowed the silky thread of it to run through his fingers. As he did so, he felt a cold breath of wind upon his bare feet.

"Clever." He muttered as he pulled the tapestry away.

Behind it was a passageway. Jamiason looked over his shoulder before slipping within.

On light feet which made no sound, Jamiason walked down the length of the dark corridor. His heart was beating wildly in his chest. He had the better sense to be terrified. The Gods alone knew what he would find at the end of this path.

What he did find, he was unprepared for.

At what appeared to be a jointed elbow of the corridor was a well lit room. Hiding himself in the shadows, he peered within and bit his tongue lest he make even the slightest of sounds.

In the center of the room was a raised pedestal upon which lay a feathered bed. Upon the bed rested the most beautiful of all Ladies. She lay sleeping with an expression which was frozen in a mixture of horror and surprise. And at her side, looking upon her with what could only be described as utter adoration, sat the King of Lords.

Jamiason stole into the shadows. If he were not careful, he would lose what was left of his waning senses.

Uncertain what he should do now that he found the truth which he sought, Jamiason leaned forward again so he could stare at the pair.

Until, that was, he felt someone grasping his arm.

He nearly screamed out. But another hand wrapped around his mouth as he was pulled back into the shadows and carried, fighting, down the corridor toward the apartment from which he had come. It wasn't until he and his assailant were on the other side of the tapestry that he was let go.

"You damn fool." The archangel, Barkiel, hissed at him. "Why are you lurking down dark halls? And, after having seen the painful truth of things, why on which moon would you linger?"

He looked upon the strangely beautiful archangel and twisted his tongue as Loki had ordered.

"What is wrong with him?" He asked of Lady Lucias.

"He slumbers." Barkiel spat, showing how little he knew of what lay beyond in yonder room. "Nothing more."

He believes that the Lady Regent is still a Lord. And he believes that she slumbers at the King of Lords' will.

Which was, precisely, what Loki had predicted.

"Heed me, demon. You cannot say a word of this! Not even to Emissary Darklief."

"But—"

"King Noliminan will level you if you spill his secrets!" Barkiel advised him. "Mind me now."

"I cannot hide this from Aiken." He advised the archangel. "Not for overlong."

"You needn't." He assured him. "Not for overlong."

Jamiason shook his head, frustrated. He loathed the politics of the Heavens and the Hells. Even more than he had ever loathed life in the Grove. There was more prejudice and betrayal here than ever he had experienced in his mortal life. At least in the Grove he knew who was his enemy and who was his friend.

Barkiel, at least, hadn't given him away. Probably due to some fealty he felt he owed to his father. Jamiason was, by extension, just another of Lucias' servants as far as Barkiel was concerned.

"Go." Barkiel urged him. "Return to Emissary Darklief. Tell him you found nothing."

"I will return to Aiken." Jamiason agreed. "But I shan't lie to him. I will merely tell him I found you here as if baring my way."

There wasn't going to be an opportunity for the lie and Jamiason knew it. The walls of the King of Lords' house shook around them with such violence that they were swept off their feet. Jamiason managed to extricate himself from Barkiel's grip whilst the rock structure began raining down upon them.

He was on the right side of the path to see to his freedom when all was soot and ashes.

-90-

"I have an idea as to how we can save Zadkiel." Prince Ishitar told Aiken.

"What idea?"

"We must awaken Lady Lucias." Prince Ishitar advised him. "She will speak with my father. She will convince him that Zadkiel was a pawn in this game."

"But how?"

"I'm not certain if it will work." Prince Ishitar admitted. "But if we were to rescue Zadkiel, perhaps he could use his magic to will her awake."

"His magic was never meant to preserve life!" Aiken laughed. Things were moving precisely in the direction that Azrael had told them they would. "It has ever been to take it!"

"How do you know?" Prince Ishitar asked. "Isn't it, at least, worth a try?"

"If you say so." Aiken shook his head. "But how will you rescue him? If he is Sappharon's prisoner, then he is most likely locked away in one of the cells in the castle at Anticata."

"By sheer force if this is the option which is left to me."

Aiken turned his head away as he bit back his smile.

-91-

Stealing into Anticata to find Zadkiel was going to be a nightmare, Aiken knew. But Azrael had instructed him that his part in this ploy was to follow whatever plan Prince Ishitar set. It was two more shifts of Countenances shadow before they actually stood in the small alcove where Lady Lucias had bidden her time in a private room at the castle.

Zadkiel was under false guard and their first attempt to take him failed.

As did many others.

He couldn't make it easy for Prince Ishitar, you see, lest the boy grow suspicious.

-92-

While Emissary Darklief and Ishitar were attempting to catch Zadkiel, I materialized at Noliminan's home and advised Barkiel that I had seen Jamiason back to the Hells where he belonged.

Barkiel was relieved by this news. "And Lucias still slumbers?"

"Lucias does." I muttered. "Where is Noliminan?"

"Still with Lucias." Barkiel pointed his chin to the tapestry.

I nodded at him and made my way to the alcove as quickly as I could. There was little time left to tie the loose ends of our plans.

"Your Grace?" He turned to face me. His expression was one of cold fury. "Barkiel has secured the hall leading to Lady Lucias."

"You are certain?" His lips thinned.

I confess, now, that I did something to Barkiel then that I have never done to any of my siblings before and will never do again under any circumstance: I betrayed him.

"He found a demon wandering around your bedchamber." I couldn't look at him. "He didn't seem to be anything more than curious so Barkiel sent him away."

"The Gods damn him!" Noliminan threw the book he was holding across the room. It slid across his bar, smashing bottles of spirits to the floor. The entire room flooded with their contents, staining the marble and bringing about an unpleasant stench that took hours of scrubbing to remove. "The demon could have led us directly to Sappharon!"

"There will be time to deal with Barkiel's stupidity later, your Grace." I swallowed, loathing myself for having gotten Barkiel into trouble. "You must go after Sappharon now. Before she has time to secure the castle on Anticata."

The lines of his face smoothed. "Stay with her until I return."

"As you will me."

I was relieved. And extremely proud of Zadkiel's ability to reason. This was precisely what he had predicted Noliminan would do.

Lady Moira must have been blessing us that day because Noliminan disappeared scarcely a flicker of a shadow before Prince Ishitar appeared with a hog-tied Zadkiel.

I really thought this last bit fitting and may have even laughed in a different situation. As it was, there was nothing funny to me about what was taking place.

Zadkiel continued to squirm and harp until I gave him the barest of nods. This had been a signal that we had agreed upon discussing the details of our plans. It was my way of telling him that Noliminan had breached the Anticata castle's walls.

Ishitar, satisfied that we would see to the task that he had set us to after we had made him our promises, dismissed himself to find his father.

When he was gone, Zadkiel stepped toward the podium upon which Lucias lay and braced himself as he looked down upon our father wearing his woman's face. It was the first time that Zadkiel had seen this face. Because of this, I understood that he needed to collect himself.

What he needed and what he had time for were two separate things, however.

"Zadkiel." I tried not to rush or admonish him. "We've the barest of shifts."

He raised his gaze and gave me a guarded smile. "I didn't expect her to be so beautiful."

"Nor did I when I first looked upon her face." I admitted. "But you can reflect upon her profile later. For the nonce, you must see to her waking."

Nodding, he returned his attention to his task.

To our surprise, Zadkiel was successful in awakening Lucias on the first pass of his fingers across her brow. The relief that passed through us both was immeasurable.

Until, that was, we realized that she awoke as a broken thing; a dragon born without wings.

This is one eventuality that Zadkiel hadn't considered.

And he was forced to face it now. We had to bring her back to herself before Noliminan and Ishitar returned. We both knew that there was only one option left to us which might, as close as we were coming to seeing our plans through, save our hides.

I wasted no time in seeking out Lord Loki at his desk, where he sat waiting for news. He held the Gods be damned Tome he had no business reading in his hands. His brow was furrowed with distracted interest as his eyes flicked over the symbols within.

"My Lord?"

He cried out and slammed the book shut. His purple eyes grew wide as he looked upward. "Damn it, Azrael. Must you lurk? You frightened me!"

"Perhaps we shouldn't be reading books which aren't meant for our eyes?" I snapped.

I was less than thrilled that, while we risked our necks, he was attempting to sate his curiosity over something that he had no business concerning himself with.

"Why are you here?" Embarrassed, he looked away. "Has it gone wrong?"

He spoke of Zadkiel's plan of course.

"Lucias needs your aide."

This garnered his immediate attention. He flew to his feet and reached across the desk to grip my hand so tightly that I thought he might break the bones of it. When he released me he asked, "How might I help her?"

"Come with me." I lowered my gaze lest he see that he had hurt me. I knew this hadn't been his intent. "I will bring you to her."

"At once."

Gingerly holding his hand, I willed us to the secret room where Lucias had been kept before she had been awakened.

The barest shift of the shadows that her eyes fell upon him, a spark of recognition flared within them. As for Lord Loki, having never seen her true face before, he stood exalted at her side.

"Oh, my Lady."

"My Lord." She whispered. "My . . . love?"

He swallowed. I watched his larynx twitch as he did so and smiled. He understood the problem at once and was deciding how he would respond to her confusion.

"Loki." He replied in hoarse tones. He wanted to be her love. He wanted it desperately. But he would not force the idea upon her. My respect for him was immeasurable in that moment given I understood he could make it be so with a single word. "My name is Loki. And, yes. I do love you."

"Yes." She smiled up at him. "Loki. You *do* love me. And I love you." She turned to look at me. I finally saw clarity within her dark eyes and was relieved beyond measure. "I remember now. Not everything. But enough."

As I had prayed that she would when she looked upon his face.

"Tell me, Zadkiel." She released Lord Loki's hands and turned toward my brother. "I beg you. Forget what might or might not become of you personally. I must know. For the sake of every other soul. Please. Tell me everything that has happened since I lost my reason."

Lucias, you see, had not obeyed the rules of her son's exile. As a result she, like each and every member of the Quorum, had lost her fair share of rounds of the game of kings' castles to Zadkiel.

She knew better than anyone that Zadkiel was one of the very few in existence who could claim to have bested her.

-93-

It was Ishitar who saw her first. He turned his gaze to the door of his father's library—where they had retired so that they might discuss the fact that they had been unable to locate Sappharon at the castle in Anticata—as he heard the knob turning so it might open.

When he saw his mother's face, he froze.

"What in the name of my Thirty Hells have you done?" She seethed.

Noliminan flew his gaze in her direction and found his feet. "Luci! Tukte lolo!"

"You carvetek mouk!" She cried. "All that has transpired! What have you been thinking?"

He went to her. He tried to take her in his arms but she pushed him away. "My goal was to make them see reason!"

"Reason that I was *wrong*!" She admonished him.

"You don't understand!"

"No, Noliminan." She agreed, her eyes darting to Ishitar. "I don't understand." Her gaze returned to Noliminan. "So put an end to your Gods be damned game of kings' castles, tukte 'aasifa. And let us see if we can find reason with one and another on the other side."

-94-

Every sky in every world was littered with Gods, angels and demons at battle after the King of Lords broke the barrier that held his army from entering Anticata. Brothers, sisters, mothers and fathers all fought one against the other in an exponential explosion as soul met soul.

Seemingly from out of nowhere, in the center of all skies in existence, came a bright and brilliant presence born of a violent, tawny light.

And from this presence spread stillness and peace.

Every warrior on every side fell still.

The bodies, for many cycles of the sun, littered each and every one of the inhabited worlds.

Mine was the last to fall.

-95-

And I, for whatever cruel reason, was the first to rise.

My mind was spinning and my legs were unsteady as I rose. I stood in Noliminan's library, which was where the conversation I had witnessed between my betters had taken place. The peace that I momentarily felt by inhabiting only one space and time was utterly destroyed as my essence exploded around me and ubiquity overtook me.

Only one moment where I was merely one version of Azrael. But that one moment has carried me through antiquity.

They sat in their chairs, looking at one another, all three seemingly at peace with whatever decisions they had come to.

Yet, I realized, almost at once, that my beloved Ishitar had changed.

His eyes trailed over me while the other two merely stared at one another. They were filled with great sorrow and even greater regret.

Had we been alone, I sensed that he would have tried to speak with me. As it was, I turned to Noliminan as he issued his command. "Take her to the Thirteenth level. Lock her up. And speak not a word as to her essence to anyone."

Frowning, I turned my gaze to Lucias. She was standing by then, granting me a guarded smile. She assured me that this is what they all agreed to and that she had earned whatever punishment Noliminan deemed appropriate. Knowing she had been sleeping throughout the entire rebellion, I failed to see how this could even remotely be the case.

But I am an archangel, as Ishitar has pointed out. Not a God. It was not my place to question my betters.

As such, I did as I was bid.

-96-

As I left with Lucias, the version of me which was forced to stand beside Ishitar heard him excuse himself to pass water. I followed him into his bedchamber and watched with guarded interest as he locked the door. When he was certain we had our privacy, he turned to me wearing a guarded smile.

I still hadn't truly spoken with him since he had put me in my place. Rather than doing so now, I crossed my arms over my chest and pursed my lips, waiting for him to be the one to say the first word.

Eventually, he did.

"Azrael . . . I . . ."

I shifted nervously from one foot to the other. But I held my tongue. He had hurt me. As his servant I would have forgiven him. As someone who thought of themselves as his parent, he owed me an apology.

"My mother is so very different from my father." He lowered his gaze. "Wrong, too. I think. But trying to be right."

He was seeking my advice. I couldn't give it to him. Not until he apologized to me.

"Their argument was violent." He shivered. "It frightened me."

I let out a long, low breath.

He raised his gaze to look at me. His brow was furrowed and his eyes were studying my face. "Why aren't you speaking with me?"

"I believe that your last words to me were that I can't possibly understand the politics of the Gods." I admonished him. "That I must mind my damn station lest you mind it for me." He flinched. "So what advice could I possibly have to offer you that won't sully your Gods be damned ears?"

Frowning, he lowered his gaze. "I apologize. That was uncalled for."

His apology was under a whoosh of breath and made with the annoyance a child bears when having to respect his elders.

"I understand." I relaxed slightly, mollified and most desperately willing to accept any words of sorrow as long as they issued from his lips. "You were with your father. It is what you always wanted."

He nodded and met my gaze. "Who is right, Azrael?"

"I cannot answer that question for you." I sighed. "You have to decide that for yourself."

"But you can tell me which side you stand on." He entreated.

"No." I advised him. "I can't." I reached for his hand and squeezed it. "If you want to know who is right, then you must walk among the people and see the inequities for what they are. No one can tell you which of your parents are right. Or even if either one of them are. You have to decide what you believe on your own."

He sighed and nodded. He understood what I was telling him to be true. "Perhaps it is time that I begin my studies amongst the Quorum."

"Perhaps." I agreed.

"Come." He held out his hand. "Everyone will be waking soon. He will call them to Council. So I must return to my Da. If, that is," he smiled wanly, "Zadkiel will allow me into our cabin."

"Zadkiel loves you, Ishy." I assured him. I was smiling stupidly but I cared not a wit. Our son was at last returned to us and my heart was singing louder than any trumpet that Gabriel would ever be able to blow.

"Do you think he'll make me a pie?"

"What flavor?" I grinned. This was a game we had long played when trying to reconcile after a fight.

"Shaweet potato, shaweet heart." He winked at me.

Laughing, I threw myself toward him and let him take me in his arms.

-97-

Metatron lowered himself onto his pillow in his waiting stance and watched as the Gods and Goddesses of the Council stumbled in. They were all still wearing their battle gear and clearly as disoriented as Metatron, himself, was.

When Zadkiel reached his pillow, Metatron stood to help him lower himself to the ground. He gave Metatron a grateful smile and leaned toward him once he was on his knees. "Ishitar has come home to me."

Metatron smiled at him. "On his own accord?"

"Ta." Zadkiel nodded as he watched Michael lower himself to his pillow and then returned his attention to Metatron. He was so beautiful when he smiled that Metatron was helpless but to reach for his hair and let it run through his fingers. "And apologetic for behaving poorly."

Metatron chuckled. "I'm glad to hear this."

"We're having dinner this evening." Zadkiel looked down the line of his brothers and sisters. "Everyone is welcome."

"I appreciate your happiness, Zad." Michael muttered. "But I have a feeling that not a one of us are going to be in a partying mood after Noliminan's seen done with us."

Metatron sighed. He loved his brother. He truly did. But why did Michael always have to dampen the mood? He was right, of course. This was not going to be a light hearted Council. Still, Zadkiel deserved to have his Gods be damned moment of joy.

It was a rare enough occurrence.

King Noliminan entered the Great Hall and they all fell silent. At his heel was Raphael, who kept his gaze lowered as he darted past the thrones and lowered himself to his pillow. His wrists, ankles and wings were bound in bandages where the nails had been driven within them. When Michael reached for his hand to bring him comfort, he pulled it violently away and turned to glare at Michael with so much loathing that it broke Metatron's heart.

Michael, taking no offense, gave Raphael an understanding smile and withdrew his hand. Raphael looked down the line of his brothers and sisters and then returned his gaze to the hands folded upon his lap.

"Michael." King Noliminan snapped.

Michael gave Metatron a terrified frown and then rose to his feet. He went to their Lord and Master and fell upon one knee before him. Metatron watched with mounting horror as Michael paled and his black eyes widened. As he stood, he looked toward the Quorum before bowing to King Noliminan and backing away and out of the room.

When he was gone, King Noliminan stood.

The silence that beat through the Great Hall was deafening. The faces of the Gods were set and strained. Even Lord Loki, who was always in good cheer, sat silent at Emissary Darklief's side, his expression drawn and heavy.

"Look around you." King Noliminan ordered them as he found his podium. "See the price of your discontentment." He swept his hand back to the thrones, three of which remained empty. "Lady Raguel has been expired. Lucias has been imprisoned." He returned his gaze to the Council. "Lady Raziel will return, though I know not in what capacity at this moment in time."

Everyone exchanged glances. Eyes fell on the many empty chairs of those Gods whose involvement in the war could not be denied. That Emissary Darklief and Lord Loki were sitting in the Council was, Metatron knew, by the hand of Lucias. They had been as involved, or more so, than anyone else. Yet they had obviously managed to be covert enough that their loyalties could not be directly called into question.

Turning his gaze to the door, King Noliminan called out, "Michael. Bring her in."

The door opened and Michael slipped in. At his side stood Sappharon, her face pale and her lips trembling. Metatron felt himself rise on his knees, so that he was no longer in his waiting stance, as Michael guided her to stand directly before the podium. She was terrified. And Metatron understood, all too well, that she had good reason to be so.

"You are to be put in your place, Sappharon." King Noliminan growled at her. "You are to be taken by every male of this court. Then I shall relieve you of your forked tongue."

Sappharon's eyes grew wide. She began to weep; albeit in silence. Metatron found himself rising to his feet. Michael began shaking his head violently at his brother, but this only served to draw attention to Metatron.

"Since we apparently have a volunteer," King Noliminan seethed as his eyes narrowed upon Metatron, "my selection of who it is to start your humiliation has been made an easy one."

"No." Metatron whispered. "Please. I cannot volunteer." He swallowed and looked away. "Nor will I bear witness to this."

King Noliminan cocked his head slightly. "I am issuing you a direct order, Metatron. Do not disobey me."

"Your Grace, I can't." Metatron heard the begging quality to his own tone. "She's my—!"

"Yes?" King Noliminan seethed. "She's your what? Exactly?"

"Sister." Lord Loki stood. Metatron found his eyes flying to him. "Though not by Lord Regent Lucias' seed, she was still made from him. It isn't right that it be Metatron or any other of the male members of your Quorum who claims her virginity."

"Stay out of this, Loki." King Noliminan warned. "You are a breath away from joining your Master in his cell. Now is not the time for your interference."

"I wish not to interfere, your Grace." Lord Loki swallowed and looked around himself. "She would be further humiliated if it were me to steal her maidenhood. She loathes me. You know she does. And I wish to prove my supplication to you." Lord Loki flicked his eyes to Sappharon. Metatron saw no animosity there. Nor did he see any desire. "Let me serve you in this."

Sappharon spun to look upon him. Her eyes were wide with their pleading. Even more confusing to Metatron, they were filled with her gratitude.

King Noliminan smiled cruelly at him. "As you will it, Loki. Have her lift her skirt. And let us see for ourselves what is so special about your Gods be damned beard."

Lord Loki's eyes darted to Sappharon. Having sex with her had been one thing. Seeing to her pleasure with his tongue was something else all together. That particular act was one that very few men admitted to enjoying, even if they did so in the privacy of their own beds. It was complete supplication to a female and it was belittling to a man's masculinity.

Not, Metatron knew, that it was to Lord Loki. His tongue was almost as famous as his beard if one were to believe the squawking of the geese who made up his gaggle.

Metatron found his gaze meeting Sappharon's, swallowing as her lips thinned. She gave him a nod, which was nearly imperceptible. It was her way of telling him she would bear this with her head held high.

Maybe. But Metatron would not.

He stormed away from his pillow and toward the door. Consequences be damned. He wasn't going to watch Lord Loki defile the mother of his child.

He couldn't stop it. He knew that. But he didn't have to bear witness to it.

When he reached the door, he found it locked to him. He pulled upon it but it wouldn't budge. Understanding that he was not going to be allowed to leave, he spun on his heel to find King Noliminan glaring at him.

"Very well, Metatron." King Noliminan seethed. "Given your sensibilities, I will give you what you want." Metatron felt his eyes grow wide. "Sappharon will be spared her humiliation." His lips curled into a tight grin. "And you shall take her place."

"Your Grace, no!" Michael cried. "You can't—!"

"Silence Michael." He rounded upon Metatron's brother. "Or you will join Loki in the taking of him."

Michael, paling, shook his head and backed away.

"I couldn't possibly." Lord Loki's voice was a hoarse whisper. "I couldn't physically."

"I said he was to ride your damned beard, Loki." King Noliminan grinned at him. "Your ability to forge your iron at the fire very obviously has little and less to do with the ability to flick your Gods be damned tongue."

"Mayhap not." Lord Loki's tone was tight. "But Metatron would never. Not with another man. His ability to forge his iron is very clearly the point."

Metatron watched with cold detachment as King Noliminan raised his hand and flicked his fingers in Lord Loki's direction. At his command, Lord Loki's essence changed.

And dear Gods, Metatron thought, *but you do make a horrifically ugly woman.*

Even the damn beard remained.

But, then, that was the point. Wasn't it.

None of this had anything to do with Metatron. No more than it was about Sappharon. King Noliminan, upon Lord Loki's insistence that it be he who put Sappharon in her place, had found a way to humiliate the one God in the court who he despised above all others.

"Your Grace, please!" Sappharon cried. "I shall see to Metatron! There is no need for—!"

"Silence!" He roared turning toward her and raising his hand to flick it at her. "As for you, from this moment forward, your lips are ever sealed!"

Her eyes grew wide as she flew her hands to her mouth. Metatron, who had heard these words before, cried out in despair. The last time they had been uttered, they had been more precise and directed at Camael. Metatron knew it wasn't merely her mouth which would never again open.

"She has to eat!" Lord Loki cried.

"No." King Noliminan shook his head. "She doesn't."

Lord Loki was about to argue the point further, but Sappharon stopped him. She flew to her knees and held her hands upward, grasped together in a pleading gesture as she began crawling toward him. If he kept talking—if he kept arguing with King Noliminan—the plight of all three of them would only escalate.

Understanding her silent plea, Lord Loki swallowed, gave her an almost imperceptible nod and then fell on his knees. Once on the ground, he turned toward Metatron and held open his arms.

Dear Gods . . . Lord Loki . . . Why?

He couldn't answer that question now. He would have to ask Lord Loki directly when there was time and the pair of them were alone. For now, understanding that—despite the disdain that lived between Lord Loki and Sappharon—Lord Loki was willing to take Sappharon's punishment was enough.

I will pay you back for protecting my Lady, Lord Loki. It is a solemn vow and a heartfelt promise. When the time comes that I may, I will pay you back.

Knowing that there was nothing else for it if some semblance of an end could ever come to the drama that was unfolding before them, Metatron rose himself to his full height and stepped, with his back straight, toward Lord Loki.

Unable to bear this humiliation while looking down upon the atrocity that was Lord Loki as a woman, his forced himself to stare at the only soul he had ever taken to his bed. Imagining her lips around him, looking deep into her blazing eyes, he buried himself in old memories he had long ago tried to deny.

And thank all the Gods that are or ever were that he was able.

Because, the Heavens help them all if this humiliating farce didn't play itself out in exactly the manner that King Noliminan insisted it must within his own mind.

456

-98-

Loki sat in his bathing pool shivering. His disgust and his humiliation were more than he could bear.

He would find a way to pay Noliminan back for this atrocity. He vowed this to himself as he spat handful after handful of water out of his mouth in his attempt to void his tongue of the charcoal taste of Metatron and his seed.

He only hoped that word regarding what he was forced to do would never reach Lady Lucias' ears.

It was a hope, he understood all to painfully, which was utterly in vain.

-99-

Ishitar listened to Zadkiel and I—both of us very clearly enraged—recount the events of the Council with a furrowed brow. Hearing about the brutality of what had taken place was confusing to him.

He didn't understand why Lord Loki had volunteered to take Metatron's place as far as raping Sappharon went. Nor did he understand why Lord Loki finally supplicated to his father's will. Yet, he understood even less why an entire Council of Gods would sit in silence to watch these horrific events play themselves out.

He posed the questions to me because, knowing everyone's mind as I do, I was bound to have the answers.

"What was the Council to do?" I sighed. "He was demonstrating his power over everyone. If Lucias can be captured and her demon can be defiled and defaced before us all, what chance do any of the rest of us have in taking a stand against him. Look to how Lord Loki and Metatron fared for their interference."

"But Loki . . ." He shook his head. "Why would he volunteer? Why would he put himself in harm's way?"

"He rose because he loves her." Zadkiel's tone was low and respectful. "He rose to prevent Metatron from being forced to rape her. And he supplicated because it is what Sappharon begged him to do."

Ishitar felt his eyes roll closed as his mind began to turn. He had listened to his mother and father argue over many things. And Loki was one of those. He was beginning, he thought, to understand why. Not only did his mother have feelings for Loki, the God was also someone who was willing to take a stand when the taking of a stand was required.

"He knew the barest moment that Metatron voiced his dissention what your father would do." I agreed. "Though he miscalculated in his understanding as to how Metatron would react, playing into Noliminan's hand." My lips grew tight. "If Metatron wouldn't have acted, the worst that would have happened would have been Lord Loki taking Sappharon with his tongue. As it was . . ." I shrugged. "Metatron forced Noliminan's hand."

"You must understand that Lord Loki is very adept at the game of kings' castles when playing on an even board." Zadkiel added. "He's very clever. He merely miscalculated Metatron's love for Sappharon. An easy enough error to make given they pretend to loathe one another."

"What choice do they have?" I grumbled. "Noliminan will destroy them both if he learns how deeply their love runs."

"Yet not knowing, Loki stood up for Sappharon?" Ishitar asked us.

"Ta." I nodded. "Lord Loki did what he thought was right. What he thought would protect Sappharon and Metatron both."

"He's like my mother." Ishitar observed. "Only not enamored by my father."

"Your mother with a conscience." I corrected him. "This is Lord Loki to the very soul. He shares her ideals but he will always temper them with what is right rather than what he wants. And he will always defend those who would be punished for naught."

"He would speak her words if allowed?" Ishitar asked, his mind ticking with an idea that had been formulating since the moment he began watching his mother and father's violence toward one another explode during their arguments. "If my father would listen to him? He would stand against him?"

I snorted. "As if he ever would."

"Lord Loki would be decimated if he were to even try." Zadkiel reminded Ishitar. "He's clever. But he's not powerful. Certainly he isn't strong enough to stand up to Noliminan!"

"Of course he isn't." Ishitar muttered and stood. "Zadkiel?"

"Yes, min 'lasupita?" Zadkiel looked up at him with quiet interest burning in his golden eyes.

"May I borrow your kitchen?" He asked.

"Of course." Zadkiel shrugged. "It's your kitchen as well." His eyes narrowed as he gave Ishitar a thin smile. "Why?"

"No reason." He replied, forcing himself to smile in response. "I merely mean to make myself a pie."

Zadkiel snorted at that, but he grinned. "Let me know when it all goes wrong, why don't you?"

Ishitar nodded at him absentmindedly and then left us both to travel to Eden. After picking a bushel of ripe gourds from his father's 'ridiculously stupid fruit tree', as Lucias was fond of calling it, Ishitar returned to Zadkiel's cottage and set about the task of making his very first pie.

-100-

Samyael opened the door and froze. Standing on the other side was a most handsome man. His long brown hair fell in gentle waves over his bare, bronzed chest and his light brown eyes danced with curiosity over Samyael's features. He wore a simple white linen shendyt, which fell to his knees. Other than that, he wore very little else at all. Even his feet were bare.

Camael would have marked at once that he had lost the jewelry which had once adorned him and questioned his new, simplistic manner of dress. Given this was the first time Samyael had ever laid eyes upon him, however, he was unaware of the change.

"Samyael." Prince Ishitar greeted. His tone was gentle. "I've heard much about you."

Samyael swallowed and lowered his gaze to the pie in the young God's hand. His brow furrowed at the strangeness of it as he raised his gaze. "My Lord. I fear you have me at the disadvantage."

"I think not." He smiled softly at him. Samyael gave him an embarrassed smile. "Is Loki in? Might I speak with him?"

"He's . . ." Samyael felt his stomach lurch. Loki was avoiding everyone at the moment. But he didn't know if Prince Ishitar understood why and he didn't want Loki to be any more humiliated than he already was. "I believe he's in the library."

Prince Ishitar nodded. His eyes searched Samyael's for quite some time before he raised his hand and set it upon his shoulder. Samyael shivered under his touch.

"My father is sometimes short sighted." Prince Ishitar sighed. "I'm sorry for what he forced you to bear witness to."

Samyael could only nod at that. How was he supposed to respond?

"You can hear this conversation." Prince Ishitar said. "I have no confidences to share."

Samyael felt his brows raise with his curiosity. "Thank you."

He gave him a guarded smile and indicated the hallway. "The library?"

"Yes." Samyael smiled at him. "Follow me."

Prince Ishitar gave him a perfunctory nod and then followed him down the hall.

Samyael raised his hand and knocked on the door. When Aiken answered, it was with a strained smile. Until, that was, his eyes landed upon Prince Ishitar. He let out a long sigh and then forced a smile. "Your Royal Highness."

"He's come to speak with Loki." Samyael advised Aiken "Is he in the mood for palaver?"

"I'm certain he'll make the time even if he is not." Aiken gave Samyael a tight smile. "Come in. I'll retrieve him from the basement."

Samyael nodded as he and Prince Ishitar stepped into the library. As Prince Ishitar looked around himself, he smiled slightly. Stepping forward he sat the pie upon the desk and crossed his arms over his bare chest. "Very masculine."

"Loki's a very masculine individual." Samyael smiled wanly at him. He hoped that his true hearted distaste for the King of Lords' actions was passed through that smile. Prince Ishitar needed to understand just how deeply Loki had been violently wronged. "Though your mother is the one who decorated these rooms. This used to be the Lady's abode."

Prince Ishitar nodded distractedly as his eyes fell upon the rows of Tomes that Lady Raziel had written over the years. Seeming to take great interest in these, he stepped forward and began running his hands over the binds of them. Samyael, watching him, felt his lips thin.

After a few shifts, the false book case opened and Loki stepped out. He offered Samyael a haunted smile, which Samyael returned, and then turned his eyes to Prince Ishitar's bare back.

"Your Royal Highness." He sounded as tired as he looked.

Prince Ishitar turned away from the Tomes to meet Loki's gaze. His eyes flicked with great curiosity over Loki's face before he stepped forward and offered Loki a bow. "Loki."

"How might I assist you?" Loki asked, his smile still tight. "Did you come to see your mother?"

"No." Prince Ishitar shook his head. "Until Noliminan decides what to do with her I am forbidden."

"Oh." Loki muttered. "Of course."

"But I've brought her a pie." He indicated the pie on the desk. "And written her a letter. Will you deliver them to her?"

"Of course I will." Loki replied, surprised. "She will be grateful for the tidings."

461

"Perhaps it will bring her some small bit of comfort." Prince Ishitar shrugged. "Forgive me, my Lords. But, as you know, I'm not to be seen. I should take my leave of you both."

"You are welcome to visit any time." Loki assured him.

"Perhaps I shall." Prince Ishitar smiled at him. "Good day."

Samyael watched his back as he took his leave. When he was gone, he turned his gaze to his Lord Loki. Loki's expression was so full of self loathing and regret that Samyael was unable to bear it. He left the room as Aiken re-entered it.

"Aiken . . ." Loki sighed.

"It's okay, Loki." Aiken muttered. "None of us judge you. You must know that."

"No, but—"

"Let us just put it behind us?" He begged. "Please? Until you are ready to talk with me? At which time I am here for you. But, for now, I desperately need your friendship. These past few days of us avoiding one another have been torturous to me."

Loki rolled his eyes closed.

These were the words he needed to hear and Aiken knew that. He didn't want to talk with anyone about what had happened. Least of all Aiken, who he miscalculated could never understand the true depths of his distaste for the task he had been forced to.

When they opened, Loki's eyes darted toward the pie. "Best I deliver the Lady her son's gift before it goes cold."

"Best you should."

Loki gave Aiken a final, guarded smile and then, pie in hand, disappeared behind the false bookshelf.

-101-

I watched with great curiosity as Lord Loki stood outside of the door to Lucias' apartment, his fingers dancing on the wood and his forehead pressed against it. He wanted to see her face, I knew. Not speak with her through the door. But he had tried to enter before, only to find it locked against him.

After almost five shifts of Lord Countenances shadow she opened the small window in the door and slid a plate through with a piece of Ishitar's pie upon it.

"Try it, Loki." She said, her voice gentle. "It's very good."

Lord Loki, frowning, took the plate. He had no intention of eating the damn pie. "Thank you, my Lady."

"Sit on the floor on your side." She suggested. "I'll sit on mine."

"You would palaver with me?" He asked, surprised. He thought she would loathe him for what he had been forced to do to her son.

"Yes." She agreed. "We must enjoy this pie while it is fresh. And I fear I can't eat it by myself. And nor do I wish to. You will have a few pieces?"

"If it's good." He hadn't eaten since the Council. He had no desire to eat now.

"It is." She muttered. "You'll like it."

I knew that, whether he liked it or not, he would eat every damn piece of it if only to have a reason to palaver with her. His love for her was overwhelming to me.

As, it must be said, was my curiosity in regard to the letter and the pie.

Still frowning, still believing that Ishitar had told her what had happened and that she was judging him for it, he lowered himself to the ground. As he did so he asked, "Did you hear about Sappharon?"

"Ishitar told me that you bravely stood up to protect her and Metatron both." She replied, her tone gentle.

He flinched.

What else did he tell you?

"Thank you for that." And then, in concerned tones. "How does she fare? Have you visited her?"

"She's very brave." Lord Loki admitted, relieved that she was more concerned about Sappharon than him. Perhaps Ishitar didn't know and hadn't told her. "She cannot speak, of course. He sealed her mouth shut. But her face is very . . ." He laughed wryly. There was no joy within him to make it a true hearted reaction. I found myself wanting to bring him comfort, but, given his sensibilities, I knew better than to try. "Expressive."

She laughed in response. "Eat your pie, Loki."

Grateful for her company, and for ignoring whatever Ishitar may or may not have told her that he had been forced to do, Lord Loki complied.

He didn't realize, even at the end of it, that he had eaten the whole damn thing by himself.

-102-

As I retell this story I do not, yet, know the effects that the pie made out of Noliminan's forbidden fruit will have on Lord Loki. Aside from the fact that, as with Noliminan, Ishitar and Lucias, within three waning moons I was no longer able to access Lord Loki's thoughts or emotions. This added a level of mystery in my mind which bore careful consideration for the future.

For now, suffice it to say, it's time to come to the point in the story where Gabriel offended Noliminan enough so that Gabe would be put on trial.

Or, shall we say, the point where Noliminan manipulated Gabriel to his advantage. Because, as with everything else I'd witnessed, I don't believe for a moment that Noliminan wasn't completely in control of his senses as this little drama played itself out.

Really, that is the last piece of the overall history as it relates to the war. And as good a place as any to stop.

Noliminan was deep into his cups and, before long, he started screaming at Gabriel about what a disappointment he was and how he'd broken his heart. Asking Gabe why he didn't love him enough to stay with him rather than defy him.

"Your Grace!" Gabriel, who had bore the brunt of Noliminan's frustrations throughout the war by being forced to take on the face of his father when it suited his Lord and Master, cried at him after the shifting of shadows passed a hundred or so. He didn't understand why, now that the war was over, he was still being subjected to Noliminan's tantrums and games. "I am not Lucias! Stop screaming at me! I've got nothing to do with what he did to you!"

"No, but you wanted to join him!"

"I *never* wanted to join him!" Gabriel, confused, cried in response to this. "I understand what he was trying to do, but I never would have—"

"I knew it!" Noliminan growled at him. "You're just like him. The minute you have the opportunity then you'll turn your back on me too!"

"That's not what I said." Gabriel shook his head, confounded. In his mind, Noliminan was running mad right before his eyes. If only he had understood that he was being played for a fool, perhaps things would have proceeded differently. "All I said was that I understand why he did what he did."

"I can't have you in my service if I can't trust you."

"Your Grace!" Gabriel walked up to him and did the only thing he knew he could do to draw him out of his raving. It was something he would regret and he knew this before he acted. He slapped Noliminan. And hard. Because that's what Lucias would have done. And behaving exactly as Lucias would had ever been the most important rule of this sick and twisted game. "I said I understand. I didn't say I'd join him or even behave as he did!"

Noliminan stood there, pretending to be stunned. He held his hand to his cheek. Finally, he cried out in false indignation. "You slapped me!"

"I had to get your attention."

"Nobody strikes me!" Noliminan advanced on him. His hands snaked around Gabriel's neck as he threw him to the floor, strangling him. He was still raging at Gabriel but none of his words made sense.

Especially not given the game of old.

Gabriel, you see, didn't understand that, now Lucias was no longer opposing Noliminan, the game was no longer required. This was simply Noliminan's way of disposing of the problem Gabriel would become should Lucias—or anyone else for that matter—learn about what had been taking place between the pair of them.

What he failed to understand was that Queen Raguel had already shared this particular abomination with Lucias. And that no one else who knew what was going on would have put Gabriel in danger by talking about it. Even amongst themselves.

I can't tell you how long Noliminan sat over Gabe, strangling him, before Raphael, lost and within himself, happened to walk in the room.

He saw what was going on, came back to himself as much as he could, screamed, and then ran forward, pulling Noliminan off of Gabriel.

Gabriel lay on the ground, writhing, struggling to make sense as to how he had come out on the wrong side of things, as Noliminan muttered something Gabriel did understand. "Call the Council on the morrow. The trial which that will decide my final punishment for those on the Thirteenth level who waged war against me shall be *his*."

"Your Grace," Raphael, terrified, whispered, "I don't think—"

He struck Raphael. Hard. Gabriel heard Raphael cry out and flew upward so that he was standing in front of him. He wanted to protect his brother after everything that Raphael had been forced to endure.

All the while Noliminan was screaming that if he wanted an opinion he'd seek out Lucias.

"Report to Loki!" He finally raved at Gabriel. "And may you be as damned as your treacherous father!"

Given everything that you know about me, do you believe that I will ever loath Noliminan more than I did in that moment?

It pains me to advise you that, yes, I will.

But that is a story that has yet to unfold.

-103-

"My Lord, you have a visitor." Loki looked up at Samyael, his brow furrowed with surprise. His mood was tempered from the evening with Lucias and Aiken, but he was still very much on edge.

Who would be calling at this hour? And without invitation?

"Whom?"

"Gabriel, my Lord." Samyael wore a strange expression. "He said it's important. He doesn't look at all well."

"Bring him in." Loki sighed.

Samyael bowed and stepped out of the room. When he returned, Gabriel stood behind him. His pallor was pale but for the red marks on his neck. Upon further inspection it appeared, to Loki, that those red marks had been made by strong, choking hands.

He rose to his feet and ran toward the archangel.

"Piss on the Gods, Gabriel!" He cried. "What has happened to you?"

Tears began streaming down Gabriel's cheeks. He raised his hands to hide his well made face as his knees buckled under his weight. Great sobs reverberated around the room. Loki fell to his knees at Gabriel's side, his hand running endlessly up and down Gabriel's back, trying desperately to avoid his wings lest he offend him by inadvertently touching them.

"What's the matter with him?" Samyael asked, his black eyes wide and his lips trembling. "I've never seen anything like this!"

"Go get the scotch." Loki ordered him. "Bring it to me." And then, when Sam didn't move, "Mind me now, Sam!"

Samyael ran out of the room as though Lucias' breath was on his heels. Loki, who didn't know what else to do, looked up to the ceiling and gave a silent prayer for help.

Somebody, anybody, please help.

No one came. That didn't surprise him much. Given Loki, himself, was a God, who did he, honestly, have to pray to?

Samyael came into the room with the bottle. Loki grabbed it from him and roughly grasped Gabriel's shoulders. He forced the archangel to sit up and put the bottle to his crying, wailing lips.

"Take a drink, Gabe." He didn't. "Please."

Loki forced Gabriel's mouth open and poured it down. He needed Gabriel calm so that he could find out what in the Sixty Realms had spurred this ballyhoo.

Gabriel desperately tried to spit it out as the alcohol burned his throat, but Loki was having none of it and pouring even greater amounts into his mouth. As Loki did so, the archangel did, for a wonder, calm down. The wailing and screaming became ripping sobs. It was horrific, but much better than what had gone on before.

Loki gave him another drink. This one he took willingly.

Perhaps five shifts later, Gabriel finally calmed down enough that Loki thought that he might get something out of him. "Alright, Gabriel. Now tell me what is going on."

"He's putting me on trial!"

Loki started. "What? Who's putting you on trial?"

"The King of Lords!" Gabriel cried. "Because I told him that I understand Lucias' reasoning! He accused me of being a traitor! He was ranting and raving and I didn't know what to do so I slapped him hoping that it would calm him down. But it only made him angrier and he . . ."

Loki's hands flew to his own throat. He didn't need him to tell him what it was that the Noliminan had done.

"Raphael got him off of me and he told him that mine was to be the trial which decides the fate of everyone who was on Lucias' side of the war!" He shook his head. "He ordered me here! He told me that you are to put me down . . ." His voice was quivering now. His finger pointed to the false shelves that were really the door to the dungeon where Lady Lucias held her damned. "You're to put me down there!"

Loki, frowning, shook his head. "I'm not going to put you down *there*."

"But he told me to tell you—"

"I don't give a flying fuck what he told you to tell me." Loki snapped at him, reverting to the vulgarity of his people, who used this term in jest against the winged centaurs as that race preferred to mate mid-flight. "My ruling Goddess is Lady Lucias. Not Noliminan. And she would never stand for this blasphemy if she were here." He clenched his teeth and shook his head violently. He wanted to scream. But he knew he couldn't. "You can stay in Sappharon's old room. But you aren't going down there."

Gabriel looked up at him with wide, haunted eyes. His voice was a distant whisper. "Do you promise?"

"I promise." Loki nodded. "You're never going down there. Not on my watch."

He understood what might happen to himself if Gabriel were damned and Loki allowed him to stay in Lady Lucias' apartment rather than to be caged in the basement. But he didn't care. He would hide the child to the end of antiquity if he had to. And, if he were found, he would take whatever punishment such a deception had earned him.

Loki would not broker what he knew was right for what would keep him alive.

Never in life.

"Do you want me to get Lady Raziel?" Samyael asked.

"The Gods pray, Sam. What in the name of the Thirty Hells are you thinking?" Loki shook his head and flashed his demon an irritated scowl. "She can't do anything about this and it's better she doesn't know I'm keeping Gabriel up here. She'd have me put in my place in the first shift of shadows. Then I'll only be forced to break my promise to him."

"I'll go make Sappharon's room comfortable." Samyael bowed to them both and made himself scarce.

Loki wished he could do the same.

"Do you want another drink?" Loki asked.

"No." Gabriel's entire body was shaking. His lips were still quivering and his eyes were still two haunted saucers that spoke volumes in regard to his disbelief. "I am not responsible for the fact that I wear my father's face."

Loki shivered.

"I should tear it off with mine own hands if—"

"Look." Loki sighed, pulling those clawed hands away from Gabriel's face. "You're safe here. And I can't believe that anyone is going to think you had any intention of joining Lucias in his war. If you were going to do that, you would have done it along with everyone else. Not now, when everything is over."

"You do not understand the true hearts of the Gods." Gabriel whispered. "They have no compassion." His haunted eyes flickered over Loki's face. The mistrust buried within them made Loki shiver. "They vote what they want. Not what is right. And nor do they regret their ill begot decisions."

"Let's just wait and see." Gabriel nodded. Loki was grateful. Because, at the end of it, Gabe was right. "Do you want to take a warm bath before bed?"

"Yes." Gabriel nodded.

"Samyael's getting you something to sleep in."

"Thank you, my Lord." Gabriel looked upon him with dark, frightened eyes. "I'm sorry, Lord Loki. I don't mean to put you out."

"None of this is your fault or doing so no apology is required."

"Why are you being so kind to me?"

"I'm a sucker for the underdog." Lord Loki forced himself to smile at the archangel.

Samyael stepped in with one of his own satin night shirts and a pair of his small clothes. He sat them on one of the tables at the edge of the room and smiled at Gabriel. "If you're scared to sleep alone tonight, you can stay with me in my room."

Loki looked on him with a brow raised with interest. Gabriel snapped his gaze in Sam's direction and forced himself to smile. "If it would be no trouble."

"None at all." Samyael smiled easily at him. "You scared me back there. That's why I didn't offer before."

"Well." Loki said. "It's settled then." He turned to Samyael, relieved despite his distaste. "Why don't you help him with his bath? I've got to go tell Lucias what has happened."

He stood, satisfied that Gabriel was in good hands, and closed the door behind himself. He didn't know how far Samyael's invitation extended because he knew Samyael rutted as easily with males as with females. But knowing this and seeing it were two separate things.

He opened the false door in the library and walked down the stairs. He ignored the damned souls who were crying to him for attention—he'd become very adept at ignoring them—and went to the door to the apartment where Lady Lucias was kept.

He knocked and he waited.

Finally, after what seemed an eternity (the barest shift seemed an eternity down here) he heard a sad, yet somehow still sultry, voice on the other side. Lucias, it would seem, was in no mood to see Loki's face. "Yes, Loki. What is it?"

"I'm sorry to disturb you so late, my Lady, but I have some news I know you'll want to hear right away."

"Yes?" She cleared her throat. He realized, then, she had been crying. "What is it?"

"Some ruckus with Gabriel." Loki said. "Noliminan attacked him and he's going on trial because he told Noliminan that he understands your position."

Silence on the other side. It was eerie. Loki didn't like it one bit.

"My Lady?"

"I heard you." She growled.

"Noliminan wanted me to put Gabriel in one of the cages until his trial but I put him in Sappharon's room instead." He turned to face the door. He raised his hand and put it against it, running his fingers down it lovingly. It was as close as he could get to touching his beloved Goddess. "I hope that's okay."

"Of course it's okay." Lady Lucias sighed. She sounded so very weary. "Is he going to be alright?"

"That depends on the outcome of the trial."

He could almost picture Lucias nodding. And when a low whistle danced between them he could very easily picture her gritting her teeth in the gruesome grin she sometimes wore when she was frustrated or upset. "Let Gabriel know that I love him."

"I will." Loki pressed his forehead against the door and closed his eyes. His palm was flat against the door. "Are you okay?"

"Not really." He listened as Lucias chuckled. "But I made my own bed." Loki nodded. "Go to your own, Loki. It's late."

"Yes, my Lady." He sighed. "Good night."
"Good night, met paken."

PART FOUR:
THE TAKING OF THE TOME

-1-

I shift uneasily, my eyes dancing over Lady Raziel's fair face. "The rest of what I can tell you, you already know."

Raziel nods at me.

"Are you going to put these things in your Tome?"

"If I'm going to save Gabriel, then I have to."

"He won't like reading about it."

"I cannot worry about that now." She snaps. "Though, I think some of it can stay out of the Tome."

"If you need help while you're writing, just ask me a question."

"I will." Lady Raziel stands and holds her hand out to me. I grasp it, raise and kiss it. It would seem that whatever anger she had harbored against me during the tale has subsided.

For now.

"Thank you, Azrael. You may have just saved us all."

I force myself to smile at her and then let myself disappear.

There is nothing more that I wish to say to her.

Nor, would it seem, is there anything more I *can* say to her.

No longer holding Ishitar's hair in my satchel, my magic explodes upon me with its curse, punishing me for every time I had opened my mouth and Ishitar's hair had protected me.

Which is to say that, after I finish telling her my story, it would seem that I am to never be heard or seen by anyone ever again.

-2-

Tristan watches from his cell as Loki walks swiftly and with a purpose from the stairs which lead from his library to the door that separates Lady Lucias' apartment from the rest of the damned. A small smile dances on Loki's lips as he raises his hand and knocks.

Lady Lucias keeps him waiting for several shifts of the shadows. When she opens the small window on the door, her dark brown eyes dance over Loki's face. Loki lowers his gaze and mutters, "My Lady, I've come to tell you about—"

"I already know, tukte 'aasifa." Lady Lucias spits. "As *you* well know. Just as I know you kept my apprentice sleeping during my pregnancy lest he see my womanly form and I grant him my favor."

Her eyes narrow; his widen.

"And what you forced him to do to Metatron for the simple turn of your amusement."

Loki, seemingly surprised, licks his lips.

"Stop your constant tricks with me by wearing Loki's face in order that I might bend to your desire, you carvetek mouk." She snaps. "And return Gabriel to his Guf where he belongs lest you ruin all of our plans."

The window snaps shut.

As it does, Loki, who Tristan understands now is not Loki at all, leans his head back and lets out a long, gratified laugh.

-3-

I learn quickly enough that even though I am unable to form a corporeal body, this does not prevent me from passing messages by way of sending them with my mind. I am grateful for this. I had left various letters explaining what I needed certain individuals to do, but it was much easier to be able to speak within their minds and impose upon them my thoughts.

Immediately after finishing my tale, I went to Gabriel, who was floundering on one of the inhabited worlds, trying to figure out how to live an existence amongst the mortals where he would not be ridiculed or shamed.

I explained to him about the hair. I explained to him about Parsiphany's brew to force the sexes, and I advised him of my plan to have Lady Lucias released so that she could protect Ishitar against his father who had, since our return from our slumbers, been paying far too much attention to Ishitar and his abilities.

Noliminan had done enough damage to the boy. Though his mother wasn't the perfect solution, her limited influence would remind him that Noliminan didn't entirely have the right of things.

By any road, whatever plot Ishitar was playing with Loki and Lady Lucias needed to work itself out. It couldn't do that if the Lady was imprisoned.

Gabriel agreed to help me once he understood what I intended to do. Though he didn't quite comprehend all of the details.

No matter.

His understanding of my reasons was the least important piece to seeing them play out. Once I had his agreement, there were far more important tasks which I had yet to see to.

-4-

When they reached Anticata, Raystlyn realized that the angels who had fought in the revolution were being delivered to the very castle that had been their home base. After assuring the others that she had a plan for them and that she would watch over all of them, Lady Theasis led him to his apartment and then bid that he come inside to talk.

Raystlyn agreed—who was he to turn Lady Theasis away given that it would be under her care he was to remain for the rest of his days—and smiled as she lowered herself very gracefully into one of Raystlyn's high back chairs.

"I need you to keep my counsel your own." Lady Theasis said as she tented her fingers beneath her chin. Raystlyn nodded and forced himself to smile. "You're going to lead your little band until they bid Zadkiel visit them. So I need you to promise me that you won't seek out Zadkiel's aide until the very last one of them is gone."

Raystlyn swallowed. He understood that that could be a very, very long time from now. "I see."

"You'll be able to mix with the mortal inhabitants of Anticata." Lady Theasis smiled softly at him. "And your descendants will become very powerful sorcerers." Her smile grew as Raystlyn's brow furrowed. "As long as you remain you shall Lord over these descendants. And you will choose your successor when the time for succession comes."

"I don't understand." Raystlyn said. "You don't intend to strip us of our powers?"

"No." She replied. "I do not. I mean that you pass them along. Having sorcerers among the peoples of this place will afford them the ability to protect themselves."

"And manipulate others." Raystlyn counseled.

"Yes, that is true." Lady Theasis sighed. "Which is why I need you to build an educational guild of sorts. So that when the time comes for your descendents—and those of your peers—to actually use their natural abilities they are trained to do so properly."

"But not attending my guild wouldn't stop them from using their powers?" Raystlyn asked.

"No." She agreed. "Not unless laws are built around that. But they would have to be agreed to by every race of Anticata. So you have your work cut out for you if you agree to accept my tasks of you."

"May I think about it?"

Not that he wouldn't, ultimately, comply. He wouldn't have a choice. He was still, as he ever would be, a servant of his God. *Goddess,* he amended, *and she will never harm me a purpose.*

"Yes." Lady Theasis nodded and stood. "But you have only until Evanbourough decides whom he will choose to take over the werefolk. Once he decides I will be forced to announce your name if I haven't heard from you yet."

"I only need a single moon." Raystlyn assured her, already knowing his answer. "You'll have my answer by tomorrow evening."

Lady Theasis looked at him for a long moment and then nodded. "Do not take the request lightly. If you need more time, I shall give it to you."

"I understand." Raystlyn replied.

"Good." Lady Theasis smiled at him. "I'll check in on you tomorrow evening, then."

Raystlyn walked her to the door and frowned as he closed it behind her.

He would be a fool to deny Lady Theasis her request and he knew that. But he was glad that Lady Theasis understood that he needed to be certain that he could actually carry through her plans before giving her an answer rather than demanding it right there and then.

He had a feeling that if he were on the other side of things, under Lord Evanbourough's care, choice would be no where in it.

Though Raystlyn had never been prejudiced against demons, as some of his brethren were, for the first time in his life he was grateful for the simple color of his Gods be damned wings.

-5-

The barest shift after Raziel finished transcribing her Tome, I made my move. She foolishly left it, and her scrolls, on her desk to fix herself something to eat. Seeing them laying there, unattended, I reached for them and took them as my own.

In their place, I left my letter to her. Within it were my instructions.

She had knowledge, I advised her, which she could use against Noliminan. She could use this to her advantage by not transcribing another copy. As for the copy in my hands, I intended to hide it for the sake of antiquity. It would reappear— and as it had been told rather than as it had been written for her gains—when it was least expected. And it would be in the hands of the person whom I intended it to belong when I had spun her my tale.

She shouldn't worry about Noliminan, I advised her. Or Gabriel. I would see to Gabriel's release. Which would, in turn, protect her current claim to the crown.

Would it surprise you to know that upon reading my letter, and upon realizing she had the upper hand by holding information which no one else but I could share, the Lady smiled?

-6-

My next discovery was that—even if I was unable to take on my own face and form—I had the ability to wear the face of another. I still couldn't speak. But sometimes a visual message is far more poignant than a verbal one.

Remember, Noliminan had ordered Raziel not to speak with me. So he was unaware that I had. Which gave me the opportunity to manipulate this situation to my greatest advantage.

I visited the river Lethe and obtained a pot of the blood which flowed there. Then I made my way to Noliminan's library.

I have no real motivation to do what I am doing given I watched Lucias order him to release Gabriel through Tristan's eyes. But I have a rare opportunity to play games of my own. Given I am no longer a physical being, what harm can Noliminan lay upon me?

Especially now that I understand that, if he tries, Ishitar will protect me.

I dipped my finger into the blood and raised it to the library wall. My message to him is simple and meant to make him understand that I have told Raziel everything. "Azrael has been forever silenced."

Grinning, I form myself into an image which will both anger and terrify him. Raguel, of course. In male form with eyes and wings missing.

When he sees me, his horror and revulsion are precisely the reaction I desired.

-7-

Ishitar advised Zadkiel that he was ready to garner his education from the Quorum. So it was that he sat in a small cottage which Zadkiel had built upon his land where he could bring in the teachers that he desired and speak with them in utter privacy.

He didn't know which of his brothers Zadkiel had asked to speak with him first. Yet, he was less than surprised as the door opened and he raised his gaze to see Gabriel on the other side.

But it wasn't Gabriel. Ishitar knew this the moment he laid eyes upon his teacher.

Small differences here and there set the pair apart from one another. Yet, he had been staring at his mother's face for long enough that he recognized her—even in her male form—the moment he laid eyes upon her.

Seeing her standing there, he smiled.

And, as his father would have said, he let the devil play her games.

CHARLIE

-1-

"You're driving me mad." Charlie grinned at his nephew as Mason guided him through the lobby toward the office where Marius Talbot was typically waiting for them. The moment they had entered the bank, Mason immediately began flirting with the tellers. Their giggling was irritating to Charlie to the extreme. "Can you not deliver me to our host *before* you start your damned peacocking?"

"Who am I to disappoint?" Mason replied with a slight chuckle. "My appearance completely makes their otherwise extremely dreary day."

"If you say so." Charlie replied, still smiling.

"We're at his secretary's desk." Mason muttered under his breath. Then he raised his voice, throwing in the charming lilt which drove the women mad. "Jennifer! How are you this afternoon?"

"Mr.—?" She seemed surprised to see them. Charlie felt his brow furrow. "Mr. Hamilton! I—we didn't expect to see you this afternoon."

"Of course not." Charlie grinned at her. "I suppose a standing appointment is required for my presence to be anything less than surprising."

"No, it's just that—" He could feel the embarrassment burning from her direction. "Forgive me, Mr. Hamilton. Let me retrieve Mr. Talbot for you."

Mason began chuckling under his breath the moment she was gone. "As entertaining as I find it to watch you play with your box, you'll forgive me if I take my leave."

"Of course." Charlie replied in amused tones. "See if you can't make other arrangements for dinner so I needn't waste my time cooking for you."

"You know better than that." Mason replied as he began to step away. "I should never deprive you the joy I bring you for taking care of me."

Charlie closed his eyes and nodded, unable to stay his laughter.

Less than a minute later, Marius Talbot was standing before him, stammering. "Mr. Hamilton! Welcome back!"

Charlie, confounded by the behavior of the two bank associates merely smiled and said, "Always my pleasure to pay your fine establishment a visit. Will you take me to my box?"

"Of course." Marius replied. "Forgive me! Come."

Charlie held out his hand. He was surprised by the hesitation from Marius to take it and put it on his arm. This was an old ritual which had ever run smoothly.

They saw to the retrieving of the box and, as ever was custom, Charlie allowed Marius to lead him to the small lounge where he could sit and allow his fingers to dance over old memories.

Generally the room was empty. Not so today. He sensed the presence of another sitting next to the chair he generally preferred. Though he found this queer, he certainly didn't want to be rude. So he took his seat and raised his face to Marius, who was apologizing that his sandwiches had not yet been spread upon the table at his side.

"No matter, Marius." Charlie assured him. "I'll be here for a while. You may bring them when they are ready."

"Of course, Mr. Hamilton." Marius replied with a smile to his voice. Finally, it would seem, he had calmed himself from whatever manner of concern he had felt at Charlie's visit this afternoon. "I shall return straight away."

Charlie nodded at him and reached into his safety deposit box.

As his hands fell upon a second strange box within—which felt as though it were made out of wood—he froze. His brow furrowed and his lips curled slightly into a frown as he lifted it out of the safety deposit box and pushed the rest of his belongings aside.

Running his fingers over the top of the box, he smiled. The envelope attached to the lid had his name written upon it in Braille.

He slid his finger beneath the envelope and pulled it upward so he might open it. A scent permeated from it which reminded him of the hot pots in Yellowstone National Park. It was a familiar enough scent to him. After all, he had been receiving packages and letters from its author for near on the full of his life.

Grinning, he pulled the letter out and read it.

C.,

My old friend. How are you? Does my greeting find you well?

As ever, I bring you another puzzle. Perhaps my last. Who can know what the future holds for me? Certainly this will be my most important. You must decide for yourself once you've solved my puzzle.

Keep in mind one thing: This particular puzzle is simple to the extreme. But it will require the dexterity of your fingers and the clarity of your mind's eye to solve it.

Sixteen marks forty three.

With ever growing respect and unconditional love, I am your dear and true hearted friend.

A.

"I hope you're wrong on that account, old friend." He muttered under his breath as he read the sentiment that this might be the last puzzle he was to receive. "I truly do."

He felt the presence next to him shift slightly. Feeling as though he had been rude, he turned toward the person—a gentleman he was certain by the size and smell of him—and gave him an apologetic smile.

"Forgive me, sir." He said. "I didn't mean to speak the words aloud."

"Forgive me, sir." The man replied. He had a deep voice which was gentle and soothing. "But you caught me off guard." Charlie detected the smile which enveloped his words. "You see I know that puzzle box. It is as ancient as the world itself. A true archeological find."

Charlie started at that. "You don't say?"

"Please do excuse me." The man said. "My name is Joshua Silverstone."

"Charlie." Charlie replied as his fingers began to dance over the buttons on top of the box. He did find the fact that the gentleman recognized the box curious. "Or, rather, Charles Hamilton."

"It is a pleasure." The man said.

"You're an archeologist then?" Charlie asked. His accent was odd. Charlie, who was an expert at detecting dialect, was unable to place it.

"No." The man replied. As he did so, Marius slipped in with a tray of sandwiches. He sat it upon the table between the two and quickly made his retreat. "But I do dabble in theology."

Charlie smiled at that. "Nonsense and childhood fairy tales."

"If you say so." The man replied, his smile clearly broadening. "May I ask who sent this to you? If it wouldn't be rude."

"Of course not." He shrugged. "An old friend. Though I've never met him and don't even know his name. He simply signs his correspondence with the letter A."

"Peculiar." The man replied. Though he was still smiling. "Forgive me, but, I must insist—if I give you my card will you let me know when you open the box?"

Charlie, surprised by this request, turned toward him. "May I ask your interest?"

"As I say," the man named Joshua replied, "it is a box I recognize. It's prize will be most extraordinary I am certain."

Charlie, whose fingers had been dancing to solve the puzzle throughout the entire conversation, merely shrugged. "Of course. Though, as my friend tells me, it is an easy enough puzzle. I should have it resolved within an hour or two, I believe."

"My afternoon is free." Joshua replied. His tone was strangely comforting. And, somehow, distantly familiar. "If I wouldn't be intruding on your privacy."

"Not at all." Charlie shook his head. "Share these lovely sandwiches with me, why don't you? He always brings out too many and they typically go to waste."

"Charlie?" Charlie turned his attention to the door where Mason was hovering. "I have to go. They found another body up Millcreek Canyon. I think it might be the Olsen girl."

Charlie let out a tired sigh. He hated his nephew's occupation. But he knew that Mason felt an inane sense of responsibility to solve the murders that often crossed his desk.

"Can you catch a cab?"

"I'd be happy to give your uncle a ride." Joshua advised him.

Charlie, who hadn't told Joshua that Mason was his nephew, frowned. Yet, he was intrigued by this man. If only to know where he came from so he could place his strange accent.

"Charlie?"

"It would appear I have a ride."

"Okay." Mason's tone was tight. "Call me if you run into any trouble."

Call me if this gent turns out to be a perv.

Charlie smiled at his nephew's silent message. But he didn't think it would be an issue. Something about Joshua brought Charlie a sense of comfort rather than fear. He had an uncanny ability to sense when he was in danger. He didn't believe that any threat lay here.

"I'm certain I shall be fine."

Not wanting to waste any time, Mason left them.

As for Charlie, he set about solving the puzzle and making a new, if very strange, friend.

485

-2-

Joshua's vehicle was a convertible which garnered much speed. And Charlie found himself enjoying every moment of the ride to his home, which was nestled in Ogden Canyon. This had as much to do with the warm wind on his face as it did with the easy conversation which fell between the pair.

Joshua was the fount of knowledge for many subjects. The most surprising of which was, to Charlie, Gilles de Rais, who was the subject of a fictional audio book Charlie was currently recording. Joshua understood the man's history as well as all of the political possibilities which surrounded him that might prove de Rais was innocent of the crimes he had been executed for. Yet he, like Charlie, disbelieved these theories and admitted freely that he believed the man to have been insane.

By the time they reached Charlie's home, he had all but solved the puzzle. After three glasses of scotch on the rocks, the lid to the box sprang upon and both Charlie and Joshua began talking madly over one another as Charlie described how the book within felt and Joshua explained how it looked.

It was written in ancient symbols, Joshua explained. Symbols he had studied since boyhood. And it was a script, Joshua warned, which very few had ever stumbled upon.

"I should be honored if I might read it for you." Joshua begged.

"Can you read it?" Charlie was surprised. If the symbols were truly ancient, how could that be? What luck had put Joshua in the bank's lounge on the very day his old friend had sent him such a book?

Yet, he knew his new friend was not lying to him. The book smelled old. Musty. And the paper and binding was so frail that it crumbled at Charlie's touch.

"Without destroying it." Charlie added. "It is so old and frail."

"I really can." Joshua's tone was one of pure excitement. He reached for the book and ran his hand over the cover. He didn't take it away from Charlie and that spoke volumes as far as he was concerned. "This is one of Raziel's Tomes! The missing Tome in fact. All others are accounted for and—"

He stopped himself. Charlie realized he felt he was saying too much.

To calm him, Charlie asked the burning question. "Have you read others?"

"All of them." Joshua replied, his tone low and respectful. "Please, Charlie. If you have been sent this particular Tome, I know it is meant for me to read it."

Curiosity overrode better sense as Charlie thrust the book in Joshua's direction.

"Fine." He said. "Read this to me. And when you are done, you must tell me about all of the rest."

"That," Joshua grinned, "is a promise."

-3-

Ishitar allowed the weight of the Tome to pass from one hand to the other before, gently, carefully, opening it. His eyes raising to look upon Azrael's mortal friend, he grinned.

It was in extremely reverent tones that he began.

"The Guf. The Great Hall of Souls. The Bird Cage. The Mortal Well. Otzer. Whichever of these you wish to call it, the Guf is located on the Seventh level of the Heavens and is the domain in which Gabriel has ever been charged to work his magic. Until today that is. Today the Guf belongs to me."

Watching Charles Hamilton react to the story as he read it, Ishitar understood with deep appreciation why it was that it had been this particular mortal soul Azrael had chosen for this lost Tome to be found.

*L*ESSON *O*NE:

Malicious Intent is the
Best Friend of Your Enemy

*A*UTHOR'S *N*OTE

I want to thank you for taking the time to read Fall From Grace.
As an author, I understand that you have a multitude of choices
available to you and it is an honor that is my scribing you've
chosen to while the shift of Countenance's shadows with.
I hope that you have enjoyed this first installment of The Scribing
of Ishitar. And I hope you enjoy future installments to come.
As an author, especially a self-published author, I depend upon
word of mouth and recommendation to promote my book. That
being said, if you enjoyed the yarn that my friend Azrael has
spun for you, I ask for but a shift or so more of Countenance's
shadow where you are concerned.
Please tell your friends and family of your interest and, if you are
able, post a review on any social media site that you are
subscribed to. Facebook, Amazon.com, Barnes&noble.com, or
any other media you have access to will be appreciated.
As far as the series itself goes, I want to assure you, you are in for
an interesting ride.
There are many questions unanswered, but I promise you that
Moira will tie off each and every knot.
If you have a particular question in regard to any one of the
installments, do not hesitate to contact me on the series'

Facebook page at:
https://www.facebook.com/#!/TheScribingOfIshitar
or
TheScribingofIshitar@comcast.net.

In so far as those who have made this dream become reality,
there is a pesky woman who insisted on reading my first draft
who I owe much and more to. I am honored to call her one of my
very best friends and thank Moira every day that the Goddess has
placed this tenacious individual on my path.

ABOUT THE AUTHOR

Carrie F. Shepherd (1971) was born in Salt Lake City, Utah but currently resides in Highlands Ranch, Colorado. The single mother of one, she enjoys taking advantage of the hiking trails when it's cool out or curling up with a book next to the pool on warmer days. Twenty years of scribing have brought the personalities of the people who most inspire her to life within the characters in these pages.

The Scribing of Ishitar:

Fall From Grace (Volume I)
Ashes to Ashes (Volume II)